PRAISE FOR WENDY CORSI STAUB

Windfall

"A winning lottery ticket, a haunted California mansion, and raging wildfires provide the tense and atmospheric backdrop for Wendy Corsi Staub's riveting and engrossing new thriller. I devoured this novel about the price of friendship and the things we'll do for love and money in one breathless sitting. Rocket-paced and full of unexpected twists, *Windfall* is a knockout! A summer must-read!"

—Lisa Unger, *New York Times* bestselling author of
Secluded Cabin Sleeps Six

"I couldn't turn the pages of *Windfall* fast enough in this twisty thriller that has it all—three friends who wrongly assumed they knew each other's secrets, a life-changing lottery ticket that could change their complicated lives for better (or worse), all in a Gothic setting on deadly cliffs shrouded by smoke from California wildfires. Nail biting, tense, and rich—in more ways than one!"

—Sarah Strohmeyer, bestselling author of *We Love to Entertain*

"A tense and moving exploration of women's friendships and lives. Reading *Windfall* is like winning the lottery of suspense writing!"

—Carol Goodman, *New York Times* bestselling and award-winning
author of *The Bones of the Story*

"When money and old secrets collide, someone has to pay. It all comes due at *Windfall*. Compelling, atmospheric, and deliciously twisted. Suspense at its finest."

—James L'Etoile, award-winning author of *Dead Drop*

T0370193

"Masterful and utterly compelling, *Windfall* is an examination of four scarred women and how the dreamlike opportunity for them to escape the unique, richly layered complications of their lives is hardly an escape at all. Staub lands every aching and triumphant emotional moment she aims for and, as the novel rushes forward, delivers a master class in page-turning suspense. Destined to be revered by readers and studied by aspiring and experienced writers alike, *Windfall* is the work of an author at the top of her game, showcasing all of her considerable skills."

—F..A. Aymar, bestselling author of *No Home for Killers*

"What's scarier than a small slip of paper holding a billion-dollar lottery win to be split between three old friends? Add in a haunted mansion on a Pacific cliff surrounded by California wildfires, no phone/internet service, and you'll get a scream in the night and someone going missing. This is not just a perfect table setting of mystery elements; it's also a complex story of three women's lives, old college friends who find themselves lost in midlife, wondering what happened to all their youthful dreams and desires. Wendy Corsi Staub is at her best with *Windfall*, keeping the reader on edge to find out who really wins it all in life and whose luck has run out."

—James Conrad, Golden Notebook Bookstore,
Golden Notebook Press

The Other Family

"Great psychological suspense with a wallop of a twist."
—Harlan Coben, #1 *New York Times* bestselling author

"A twisty ride steeped in betrayal. The perfect winter read!"
—J.D. Barker, *New York Times* bestselling author of *A Caller's Game*

THE
FOURTH
GIRL

The Stranger Vanishes
Dog Days

The Foundlings Trilogy

Little Girl Lost
Dead Silence
The Butcher's Daughter

The Mundy's Landing Trilogy

Blood Red
Blue Moon
Bone White

Social Media Thrillers

The Good Sister
The Perfect Stranger
Cold Hearted (e-novella prequel to The Perfect Stranger)
The Black Widow

Nightwatcher Trilogy

Nightwatcher
Sleepwalker
Shadowkiller

Live to Tell Trilogy

Live to Tell
Scared to Death
Hell to Pay

WOMEN'S FICTION

Written as Wendy Markham

Stand-Alone Titles

Hello, It's Me
If Only in My Dreams
The Best Gift
Love, Suburban Style
Mike, Mike & Me
Thoroughly Modern Princess
The Long Way Home

"Slightly" Series

So Not Single (formerly Slightly Single)
Confessions of a One Night Stand (formerly Slightly Settled)
Did Someone Say Fiancée? (formerly Slightly Engaged)
Happily Ever After All (formerly Slightly Married)
What Happens in Suburbia (formerly Slightly Suburban)

Chickalini Family Series

The Nine Month Plan

Once Upon a Blind Date
Bride Needs Groom
That's Amore

YOUNG READERS

Stand-Alone and Short Stories

Scream and Scream Again
Witch Hunt
Halloween Party
Summer Lightning
Real Life: Help Me
Turning 17: More Than This
Turning 17: This Boy Is Mine
Charmed: Voodoo Moon

Lily Dale Series

Lily Dale: Awakening
Lily Dale: Believing
Lily Dale: Connecting
Lily Dale: Discovering

Teen Angels Series

Mitzi Malloy and the Anything But Heavenly Summer
Brittany Butterfield and the Back to School Blues
Henry Hopkins and the Horrible Halloween Happening
Candace Caine and the Bah, Humbug Christmas (Coming Soon)

College Life 101 Series

College Life 101: Cameron

THE
FOURTH
GIRL

A NOVEL

WENDY
CORSI STAUB

THOMAS & MERCER

Text copyright © 2025 by Wendy Corsi Staub
All rights reserved.

Published by Thomas & Mercer, Seattle

www.apub.com

Amazon, the Amazon logo, and Thomas & Mercer are trademarks of Amazon.com, Inc., or its affiliates.

ISBN-13: 9781662523816 (paperback)
ISBN-13: 9781662523809 (digital)

Cover design by Erin Fitzsimmons
Cover image: © Wirestock, Inc. / Alamy; © Avesun,
© Vladimir Gjorgiev / Shutterstock

Printed in the United States of America

For my sweet, hilarious, and brilliant firstborn son,
Morgan,
on his milestone birthday—cent'anni!
And for Brody and Mark, with love.

CHAPTER ONE

June 14, 2000
Mulberry Bay, New York

He walks.

The streets are quiet.

Darkness comes late at this time of year. Well past eight thirty, maybe even after nine o'clock.

He has no way of knowing the exact hour. He used to rely on the clock tower atop the Municipal Building, but like so many things in Mulberry Bay, it's fallen into disrepair. The hands have been stuck at a few minutes after twelve for weeks. Perpetual noon, or perpetual midnight?

He prefers the latter. He prefers the night, when he can walk the streets and shoreline alone, eating mulberries and nuts and thinking about things.

Tonight, the lake is choppy. Blue-black water laps at the pilings, its surface pocked with the first raindrops. Low, misty clouds veil the opposite shore.

But this isn't going to be a storm. Not like a few nights ago, when trees snapped and cracked like gunshots.

This won't be like that.

Like the war.

It's just rain.

He breathes the damp, green scent of lake and woods and rain, laced with fryer grease from the Landing restaurant and underlying hints of the perch rotting in the rocky shallows and overripe fruit rotting beneath the mulberry trees.

He likes the rain's sheen on wet pavement, the way it washes away the fallen berries. He likes the way it scrubs everything clean and glosses over the cracks.

Tilting his head back, he wonders if it might do the same for his face. He recently spotted a weathered, vaguely familiar stranger returning his gaze in a men's room mirror.

His grandfather's face, perhaps, though he can't quite picture the man. He remembers only the things that matter, discarding the rest like the documents, keys, and other cumbersome items he'd carried in his satchel long after they'd served their purpose.

Habit, he supposes, or nostalgia. Or maybe he'd clung to remnants of the old life in case he ever changed his mind about this new one.

He never has.

He never will.

He's content to live out his life in this far-flung corner of Ulster County. Mulberry Bay has seen far better days, but then, so has he.

Walking along the pier, he listens to the patter of rain, occasionally punctuated by a burst of loud music coming from the Dive Inn tavern.

Then another sound reaches his ears.

A high-pitched scream.

It sounds like it came from nearby. Not in town, but on this side of the lake.

It wasn't an owl or coyote, though both are plentiful around here. He supposes it might have been a bobcat, but—

When it comes again, he recognizes it as human. A woman's scream, from up in the woods near Haven Cliff.

CHAPTER TWO

"John, Paul, George, and Ringo," Talia Shaw says from the back seat as they wait for the light to change at the intersection of Main and Center Streets. "Jerry, Kramer, George, and Elaine . . ."

Kelly Barrow, in the passenger's seat, says, "Okay, we get it! Enough!"

But Talia is on a roll. "Carrie, Samantha, Charlotte, and Miranda . . ."

Behind the wheel, Midge Kennedy asks, *"Who?"*

"The main characters on *Sex and the City*. They're an iconic foursome, like we are."

Like we were, Midge thinks, clenching the wheel.

Talia, Kelly, Midge, and Caroline.

And then there were three.

Kelly groans. *"What* is going on? Is this light ever going to change?"

"My dad says the cycle is only one hundred and twenty seconds."

The others don't question why Midge's dad would know that fact, or its validity. As the Mulberry Bay police chief, he's a regular font of information, which has both its benefits and drawbacks, as far as Midge is concerned.

"It's probably broken, like everything else in this town." Kelly reaches for the radio dial. "Just go, Midge."

"I'm not driving through a red light."

"Who's going to know? There's no one around."

It's true. On this drizzly weeknight, even the Walking Man—an enigmatic local who travels the streets at all hours—is nowhere to be seen. Midge's Honda Civic is the only car on the road. The deserted business district is bordered by empty parking spots and darkened storefronts.

But Mulberry Bay wouldn't be bustling even if it were high noon on a summer Saturday. There's nowhere to shop except the gas station minimart, nowhere to hang out if you're not old enough to get into the Dive Inn, the local tavern, and there's absolutely nothing worthwhile to do unless you count going to church.

Midge does not, though her parents insist that she accompany them to mass at Saint Bart's every Sunday as long as she's living under their roof.

It isn't that she minds so much on a spiritual level. Sometimes, she's able to lose herself in the rhythmic ritual of mass, and faith brings comfort. Especially when her mother's brother, Uncle Father Tom, comes from his own parish across the river in Dutchess County to fill in for the aging pastor at Saint Bart's.

But inevitably, guilt washes over her as she, along with the rest of the congregation, intones prayers for forgiveness, confessing to Almighty God and everyone present that she's a sinner. Words she's recited every Sunday of her life have taken on new significance ever since Caroline went missing.

Kelly fiddles with the radio dial.

Static . . . insurance company jingle . . . static . . .

"Midge, seriously!" she says. "This is never going to turn green. Just go."

"No! Don't go!" Talia leans forward, putting a hand on Midge's shoulder as if to hold her back. "Some kid my roommate knows did that a few months ago and—"

"Yeah, um, this isn't a train crossing, Talia," Kelly cuts in. "People run traffic lights all the time."

4

Midge keeps her own gaze fastened on the red light beyond the windshield, but she can feel Kelly's eye roll.

In the three weeks since Talia has been home after finishing her freshman year at Sarah Lawrence, she's made constant references to people and places her hometown friends know nothing about.

Both Midge and Kelly find it irritating, but . . .

Is it her, or is it us?

Lucky Talia, with a promising new life elsewhere. Midge still lives at home and goes to community college, majoring in criminal justice. Kelly, after grudgingly attending her parents' alma mater, Dartmouth, dropped out after one semester. Or perhaps failed out.

She doesn't talk about it.

Talia never seems to *stop* talking. "No, you guys, this kid didn't just run a traffic light. He was at a railroad crossing and the signal was still flashing after the train came through, so he thought it was broken and drove around the gates and *bam*. A train blew through from the opposite direction. The kid and his friends were wiped out. Dead, all four of them. Just like that."

Dead.

The word marinates in radio static as Kelly's hand freezes on the dial.

She, too, is thinking about Caroline, Midge knows.

They all are. Reminding themselves that their friend didn't *die* a year ago tonight, no matter what anyone thinks. She's just . . .

Gone.

The rest of the world may believe she drowned after a late-night swim, but they don't know the whole story. Not even Caroline's boyfriend, Gordy, knows what really happened to her.

Midge, Kelly, and Talia will never tell.

A secret is a secret.

A promise is a promise.

CHAPTER THREE

Present Day

The call comes in just past dawn.

It's a medical emergency, a traumatic injury involving a fall down a flight of stairs.

The sun is coming up, setting treetops, rooftops, and mountaintops aglow as Midge races through the business district, siren wailing, dome light flashing.

Long gone are the days when Mulberry Bay was deserted at this hour—at all hours. Even at five thirty in the morning, there are cars, double-parked delivery trucks, joggers, and dog walkers. Commuters are lined up at Center Street Grind and Lakeside Coffee Roasters to grab lattes and espressos before heading to Albany, Poughkeepsie, or Rhinecliff, where many will catch an express train to Manhattan.

Midge makes a right, then a quick left onto Shore Street, which will be less congested.

She slows for the crosswalk speed bumps at the new state-of-the-art complex that houses an elementary school, a middle school, and a high school. It doesn't seem so long ago that they were all under one roof in the original building, now being used as the district administration offices.

She waves at the Walking Man, ambling along in his army jacket with a tall stick in hand and backpack over his shoulders. He nods in return, then stoops to collect some sidewalk treasure as she drives past. He was never a large man but seems to be shrinking with age. Always walking, never talking, he remains a local fixture.

Boaters are setting out on the water with fishing gear at the newly built marina adjacent to the Landing restaurant, where a seafood wholesaler is unloading crates of lobster and oysters at the service entrance. Out front, a sign advertises the WORLD-FAMOUS SURF AND TURF and happy hour specials at the tiki bar. The ocean is nowhere near Mulberry Bay, but the place is cultivating a New England boardwalk meets tropical island vibe.

Painters are touching up the pink gingerbread trim at the Dive Inn, which occupies a ramshackle waterfront building that was once a Victorian hotel. The name was meant to be ironic, as the previous owners had never aspired to anything more than, well, a dive bar.

The new ones had retained the name but made the place over into something out of a Hallmark movie. It's painted in rainbow sherbet shades, with petunias rippling from window boxes and pedestal planters. The formerly rutted dirt parking lot has been paved in white stones that look like gleaming crystals when the sun catches them. Wooden rocking chairs line the wide veranda that once was cordoned off for a year because someone fell through the rotting floorboards.

As a longtime regular, Midge can't help but miss the dump it once was. A lot of memories there.

Memories everywhere, in Mulberry Bay.

Change too.

Out on Route 28, pickup trucks and contractor vans fill the left turning lane for Home Depot and the right for Lowe's. At the Starbucks that replaced the old KFC, overflowing drive-through traffic blocks the entrance to the former Family Video building next door, which is currently a high-end chain steak house. It doesn't open until lunchtime, and then will be mobbed till late tonight, just like every other restaurant in town.

Midge passes Wildgreen, the new locally owned organic supermarket that opened on the old A&P site, then veers around a dump truck with flashers on as it follows a backhoe into the ever-expanding strip mall's new satellite parking lot. A landscaper's truck loaded with burlap-wrapped shrubs and saplings pulls into the new town house community that replaced the senior citizen apartments that many years ago replaced the trailer park.

Past that development, the road maintains its rural origins.

She keeps an eye out for deer along the wooded roadside as she speeds along, aware that they're most active at this hour. She's been forced to humanely dispatch a number of injured animals that were hit by vehicles along this rural stretch. Many times, it's a doe that was chasing its fawn.

This job isn't for the faint of heart, but it's the only thing Midge has ever wanted to do.

Law enforcement is in her blood.

Maybe, too, all these years of doing the right thing and ensuring that other people do the right thing are her way of making up for the very wrong thing she did in her youth.

She instinctively slows at the spot where the old streetcar tracks had ridges in the road. Now they lie beneath layers of smooth blacktop.

If she drove a little farther, she'd be at Haven Cliff, where twenty-five years ago tonight . . .

But she's reached her destination.

She takes a deep breath, preparing herself for what lies ahead. She's worked a lot of critical trauma cases over her twenty years in law enforcement, and it's always difficult. Especially when a spouse and children are involved. Especially when she knows the victim.

Knew. She hasn't talked to him in years—just seen him around town, always from a distance. Like his old Dutch farmhouse that sits on a large swath of steep, wooded acreage with no sight line to neighboring homes.

The ambulance is already there, parked behind a pair of Volvos.

Two lanky teenage boys and a blond woman are out on the sloping front lawn. Midge doesn't know her personally, but she's seen her around town. She seems like a prim and proper person who rarely cracks a smile, raises her voice, or has a hair out of place. Now, she's crying hysterically. Her younger son has an arm around her. The older son is pacing, talking on his phone.

Midge parks behind the ambulance, which is unoccupied, and strides toward the two-story house, gray shingled with blue shutters. The garden beds are precision edged and mulched. Clumps of bearded purple iris bloom along the stone foundation, and red geraniums and ivy trail from window boxes.

The front door is wide open, providing a clear view of a wooden staircase. There's no sign of the medics or the victim, who reportedly fell down a flight of steps.

Midge turns her attention to the family.

Even in the dim morning light, Midge can see that the woman's white nightgown is streaked with what can only be blood.

Midge flashes her badge and introduces herself, then asks the woman, "Are you Amy?"

She wails a yes.

"What's your name?" Midge asks the boy.

"Noah."

"You're the one who called 9-1-1."

He nods, poking a finger behind his glasses to wipe tears from his blue eyes.

He looks so much like his father did as a teenager.

She glances at Amy. Her head is bowed and she's whispering to herself. "Dear Lord . . . oh, dear Lord . . ."

"And your brother's name is . . . ?" Midge indicates the other boy. He's ignoring them, pacing the yard with his phone still pressed to his ear.

"Mike."

"Do you know who he's talking to?"

"His girlfriend."

"And none of you are injured, right?"

"Yes. I mean, yes, right. We're not injured."

"When did your dad fall? Just the approximate time?"

"I was asleep, so . . . I heard Mom screaming, and so did Mike, and we got up, but . . ." Noah looks at his mother. "Mom? What time—"

"I don't know! He wasn't in bed, and he wasn't downstairs, and then . . . I found him . . ." She presses a trembling fist to her mouth, shaking her head.

"So no one witnessed the fall? There's no one else on the premises?" Midge asks Noah. "Aside from the medics, I mean."

"Just my dad."

Amy moans. "He wasn't breathing. He's dead."

"Stop saying that!" Mike shouts, shoving his phone into his pocket and raking a hand through his hair, which is already standing on end. "Mom, please! You don't know that!"

Amy's desolate, tear-flooded eyes meet Midge's gaze. She does know. Her mouth moves, but nothing comes out.

"Okay," Midge says quietly, and looks at Noah. "Where . . . ?"

"Out back." He points to a flagstone walkway that leads around the side of the house. It passes beneath an arched white trellis covered in pink roses.

"All right. I'm going to go see what's what."

"Uh . . ."

Midge turns back to Noah. "Yes?"

He hesitates, as if he wants to say something, then shakes his head. "Never mind."

"Just sit tight for a minute."

She walks to the backyard. Songbirds chirp from overhead boughs and take turns swooping to a feeder. The landscaping is natural, with more trees, shrubs, and large rock outcroppings than lawn. But what there is has recently been mowed. The sweet scent of grass clippings mingles with cedar mulch.

Midge eyes the open sliding glass door to a low deck that runs the length of the house, with three wooden steps leading to the backyard.

Amy had to be mistaken. It's impossible to imagine a grown man being killed falling from that height. And even if, in some freakish twist, her husband *is* dead, the medics wouldn't have moved him from the spot. There are procedures, protocols. They'd have had to wait for the medical examiner to get here.

All right, then. He fell down the steps, and he got banged up, and they're probably tending to him inside the house. That's all it is.

Midge tilts her head to the sky as relief courses through her, closing her eyes and saying a quick prayer of gratitude.

When she opens them, she sees a large winged creature circling high overhead. Not a songbird.

A hawk, maybe, or . . .

A vulture?

She remembers the blood staining his wife's nightgown, and the boys' stricken faces.

Then she hears a squawk. Not the bird, but a two-way radio. It's coming from nearby. Not inside the house.

Slowly turning, she eyes a tall wooden lattice fence along the back of the yard, bordered by trees and shrubs. The gate is ajar.

She walks over. Beyond the gate, terraced stone steps descend fifteen, maybe twenty feet to a bluestone terrace with a firepit surrounded by chairs.

At the base of the steps, one paramedic is talking on the phone as the other unhurriedly packs away the lifesaving equipment that was obviously unnecessary.

Between them, a man lies face down on a bloodstained bluestone slab. He's barefoot, wearing a pastel-yellow T-shirt and blue-and-white-striped pajama bottoms. His head is badly fractured, and his neck twisted at such an unnatural angle that his wife must have known at a glance that he was dead.

"Oh, Gordy," Midge whispers. "What happened to you?"

CHAPTER FOUR

June 14, 2000

Talia is still talking about college. Talking, talking, talking.

"... and then my roommate said we should ..."

Kelly is still twisting the radio dial. Twisting, twisting, twisting.

Static ... commercial ... country music ... heavy metal ... static ...

Midge is still waiting, waiting, waiting for the light to turn.

She cracks her window—not enough to let in the rain, but to get some air. Suddenly, it all feels so claustrophobic—the car, and these people.

"Green!" Kelly announces as the light changes at last. She adds, "You can go," as if Midge might be wondering what to do next.

She, too, has been getting on Midge's nerves these days.

Maybe that's just how it is with childhood friendships. Growing pains, growing up.

Or maybe it's because their personalities don't quite meld without Caroline in the mix.

If Caroline were here, Midge wouldn't blurt, "No!" when Kelly lands on a radio station playing "Oops! . . . I Did It Again."

Britney Spears is everywhere lately, a pervasive reminder that Caroline, an avid fan going back to the singer's *Mickey Mouse Club* days, is nowhere.

Kelly twists the dial, silencing Britney.

Static . . . static . . . Aaliyah's "Try Again."

"Ooh, good song!"

Kelly jerks the volume knob, and the music blasts, drowning out further conversation, and she bops her head to the beat. She recently bleached her long blond hair platinum and had it cut into short, spiky layers, as if to further distance herself from the elegant Ivy Leaguer her parents groomed her to be.

Driving on through the sleeping village, they pass the town square littered with broken glass and graffiti, the bandstand that hasn't held a concert in ages, and the Landing, which is now a greasy spoon with Talia's mom as the only waitress.

A rent-to-own store is the latest in a string of businesses that have occupied the first floor of the old savings and loan building that's never been a bank in Midge's lifetime.

Two doors down, above a tanning salon rumored to be closing soon, MULBERRY BAY JEWELERS is still faintly legible on the brick facade where the scrolling sign hung for years.

On the next block, a tattoo parlor recently replaced the dollar store that had been the lone successful retailer. But it had outgrown its space, so locals looking to stock up on off-brand condiments, plastic picture frames, and vinyl handbags will now have to visit the expanded store, which anchors a mostly vacant shopping plaza out on Route 28.

This, according to Midge's father, is the final nail in Mulberry Bay's coffin.

Born and raised here, Bobby Kennedy—not *that* Bobby Kennedy—frequently brings up the good old days, usually at the family dinner table.

"It used to be a JCPenney," he said of the dollar store's new location.

"Wow, next best thing to Saks Fifth Avenue," Midge's wiseass sister, Patty, commented under her breath.

"Every year on Labor Day, my mother brought us there for our back-to-school shoes," he waxed on.

"And your mother's always talking about how *her* mother bought *her* back-to-school shoes at an actual shoe store downtown on Center Street," Midge's mom reminded him. "Everything changes. Everyone is nostalgic."

"I doubt our kids will ever be nostalgic for a strip mall dollar store, Gena. And that damned tattoo parlor is going to bring in every kind of riffraff."

From Patty: "How many kinds of riffraff are there, exactly? Ten? Fifty?"

"Too many. And only an idiot would pay to be branded like a cow."

Ordinarily, Midge would have pushed back against her father's comment. But she kept her head down and ate meat loaf, her own tattoo threatening to sear a hole through her bra strap and make itself known.

It was meant to be indelible as the friendship between Midge and her three best friends.

Now Talia's future lies elsewhere, Midge and Kelly don't see each other as often as they might, and Caroline . . .

Everything changes. Everyone is nostalgic.

The residential neighborhood falls behind as they head out on Route 28, the two-lane highway that traces the lakeshore out of town toward Phoenicia and the mountains. They pass Kentucky Fried Chicken, Family Video, the strip mall, a trailer park. The road becomes darker and more rural, bordered by fields and woods, Catskill peaks looming like sleeping giants.

She brakes just ahead of the parallel ridges in the pavement that mark ancient streetcar tracks. A rusted grillwork sign on the shoulder reads TROLLEY PARK BEACH, though it's one of those things you only know if you know. The text is all but obscured by weeds and vines, marking the overgrown lane that once led to a waterside amusement park.

Three-tenths of a mile past the sign, she brakes again.

Kelly takes that as a cue to turn off the radio.

In the silence, Midge hears Talia suck in a breath and release it slowly, as if she's steeling herself for what lies ahead.

They all are.

Another tenth of a mile and Midge flips on the turn signal. After glancing in the rearview mirror to make sure there's no one behind them, she pulls into a shadowy dirt lane flanked by massive stone pillars connected by an arched iron banner that reads HAVEN CLIFF.

The estate was built in 1892 as a summer retreat for Caroline's great-great-grandfather, New York industrialist Asa Winterfield.

After Asa and his wife, Edith, were brutally murdered here, the eldest of their seven offspring, Lester, inherited everything. The house sat deserted until 1909, when New York state mandated that every county must open at least one sanatorium to address the tuberculosis epidemic.

Lester, living in New York City, donated Haven Cliff for that purpose. Its lakeside location was deemed ideal for a macabre reason: bodies of the dead could be removed from the premises via boat rather than transported through the town.

With tuberculosis cases sharply declining in the 1920s, Haven Cliff was converted to a so-called "lunatic asylum." In a tragic twist, one of Asa and Edith Winterfield's daughters was committed to the mental hospital that had once been her family's private home. Her mysterious death soon afterward was either a gruesome accident or suicide, fueling rumors of the Haven Cliff curse.

The asylum operated into the 1980s. The house and grounds have been abandoned ever since.

In the headlights' misty glow, Midge can see rain-soaked NO TRESPASSING warnings posted on the trees, edges flapping in the wind, and a FOR SALE sign with the name and phone number of a local real estate company.

If this were a weekend night, or even a weeknight with nice weather, cars would be parked along the lane leading to the mansion's ruins. There are always high school parties up here—not just on prom night.

"You'd have to be out of your mind to buy this place," Kelly mutters. "Even Caroline's parents aren't trying to get their hands on it, and they're the only Winterfields left in this town."

"Yeah, but they're not rich," Midge points out.

The youngest of the seven orphaned Winterfields, Caroline's great-grandfather was a toddler when his parents were murdered. He was found at the scene, crying and covered in blood, trying to wake up his dead mother.

"There's no way they'd want it now, even if they could afford it," Talia says. "I'm sure they're glad it's condemned. They'll probably be relieved when it's knocked down later this summer."

Midge shakes her head. "My dad said the Preservation Society will never let that happen. And my mom heard that some investment banker from Manhattan made an offer on it. I guess he wants to restore it and use it as a private vacation home."

"Here?" Kelly asks.

"Yes, *here*," Midge says. "Back in the late eighteen hundreds, all the rich New York City tycoons built mansions in the Hudson Valley."

"Not *all*," Talia says. "My roommate's uncle is really good friends with this guy who—"

"Not now, Tal," Midge cuts in, as gently as she can. "Please? We have to focus on what we need to do."

"I don't think I want to do it anymore."

"You have to," Kelly snaps. "We're here. We're not bringing you back home."

"Then I'll wait in the car."

Midge glances at her in the rearview mirror, noting the stubborn set to her jaw. "Come on, Talia, don't be like that. We promised Caroline we'd do this."

Kelly nods. "Right. All three of us, together. That's what we said."

Silence from the back seat.

"Don't be a candy-ass," Kelly says.

"I'm not!"

"Then we're doing this."

Midge navigates the last bend in the rutted lane, and they emerge into a wide clearing, startling a herd of deer grazing there. The animals disappear into the woods beyond the remains of the three-story mansion.

Shrouded by a filmy veil of rain, the crumbling granite facade wears its pillars and balustrades like a crone in a tattered ball gown. There are traces of former architectural grandeur in the brick chimneys and stone turrets rising from an elevated foundation, and in the raised stone terrace facing what's left of a courtyard. Weeds shroud marble fountains, and statues rise like ghostly sentries from a tangle of brambles that were once a formal garden.

Midge pulls to the edge of the clearing, alongside a stand of overgrown mock orange. She shifts into park and takes a deep breath, filling her lungs with the shrubs' sweet, old-fashioned scent.

"I love this smell."

"Seriously? I think it's disgusting," Kelly says. "It's like a whore's bath."

"A what?" Talia asks.

"You know, spraying perfume to cover up something nasty. Which pretty much suits this place, when you think about it."

Midge does think about it. About the terrible things that have unfolded at Haven Cliff—beginning and ending with the Winterfields.

"Do you guys think she's really going to show?" Talia asks.

"If she doesn't, she's dead," Kelly says.

Midge shudders. "Please don't use that word. She's not—"

"Not *dead* dead. I didn't mean it like that. Just . . . we kept our promise. She'd better have kept hers, that's all."

"She made it a long time ago, though. A whole year."

A year. Yes. Pretty much to the minute.

Midge glances at the dashboard clock, turns off the engine, grabs a flashlight from the glove compartment, and opens her door.

"Let's go," she tells the others. "It's almost midnight. We're right on time."

CHAPTER FIVE

He walks as the rain pours down beyond the remnants of a century-old wooden awning. This was once the facade to a penny arcade, and the splintered planks beneath his feet were part of the Trolley Park Beach boardwalk.

One of the region's most popular amusement parks, it was a smaller-scale Coney Island, with rides, games, concessions, and vaudeville entertainment. Closed during the Depression era and war years, it reopened in the 1950s but never quite caught on again.

He learned all this information at the Historical Preservation Society, combing over sepia photos depicting the park's halcyon days.

He's seen the carousel and Ferris wheel filled with gleeful children— little girls with corkscrew curls and huge floppy hair bows, little boys in knickers and newsboy caps. He's seen young women in bathing costumes wading in the shallow water beside the boardwalk, and mustachioed anglers in brimmed hats on the long fishing pier.

He spends a lot of time at the historical society. The faces and places of Mulberry Bay's distant past—one he never actually experienced—are far more familiar to him than the ones that populated his own.

He mourns the long-dead carousel children—all of them, really, all the people in those old photographs—more than he does the ones he's actually known. He even mourns the carousel ponies interred beneath a heap of wood and twisted metal. Mourns the Ferris wheel whose rusted spokes rise like gnarled claws, and the arcade that lies behind him in rubble, and the fishing pier reduced to a rickety wooden platform about fifty yards out in the water, with another in the shallows off the pebbly beach.

Tonight, a canoe is tied up to one of the pilings.

It's blue, with a white number four on the bow, and red lettering that spells out WOODY LO-HI. That's the name of the sleepaway camp across the lake, also captured in photographs he's seen at the historical society.

But the camp is part of a more recent history. It operated from the 1950s until just a few summers ago. Now it's on the market, advertised on a faded flyer taped to the window at the local real estate office: *Bucolic summer resort with ten charming cabins, dining hall, administration building, indoor and outdoor recreational facilities. Includes all furnishings and recreational equipment.*

The canoes are stored in the small crafts shack with a broken padlock. There are six, each bearing a number and painted in a different color scheme.

He knows this because he's explored the abandoned camp, just as he's explored this abandoned park and the abandoned estate nearby.

Haven Cliff.

Someone must have taken canoe number four and rowed across the lake. It happened tonight, because he's been by here several times today, making his rounds, and he'd have noticed it.

He remembers the things that matter.

Remembers that this same canoe—the one painted in patriotic colors—was here once before, in this very spot. Exactly one year ago tonight.

CHAPTER SIX

Present Day

Every morning, Kelly hikes alone along a trail that was once a walkway to Haven Cliff's outbuildings and amenities. There had been a carriage house, a greenhouse, tennis courts, a swimming pool, and, perched at the highest point, a picnic pavilion with a beautiful view of the lake.

After the Winterfields' double homicide, the manor was abandoned, and the surrounding forest encroached on Haven Cliff like a predator that had been lurking all along.

Every morning when she's out here, phrases about the dark, deep woods and promises to keep flit in her mind like moths in a dusty attic. They're from a poem she used to know by heart, but now she can't even recall the title—only that she and Caroline memorized it for a sophomore English project back in the spring of 1997. Two years before Caroline disappeared—around the time that Caroline's sister Mary Beth—

Hearing distant sirens, Kelly pauses to listen.

Another fender bender in town, most likely. There are so many city people around here now, unfamiliar with traffic patterns, speeding around, honking, too impatient to wait for lights to turn green.

Kelly herself was one of them a few short years ago, infused with urban edginess, unaccustomed to life in this place, at this pace, after two decades away. Gradually, the urban edginess subsided, and Mulberry

Bay became home. Home *again*, though she's settled here in a way that she never was in her reckless, restless youth.

The sirens aren't quite so distant now. Maybe the fender bender was nearby, on Route 28. Or maybe it was something more serious.

She walks on, ignoring a prickle of apprehension, trying to focus on the dawn chorus emanating from treetops shrouded with early-morning fog.

She spent over a decade living in San Francisco, where it wasn't unusual for a wall of swirling gray to obliterate a clear blue sky without warning and linger all day. But it strikes her as an ominous sign here, alone in the woods at Haven Cliff—on this day, of all days.

She reminds herself that the fog has nothing to do with that; that it will quickly dissipate with the sunrise; that there's a beautiful day in the forecast. There's no reason for the apprehension that dogs her now along the path she follows most mornings at this hour, steeping her soul in nature, exercise . . .

Oh, and coffee. A whole lot of coffee. She'll be on her third cup when she gets back to the house.

Long gone are the days when she could party all night, fall right to sleep, and not stir till morning—or, on good days, afternoon.

At forty-three, she's become one of those women who can barely keep her eyes open past nine, only to wake in the wee hours, plagued by insomnia, and pain.

Every part of her body aches these days, even though the bulk of the physical work has been over for a while now. Last winter and into the spring, she pitched in with the crew on tasks like painting and staining woodwork, carrying boxes, moving furniture. Sometimes it was because she wanted things done right, and sometimes it was just to expedite the process. At the time, she didn't experience sore muscles, creaky joints, headaches, or fatigue, but they've caught up with a vengeance.

Maybe this, like her forgetfulness, is due to age or the stress that comes with the gargantuan project she took on when she bought this property.

"But *why*?" Midge asked her back in 2021, when she first confided that she'd set her sights on Haven Cliff.

She considered telling Midge about the psychic reading she'd had a year earlier, while she was still living abroad.

Kelly herself never put much stock into fortune-telling before moving to Paris, where she stumbled across an exhibit in le Musée français de la carte à jouer, a museum devoted to playing cards. After learning about the fifteenth-century European origins of the tarot, she had her first reading with Madame Céline—and became a monthly regular thereafter.

Three memorable cards came up for Kelly at that last reading, immediately preceding the phone call that changed everything: the tower card, which Madame Céline said indicated sudden upheaval looming; the six of swords, which was connected to letting go of the past; and the reversed moon card, advising her to trust her instincts regarding a significant investment.

Midge, who deals in facts and concrete evidence, would dismiss the tarot as bunk, so Kelly said only, "I can't keep living with my mother. And I can't live far from her either. If I have to stay in Mulberry Bay—and I do, for the foreseeable future—then I need a place of my own. This is a great real estate investment."

"That's BS. There are plenty of other places around here. You have the money to get a big piece of property and build a brand-new house."

"I don't want a brand-new house, Midge. I lived in a brownstone in New York, and a Victorian in San Francisco, and a belle epoque *maison* in Paris. I like a place with history."

"But *this* history? With everything that happened at Haven Cliff . . . with Caroline . . . isn't there some other place you can—"

"There isn't," Kelly said with a shrug. "I want this *because* of Caroline. Haven Cliff was her family's home. It's the last place we saw her. She promised to come back here. This is the only way we can make sure that it's still here when she does."

When.

Not *if.*

"I'm meeting with the owner next week in New York to talk her into selling. Wish me luck."

"You don't need luck, Kelly. When you want something, you always find a way to get it."

"Yeah, but it was a lot easier when I had some man wrapped around my finger to make sure of that. Like my dad."

"Or all those ex-husbands?"

"There were only two."

The second was even wealthier than the first, which meant that Kelly could certainly afford Haven Cliff. Not that it was on the market. But everything has a price, and Kelly had done her homework.

Joseph Andover, a New York financier, bought the property in 2000. He promptly applied for permits to raze the existing structures, clear the wooded peninsula, and build a condominium complex. The town board took over a year to grant them.

On September 10, 2001, the paperwork was finally in place, and demolition was scheduled to begin. But the weather was stormy, and the work was postponed.

The next morning, Andover was presumed to have been in his ninety-fifth-floor office, precisely where the first terrorist-hijacked plane slammed into the World Trade Center's North Tower. His remains were never recovered.

Work was halted as the New York–based construction crew joined the recovery efforts at ground zero. Andover's widow had no interest in resuming the Haven Cliff project and did little more than pay the taxes on it for twenty years.

Kelly met Kathryn Andover at her penthouse on the Upper East Side. The view of the park was spectacular. The view of the cityscape to the south likely would have been spectacular, too, but the drapes were drawn across those windows, facing the altered skyline where the Twin Towers had once stood.

Two decades after they fell, almost to the very day, Kathryn accepted Kelly's offer, and Haven Cliff was hers.

She doesn't believe that Joseph Andover was a victim of the curse that, according to local legend, was spawned when New York City tycoon Asa Winterfield knowingly built the mansion on the site of an eighteenth-century settlement graveyard.

Supposedly, its vengeful spirits instigated Asa and Edith's 1894 double homicide, as well as every tragedy and mishap related to the property ever since, including Joseph Andover's death and, of course, Caroline Winterfield's mysterious disappearance from the grounds in 1999.

Asa and Edith supposedly haunt the place to this day, along with patients who suffered and died here when it was a tuberculosis sanatorium, tortured souls involuntarily committed within these walls when it served as an asylum, and a little boy who fell into the lake from a rowboat during a Sunday school picnic back in the early nineteen hundreds.

He went underwater and never resurfaced. He didn't struggle. Didn't cry for help. He was simply swallowed by the depths, and his remains were never found.

For weeks afterward, as the tale goes, his distraught mother wandered out here in the dead of night, calling his name. She was pulled from the water time and again, fully clothed and searching in vain for her child. Finally, she, too, disappeared into the icy depths, and both their spirits are said to haunt the lake.

Kelly first heard that particular ghost story back in kindergarten. She found it far more disturbing than the others because it involved a child. She was terrified to go to swimming lessons at the lake until her parents convinced her that it wasn't true.

Turned out, it was.

Well, maybe not the haunting part. But recently, having embarked on Haven Cliff's restoration, she stumbled across old news accounts about the ill-fated mother and son in the historical society's archives. They were real, and the details about their deaths were accurate.

She often wonders if that ghost story is still circulating among Mulberry Bay kids.

Wonders, too, whether Caroline Winterfield is said to be haunting the lake.

She isn't, of course.

But if she *were* going to haunt Haven Cliff from the afterlife, Kelly is certain this is where Caroline would be—here, at the spot where she walked into the woods that fateful night and took her place in Haven Cliff lore.

CHAPTER SEVEN

When the sirens sounded, Ceto was in bed but not asleep.

You don't sleep after something like that. You lie awake for hours, adrenaline still pulsing through your veins, and you relive everything that happened. Everything he said and wouldn't say. Everything you *did*.

Your whole body is clenched, and you're bracing yourself for whatever is coming next. For a police car to pull up outside, casting the room in fluid red light. For footsteps, voices, a knock on the door. They'll take you away, asking questions you'll refuse to answer until you have a lawyer present. You weren't born yesterday. You know your rights.

Yeah, but none of those things happen.

Only sirens, screaming in the night.

Rather, morning. Just past five thirty, according to the clock on the nightstand.

Ceto sits up, heart pounding.

It might be something else—a fire, a robbery, an accident . . .

But more likely, they've found the dead man.

CHAPTER EIGHT

Midge recognizes both paramedics who are standing over Gordy Klatte's corpse.

Louie Felch is a gruff old-timer who's been working this job since Midge's father was chief of police, and probably long before.

Janna Torres was married to one of the players on Midge's softball team, though they're no longer together. That's for the best, as Janna is a wonderful person and her wife was a serial cheater.

Midge jots down notes as they fill her in on what they know, which isn't much. Injuries consistent with a fall. Rigor mortis has set in, and he's probably been lying here for several hours.

As often happens on the job in Mulberry Bay, Janna and Louie also know—knew—the deceased.

"I don't know him well," Janna tells Midge. "Just from around town."

"Yeah, his dad is my dentist," Louie says. "Odd duck, Dr. Klatte. Like father, like son."

Janna swats his arm. "Don't speak ill of the dead. Sorry, Midge. Did you know him too?"

"He's . . . an old friend. High school. He, uh . . ." She swallows the rest of it. There's no need to bring the past into this conversation when the present is disturbing enough.

The summer after Caroline's disappearance, Gordy went away to college in Pennsylvania, as both he and Caroline were planning to do. If he ever came home to visit, Midge didn't run into him, which wasn't surprising. He wasn't into sports, and he didn't drink, and back in those days, she spent her free time playing softball and basketball in the rec leagues or having beers at the Dive Inn. Still does.

Funny, how you can share a past and a small town and not cross paths until . . .

Well, until it's too late.

"The ME's on the way," Louie tells her, pocketing his phone. "He can notify the family, if you want to wait, but it might be a while."

"They already know. They saw him. His wife did, anyway. I don't know about the boys."

"I hope not." Janna coils a cord around her hand. "Poor kids."

"Damned shame." Louie takes a bag of chocolate-covered peanuts from his pocket and eats a few, then shoos away a couple of flies buzzing around the dead body before offering the bag to Midge and Janna.

Midge shakes her head and looks again at the sky. Now there's another large bird circling with the first, high overhead.

Don't vultures eat people? she asked Gordy so long ago. He said yes.

She hasn't thought about that exchange in years, but it comes back to her in this moment.

As she shifts her attention away from the sky, Midge spots a clean-shaven man in a dark suit peering down at them over the lattice fence. She sees him see Gordy. His face registers shock, then sorrow.

He tilts his head back, eyes closed, lips moving, hands clasped in prayer.

"That's Reverend Parker," Louie says low, under his breath. "He's a real holy roller, that guy."

Janna pokes Louie with the end of the cord.

He flinches. "Hey!"

"Shh!"

"What? He's busy talking to God. He can't hear me."

Midge gives Louie a stern look. He goes back to his candy as she climbs the stairs toward the newcomer. When she reaches the top, he opens his eyes, and she sees tears in them.

"I'm Detective Sergeant Imogene Kennedy," she says. "Reverend Parker, is it?"

"Yes."

"How did you hear?"

"The Klattes are congregants at my church. Noah called me right after he called the ambulance. He told me that his dad had had an accident and that they needed me to come right over. I assumed . . . I thought it was a car accident, not . . ." He glances at the body and releases a shuddering breath. "Gordon was a wonderful man."

"I'm so sorry for your loss, Reverend. I was just going back to speak with the family. I think it might be a good idea if you can accompany me when I confirm the death."

"Of course. Do you know how this happened? Or when?"

"It looks like he came out here in the dark and lost his footing on the stairs."

"It does," the man agrees, rubbing his hairless chin and gazing down at Gordy. "It does look like that, but we don't know for sure, do we?"

"You don't think that's what happened?"

"What?" He flicks a startled gaze at her.

"It's just the way you said that it *looks* like that . . ."

"You're the one who said that, Detective. I merely agreed and pointed out that we don't have that information. Only God knows. Only God was with him in the end."

Let's hope so, Midge finds herself thinking, with a glance at Gordy.

Of course no one—God aside—was out here with him under cover of darkness, watching him fall to his death . . .

Pushing him to his death?

There's no evidence of foul play, and the preliminary conclusion is that this was nothing more than a tragic accident.

An accident that occurred on the twenty-fifth anniversary of his high school sweetheart's disappearance.

CHAPTER NINE

Kelly gazes at one of the few spots on the property that has remained unaltered since the night Caroline disappeared into the woods here. Four splintered pillars and a bluestone platform mark the original picnic pavilion, along with corroded iron tables and benches and an old stone fireplace. Nearby, a tire swing with rusted chains dangles from a low-hanging branch.

The trail continues on along the wooded slope to wide stone steps down to the water. The original handrails are long gone, but back then, there were makeshift ones, constructed from fallen limbs and old planks. Those have since rotted away.

So have the boathouse and icehouse that once stood near the lake, and the remnants of the Trolley Park wooden fishing pier.

For as often as Kelly has come out here in the three years since she bought Haven Cliff, she's ventured down there only a handful of times. For her, the beach and water hold no memories. Nor does the rebuilt house itself.

But the woods . . .

The woods hold memories. For better or worse. The woods remind her of Caroline, and that night, and that damned poem . . . whatever it was.

It seems to happen a lot lately—this forgetfulness. Maybe it's because she's been so busy, a million details on her mind as the massive renovation project nears completion.

Or maybe it's just that she's getting older.

As long as that's *all* it is.

She's started making lists, jotting down ideas and thoughts as they occur to her. But she doesn't carry her little notebook and pen on her hikes.

She turns and heads back toward the house, breathing the sweet smell of flowers. Many of Edith Winterfield's horticultural specimens escaped their Victorian beds to creep along paths and scale stone walls. At this time of year, a sea of mock orange blooms transforms the property into a fragrant oasis.

She reaches the pool. The original one, with its cracked Italian tiles, was filled in the summer after Caroline's disappearance. Now the site is staked off and ready to be reexcavated.

Masons have already completed restoration on the brick colonnade. Beneath each of the four archways, stone pedestals are etched with the names of the Greek water gods whose statues once perched there: Poseidon, Oceanus, Hydros, and Ceto.

Wisps of morning mist drift like apparitions as Kelly pauses to stare at the spot, remembering.

Each of the girls claimed her own pedestal, back when they first started hanging out up here. Kelly was Poseidon, Talia was Oceanus, Midge was Hydros, and Caroline was Ceto.

Kelly considered commissioning new statues to replace them, but it doesn't feel right. Nor does removing the pedestals.

She would prefer to leave the pool site untouched altogether, building a new one in a sunnier spot, but discovered there's a reason it was positioned in this location. The property is wooded, perched on deep layers of bedrock and pocked with massive boulders.

Raoul, the contractor from Aquascapes, told her that relocating the pool would involve geological surveys and trying to get permits for blasting bedrock and removing ancient trees.

"If you keep it right where it is, it'll be ready by the first day of *this* summer. If you want to move it to another spot, you're looking at next summer at the earliest."

"I'll keep it right where it is, then. When can you start?"

At first he said April. Then it got pushed back to May. She's learned that that's the way it often goes with these things—delays due to weather, workman or equipment shortages.

The first day of summer is only a week away now. But Aquascapes is starting excavation this morning. Raoul promised they'll work all this weekend and next to ensure that she'll be swimming in a couple of weeks.

"You can have a pool party on the Fourth of July," he told Kelly.

Party . . . Fourth of July . . .

Happy birthday, Caroline . . . wherever you are.

CHAPTER TEN

July 4, 1997

"Could this be any more depressing?" Kelly asks as she walks with Midge and Talia along Main Street beneath an overcast sky, chilly even in jeans and a windbreaker.

"You just said five minutes ago that you're over it," Talia says.

"The breakup? I'm totally over *that*." Jason may have been her first real boyfriend, but he was also a cheating jerk. "I'm talking about the weather. It feels more like March than the Fourth of July."

Midge shrugs. "Who cares? We're going to a party."

Caroline's annual family birthday picnic isn't Kelly's idea of a party, but she says only, "We can't even go swimming."

"Swimming!" Talia shudders. "There's probably still ice floating around the lake. My leg cramps right up if I even stick a toe in that water at this time of year. Anyway, it's not supposed to rain."

"I guess that's good, but everything seems so gloomy. I wish the sun would come out."

Midge, a fair-skinned ginger, shakes her head. "Not me. I'm glad I'm not getting third-degree burns today."

"And it sucks that there's not even going to be fireworks tonight," Kelly goes on, stepping around a ripe mulberry someone else's shoe squashed.

The town was named for the trees that grow rampant around the lake. It sounds charming, and maybe it's nice if you actually like the fruit. Kelly does not. But the birds sure do. At this time of year, their droppings make a terrible mess, mingling with the fallen fruit that stains the sidewalks like blood.

"My dad is glad they're not doing fireworks here this year," Midge says. "He thinks it was getting out of hand, with so many out-of-towners coming here to see them."

"What's wrong with out-of-towners? If there were fireworks, I'd be working today for sure," says Talia, who just started a summer job waitressing at the Landing. "My mom says tourists are good tippers."

Midge shakes her head. "Not these kinds of tourists. A lot of them are just here to cause trouble. Do you know how many people were arrested last year on the Fourth?"

"I think trouble sounds like a lot more fun than this lame birthday party we have to go to every year," Kelly says, and immediately wishes she hadn't.

"Kelly!" her friends say in unison.

"What? You know I love Caroline. But we're sixteen now! Don't you think that's too old for a family picnic with stupid games and cupcakes?"

"Maybe, but I doubt her parents are going to throw her a kegger," Midge says.

Kelly rolls her eyes. "I bet they got her a chastity belt for her birthday."

Mr. and Mrs. Winterfield make Midge's police chief father look permissive. They've always been strict with their four daughters.

The eldest, Eve and Joanna, are drab twins—fraternal, they like to remind everyone, to which Kelly once replied, "I was thinking Siamese."

Yeah, they weren't amused.

They're never amused. They've always been humorless and have always done everything together—which mostly involves studying, church activities, and chores. Now in their early twenties, they're married to equally drab guys, both named Jim.

At seventeen, the next Winterfield daughter, Mary Beth, is only eighteen months older than Caroline. The two of them look far more alike than their twin sisters, but the resemblance doesn't extend to their personalities.

Mary Beth is vivacious, athletic, and popular, especially with the boys. Not that her parents allow her to date.

And not that Mary Beth ever let their rules stop her.

Caroline, though . . . she's the model child. So good, and kind, and sweet.

They round the corner onto Shore Street, a wide semi-industrial area dotted with smaller homes and waterfront warehouses. It runs along the lake, parallel to Main Street, before merging into Route 28.

Over at the Landing, Talia's mom's beat-up Honda is one of the only cars in the parking lot. The lake is gray and choppy today, and a cool breeze threatens to whip the American flag right off its tall pole on the concrete pier. The bandstand is forlorn, draped in patriotic bunting as in holidays past, but without the prospect of the annual concert and fireworks.

The Walking Man is there, poking around a weedy patch with his long stick.

"I wonder what he lost," Midge says.

"His mind, obviously."

"Kelly!" Talia shakes her head. "Geez, leave the poor guy alone."

"I don't mean it in a bad way. But it's the truth."

"I don't think he's crazy," Midge says.

"He just walks and walks and walks without ever going anywhere," Kelly points out. "How is that not crazy?"

"He wears military camo," Talia says. "My mom thinks he's a vet. Maybe homeless."

"Great. My dad said you only used to see bums in big cities, but now they're everywhere."

"Kelly! You can't call the Walking Man a bum," Midge says. "That's so mean."

"Okay, he's a vagrant."

"Why are you being so heartless toward him, Kelly?"

"Why are you defending him so hard, Midge?"

"Because he served our country! And he's a human being! And sometimes *you* aren't—"

"Human?"

"Humane."

Midge is right, but Kelly can't help cloaking her remorse in snark. "Okay, okay! I'm sorry, Saint Midge."

"My mom sneaks him a sandwich sometimes," Talia comments, "and she said he always seems to be starving, but he still breaks off pieces of bread to feed the birds."

"Does she talk to him?" Midge asks.

"She tries, but he never says anything. She doesn't think he can speak."

"Can't? Or won't?" Kelly asks, and Midge makes an exasperated sound. "What? I'm just asking an honest question. I'm curious."

"So am I," Talia says. "But I don't know the answer."

They cross the road toward the small waterfront park, where red and blue Mylar balloons mark the usual picnic shelter.

Caroline's uncle Chuck is unloading coolers from the car, her mother and aunt Deb are wrestling with a plastic tablecloth in the breeze, her younger cousins are playing on the swings, and her dad and an unfamiliar man are firing up a barbecue grill.

"Looks like the gang's all here," Talia says.

"Except Mary Beth."

"Well, she's away for the summer," Midge reminds Kelly.

Right. Down south, or maybe it was out west, visiting relatives. That's what Caroline told them. But Kelly spent some time at Caroline's house this spring working on their honors English project and Mary Beth was excited about a summer nanny job she'd lined up. It seems strange that she left so abruptly.

"Hey, who's that with Caroline?" Midge asks.

Following her gaze, Kelly sees the birthday girl, pretty and petite, with glasses, wearing a white dress, white cardigan, and white flats. Her long brown hair is pulled back in a wide white headband with a white bow.

The guy she's talking to is scrawny with bad skin and a pronounced Adam's apple.

"One of the Jims?" Kelly suggests, referring to Caroline's two brothers-in-law.

Talia shakes her head. "No, isn't that Gordon Klatte?"

"Who?" Kelly asks.

Midge nods in recognition. "Oh! You're right. It *is* Gordon Klatte."

"*Who?*" Kelly asks again, peering at him. "How do you guys know him?"

"He's in my homeroom. Alphabetical order. Kennedy, Klatte."

"He's in marching band with me," Talia says. "He plays the sousaphone."

"The *what?*"

Talia rolls her eyes. "It's a musical instrument."

"Where, in Whoville?"

"Not *Seuss*, Kelly! Sousa. As in John Philip. He was—"

"Never mind, Tal; I really don't need to know."

"What *I* need to know," Midge says, "is what's he doing here?"

"Maybe he was jogging by and stopped to say hi," Kelly says.

"He isn't dressed like he was jogging," Talia says, indicating his khaki pants and short-sleeved button-down that someone's dad might wear on vacation.

"It was a joke, Tal. He doesn't look like he's capable of jogging. He looks like he's pinch-hitting for Reverend Statham."

Caroline has spotted them, and waves. Gordon turns around, and Kelly gets a better look. He's gawky, with a swoop of bad blond haircut above a prominent nose. Yeah, he seems vaguely familiar.

Caroline says something to him and heads toward her friends as they approach. Gordon hesitates for a moment, then trails after her.

"Yay! Now the party can start," Caroline says.

"Break out the JELL-O shots!"

Kelly is joking, of course, but Caroline immediately swivels her head to see if her family overheard. No, but she jumps, as if she didn't realize Gordon was right behind her.

Turning back to her friends, she appears flustered, eyebrows raised and cheeks puffed. Kelly can't tell if it's in a good way, or in a *why won't he leave me alone* way. Probably the latter, considering that Gordon's demeanor strikes Kelly as "puppy hoping for a treat."

Midge wraps her in a huge hug. "Happy sweet sixteen!"

"Thank you. You guys know Gordy, right?"

So he's Gordy, not Gordon—to Caroline, anyway. Interesting.

"I do, from band." Talia hugs Caroline before turning to Gordon. "You play the sousaphone, right?"

"Right."

"And you're in my homeroom," Midge says.

"Yeah," he agrees, and shifts his attention to Kelly, who's taking her turn to hug the birthday girl.

Meeting his gaze, she shrugs. "I don't know you."

She means it to come out in a fun, teasing way, but it doesn't. It sounds completely dismissive, as though she doesn't *want* to know him. Which may be true, because why is he here, hanging around with Caroline on her birthday? Still, she forces a smile and does her best to smooth things over. "I'm Kelly Barrow. You're Gordy . . ."

"Nobody calls me that."

"Oh, I must have misheard Caroline, then?"

"Caroline calls me Gordy. No one else, though."

"That's Caroline for you," Midge says. "She's the one who started calling me Midge, and now everyone does. Even my parents."

It's true. Caroline has nicknames for all of them. When she's feeling affectionate, Kelly is K. K., and Talia's Tally. But nicknames are for people who are closest to her, and Gordon Klatte is just some random guy.

"You two know each other from school?" Kelly directs the question to Caroline.

"Well, since Sunday school, when we were little kids. Our parents are good friends." Caroline indicates the polo-clad man with her father at the grill, and a woman in pearls and pumps setting out plastic-wrapped salads in the shelter.

There's an awkward pause.

Then Talia says, "You look so pretty. I love your dress."

"Thank you."

"So do I! So pretty," agrees Midge, who hates all dresses.

Kelly hands Caroline the tissue paper–bedecked bag holding the presents they picked out together at the mall yesterday. "It's from all of us."

"Aw, thanks, you guys! I can't wait to open—"

"Hey, look!" Gordy cuts in, pointing at a large winged creature arcing against the monochrome sky. "Do you know what that is?"

"A bird?"

He scowls at Kelly. "Duh."

"What kind of bird is it?" Caroline asks.

"I thought it was a turkey vulture, but it's not! It's a black vulture! Can you believe it?"

"Is that unusual?" Talia asks.

"Of course! Until recently, they weren't found this far north."

"No way, *really*?" Caroline asks, sounding like her mother, who tends to speak in a high-pitched, girlie tone that gets on Kelly's nerves.

"Wait, don't vultures eat people?" Midge asks.

"Yes."

"Cool," Kelly says in a tone that is decidedly *not* girlie, and the others shudder.

Gordy goes on to tell them more than anyone could ever want to know about that, and Kelly can't wait to get Caroline alone and ask her what's up with this teenage ornithologist crashing her birthday party.

But Gordy has adhered himself to their friend like a bodyguard. He joins them on the playground to keep an eye on the young cousins, and he sits with them when it's time to eat, apparently unaware or unbothered that he's the fifth wheel.

He doesn't have much to offer, conversation-wise—not to Kelly, Midge, and Talia, anyway. He's the kind of person who sits in a group but only addresses one person—Caroline—about people, places, and things the others know nothing about.

It isn't entirely bird talk. Most of the topics he broaches seem to involve academics, even though the school year is behind them, or church activities, or the Reverend Statham's kidney stone.

Oddly, Caroline doesn't seem to mind any of this.

There are moments when Kelly wonders if she, Midge, and Talia are the third, fourth, and fifth wheels.

Moments, in this first day with Gordy, that will later come back to haunt her.

CHAPTER ELEVEN

Present Day

Ceto was correct about the sirens.

They've definitely found the body.

First responders' vehicles now clog the Dutch Colonial's driveway.

She drives on past, wondering if Midge Kennedy is among them. If she isn't, she'll find out soon enough.

When she does, what will she think?

Not just Midge, but the others too. The so-called lifelong friends who weren't there for each other—or for Caroline—when it mattered most.

Just like Gordon Klatte.

Things could have been so different if they'd bothered to look at her, really look. All they had to do was look, listen, ask questions—just pay attention to what was going on right under their noses.

They could have helped her. They could have changed everything. Especially Gordy.

"I don't even know what you're talking about," he said last night when she pointed that out.

He was lying, though. Of course he was. She told him she was aware of that.

He had the nerve to say, "I can't have this. It needs to stop."

As if she were disrupting his perfect life.

As if he weren't responsible for destroying hers.

Partially responsible, anyway.

He refused to see it that way, and he paid the price.

As for the others . . .

Up ahead on the left, Ceto spots the stone pillars that flank the driveway that leads to Haven Cliff.

Driveway? More like an actual road.

It must be nice to live on a grand estate. To go through life using other people's money to buy whatever you want—even the things that rightfully belong to someone else. To tell yourself that you aren't responsible for the misfortunes of others—even when they're your friends.

The pillared entrance is looming.

Ceto slows down and flips the left turn signal.

It's time they were reminded that not everyone has been so fortunate.

CHAPTER TWELVE

Westchester County, NY

"Let's go, guys!" Talia calls from the foot of the stairs. "You'll have to walk if you miss the bus, because I can't drive you today!"

A lie. She will if she has to, though Westbrook Elementary School is a mere fifteen-minute stroll from here.

Half that, if you cut through the woods at the end of the cul-de-sac.

Not that anyone would. Student walkers stick to residential sidewalks and are always accompanied by entourages: nannies or parents, leashed dogs, siblings in strollers, neighbors. The others ride on yellow buses or in a brigade of luxury SUVs and EVs.

Kids around here don't go anywhere without supervision.

Things might have been different years ago in this leafy suburb where, according to local Realtor lore, Nobody Locks Their Doors and Nothing Bad Ever Happens.

Another lie.

They do. Bad things happen, even in beautiful small towns like Westbrook.

Like Mulberry Bay.

Talia may have called it home for the first two decades of her life, but when she left in 2001, she vowed never to return. She's kept that promise to herself ever since, but—

"Here I am, Mom!"

It's Hayley, appearing at the top of the stairs like a leading lady taking the stage. She recently informed Talia that *Mommy* is too babyish and she would hereafter refer to her as *Mom*.

"It could be worse," Ben said when she told him. "Imagine what she'll call you when she's a teenager."

"Only behind my back. I was hoping to get at least another year out of *Mommy*. I never stopped calling my own mom that."

"Things were different then," Ben pointed out. "I guess our girl is growing up."

And then some.

Hayley descends the stairs on long, lean legs, white sandals revealing her glossy red pedicure. She's wearing denim cutoffs she's cuffed to make shorter and a ruffly off-the-shoulders red-and-white-checked peasant top that had seemed adorably girlish in the store but now strikes Talia as Kardashian-esque.

"I thought you were going to wear jeans and red sneakers?"

"It's way too hot."

Talia can't argue with that. This is mid-June, with humid sunshine forecast for the third day in a row. And a clothing swap would be complicated, as the students were instructed to wear patriotic colors for the annual Flag Day field games.

It's getting late. They have to go.

"Where's Caleb?"

"I told him to hurry up because you're going away, and he told me to shut up, and I said, 'We don't say "shut up" in this house,' and then he told me to shut up *again*." Hayley rolls her green eyes and pushes her thick brunette hair back behind her ears.

She may look like Talia, but at her age and well beyond, Talia and her friends were steeped in innocence, collecting Beanie Babies and Polly Pocket dolls, on the cusp of their Backstreet Boys and Spice Girls years. Even Kelly, the most worldly and advanced of the four, seems downright wholesome by today's standards.

Hayley is eleven, going on eighteen. She's got a training bra, a cell phone, and her father's self-assurance.

At six, Caleb seems much younger, a timid, anxious little boy. That's why Talia waited to tell him she's going away for the weekend until last night, after they got home from Hayley's band concert. After begging her not to go, he finally cried himself to sleep, then crawled in with her and Ben after midnight.

It's not a new trend. This time, though, she allowed him to stay, cocooned in her arms until he was sleeping soundly enough for Ben to carry him back to his own room. She lay awake the rest of the night, steeped in guilt and unsettling memories.

If Ben knew what was on her mind—not just what she did, but what she's about to do—he wouldn't have been snoring peacefully by her side.

"Make sure you take away Caleb's screen privileges for saying bad words two times, Mom," Hayley tells her as she starts up the stairs.

A weekend without Talia *and* without video games and television? Yeah, no.

"Grab your backpack and your lunch bag and wait right here by the door, Hayley. I'll be right back."

The worn stair treads creak and squeak as she hurries up. The Queen Anne Victorian has original floors, moldings, doors, and hardware, with gabled ceilings on the second floor, and only one bathroom. They intended it as a starter home / fixer-upper when they bought it—a budget stretch at the time, but already worth considerably more now. So here they've remained, ambitious remodeling blueprints relegated to the bottom of a drawer while they work their way through a never-ending list of upgrades and repairs.

Old houses have character. This one reminds her of her childhood home in Mulberry Bay, a third-floor apartment with water-stained gabled ceilings and cast-iron radiators.

She wishes she'd asked her mother whether that Victorian rental house on Fourth Street is still standing, along with the Winterfields' house next door. Maybe both houses have been condemned and razed, like others on that block were, even while they were all still living there. But if they survived to see the town's long-awaited renaissance and booming real estate market, those houses were probably snapped up and restored to their former glory.

Checking her watch as she reaches the second-floor hall, she sees that she has eight minutes to get the kids on the bus.

On Caleb's closed door, painted wooden letters spell out A-L-E.

Talia is reminded of something.

Should she . . . ?

Yes. *Yes.*

She hurries to her own room, opens a bureau drawer, and retrieves a small rectangle from way in the back, behind her winter sweaters. It's not one of those hinged velvet jewelry boxes but a white cardboard one gold stamped MULBERRY BAY JEWELERS.

Inside is a silver bracelet with four lowercase initial charms. It's badly tarnished, and the clasp is broken, but unlike Caleb's bedroom door, its letters are all accounted for: a *t*, an *i*, a *c*, and a *k*.

The same letters are inked on her skin, above her heart.

Talia has never regretted the tattoo. Only the lie she told Ben when he first saw it, back in college, the first time they were together.

"Tick?" he said, tracing the ink letters with a fingertip. "Why do you have this?"

"Why does anyone have a tattoo? It's to remind myself of . . . something."

"Of what? Lyme disease? It's rampant around here, right?"

"Not that kind of tick." She took a deep breath, glad she'd long ago come up with a logical explanation for situations such as this one. "It's about cherishing every moment, because you never know."

"I don't get it. Tick?"

"Like a clock. You know . . . tick . . . tick . . ."

He grinned. "A clock, or a bomb?"

Oh, Ben. If you only knew.

She takes the bracelet, shoves the box back in her drawer, and returns to Caleb's door.

The *C* and then the *B* dropped off his door and disappeared months ago, leaving dingy rectangles where they'd been attached with double-sided tape. Now the *E* dangles by a thread. But Caleb's the kind of kid who'd rather live behind a door marked A-L than retire the letters to the plastic tub filled with other toddler relics.

"Why don't we put them away now that you're a big first grader?" Talia suggested on an August afternoon spent back-to-school shopping and helping the kids organize their desks for homework season.

"I can't because Granny put them there."

Talia's mom had been gone a year at the time. Now it's going on two.

"Granny would understand that you've outgrown them."

"No. I need them." He hesitated. "Can you keep a secret?"

Even then, the question triggered an uncomfortable memory of a dark night by the lake.

Can you keep a secret?

She thought of the two huge ones she's kept for more than a quarter of a century.

Caleb stood on his tiptoes and whispered, "I need the letters on my door because I'm scared."

Oh, Caleb, frightened of so many things. But that time, it wasn't about burglars or thunderstorms or bullies. That day, he confided, "I'm scared that I'm going to forget her."

"Sweetie . . . you won't forget—"

"No, Mommy, sometimes I do! And then I see the letters on my door, and they help me remember."

"I know," she said, thinking of the bracelet with the broken clasp.

Now, it's tucked into her pocket.

She knocks on the door, opens it a crack, and peers in. "Caleb?"

He's sitting on the bed, ready for school in a red T-shirt, white shorts, and blue Yankees cap.

"I don't want you to go, Mommy." He meets her gaze, and she sees that he's been crying. "Why can't you do your yoga here like you always do?"

Her gut clenches. "It's only for the weekend. I'll be home Sunday night, and Daddy will take good care of you and Hayley while I'm gone."

"But Hayley will be gone too. She's sleeping over at Chloe's."

She is, and then Chloe's mom will get the girls to dance class in the morning and soccer in the afternoon. Her offer to keep Hayley all weekend is still on the table. The girls are at that inseparable age, and Chloe is leaving for sleepaway camp as soon as school is out.

"Daddy will be here with you every second, all weekend," she assures Caleb. "He'll read your bedtime story, and take you to T-ball tomorrow, and out for ice cream. Now come on. You'll have a blast at school with the field games."

"But I don't want—"

"You're going, Caleb."

And so am I.

Five minutes later, they're at the bus stop with a gaggle of parents and patriotic kids. Caleb won't hold Talia's hand in front of the others but remains glued to her side as Hayley and Chloe embrace like long-lost relatives.

"Hey, Talia! I thought you were going to the beach for the weekend!" Chloe's dad, T. J., announces.

"The beach? Without the kids? How lucky are *you*?" That comes from Bree, a mom with a baby in a sling, a toddler in a stroller, a go-cup of coffee, and a voice like a bullhorn.

"You're going to the *beach*?" Caleb asks, brown eyes radiating dismay and betrayal.

"No! I mean, I'm going to a yoga retreat, and it's near the beach, but . . . it's just yoga."

"The Hamptons?" Bree asks.

"Jersey Shore."

Another question from Bree: "With Ben?"

"Just me."

"So, wait . . . you're leaving Ben alone with the kids for Father's Day weekend?" T. J. asks. "Shouldn't he be the one going away?"

Talia shrugs. "Shouldn't fathers spend Father's Day with their kids?"

Hearing the familiar squeak of brakes, she spies the school bus rounding the corner, lights flashing. She extracts herself from Caleb with a hug and forces one on Hayley.

Watching them board the bus with the other kids, she notes that everyone but Caleb is chattering excitedly about the Flag Day festivities. His face is pressed against the window, hands cupped over his forehead to shield his streaming eyes from his seatmate.

Talia pastes on a bright, confident smile and gives him a thumbs-up, then quickly turns away so that he won't see the tears brimming in her own eyes.

Oh, sweetie. I'm so sorry. But I have to do this. I promised Midge and Kelly . . .

And Caroline.

Back home, she finds Ben in the kitchen, barefoot and wearing the shorts he slept in, but otherwise ready for his early-morning meeting with a European client. It's virtual, and his colleagues will only see him from the waist up, clean shaven, in a Brooks Brothers button-down.

About to pour what's left of the morning coffee into his mug, he looks at her. "Did you want to take a cup for the road?"

"No, you can have it. I'll get some on the way."

"There's a Starbucks at the Judy Blume, remember?"

Starbucks . . . Judy Blume . . . ?

It takes her a moment.

The rest stops on the Garden State Parkway are named after famous New Jerseyans. Last summer, on their annual trip to the Outer Banks, she insisted they stop at the one named for the author, though they weren't even a hundred miles into a twelve-hour road trip and the kids were asleep in the back.

"Right. Good idea," she says now, not meeting his eyes.

He takes a carton of oat milk from the fridge.

On the door, pinned beneath a calendar magnet from the garbage collection company, are the two pages of a yellow legal pad she filled with instructions for getting through the weekend without her.

"Ben? Do you want to go over the list one more time in case you have any questions, since I'll be unplugged for the weekend?"

"No, I promise I've got everything under control here. Now *you* need to promise me you'll have a good time, or a zen time, or whatever time one has at a yoga retreat, and not stress about anything here. Okay? Promise?"

She forces a smile and agrees, though she likely can't keep the promise.

Not like she keeps secrets.

"Good. Now get going. There's going to be a lot of beach traffic."

Beach traffic. Right.

He walks her outside, opens the back of the SUV, and lifts her rolling bag inside.

"You're taking the Tappan Zee, right? Not the George Washington Bridge?"

"Tappan Zee. Right." She opens the driver's-side door and busies herself looking for something—anything—in the console.

"And remember that there's construction on the southbound Saw Mill Parkway. It goes down to one lane. Maybe you should take the—"

His phone buzzes in his pocket. He checks it.

"It's a client. I should—"

"Go ahead and take it." She closes the console, turns, and gives him a quick hug. "See you Sunday night. Love you."

"Sunday night. Love you." Into the phone, he says, "Ben Adler."

She drives away, resisting the urge to look in the rearview mirror.

Of course Ben isn't suspicious. They've both made plenty of solo trips throughout their marriage. Business travel, college reunions, Talia's visits to Florida to see her mother . . .

Last winter, following a Palm Springs golf weekend with his college buddies, Ben suggested that Talia do something similar.

"How about a girls' getaway? Or a yoga retreat?"

So yes, it was his idea. She'd just had no intention of actually doing it . . . until it provided the perfect cover story.

Now she's leaving town on a string of lies, with the past on her mind and a tarnished bracelet in her pocket.

Spotting the entrance to the Saw Mill River Parkway ahead, she turns off her cell phone and checks the rearview one last time. All clear.

She passes a car waiting to turn into the southbound on-ramp. It has a surfboard strapped to the ski rack, heading toward the beach.

Talia gets on the parkway heading north, toward the Catskills, and Mulberry Bay, and Haven Cliff, and the memory of the June night twenty-five years ago when Caroline asked Talia, Kelly, and Midge the pivotal question.

Can you keep a secret?

She had. They had.

But the other secret—the first one—had just been between Talia and Caroline.

CHAPTER THIRTEEN

Midge has learned, on the job, that even when devastating news isn't news, the victim's loved ones often react as if it's a shocking blow.

Maybe it's human nature to hold out impossible hope. Maybe we're wired to protect ourselves from the inevitable for as long as we can.

Gordy's wife and sons are shattered anew at the confirmation of his death. Relieved that Reverend Parker is with them to provide comfort, Midge returns to the backyard and avoids looking at Gordy as she steps carefully around him onto the patio. There are more flies now, buzzing around, and Louie has moved on from candy to a bag of Fritos, which he offers to Midge.

"No, thanks. I don't know how you can eat in this situation."

"*Nothing* kills his appetite," Janna says.

"Hey, I've got low blood sugar."

"You've got low blood sugar all day, every day. I think you should get that checked out."

"You want me to go to the doctor and tell him, what? I'm hungry a lot?"

"It might be a symptom of an underlying problem, Louie!"

"It *is* a symptom of an underlying problem, and that's you always telling me that this isn't healthy and that isn't healthy, and why don't I eat some baby carrots with that brown sludge instead of—"

"Hummus! It's hummus!"

"Well, it doesn't fill me up. And if I don't get filled up, I'm hungry. I don't need the doctor to tell me that."

Ignoring the bickering, Midge looks around the area, making sure she didn't miss anything, wondering why Gordy was out here late last night.

Maybe he was coming down to sit by the firepit, or for a night swim, ironic as that would be, given the circumstances.

A wood chip–carpeted trail leads away from the patio, off through the mulberry trees toward the lake. She knows it's back there, though she can't see it. Knows, too, that there's a waterfront walking path that stretches out here from town. It stops just short of Haven Cliff, but you can still get there from here if you keep walking along the gravelly shore.

Louie kills a fly with his bare hand on the wooden railing above the corpse. "Gotcha!"

"Tell me you're not going to keep eating with that hand," Janna says.

"Well, yeah. I'm a lefty."

"You're disgusting, is what you are."

A lefty.

Caroline was left handed.

Caroline . . .

Maybe Gordy, aware of the date, simply decided to pay a memorial visit to the spot where Caroline had presumably drowned.

Does that matter to anyone but Midge, in the grand scheme of things?

It certainly wouldn't bring comfort to his wife.

But I need to know.

Midge makes a beeline for the path, calling over her shoulder, "I'll be back. I'm just going to go down to the lake."

Locard's Exchange Principle—that wherever we go, we leave something physical behind and take something with us—has never failed Midge yet. If Gordy was down here last night, there will be microscopic evidence in the area and on his body.

If this were a criminal case, it would be important, requiring expensive lab tests that take weeks, often months, to yield results.

With luck, Midge will find something more tangible to satisfy her own curiosity.

Her footsteps are hushed as she makes her way over the dense mulch, looking for disturbances beneath her feet and in the woodlands bordering the path. Noting the cloying, sweet stench of fallen mulberries and blooming mock orange, she hears Kelly's voice, on that long-ago night. "It's like a whore's bath . . . spraying perfume to cover up something nasty."

She reaches the lake. The opposite shore is wooded hillside with mountains off in the distance. There are a few houses up there too—cabins, mostly. Prime real estate these days.

To her left, a large crane pokes high above the tree line at the old Trolley Park Beach site. The new owners plan to build a waterfront recreation complex but had to halt construction to wait for permits that may never come. The town planning board largely consists of longtime locals fed up with the influx of developers, newcomers, summer people, tourists, and day-trippers.

Beyond Trolley Park and a stretch of wooded shoreline, tall mansard rooftops and steeples are set back from the water where the bay curves in, marking the town proper and the flattest part of the shore.

To Midge's right, past a smattering of houses and more woods, the terrain rises steeply.

In the old days, in the dead of winter, Haven Cliff's crumbling turrets were visible from pretty much any spot on the lake. This past winter, with the mansion's exterior fully restored, it was a glorious sight.

But it's summer now, and Kelly's new home is shrouded by forest.

There were no Amber Alerts back when Caroline went missing. Search parties combed the woods and trails surrounding the lake in case she'd taken a wrong turn, gotten lost, perhaps fallen and been injured.

They found no sign of her.

She said she was going swimming. The logical conclusion was that she drowned trying to reach the "Island," a rickety wooden platform that was once the end of an old fishing pier off Trolley Park Beach. During illicit parties at Haven Cliff, kids always swam over there to hang out. It wasn't particularly far out, maybe a couple of lap pool lengths, at most.

Midge's father warned her never to do it.

"I don't care how strong a swimmer you are. Only an idiot would go out there in cold, dark water in the middle of the night."

Of course, Midge ignored the warnings, as did her brothers before her. Her father's "only an idiot" speeches always went in one ear and out the other. Besides, teenagers are immortal, or so they believe.

There was a group of kids on the Island that night twenty-five years ago. Questioned by the police, they all said they never saw Caroline on the beach or swimming toward them. But it was prom night, fueled by beer and weed. The lack of witnesses surprised no one, including Chief Kennedy.

"I always said someone was going to get hurt out there, or at Haven Cliff," he was quoted as saying. "This rips my heart to shreds. We need to prioritize safety for our children. That means removing and/or securing existing hazards."

Shortly after that, the town demolished the Island.

Standing at the water's edge, Midge gazes out over the shimmering ripples at the spot where it once was.

Even close to shore, this part of the lake is far more hazardous than the town's bay beach, where she'd been a lifeguard. There, the roped-off swimming area is flat and pebbly, gently sloping toward the depths. Here, there are jagged rocks just beneath the surface in the shallows, slick with moss and algae, treacherous even for waders. Beyond, the water grows murky, and there's a steep drop-off.

Divers scoured the lake for Caroline but didn't find her. That wasn't unusual.

Midge has since learned, via her aquatic death investigation training, that drowning victims typically sink to the bottom of a body of water, then resurface three to five days later. That's if the submerged remains don't get caught in the tangle of boulders, felled trees, sunken boats, and other debris that litter the bottom. Especially in this lake.

The obvious conclusion was that Caroline drowned.

Gordy Klatte, along with everyone else in Caroline's orbit, including Midge herself, was questioned and cleared of any wrongdoing. If some terrible fate befell her, there was no one to blame. It was an accident.

And now, against nearly impossible odds, on the same date, the same is true of Gordy.

CHAPTER FOURTEEN

July 4, 1997

Until now, Talia has never paid much attention to Gordon Klatte, other than during sousaphone solos in marching band. Okay, not even then, because he isn't super talented. Nor is he untalented. He's mediocre, like everyone else—except Paul Liccione, the woodwind captain, who plays a nimble clarinet on top of being nice, funny, and super handsome.

If Caroline was going to finally invite a guy to her birthday party, why couldn't it have been him? Why Gordon Klatte?

Talia isn't the only one who's wondering about that, but it takes a group excursion to the bathroom pavilion for her, Midge, and Kelly to get the birthday girl alone.

"*What* is going on?" Kelly asks Caroline as soon as she comes out of her stall.

"What do you mean?"

"Gordon!" They say it in unison.

"Oh—what about him?" She turns on the tap, avoiding their eyes, staring at the obscene word scrawled on the mirror, or maybe at the even more obscene phrase spray-painted on the stall door reflected there.

"What's up with him?" Talia asks. "Why is he here?"

"I told you; we've known each other since we were little Sunday school kids." Caroline presses the soap dispenser. Nothing comes out.

"You've known a lot of people since then. Why'd you invite him to your sweet sixteen?" Kelly asks.

"I didn't. My parents did." Caroline is washing her soapless hands like a surgeon scrubbing in.

"I thought you weren't allowed to date," Talia points out.

"It's not a date."

"Are you sure?" Midge asks.

"Yes! It's my birthday party, okay?"

Talia changes the subject. "Let's go for a walk around the lake. I think the sun is trying to peek out."

"Sounds good." Caroline turns off the tap and reaches toward the towel dispenser. It, too, is empty. "I'll run back to the shelter and get—"

"*Without* Gordon," Kelly says.

"Oh." Caroline wipes her hands on her white dress. "I'm not sure if . . . I mean, I can't just leave him alone."

"It kind of seems like the opposite," Midge tells her. "He hasn't left you alone for a minute all day."

"I'm sorry, guys," Caroline says. "I'm just trying to do the right thing."

"If it's a date, then the right thing is to be with him," Midge says. "But if it's not, like you said . . . then you're not obligated."

"Not *obligated*, but it wouldn't be polite to ditch him."

"It's even less polite to stalk the guest of honor," Kelly points out.

"Stalk! I think it's nice that he's so attentive."

Talia grins. "It's totally a date."

"It isn't!"

"Then what is it, a hostage situation? Are there guards posted outside?" Kelly peeks out the door and turns back. "Whew. The coast is clear. Let's make a break for the border."

They all laugh, even Caroline.

"I'm just trying to be a good hostess," she tells them.

"You're supposed to be trying to have a good time," Kelly says. "This is your day."

"I'm having a great time. Really. Gordy's fine. He's nice."

"Okay, well, we should have a signal or a code word if you need us to get you away from him," Midge suggests.

"Or from your parents," Kelly says, "or your cousins. They keep hanging on you and getting grimy little kid fingerprints all over your vestal virgin outfit."

They laugh again. Even Caroline. But not quite as heartily.

"I don't mind. You know how much I love kids."

Talia grins. "Understatement of the year, Mary Poppins."

Caroline is the most popular babysitter in town, showing up for her jobs with a tote bag full of crafts and games. She wants to become a music teacher one day.

Like Talia, she also intends to get married and have lots of babies.

When they were little girls, they spent hours playing "house," a game in which they were both married mothers. An assortment of dolls served as their children, and a mop and broom stood in as husbands until Caroline's sister Mary Beth caught them practicing kissing on the wooden handles. After that, the husbands were imaginary.

On Talia's first day of middle school, she was overwhelmed by the newness, and the scale of it all. Relieved to spot a familiar face in a crowded corridor between classes, she thought for a moment that it was Caroline.

But no, it was Mary Beth, a grade ahead, infinitely cooler, and flanked by a couple of boys. Seeing Talia, she grinned and waved. Then she grabbed a mop from a nearby janitor's bucket, crooned, "Hello, lover," and feigned making out with it, with exaggerated kissing noises.

Talia was mortified. Before she could escape, Mary Beth gestured at her, apparently explaining the situation to the snickering boys.

"I hate your sister," she told Caroline that day at lunch.

"Which one?"

"Mary Beth."

"Who doesn't?" Kelly asked. "She's amazing at everything—gymnastics, piano, academics . . . she's so perfect it's sickening."

"She's soulless."

They just stared at Talia.

"Come on, you guys can't all think she's perfect!"

"She's not the sweetest person I've ever known," Midge admitted. "In fact, she can be really nasty. But *soulless* is a strong word."

"What'd she do?" Caroline asked.

Feeling a bit like a tattletale, Talia just shook her head and muttered, "Forget it."

But she wasn't the only one having problems with Mary Beth Winterfield.

This past spring, when the weather warmed up and the windows were open, Talia overheard more than the usual arguing next door between Mary Beth and her parents. Things are definitely much more peaceful now that she's gone.

Walking back to the picnic shelter with the others, Talia spies Gordon perched alone on the bench where they left him, watching for them.

"Okay, seriously, Caroline?" Midge says. "If you need rescuing, it's a two."

"Huh? A two what?"

"A code two. It means urgent."

"What are you even talking about?" Talia asks. "Code two?"

"Oh—it's cop code!" Kelly says. "Right?"

"Yup. My dad uses it. If someone is in trouble, it's code two, and if no assistance is needed, it's code four. Got it, Car'? Two is help, four is don't worry, I'm fine."

She laughs. "Four! I'm fine!"

"Right now you are, but when you're back in his clutches, you'll have to signal us."

"Gordy does not have clutches!"

"We can't be sure." Kelly looks at Talia and Midge. "So, like, what's the plan? We'll wear police radios?"

"That's probably not practical." Midge is equally deadpan. "Guess we'll have to find some other means to communicate."

"Maybe she can blink two times if she needs help and four times if she doesn't," Talia suggests, giggling. "Or hold up two fingers, or four. Or drop two pennies, or—"

"You guys are crazy!" Caroline cuts in, but she's laughing too. They all are.

Gordon is on his feet, trying to act as though he hasn't been waiting and watching. "Hey, what took you so long? I was starting to get worried."

"Don't worry, we're fine." Kelly slow blinks at him, four times, and everyone cracks up except Gordon, who looks bewildered.

Back in the shelter, the birthday girl opens her presents.

Caroline's parents give her a large gold cross on a chain, and she thanks them politely.

Gordon's parents give her an electric toothbrush. "With all the bells and whistles," his dad says, beaming. Caroline thanks him, and her mother and Mrs. Klatte inform everyone that her husband is a dentist.

Yeah, like *that's* an excuse.

Next up among the contenders for Worst Present Ever is a stupid book from stupid Gordon, who explains that his aunt bought this copy for him in London just last week and he read it in one night.

"You'll love it. It's a British author, debut novelist," he says. "It's about a boy wizard."

"Ooooh!" Caroline says again, as if she's a huge fan of regifted books about boy wizards.

She opens the package from Midge, Talia, and Kelly.

"Cucumber-melon! Aw, you guys—you know it's my favorite."

"Salad?" Gordon asks.

"What? No! Lotion! It's lotion!" She waves the pale-green bottle.

He reddens. "I know; it was a joke."

"Oh!" Caroline emits a gratuitous laugh, then a genuine delighted one as she reaches back into the bag and pulls out a pastel-yellow box. "A Tamagotchi? Oh my G—gosh," she amends, with a glance at her parents.

Mrs. Winterfield leans in, eyeing the plastic device as if it's the devil's handiwork. "What in heaven's name *is* that?" Her voice is even higher pitched than usual.

"It's some kind of foreign toy," Gordon, who just gave Caroline a *foreign* children's book, says with a hint of disdain.

Kelly, Midge, and Talia exchange an equally disdainful glance, and it isn't directed at the Tamagotchi.

"It's a digital pet!" Caroline's ten-year-old cousin Veronica is bouncing with excitement. "This is the egg, and you have to take care of it, and it grows up, and you have to keep it alive."

"But it's not alive," Gordon's mother says. She, too, has an annoying little-girl voice.

"No, it's virtual," Talia explains.

"Virtual? Virtually what?"

"Alive."

"How can anything be virtually alive?" Mrs. Klatte seems angry—if not at Kelly, then at something, or someone.

"I want one!" Veronica says. "Mommy, can I please have one?"

"Absolutely not."

Caroline's aunt Deb is the kind of woman whose natural state is *put upon*, and she has a little-girl voice like her sister and Mrs. Klatte.

What is up with these women? Kelly wonders. And why is Caroline starting to sound just like them?

Caroline reaches back into the gift bag, pulls out the gift certificate, and squeals. "Contempo Casuals! My favorite!"

"Salad?" Midge asks, getting a hearty laugh out of everyone but Gordon.

"Thank you all so much. I love you guys." Caroline reaches to pull her friends into a group hug, the sun glinting on the familiar silver charm bracelet on her wrist.

CHAPTER FIFTEEN

Present Day

In her second-floor suite, Kelly peers at the black wood splinter embedded just under the skin of her right thumb.

No wonder.

All morning, she's been vaguely aware of this new pain, but until now hasn't separated it from the rest. Her head aches, her shoulders are sore, and every muscle is stiff, even after a long, hot shower.

She slips her feet into heeled sandals and chooses sunglasses from a drawer filled with designer pairs. After propping them on her blond head, she checks her reflection and decides she looks a hell of a lot better than she's feeling.

In the adjacent bathroom, she opens the medicine cabinet and finds a bottle of ibuprofen, but there are no tweezers for the splinter.

After swallowing a couple of pills, she returns to the bedroom and steps to the window to examine it in better light. It's in pretty deep. How, where, when did she even get it? She attempts to use the manicured nails of her left thumb and forefinger as forceps, squeezing the throbbing skin to force it out, but it won't budge. Oh well. She'll just have to—

Hearing the front door open and close below, she glances out the window, wondering who's coming, or going.

Beyond the overhanging portico, she can see a workman riding a mower on the vast green lawn, and another clipping the boxwood hedgerow.

Unfazed by the human presence and buzzing equipment, several deer are grazing on the greenbrier vines growing over a low rock wall. It's an invasive plant, according to the landscaper, who's hoping that it and the poison ivy growing nearby will keep the herd from feasting on the ornamental shrubs and flowers.

"If that happens, we're going to install a perimeter of mesh fencing to keep them out," he said.

"No, I don't want to do that. The fencing is ugly. The deer are beautiful."

"They're pests."

"Most beautiful creatures are," Kelly replied with a wink.

As she watches, a figure emerges from beneath the portico and descends the front steps—probably one of the workers taking care of a few more finishing touches this morning—a drawer pull here, a towel bar there.

The private chef she hired for the weekend is unloading a crate of fresh produce down in the kitchen. The florist is placing fresh arrangements throughout the first floor. A maid is making up the bed in the suite where Talia will be staying.

When she agreed to come for the weekend, she asked Kelly and Midge for hotel recommendations. Kelly wouldn't hear of it.

You're staying here, at Haven Cliff, with me.

Talia texted back, Same old bossy Kelly, following that up with a smiley face and her gratitude for the hospitality.

Kelly isn't the same, though. She, like Haven Cliff, has come a long, long way.

About to turn away from the window, she pauses.

The person below is wearing a baseball cap and a boxy jacket, head bent, shoulders hunched, scurrying away from the house like a roach scurrying from a kitchen light. He—or she?—bypasses the vehicles lined up in front of the house and disappears around a curve in the long driveway.

Kelly frowns.

No one arrives at Haven Cliff on foot, located as it is on a rural stretch of highway.

Maybe it's a worker who parked farther down along the drive, unfamiliar with the property. Maybe it's a summer person who made a wrong turn. Or a lost hiker—though they weren't dressed for it.

She shrugs, turns away from the window, and leans in to pet the drowsy cat curled up on her bed.

"Sorry, Bibi. I have to leave for a little while, but I'll be back."

He regards her through copper-colored eyes as she strokes his blue-gray fur.

He's a French Chartreux, adopted last year as a kitten and named for her beloved Bijou, left behind in France for what she'd assumed would be a quick overseas trip back in 2020. She couldn't have known that her mother's seemingly innocuous hospitalization was far more momentous than it seemed, or that the entire world was about to be locked down, stranding her in the States indefinitely.

But this has become her home once more, and she intends to stay forever. Here in Mulberry Bay. Here, at Haven Cliff.

She retrieves her spiral notebook from the bedside table, aware that she meant to write something in it, but not certain what that was.

She bought the notebook at La Papeterie, the fancy new stationery store in town, along with a diamond point pen she recently misplaced. Now there's a pink pen stuck into the coiled binding, a signature item from the Langham Hotel in London. She hasn't been back to Europe since the pandemic. How is it that she remembers getting the pen on that trip but she has no idea what she's supposed to be writing with it now?

She ponders for a few moments, decides it couldn't have been important, and tucks the notebook and pen into her leather purse.

In the doorway, she hesitates, looking back at the window, thinking about the furtive figure she saw leaving the house . . .

Or *believed* she saw.

Sometimes, when Kelly's alone in the house, especially late at night, she hears distant voices echoing. She sees flickers of movement out of the corner of her eye.

She never gave it much thought until lately. Why would she? She never saw things or heard things until she moved into Haven Cliff.

Maybe it's her imagination. Maybe she, like her mother, is suffering from dementia. Such things are hereditary, and it's one of the warning signs.

Warnings . . .

She thinks of the Enchanted Chalet, a little shop in Woodstock she's occasionally visited for spiritual readings. The psychics there use cartomancy, a method that involves regular playing cards instead of tarot cards.

It's a similar premise. Every number and face card has meaning, and the suits correspond to tarot symbols—hearts to cups, spades to swords.

Last time Kelly was there, she got a four of spades—illness, the reader explained.

Taken aback, Kelly asked, "Are you sure?" though she knew better than to question it. While tarot readers rely on intuition to interpret the messages, there is no ambiguity in cartomancy, and the college-aged woman performing her reading was no Madame Céline.

"It doesn't necessarily mean serious illness," she explained, as her cell phone pinged and buzzed in the pocket of her Bard hoodie. "It might just be that you're coming down with a cold. Be, uh, be mindful of your health."

What if it's something far more serious, though? What if it involves her mental health and not her physical health?

Kelly would prefer to think that the place really is haunted, or cursed.

That the past leaves as indelible a mark on places as it does on people.

Haven Cliff was, after all, the site of so much anguish for so many people, from the Winterfield murders to its role in the deadly tuberculosis epidemic to its incarnation as a so-called lunatic asylum.

Maybe the intense emotional and physical anguish humans expel when confronted by tragedy and illness, trauma and death—maybe all that energy doesn't just evaporate without a trace.

Maybe it lingers, like dust drifting in the air long after demolition.

CHAPTER SIXTEEN

January 18, 1997

Kelly has long been looking forward to turning sixteen this month—old enough to drive, at last!

Turns out, you have to pass a written test to get your learner's permit, which took her a couple of tries. There are a lot of stupid rules and laws you need to know in this state. And then you have to practice driving for at least six months before you can schedule a road test, and you have to take a driver's ed course if you want to be allowed to drive at night at seventeen instead of eighteen . . .

Somehow, Kelly didn't realize any of this. Somehow, she assumed she'd turn sixteen, get her permit, get her license, and boom—she'd never again have to rely on her parents to cart her around.

Or, worse, on Mrs. Verga, she thinks, climbing out of the housekeeper's car in front of Caroline's house,

"I'll pick you up at four o'clock sharp. Make sure you're ready and watching for me. I don't want to have to chase you down again at all hours."

"That was months ago," Kelly reminds her. "And this isn't a party, and four o'clock is the middle of the afternoon."

She's already pulling away, leaving Kelly on the curb.

She heaves a sigh, her breath puffing white in the frigid air, and wishes she were wearing a warmer coat. As much as she hates to admit it, Mrs. Verga was right—a jean jacket over a short-sleeved T-shirt really is ridiculous clothing for single-digit temperatures.

She glances over at the house next door. Talia lives in the top-floor apartment. Maybe Kelly can borrow a sweater or something—though Talia and her mom are just getting over a nasty flu.

Yeah, never mind. Kelly would rather risk death from exposure than exposure to germs.

She slings her backpack over her shoulder and heads toward Caroline's house. The railings are still festooned with tinsel garlands now shredded by the mountain winds, and the front door has a bedraggled wreath with a crooked red velvet bow tied with frayed gold cord.

In previous years, the Winterfields' Christmas decorations consisted of a plastic crèche they used to set out on the lawn.

But the neighborhood is changing, like the town itself. At first, the nativity scene was the subject of pranks—kids, probably, creating obscene tableaux with the plastic statues. Then vandals struck, with spray paint one year and a blunt force object the next. Last year, the entire thing was stolen. Not surprising, as there have been other burglaries lately—nothing major, but missing cash, and jewelry and electronics stolen while people are out.

"My parents can't afford to replace the crèche again," Caroline told Kelly. "They're really upset over what's happening to this town."

"It's disgusting. No wonder people don't want to live here. I can't wait to get out."

"But that's why it's happening. If all the good people leave, it's only going to get worse."

"No one ever called me a good person," Kelly cracked, but Caroline was earnest.

"Well, you are, deep down inside. And you should stay forever, like me."

"Forever? Why?"

"Because I'm going to make it better. And because it's home."

Climbing the front steps, Kelly can't recall the last time she was even here.

No one, including Caroline, wants to hang out at her house. The Winterfields have way too many rules. You can't gossip about anything worthwhile, like parties and boys, because one parent or another is always in earshot. They never have good snacks, and there's no cable TV, no video games, no CD player . . .

Really, there's nothing to do at Caroline's house unless you're working on a school project, as Kelly is today. And Caroline isn't allowed to come to her house because Kelly's father's away on business and her mother is skiing and the Winterfields don't trust the housekeeper to provide "sufficient supervision."

That's fine. Kelly would just as soon avoid Mrs. Verga herself. Plus, she always welcomes the opportunity to see Caroline's sister Mary Beth. She's the kind of girl an underclassman needs to know.

Caroline mentioned in an earlier phone call that her sister's home today, so they might not be able to work on their sophomore honors English project in the bedroom Caroline shares with her.

"I thought she was going on the French Club trip to Montreal this weekend!"

"She was, but she's grounded."

"Again? What'd she do this time?"

"Who knows? She's Mary Beth."

Climbing the front steps, Kelly can hear piano music from inside.

Mrs. Winterfield answers the door, wearing a scratchy-looking olive-green cardigan and blue pants that can only be called *slacks*. Unlike the other moms in town, including Kelly's own, she never wears jeans, sneakers, or any clothing that looks remotely comfortable and casual.

And unlike the other moms, she doesn't seem to have gotten the women's lib memo back in the seventies. Kelly has actually heard her refer to herself as a "housewife," in that little-girl voice she so often uses.

Not that Kelly's own mother has held a job since she got married and had Kelly—but Beverly Barrow wouldn't dream of calling herself a *housewife*.

"So lovely to see you, Kelly," Mrs. Winterfield says, as always, sounding as though she doesn't quite mean it, as always. "The girls are just finishing piano practice."

"I hear it. They sound great. Is that Debussy?"

"Yes." She looks mildly impressed. "Do you play?"

"I don't, but I recognized it. I just love classical music. I'll go listen." She heads for the living room.

"All right, but please don't disturb them until they're done."

"Wouldn't dream of it." Kelly smiles sweetly, and Mrs. Winterfield nods and retreats down a long hall toward the kitchen.

The house is old. Not *charming* old—*old* old. It smells musty and is full of uncomfortable furniture, dark wooden paneling, closed doors, and drawn curtains. It's always cold and drafty in winter because Caroline's father controls the thermostat, like everything else.

In the living room, Caroline and Mary Beth are seated together at the upright piano, fingers flying in synchronicity over the keyboard.

Caroline's long hair is neatly brushed and pulled back in a head-band, while Mary Beth's falls in unkempt waves. Caroline is wearing a cream-colored sweater, and Mary Beth has on a black turtleneck, probably to hide the hickeys Kelly spotted on her neck at school yesterday. Their performance styles are dissimilar—Caroline seems to stroke each note, while Mary Beth bangs them out—but somehow, it's a perfect duet.

"You're so full of BS, Kelly Barrow," Mary Beth says without turning her head or missing a note as Kelly enters the room. "You don't know Debussy from Gary Busey."

"I do so. Gary Busey played Radar O'Reilly on *M*A*S*H*," she says, having watched reruns with her dad.

"That's Gary Burghoff, which makes that three things you don't know."

71

"Okay, Debussy was a lucky guess because Caroline has been talking nonstop about the recital, but don't tell your mom. She loves me now."

"Our mother will never love *you*!" Mary Beth says. "She doesn't even love me."

Before Kelly can digest that comment, Caroline protests, "I haven't been talking *nonstop*. I'm just excited."

Mary Beth rolls her eyes. "You really need to get a life, Car'."

"I have a life. I love my life. I love piano music and I—" At a discordant plink, she breaks off speaking, and playing.

Mary Beth throws up her hands. "I hate *this* piano and that stupid F key that won't stay in tune. If they're going to make us take stupid piano lessons, they should buy a decent piano."

"You know they can't afford it," Caroline says. "I'll go get the glue and fix it again."

"Forget it. We were almost done anyway, and your friend is here," Mary Beth says.

"It'll take two seconds." Caroline stands and hurries out of the room.

Mary Beth looks at Kelly. "Wow. She needs . . . *something*."

"Glue, she said."

"No, I mean, she needs to go to a party, or on a date, or have a beer . . . We need to save her from my parents' rules or she'll never know how to have real fun."

We—as if Mary Beth considers Kelly someone who knows how to have real fun.

Flattered, she agrees, "We really do. I love parties, and beer, and . . . uh, dates."

Mary Beth laughs. But not in a mocking way.

The room is filled with her signature scent. No fruity Bath & Body Works for her. She wears real perfume, Donna Karan's Cashmere Mist. It's expensive. Kelly asked for, and received, a bottle for Christmas.

Peering at the concert T-shirt Kelly's wearing under her jean jacket, Mary Beth asks, "Hey, is that Stone Temple Pilots?"

"Yes! I saw them in New York in November."

"Cool. They're playing Syracuse in April with Cheap Trick opening for them. I can't wait."

"Wow! Your parents are letting you go?"

Mary Beth holds a fingertip to her lips. "I have a gymnastics tournament there. But I've got friends at 'Cuse, so I'm going to sneak out that night and meet them at the concert. That's where I'm going to college."

"Caroline said you were going somewhere in Pennsylvania."

"Oh, please. My parents want to send me to the rinky-dink Bible college where my sisters went, but my guidance counselor thinks I might be able to get a scholarship. Plus, I've been saving my babysitting money, and I've got a full-time nanny job lined up when school gets out, working for rich summer people from New York."

"I didn't think there were many of those left around here. So your parents will let you go to 'Cuse if you can afford the tuition?" Kelly asks, using the abbreviation as if she's as cool and familiar with the university as Mary Beth is.

"They'll have no say in where I go if they're not paying, right? It's my life and my money, and I'll be able to do whatever I want. How about you?"

"My parents want me to go to 'Mouth."

"Mouth?"

"Dartmouth," Kelly clarifies, feeling lame. Maybe it's not cool to abbreviate all universities.

"What do *you* want to do?"

"I don't know. I mean, it's only sophomore year."

"If you want to do something other than what your parents want you to do, you need to figure it out *now*. Make a plan, and put it into action. That's what I've been trying to tell Caroline. They're running her life, and she's letting them. She's afraid to push back on anything."

Feeling the need to stick up for her friend, Kelly says, "I don't think she's *afraid*. I think she's just . . . easygoing. She wants to make everyone happy."

"What about *herself?* Is she making herself happy?"

"She seems happy to me."

"Yeah, well, you don't live in this house with us, do you."

"What do you mean?"

"I mean, four daughters, and we're all supposed to be deferential, like my mother. We're taught never to speak up if we don't agree with something, or, God forbid, to talk about anything with 'outsiders.' So I'm not surprised that my sister doesn't complain to her friends. But maybe you should ask her how she really feels."

"About college?"

"About everything."

Before Kelly can digest this, Caroline is back with the glue, asking, "Mary Beth, where's my stapler?"

"How would I know?"

"Because it's not in my drawer. And you're always helping yourself to my stuff."

"I am not." Mary Beth rises from the piano bench. "I'm going upstairs, if you guys want to come up and hang out."

"We can't." Caroline opens the piano and peers inside. "We have to pick our poet."

Mary Beth cups a hand to her ear. "What? You have to pick your noses?"

"Our poet!" Caroline says. "We have to choose a poet for an intensive study for an English project for the rest of the school year."

"Pick Sylvia Plath," Mary Beth says, on her way out of the room. "She's the best. I'm obsessed with her stuff."

"Sounds good. Let's just do Sylvia Plath," Kelly tells Caroline.

"No way. She's the worst."

"I love her."

"Do you even know who she is?"

74

"Of course I do. She played Radar O'Reilly on *M*A*S*H*."

Caroline laughs, dabbing glue on the broken key.

"Seriously, let's just pick her."

"That would be way too dark and depressing. I think we should go with something more upbeat."

Kelly considers this. "Caroline . . . you don't always have to be so upbeat. You know?"

"What do you mean?"

"I mean . . . we're friends, right? We've been friends forever, right?"

Caroline looks up, frowning. "Of course we're friends."

"You can be yourself with me. You don't always have to act like everything's all hunky-dory."

"What are you talking about, K. K.?" she asks, and then her eyes narrow. "What did Mary Beth tell you? Were you guys talking about me?"

"We were just talking about concerts, and college, and how it really bothers her that your parents are so strict."

"'Bothers her' is putting it politely."

"Does it bother you?"

"Not as much as it does her." Caroline looks as though she wants to say something else, then shakes her head and puts the cap back on the glue. "Forget it. Let's just pick our poet. If you really want to spend the next six months on a suicidal poet . . ."

"I don't," Kelly says. "You pick. I'll go with whatever you say."

But I'm going to spend the next six months paying more attention to what you're not saying.

CHAPTER SEVENTEEN

Present Day

At the Klatte home, the medical examiner's van and another squad car are now parked behind Midge's car and the ambulance.

Midge stands in the entryway, keeping an eye on the proceedings outside and in.

Having regained their composure, made the necessary calls to family and friends, and gotten themselves dressed, Amy Klatte and her sons are huddled miserably on the sofa. Reverend Parker is pulled up in a wingback chair facing them, praying with them for Gordy's salvation.

A uniformed officer is posted on the driveway, prepared to greet arriving family and friends who have been summoned, and to deal with curious onlookers if necessary. There are invariably a few ghouls who show up in situations like this.

In the backyard, the medical examiner's transport team are documenting evidence, taking photos, filling out paperwork, and preparing to remove the body. It's all in a day's work for the authorities, Midge included.

She frequently finds herself inside people's homes when they least expect it. She's accustomed to stumbling into domestic chaos—piles of clutter, sinks filled with unwashed dishes, accumulated laundry, and sometimes, far, far worse. What you find behind closed doors can tell you a lot about the people who live there.

She's seen Gordy around town over the years, but all she really knows about him is that he was a family man, married with kids.

His home reflects a steadfast, stable life. Every room is clean and tidy, not a fleck of dust or a crooked scatter rug in the place. The air smells faintly of home cooking, of the unlit vanilla-scented Yankee Jar Candle on a nearby console, and of the Mrs. Meyer's multisurface cleaning spray Midge can see on the kitchen counter.

The decor is folksy and bland—brown wood, pastel fabrics, floral prints, white walls. In the dining room beyond the archway, there's a glass cabinet filled with porcelain bells, the kind you find in souvenir shops, each imprinted with a tourist attraction. Niagara Falls, Cape Cod, Disney World . . . nothing off the beaten path for this family.

The wall above the stairs is lined with photos in gold metal frames. They're not candid shots, but professional ones, most featuring the Klatte boys as babies, toddlers, gap-toothed kids, awkward adolescents. There's a formal wedding portrait of Amy enveloped in white tulle, and a posed family photo probably taken a few years ago, with a paunchy, balding Gordy.

Farther up the wall, there he is in a maroon and white cap and gown—Mulberry Bay colors. Midge has seen that picture in her own yearbook; recognizes that Gordy from her past; remembers what unfolded around him, around all of them, in the summer of '99.

At that time, a lot of people in town—her father included—believed he had something to do with Caroline's disappearance.

Lurking in the hall outside her parents' bedroom, Midge overheard them discussing it in hushed tones.

"That kid knows something about this, Gena," her father said, and at first, Midge was certain he was talking about *her*.

She froze, wondering how they'd figured it out.

"What do you mean?" her mother asked.

"There's just something off about his reaction."

"Bobby, he's, what, seventeen? His girlfriend vanished into thin air, and he's being questioned like a suspect. Everything is *off* about this."

"But he's too quiet. When you talk to him, he stares at you, or through you, like he's not even listening."

"Well, the poor boy is traumatized, just like Midge. How would you feel if people were going around saying there's something off about *her* reaction?"

"Trust me, no one is saying that about my daughter, and I'm not *people*—I'm the chief of police. I know what I'm talking about. I've been doing this long enough to listen to my instincts. My instincts are telling me that this Klatte kid isn't sharing everything he knows."

All these years, the comment has dogged Midge. She knows a thing or two about police work and trusting your instincts—but she also knows the truth about Caroline's disappearance.

In the next room, Reverend Parker, who's been reciting disquieting Bible verses about punishment and mortality, tells Amy Klatte and her children, "Let us not forget Corinthians 15:56: 'The sting of death is sin.'"

Peeking into the room, she sees Amy wiping her eyes with a crumpled tissue. Mike is motionless, staring at the floor, or perhaps at his phone in his lap. Noah meets Midge's gaze, then quickly looks away.

". . . and that each of us, from the moment we are born into this world, has been sentenced to death," Reverend Parker is saying in the living room.

His words intermingle in Midge's brain with her father's, so long ago.

Gordon Klatte isn't telling us everything.

CHAPTER EIGHTEEN

June 14, 1997

Kelly and Caroline kneel on the floor beside a large white poster board they're using to create a map for the final project of their sophomore poetry study, intended to illustrate Robert Frost's "The Road Not Taken."

"We can draw a bunch of trees," Caroline says.

"But it's supposed to be woods. That's a lot of trees."

"It'll go fast. They don't have to be fancy. And we can just draw lines for the paths and stick figures to represent all of the different scenarios we want to show."

"Are you sure you don't have some magazines or catalogs so that we can just cut out stuff and glue it on?"

"Do you *see* any magazines or catalogs?" Caroline gestures around them.

As teenage girl bedrooms go, the one she shares with Mary Beth is unusually sparse. It's not just the lack of frills, stuffed animals, and posters that strikes Kelly, because she has long since rid her own room of those things.

But Kelly has a television, CD player, and desktop computer, along with framed photographs, yearbooks, and a bulletin board that holds mementos like ticket stubs and invitations.

Aside from the built-in shelves crammed with Caroline's books, this room has few personal touches. The furniture is boring rectangles—two bureaus, two desks, two wooden chairs, and a nightstand between a pair of twin beds. Caroline's is always neatly made and the white chenille bedspread spotless, while Mary Beth's is usually smudged and rumpled. The only art on the walls is a gory portrait of Jesus on the cross.

Both bureaus hold old-fashioned piggy banks and jewelry boxes. On Mary Beth's, there are cosmetics and that pricey bottle of Cashmere Mist. On Caroline's, there's a novel with a bookmark in it.

"Did you ever consider redoing this room, Car'?"

"No. Why?"

"To make it look a little more homey."

"Homey?"

"There are no knickknacks or anything. Like, where's your Caboodle?" she asks, looking around for the fuchsia-and-pink plastic makeup case she gave Caroline for her last birthday, after Caroline had long coveted Kelly's.

"It's hidden way back in the closet. Not that I don't love it," Caroline adds quickly. "But Mary Beth was always going through it, helping herself to my stuff."

"Just tell her not to. This room is so boring. All you have is a bed, and a desk, and books."

"Well, bedrooms are only supposed to be used for sleeping, reading, and doing homework."

"What about sex?"

"K. K.!"

"*Caroline!* Who says bedrooms are only for sleeping, reading, and doing homework? Your parents? But you *do* know they must have done it at least four times." Kelly grins. "Wait—maybe just three, since they've got twins. Unless they—"

"Stop!"

Seeing her expression, Kelly clamps her mouth shut.

Caroline gets up, plucks a tissue from the generic-brand box on the nightstand between the twin beds, and dabs at her eyes.

"Hey, are you crying?" Kelly jumps to her feet and hugs her friend. "Car', I'm so sorry. I was just teasing you. I didn't mean to—"

"I know, it's just . . ." She swallows, sniffles. "Never mind."

"No, tell me."

"It's nothing. I'm fine."

She *isn't* fine.

Kelly remembers, with a twinge of guilt, what Mary Beth said on that January day, about how Caroline always puts up a good front. She'd vowed then to pay more attention to signs that her friend is keeping her troubles to herself, but there haven't been any.

Or have there?

Maybe Caroline has seemed a little off lately. Quieter than usual.

Not that they've seen much of each other. English is the only class the two of them have together at school—they've both always excelled at it and are in the honors section. They haven't been hanging out with the others as a group either. Midge has been busy with the varsity softball team, and Talia is working at the Landing, and Kelly has been spending time with Jason Owens. Technically he's not her boyfriend, but he's not *not* her boyfriend either.

Has she been too preoccupied with him to notice that something's wrong with Caroline?

"Come on, Car'. I just spent twenty minutes talking about Jason, and you listened. Now it's my turn to listen to whatever's bothering you."

"Nothing's—"

"Stop it! You're *crying*. I'm your friend. What's going on?"

Caroline takes a deep breath. "It's just . . . things have been kind of rough lately."

"Rough how?"

Caroline just shakes her head.

"Car'? I'm here for you. Whatever it is . . ."

"It's not a big deal. It doesn't matter."

"It matters to me. What's going on?"

"I don't know. I guess I'm just not feeling great."

"Are you sick? Is it PMS?"

"No. It's not like that."

"School?"

"No. Forget it, K. K., it's not—"

"Family stuff?"

Caroline says nothing.

"Family stuff. Your parents? Are you not getting along with them? Are they mad at you for something?"

"Me? No."

"Then is it . . . oh. It's Mary Beth."

Caroline flinches.

Nailed it.

"What did she do this time?"

"Long story. I don't want to get into it."

"Where did you say she is today?"

"I didn't."

Kelly looks over at Mary Beth's bed. It's as neatly made as Caroline's, and the bedspread is pristine.

"Is she away? A gymnastics tournament or something?"

"She dropped gymnastics."

"What! Why?"

"We're supposed to be talking about Robert Frost. Not about my sister."

"But—"

"We are working on this project." Caroline kneels on the floor and points to the poster board. "Let's get busy."

"Yeah, okay."

Kelly looks again at Mary Beth's neatly made bed.

It hasn't been slept in, and there's an air of emptiness about it—about the room itself, and the house. Not a hint of Mary Beth's chaotic presence. Not a whiff of her signature perfume, which tends to linger after she's vacated a space.

Where is she?

82

CHAPTER NINETEEN

Present Day

Sinking into a chair across the dining room table from Midge, Amy Klatte is still in her bloodstained nightgown, clutching a tissue box someone handed her. Her eyes are red and swollen.

"I'm so sorry, Mrs. Klatte," Midge says, taking out her notebook and a fine-tipped Sharpie. "I just need to ask you a few routine questions for my report, and then I'll leave you alone, okay?"

Alone—perhaps the wrong word choice to use with a newly widowed wife. In this moment, with a houseful of people, Amy is far from alone, though Midge suspects that she'd prefer to be.

"Do you have family in the area?"

"My in-laws. They, uh . . . they live a few miles away."

"And you've spoken to them?"

"No, they're out of the country on a church mission. My husband's sister lives in Rhinebeck. She's going to try to get ahold of them." She pauses, clears her throat, wipes more tears. "My mom and dad are going to drive up. But they won't get here until later this afternoon."

"From where?"

"Pennsylvania. It's where I'm from. It's where I met my husband." Her voice breaks on the last two words.

Gordy went to a Bible college somewhere near Philadelphia, Midge recalls. She wasn't surprised, years ago, to hear that he got engaged as an undergrad and married shortly after graduation. He was always going to marry young.

It was supposed to be Caroline.

Midge wonders what, if anything, Amy knows about his missing high school sweetheart, and why Gordy returned with his bride to settle down here, of all places. You'd think that after he escaped the eye of the storm, he'd have had no intention of ever coming back. Talia never had, and Kelly certainly hadn't planned on it.

What about you? You never left.

No. Midge stayed because this was home.

Maybe Gordy felt the same way.

Midge flips a page in her notebook and uncaps the Sharpie. "Why don't you tell me about last night, Mrs. Klatte?"

"Last night?" Her eyes are flooded with tears, and Midge knows what she's thinking. Last night was, well . . . the *last* night. The last time they'd be together as a family. The last time she'd ever see her husband, and the boys their father.

Midge has already spoken to the boys about it, just briefly, as they were the last ones to see Gordy alive. The game ended after midnight. They left their father on the couch in front of the TV and saw and heard nothing unusual until their mother's screams woke them.

According to Noah, when he headed to his room, he left his father holding the remote and channel surfing. According to Mike, Gordy was holding his phone, scrolling through it. If this were a homicide investigation, Midge would take a closer look at the discrepancy, but it's minor in this case. Maybe they didn't leave the room together, and thus both claims are accurate. Or one of the boys might be mistaken.

They agreed, however, that he was barefoot, wearing blue-and-white-striped pajama bottoms and a yellow T-shirt.

She asked Noah if there was anything else he wanted to share with her, sensing that there might be something. He seemed to hesitate, then shook his head and asked if he could rejoin his friends.

"The boys said you were home all evening?" she asks Amy.

"Me? After work, yes . . . I was here. We all were."

"Just the four of you, then?" Midge asks. "No visitors?"

"Yes. Just . . . just the four of us." She cries into a wad of wet tissue.

"I'm sorry. I know this is hard. Can you tell me how you spent the evening? Take your time."

Amy breathes in and out a few times.

"You know . . . we had dinner, cleaned up the dishes. Gordon and the boys watched TV."

"You didn't?"

"No, I'm not around here much during the workweek, so I was busy doing the laundry and ironing, and I went through the week's leftovers in the fridge—I . . . you know. I do that every Thursday night."

Midge nods, but she does not know. Her own fridge probably contains leftovers from Christmas dinner.

"Where do you work?"

"In Albany. For the state."

"That's a long commute. And your husband?"

"He's in data support. He works from home, and he . . ." Her voice breaks. She closes her eyes for a moment. "I'm sorry, but why . . . why are you asking me all these questions?"

"It's routine."

"But I kind of feel like . . . I mean, why does any of this matter? Gordon is . . . he's . . ." She swallows audibly.

"It's difficult, I know. I just have to file a report. I'll make it as quick and painless as possible. It sounds like you and your family had a typical evening? And your husband was feeling all right, behaving normally?"

"What do you mean?"

"I'm just confirming that there were no underlying health issues that might have caused his accident."

"No." She's crying again. "Everything was normal. Everything was good! In fact, Gordon did the sweetest thing last night. He and I usually cook dinner together when I get home from work, but when I got here, he was out—turned out he'd gone to pick up takeout from the new barbecue place as a surprise."

"The Smoke Shack? On Main?"

She nods, plucks a tissue from the box, and presses it to her eyes. "He never does that."

"So it *was* unusual?"

"No! It wasn't unusual, it was . . . a *treat*. For all of us. He doesn't like to spend money on restaurant food lately. The boys have such big appetites, and we have college coming up for both of them. But Gordon just said he knows how tired I am after a long day, and he wanted to give me a break from cooking."

"Okay." Midge nods and makes a note. "The rest of the night was routine, though?"

"Yes. Completely routine."

"When was the last time you saw him, Mrs. Klatte?"

"When I went to bed."

"What time was that?"

"I don't know—maybe ten? I have to be up at five. I left Gordon and the boys watching the game. It started so late, but they all wanted to see it because it was, um . . . the team that just won the World Series."

"The Texas Rangers?"

"Right. Gordy and the boys love them."

Midge, who does not, watched the same game last night with her own father, both of them rooting for the Los Angeles Dodgers. It was played on the West Coast and didn't start until ten o'clock.

"Did your husband come to bed after the game ended?"

"I . . . I don't know! I'm a sound sleeper!" Amy wails, as if apologizing for some grave mistake. "When the alarm went off at five, he wasn't there, and I couldn't tell whether his side had been slept in, because he always makes the bed as soon as he gets up."

"But he wouldn't have made the bed with you in it." Seeing her expression, Midge adds, "He *would* have?"

"Just his side. It's an old habit."

"So you got up at your usual time, and what did you think when your husband wasn't in bed?"

"That he'd fallen asleep on the couch and was still down there, I guess."

"Was that unusual behavior for him?"

"It wasn't *usual* behavior, but it's happened a time or two."

"Did you look for him downstairs, then?"

"Yes. And . . . he wasn't on the couch." She pauses, takes a shaky breath, and goes on. "So I checked to see if his car was still in the driveway. It was, so I figured he must be around here somewhere, but . . . he wasn't. And then I saw . . . I saw that the back slider was unlocked."

"And that was unusual?"

"Yes. I locked it last night after I stepped out with the garbage after I cleaned out the fridge. And Gordon always checks it before he goes up to bed. He checks it a few times, actually, just to make sure."

"So you assumed he'd gone outside?"

"Yes. I went out to look for him. I was calling for him, you know, not loudly, because it was so late—well, early . . . and then I saw that the gate was open . . ." She shakes her head, wipes her eyes with a tissue that's disintegrating in her hand, leaving a white shred on her cheek and another on the gleaming table. "And I went over to look, and that's when . . . I saw . . ." She breaks off, rocking back and forth, racked with sobs.

"I'm so sorry, Mrs. Klatte." Midge reaches across the table, plucks several fresh tissues from the box, and presses them into her hand. "Take your time."

"But . . . what else do you want to know?"

About to apologize again and remind her that the details are necessary for the accident report, Midge hesitates.

Is that the whole truth?

Or is there some part of her that's compelled to piece together Gordy Klatte's final movements out of . . .

What? Duty? Guilt? Morbid curiosity?

Suspicion.

That's it.

If it were any other victim, or any other place, or any other day of the year, she'd be taking everything about this death in stride. But under these circumstances, how can she ignore even a minuscule shred of doubt?

She needs to know—if only for her own peace of mind—that Gordon Klatte's fatal fall was nothing more than a tragic accident.

CHAPTER TWENTY

Descending the grand staircase, Kelly trails a hand along the smooth rail. The splinter in her thumb certainly didn't come from this.

While much of the mansion's original woodwork was left to rot amid the ruins, she recovered the perfectly preserved and polished banister from a Saugerties barn turned residence. It's intricately carved of mahogany, like the massive front door below.

Finding and retrieving these and other architectural relics entailed painstaking research and detective work.

Bits of Haven Cliff were scattered about Ulster County like branches in a storm. She found the dining room's marble mantelpiece in a salvage yard near Kingston's Rondout, the old built-in rosewood breakfront being used as a tool chest in a local garage, and the front door in a three-story, suitably Gothic Victorian in Mulberry Bay. Kelly knocked on it and convinced the owner to sell it, much like she'd persuaded Kathryn Andover to sell her the property itself.

Using period photos of the mansion and grounds from the historical society's archives, her restoration team recreated the house as it had been when the Winterfields moved in, with period wallpaper, fixtures, draperies, and antiques, some of which had actually been in their home.

Upon his parents' deaths, eldest son Lester inherited the entire estate, including the contents of their homes—*and* the Haven Cliff curse, if you believe in such things. It shadowed Lester and his offspring for the rest of their lives, some of which ended as violently and myste-riously as Asa's and Edith's had.

Rather than keep his siblings together, Lester shipped them off to boarding schools, and the youngest, Caroline's great-grandfather, to an orphanage. He sold off the family heirlooms.

Kelly bought everything she could find, including a forgotten attic trunk filled with keepsakes that had no real value—photographs, dia-ries, the family Bible. One of Lester's descendants was happy to sell it to her for a steep price.

Now, the mansion is a gleaming replica of the Gilded Age show-place it once was, ready to be bestowed upon a far more deserving Winterfield heir.

At the foot of the stairway, a gilt-framed sepia portrait of Asa and Edith Winterfield is propped against the wall, waiting to be hung.

According to the faded notation on the back, they were photo-graphed in 1892, in the drawing room of their Fifth Avenue mansion. At the time, Haven Cliff was under construction, to be used as their summer home.

Gazing into their faces, Kelly looks for some resemblance to Caroline. She's seen a hint of it before, in other photos. There's one of a younger Edith in a white dress with a lace parasol, where she seems to exude the same sweet femininity as her great-great-granddaughter, and they share a petite build. In another, Asa is seated in his study holding an open book, and there's a familiar hint of perturbed distraction in his gaze, as though someone interrupted him while he was reading.

"Hang on," Kelly can hear Caroline saying, looking up from a book with a similar expression. "Just let me finish this paragraph . . ."

This page, or this chapter . . .

Sweet Caroline, so often lost in some imaginary world long after the rest of them had discovered that the real one was far more com-pelling. For her, forbidden to do so many things, fiction wasn't just a diversion—it was an escape.

Staring up at the somber, stiffly posed Winterfields, Kelly sees a hint of the Caroline who manifested in those last months they were all together. Especially in Edith, jaw set, hands clasped, everything about her restrained and confined—maybe by her stiff corset and high collar, maybe by something more.

Is it just that nobody ever smiled for photos back then? Or had she somehow sensed the doom that would befall her not long after she moved into this house?

Maybe it had been a bit of both.

Wondering what she'd think of her home's restoration, Kelly almost expects to see a subtle shift in Edith's solemn expression—approval? Disapproval?

Of course there's nothing. It's a mere photograph, and its subjects are long dead.

Murdered.

"Are you Kelly?"

She gasps and turns to see a stranger crouched in the shadows at the base of the staircase like a cat waiting to pounce.

Then she sees the screwdriver in his hand and realizes he's a workman, installing a custom wooden switch plate that matches the wainscoting surrounding the electrical outlet.

"Sorry—didn't mean to scare you."

He gives the screwdriver a final twist and stands. He's lean and muscular with shaggy blond hair, wearing a Hudson Valley Renegades T-shirt and tattered Levi's faded to near-white.

"You're Kelly," he says with a nod. "I recognize you."

"From . . . ?"

"That article in the newspaper, about how you were fixing up this place." He reaches into his pocket and pulls out an envelope. "Someone just delivered this, and I'm supposed to make sure I give it directly to you."

She takes it. It's a white envelope with *Kelly Barrow* scrawled on the front in black Sharpie.

"Who dropped it off?" she asks, sliding a forefinger under the flap.

"A woman. I offered to check and see if you were around, but she didn't want to wait."

She pauses. "A woman? Did she have on a dark sweatshirt? Hood up?"

"Right."

Probably a subcontractor leaving a bill, Kelly thinks, opening the envelope.

Then, seeing what's inside, she frowns. "What in the world . . . ?"

CHAPTER TWENTY-ONE

August 30, 1997

Talia's mother rarely goes away—certainly never without Talia. But an old friend who lives in Niagara Falls invited Natalie to visit this Labor Day weekend, and Talia encouraged her to go.

"I hate to leave you alone for a holiday," she said.

"Mommy, it's not Christmas! Who cares about Labor Day? And I'll invite the girls over to keep me company. We'll have a slumber party to celebrate starting junior year."

"Their parents might not allow them to stay over if I'm not here."

"I'll make sure they get permission."

That went predictably. Kelly's parents didn't have a problem with it. Midge's agreed with myriad conditions. And Caroline didn't tell hers about Natalie's absence.

It's like old times, Talia thinks as they rummage in the kitchen for snacks, discussing the stack of new releases they rented from Family Video.

"I think we should start with *My Best Friend's Wedding,*" Caroline suggests.

"We all already saw it in the theater when it came out," Midge says.

"I didn't."

"That's why we rented it," Talia reminds them. "Caroline wasn't with us."

"When was it?"

"Does it matter, Car? You're never with us anymore," Kelly says.

"I'm here right now."

"But you haven't been around all summer," Midge points out.

"Well, you guys have been busy too. You're lifeguarding, and Talia's waitressing, and Kelly's always jetting off to Hawaii or something."

"That was one time, for a week," Kelly says, rooting around in the freezer.

"We just miss you, that's all," Talia tells Caroline. "It's always so much fun when the four of us are together."

She hesitates, wondering whether she should bring up the rest of what they've been discussing lately—about how Caroline's relationship with Gordy seems to have eclipsed their friendship.

It would be better coming from Talia than from straight-shooting Midge, or from Kelly, who even when she's aiming for the right thing manages to say it the wrong way.

"Ice cream!" Kelly shouts, plucking a carton from the freezer. It's coated in ice crystals. She scratches with her fingernail. "Please be chocolate fudge brownie with caramel swirl. Please be . . . Eww! It's rum raisin."

"Who puts rum and raisins in ice cream?" Midge asks.

"I mean, the rum part would be great," Kelly says. "I don't suppose we can make cocktails?"

"We cannot." Talia tosses the ice cream into the garbage, grabs two bags of chips, and shepherds them all into the living room. "And we're watching *My Best Friend's Wedding* first because it's my favorite."

Caroline smiles. "Oh, Tally. You and your happily ever afters. I love that you believe in all that."

"You don't?"

She shrugs.

"*I* don't." Kelly points to herself. "*This* girl just wants to have fun. Which reminds me . . . Did Mary Beth have a good summer, Car'?"

"I guess so."

"You don't know?"

"I haven't talked to her, so . . . no. I don't know."

"How have you not talked to her?" Kelly asks. "She has to be back by now. School starts Tuesday."

"She's going to stay out there."

"She's dropping out?" Kelly asks.

"No! There are other schools."

"But her class already voted her Miss Mulberry Bay High," Talia says.

"So? That's just yearbook superlatives. It doesn't mean she has to stay and graduate."

"*Where* is she again?" Midge asks.

"Down south, with our cousins. Why?"

"You said 'out there.' Not 'down there.'"

"Are you serious, Midge?"

"Which cousins?" Kelly asks.

"You don't know them. They've never been here to visit."

Midge furrows her brows. "Then how do *you* know them?"

"They're family! What is this, an interrogation, Detective Kennedy?"

"Forget it." Midge goes back to the bag of chips, shaking her head.

But Kelly isn't about to drop it. "How long have you known this, Caroline?"

"I don't know. Awhile, I guess."

"And you're just telling us now? Is it supposed to be some big secret?"

"Why would it be a secret?"

"Because sometimes it seems like you don't share stuff with us."

"Well, I've barely seen you guys all summer."

"Whose fault is that?" Kelly asks. "We've all been here, hanging around, same as always. It's almost like you've been avoiding us."

"*Avoiding* you? That's ridiculous! I've been babysitting, and I went away with my family—"

"Minus Mary Beth," Kelly says. "But *plus* Gordy."

"Are you jealous that I've got a boyfriend? Is that it? Because you and Jason broke up and—"

"Jason is ancient history. I'm going out with Derek Bennett, which you would have known if you'd been around, and if you asked, and if you cared!"

"Of course I care, K. K.," Caroline says, looking as if she's about to cry. "I love you. All of you."

Talia reaches out and touches her arm. "And we love you. We just miss you, and it's kind of surprising that we didn't know about Mary Beth, that's all."

"Well, it's really not a big deal. I mean . . . Lacey Alexander is going to China for a year—are you guys quizzing her sister too?"

"She's going for the foreign exchange program! This is different."

Caroline holds Kelly's pointed gaze for a moment, then looks away and does a double take at the television. "Hey, there's breaking news! What's going on?"

Diversion tactic, Talia assumes.

But then Midge says, "Holy crap!" and Talia follows her gaze.

". . . has died after a car crash in Paris," a somber announcer is saying.

"The queen is dead?" Kelly asks.

"No! Princess Diana!" Midge says. "Shh! Listen!"

". . . with her boyfriend, Dodi Al Fayed, also killed in the crash, along with their driver. According to eyewitnesses, their chauffeured Mercedes-Benz was being chased by paparazzi when it went into the Pont de l'Alma tunnel at high speed. A fourth passenger in the car, Diana's bodyguard . . ."

Talia wonders if her mother has heard the news about her idol. She's going to be absolutely devastated.

Natalie grew up in an impoverished family that moved from place to place, sometimes in the middle of the night to escape landlords looking for overdue rent. She figured she'd never amount to anything until she, like a lot of other young women, became captivated by Prince Charles's romance with a commoner.

When she was about the same age Talia is now, Natalie said, she called in sick to her summer waitressing job so that she could get up before dawn and watch the royal wedding.

"It gave me hope, you know? Not that I'd marry a future king, but just that . . . well, maybe a real-life Prince Charming would come along and sweep me off my feet," she told Talia. "But we both got screwed over in the end, me and Di. Only her rich ex was a prince who put a ring on her finger, and mine didn't even stick around till the baby was born."

"There's no way," Kelly says, shaking her head. "She didn't die in a car crash."

"Yes, she did!" Talia gestures at the television, where there's a close-up shot of the blond beauty in a tiara above the chyron DIANA, PRINCESS OF WALES, 7/1/61–8/31/97.

"Oh, come on. Are we really supposed to believe that the most famous woman in the world died in some stupid car crash like a regular person?"

"She *is* a regular person," Midge says, crunching her way through a bag of Doritos. "I mean, she's a princess, but she isn't superhuman."

"What if she faked her death?" Kelly asks. "Who would even blame her? Her life is hell. Her husband dumped her for another woman, and the royal family doesn't approve of her new boyfriend, and she gets chased by the press everywhere she goes."

"She wouldn't do that to her sons," Talia protests. "She's a really good mother."

"How do you know that?"

"Everyone knows that, Kelly!"

"Well, I bet it's a massive cover-up, like Elvis."

Midge stops crunching, hand poised in front of her mouth with a handful of chips. "What do you mean?"

"He's not dead either. He just wanted to escape."

"That's impossible," Talia tells Kelly.

"Anything's possible. Especially when you have enough money." Kelly shakes her head. "You shouldn't always believe what you hear. And if you don't witness something with your own eyes, it might not be true."

"Well, this is true," Talia says glumly. "Diana is dead."

Midge nods. "So is Elvis."

Caroline, though . . .

Caroline says nothing at all, just sits staring off into space.

CHAPTER TWENTY-TWO

Present Day

"Mrs. Klatte, you didn't . . ." Midge avoids looking at the blood on that otherwise pristine white nightgown and rephrases the question. "When you found your husband, did you try to move him?"

"No. I, uh, I knelt down beside him, but as soon as I touched him, I knew . . . I knew it was too late. I . . ."

"I'm so sorry."

Watching the woman bury her face in her hands, sobbing, Midge has had enough.

She puts the cap back on her Sharpie and is about to close her notebook. It's time to leave Amy Klatte to grieve in peace.

But then Amy lifts her head and looks at her. "It just doesn't make any sense."

"What doesn't?"

"Why would he have gone outside alone in the dark in the middle of the night?"

Midge removes the cap again.

"I would wonder if maybe he took the dog out or had to find an indoor cat that escaped . . ." Midge has dealt with both issues in the wee hours at her own place, but she's pretty certain this sterile-looking household is pet-free, and Amy Klatte confirms it.

"We don't have a dog or cat."

"He has no history of sleepwalking, does he?"

"Sleepwalking!"

"No sleepwalking. Got it. Okay. Do you think he might have . . . I don't know, heard a noise and gone out to investigate?"

"What do you mean?"

"Raccoons, coyotes, bears getting into garbage? It happens all the time at my place."

"We keep the cans locked in a shed."

"Maybe he heard neighbors making noise, then? Or fireworks? We've had a problem with illegal fireworks for the last few weeks. It's been so dry, and wildfires are a concern."

"He'd never go outside in the dark for something like that."

"Could it have been kids cutting through the yard or partying in the woods? That sort of thing?"

"It was a school night," Amy says, as if that rules out the suggestion. "But even if that were the case, he would have turned on the lights out there, and they were off."

"You're sure about that?"

"Yes. I had to turn them on when I went out, and that's why I was thinking he wouldn't be out there, but I had to check. I didn't know where else he could be."

"Is it possible he got a call or a text? Maybe a neighbor asking him to check on something?"

"I don't know. I guess so, but it had to be before he came upstairs, if he did." She turns her head toward the family room, peering at something.

Midge follows her gaze and sees a charging cord dangling from an outlet.

"He always leaves his phone plugged into that charger overnight. I always put mine there when I get home from work, and when I unplug it, he plugs in his. He doesn't like having it in the bedroom. He says it keeps him awake. The boys showed him how to put it on Do Not Disturb, but he doesn't like to do that."

"Why not?"

She shrugs. "He's a creature of habit."

Either Gordy broke the habit last night and left the phone in a different spot, or he had it with him when he went outside.

"Speaking of habits . . . did he like to sit by the firepit at that hour?"

"Alone? No."

"Could he have been going down to the lake for a swim?"

"No way," Amy says with an unequivocal shake of her head.

"Ah, you're right. He would have changed into his bathing suit."

"It's not just that. Gordon hates the water."

"Then why live on the lake?"

"I fell in love with this house when we looked at it, and I talked Gordy into it. The lake access was the only drawback for him. He never goes down there if he can help it."

Then why last night? Midge wonders.

"Why do you think he hates the water, Mrs. Klatte?"

"He's afraid of it. He said he never learned how to swim."

Midge digests this in silence.

Why would Gordy Klatte lie to his wife?

And if he lied about something so innocuous, then what else was he keeping from her?

CHAPTER TWENTY-THREE

Talia estimated that the drive upstate might take four or five hours with Friday traffic, bridge congestion, and the inevitable summer construction. Despite all that, she reached the Thruway exit in Kingston in just over two.

Memory, however, is a tricky thing. She assumed she could find her way to Mulberry Bay from there without relying on her phone for navigation, but she's made a number of wrong turns on the back roads. Old landmarks are no longer where they used to be, are unrecognizable, or have vanished altogether. Stewart's has moved to a different intersection, the Hess gas station has tripled in size and become a Speedway, and the old Pizza Hut is gone, building and all. At least, she's pretty sure it is. Either that, or she's more lost than she thinks.

Stopped at an unfamiliar crossroads, she sees a gas station minimart and wonders if they carry road maps. Probably not.

It would be much simpler to just turn on her phone and check Google or Waze. She doesn't really think Ben might somehow track her and find out she lied about where she's going this weekend . . . does she?

Maybe not deliberately.

But when they bought Hayley a cell phone, they installed an app that allows them to track her phone's location with their own. So if Ben wants to see where their daughter is at any given time this weekend, he'll also see where his wife . . . isn't.

When she warned him that the cell service was reputedly sketchy at her fictional yoga retreat, he said that was probably a blessing.

"Even if the service is perfect, just turn off your phone and leave it in a drawer while you're there. If you're reachable, Caleb is going to want to call you every five minutes. The pediatrician says he needs to get used to the idea that loved ones come and go. That you may be unavailable to him for a few hours, or even a few days, but you'll always come back."

It isn't entirely true. Sometimes people leave and you never see them again.

Talia didn't say that.

She's making herself unavailable to her family for the next few days with the doctor's blessing, and her husband's, but she's positive neither of them would approve of her lie about where she's going.

It's the only way to do this.

Is it?

Okay, it's the least complicated way to do this.

She doubts Ben even remembers that back in college, long before they were a couple, she once mentioned having a friend who'd gone missing. Or maybe she didn't even say *friend*. She might have down-played it, saying it was just a girl from her town. Caroline was part of another time and place, and she didn't want that dark episode to taint the present.

If she'd realized that Ben would ever be more than a casual pal, she might have elaborated, or brought it up again later.

Or not.

"Never tell a man all your secrets, Talia," Mommy had counseled her, long before Talia had a man; long before Caroline disappeared. "That's how I lost your father."

As a teenager, Natalie admitted to him that she wasn't a virgin. When she got pregnant, he accused her of sleeping around. It wasn't true, and Natalie was positive the baby was his, but he refused to accept responsibility.

All because she'd been too honest.

Talia was in her midtwenties by the time she and Ben found their way back to each other and fell in love. She saw no reason to bring up the past, and Caroline. Mulberry Bay was a distant memory, and everything was within her grasp: husband, children, a home, career, money, stability . . . the whole damn fairy tale that had eluded her mother, who'd sacrificed so much to ensure that Talia's life would be different.

For a long time, it was.

She went into marriage as a corporate VP and motherhood as a seasoned daily commuter. She thought nothing of the forty-five-minute daily train ride to Manhattan, or of hiring a full-time babysitter for her firstborn.

The pandemic permanently shifted her career to her home office, which meant juggling work obligations with domestic chores and homeschooling the kids. When the company took a financial hit, she welcomed being reduced to part time, and was relieved to be laid off last year.

But they need a second income, so she's been looking for something else, especially now that Ben's advertising sales position is fairly flexible, with far less travel and only a few days a week in the city. She's had interviews at multiple companies, and multiple interviews at some. It seems no one wants to hire a forty-three-year-old mom to be a digital media director.

"It'll happen," Ben says, every time she gets an email—an email, not a phone call—informing her that the "team" has decided to "go in a different direction."

"I know it will," she tells him, shrugging it off like she's just lost a game of Monopoly to one of the kids. "I'm not worried."

More lies to add to the growing heap.

Making a decision, she pulls into the gas station, which is surprisingly busy for the middle of nowhere. She bypasses the pumps, which are all occupied, to grab the only open parking space in front of the minimart.

Heading inside, she holds the door for an exiting young family. The pregnant mom is carrying a designer handbag, holding the hand of a toddler who's focused on an iPad. Dad is clad in Filson, juggling a case of Evian and a bag of groceries that has leafy greens poking out of the top.

Summer people, driving a Range Rover with Massachusetts plates.

Things sure have changed around here, Talia thinks. In stark contrast to the minimart where she and her mom used to scrounge up some semblance of dinner, this one has an organic produce section, an espresso bar, a refrigerated case with paninis, grain bowls, and sushi, and fresh florals.

She grabs a bouquet of wildflowers as a hostess gift for Kelly and joins the line waiting by the register. She scans the counter area for road maps but finds only candy, vape supplies, lottery tickets, a glossy *Hudson Valley* magazine . . .

And a flyer stamped MISSING above a photo of a pretty teenage girl.

Talia's heart stops.

Caroline.

But she blinks, and of course the girl is a stranger.

Edging closer, she can read the text. She's seventeen . . . last seen hiking in Elizabethville in April . . . family is offering a reward . . .

Talia's heart pounds.

The missing girl isn't Caroline. She looks nothing like her. She has nothing to do with her, or with Talia.

But you can't erase the past any more than you can change what happened, or that you allowed it to happen.

What she, Midge, and Kelly did was wrong, though she never grasped *how* wrong until she became a parent.

"All set?" the gray-haired man behind the register is asking, and she realizes that he's talking to her. That he's seeing her see the Missing poster.

"Oh . . . yes. I'm . . . yes, just the flowers. Oh! And . . . do you have a map, by any chance?"

"Not in years. Nobody knows how to read them these days," he adds, with a wry smile. "They just use their phones. Where are you trying to go?"

"Mulberry Bay."

He points out the window. "It's three minutes down the road. Bear right when you come to the fork and that'll put you on 28. You'll see the signs."

"Three minutes? That's all?"

"Depends on how fast you're driving," he says with a wink. "Me, I obey the speed limit. The MBPD likes to enforce it."

Midge is the MBPD. And if Talia's destination is only three minutes away, she's essentially back in Mulberry Bay already.

"That'll be sixty-three dollars even," he says, ringing up the flowers.

"*Sixty*-three?" She opens her wallet, wishing she'd checked the price first and that she'd gone to the ATM before she left home. She rarely carries much cash. And Ben will be able to see her debit and credit card transactions.

Only if he makes a point of looking, though. She's the one who handles the household bills and banking.

She hands over a credit card.

The man glances at it and chuckles. "We may have remodeled this place, but it's not quite Pottery Barn."

"Oh! Sorry, wrong card."

He reads the name on the card as he offers it back to her. "Talia Shaw?"

Dammit. She opened that account years ago, when she was still single, and never got around to changing it to her married name. Around here, Talia Shaw will get her recognized.

So what? It's not like she's an escaped convict. Even if he—or the many customers in earshot—remember her, and that she was friends with Caroline Winterfield, they wouldn't suspect she had anything to do with her disappearance.

"Talia is a pretty name," he comments as she swaps the card for an Amex that reads Talia Adler. "My daughter and her husband are expecting their third daughter. They've already got Tempo and Tesla and they're looking for another unusual *T* name, and you don't want to *know* what's on their list. I'll convince them to add Talia."

She exhales and forces a smile. So that's all it is.

Of course that's all it is. He doesn't know her. He just doesn't want another grandchild named after a car.

Three minutes later, she rounds a bend and spots a familiar cluster of rooftops and steeples against a bright-blue sky.

A wooden signboard painted in shades of blue and violet reflects the colors of the lake, the ripe berries in the mulberry trees, and the mountains in the distance.

It reads: WELCOME TO MULBERRY BAY.

Yes. Welcome to the past.

Welcome to the long-overdue reunion with her oldest friends.

Welcome to the chance to finally accept responsibility for their actions and do what they can to make things right—even if that means sharing the one thing Talia knows about Caroline's disappearance that Midge and Kelly never did.

CHAPTER TWENTY-FOUR

February 27, 2020
Paris, France

". . . cases in northern Italy as the crisis escalates in Europe. An infectious disease specialist is advising—"

Kelly turns away from the television as her phone rings, somewhere on her unmade bed amid the piles of clothes surrounding an open suitcase that so far contains only her cat, Bijou. He climbed in as soon as she started packing, as if to preclude her departure.

"You'll be fine, Bijou," she assures him as she slips a hand under the suitcase, finding only the TV remote. "Michel and Pierre always take such good care of you."

The couple's flat is below hers in this charming 8th arrondissement building, tucked along a wide boulevard overlooking the Seine.

From her scrolled wrought iron balcony, Kelly has an unobstructed view of the mouth to the Pont de l'Alma tunnel. Every time she looks at it, she thinks of the night back in 1997 when news broke of Princess Diana's fatal accident there.

She remembers saying, "She's more of a prisoner than a princess. Her life is hell."

Just like Mary Beth Winterfield.

Seeing the look on Caroline's face, she was pretty sure she was thinking the same thing—and that the story she told them about her sister spending her senior year down south with family wasn't the whole truth.

None of the truth, she learned a little over a year later, when she and Caroline made the trip to that seedy Syracuse row house to deliver the money Mary Beth left behind.

Such grim memories aren't welcome here, in Kelly's new life far from Mulberry Bay, but she's learned that unpleasant reminders of the past have a way of popping up no matter where you are.

Anyway, in addition to the tunnel where Princess Diana died, the balcony also has a classic Parisian Eiffel Tower view.

Aiming the remote, she turns off the current news bulletin about the virus outbreak. Bijou meows, perhaps in protest, as if he were hoping the dire report would keep her from flying to Milan for a long-awaited Alpine ski vacation.

The cat is a French Chartreux, a breed she chose because they're known for being extra affectionate and bonded to their humans. That suited her needs in the lonely aftermath of her second divorce, and continues to do so, for the most part. But he heaps on the guilt every time he senses she's about to travel and always gives her the cold shoulder for a solid twenty-four hours upon her return.

Cats, however, eventually forgive and forget. Unlike ex-husbands, and ex-friends.

Ah, there's the phone. Kelly answers quickly, without checking caller ID, to keep the call from bouncing to voicemail.

"Bonjour?"

A pause.

"Kelly?"

"Mrs. Verga."

In the three decades she's worked for Kelly's parents back in Mulberry Bay, the woman has never been the warm and fuzzy type.

But her demeanor toward Kelly has been downright frosty over the past decade.

"I think you'd better come. Beverly's just been taken to the hospital in an ambulance."

"What happened?" Kelly asks, bracing for the worst, flashing back to a similar summons back in 2010.

At that time, she was living in San Francisco with her second husband, and the call came from her mother.

Kelly was too late. By the time she got there, her precious, precious father was gone—dead of a massive heart attack, not yet sixty.

"She slipped and fell on the ice and twisted her ankle," Mrs. Verga says now.

Kelly heaves a sigh of relief.

"Oh! You scared me! I thought this was some kind of emergency. Give Mom my love, and I'll check back later. I've got a flight to catch this afternoon, and I'm running late, so—"

"I assure you; this *is* an emergency."

"A twisted ankle? Look, the next time I talk to Mom, I'll tell her it might be time to hang up the ice skates, but—"

"Ice skates?"

"You said she slipped on the—"

"Not at the skating pond! Do you know what time it is here?"

She checks the clock on the bedside table, and it takes her a moment to do the math. A little past five in the morning.

"Someone found her lying in the road," Mrs. Verga goes on.

"*What?*"

"She was in her nightgown."

"*What?*"

"God knows how long she was out there. It's twelve degrees. She could have died of exposure."

Speechless, Kelly sinks onto the bed. Bijou, the most empathetic companion she's ever had, climbs out of the suitcase and nuzzles his face against her. He knows something's wrong.

Terribly wrong.

"The man who found her called 9-1-1. The police called me, since I'm the emergency contact in her phone," Mrs. Verga informs her, with a pause so Kelly can digest the news that *she*, the daughter, is not the emergency contact. "They want to talk to you."

"But—"

Then a voice Kelly hasn't heard in two decades comes on the line.

"Kelly? It's—"

"Midge! What are *you* doing there?" she asks, forgetting for a split second that Midge isn't merely her former friend; that she isn't there because she's letting bygones be bygones; because she loves Kelly unconditionally and sensed she'd need some support in a time of crisis.

That's Bijou's job.

Midge is a cop, and this is hers.

"I responded to the accident call," she tells Kelly.

Her tone is so unfamiliar in its dead seriousness that a terrible thought pops into Kelly's head. What if . . .

"Is my mom . . . is she . . ." Her voice breaks. "She's not . . . dead?"

"Dead? No!"

"Are you sure? Because when my dad . . . when he . . . they didn't tell me. I called from the airport, and he was already gone, and they didn't tell me."

"Your mom is alive, Kelly," Midge says. "She's on her way to the hospital in an ambulance. And I'm so sorry about your dad. I wanted to come to the wake, or the funeral, but . . . I couldn't."

To her credit, she doesn't offer an excuse, just provides additional details about Beverly's accident, which are sketchy.

"Do you think I should come? You know how Mrs. Verga is," Kelly adds, and then wishes she hadn't.

Right now, she doesn't want to remember all those years they spent as the best of friends, privy to every detail about each other's families and households. She doesn't want to remember that Midge used to do an *SNL*-worthy imitation of the ever-disapproving Mrs. Verga.

There's a pause on the other end of the line, and then a quiet "Yes."

"Yes, you know how Mrs. Verga is? Or yes, I should come?"

"Both," Midge says. "Get home, Kelly. Get home today."

CHAPTER
TWENTY-FIVE

Present Day

"No, a little to the left," Kelly tells the man at the top of the very tall stepladder—is his name Ray? Roy?

He introduced himself earlier, but she'd been preoccupied by the strange contents of the envelope he'd just handed her.

Why would anyone give her a card? One card—not a greeting card, or even a tarot card.

Just a regular old playing card, a two of spades imprinted with a Mulberry Bay photo montage on the back. The decks are sold in local boutiques like La Papeterie, where she bought her notebook, and perhaps the Enchanted Chalet in Woodstock.

Maybe that's where it came from. Maybe it's a cartomancy message for her, delivered by the girl in the Bard sweatshirt.

That makes sense . . . doesn't it?

As much sense as anything else today.

She looks up at Ray/Roy, inching the gilt-framed portrait along the wall.

"What did she look like?"

"Who?"

"The person who delivered the envelope!"

"Oh. She looked . . . you know . . ."

"I don't know! That's why I'm asking."

"Sorry. I wasn't paying much attention. Should I have been?"

"Of course not." Reminding herself that he's not her doorman, nor her butler, she softens her tone. "It's just . . . I have no idea who she was, and it seems kind of strange that she didn't want to hang around and talk to me."

"Do delivery people usually want to talk to you?"

"No," she admits, again. "Forget it. Can you just slide that frame a tiny bit back to the right? Wait—not that much."

"Sorry."

"It's okay. I know I'm being a pain in the butt, but it's the first thing people will see when they walk through the front door, so I want it to be perfect."

"If they've ever been here before, then they'll be blown away by what you've done. I know I was."

"You've been here before?"

He takes a pencil from behind his ear to mark the wall. "Yeah, we used to sneak up here to explore the ruins when I was a kid. And then in high school, there were always parties. Guess those days are over."

"They are."

"You're not planning to live here all alone, are you?"

"Nope. I have a cat."

"This is a whole lot of house for one person and one cat."

She shrugs.

"And you don't seem like the middle-of-nowhere type. You used to live in Paris, didn't you?"

"How'd you know that?" she asks.

"Doesn't everyone in town know everything about everyone?"

"Not *everything*." Not by a long shot.

Yet he turns to look at her, and it's almost as if . . .

Does he know? About that night, and Caroline?

"Why'd you come back here?"

"A lot of reasons," she says, and offers the most innocuous—a lie. "Guess I was homesick."

"Yeah? How long were you gone?"

"I was twenty when I left."

Twenty, and eloping with the wayward scion of a wealthy New York banking family because her parents refused to give their blessing. The marriage lasted a little over a year. The divorce left her with a fat bank account, an overwhelming sense of relief, and the realization that sometimes, the goals our parents set for us become the goals we want for ourselves.

She reconciled with hers and went back to college. Dartmouth wouldn't have her, but Berkeley would, and she was happy to have a continent between her and Tad.

She went on to Stanford Law School, joined a premier San Francisco firm, and met her second husband while representing his tech company in an antitrust lawsuit, which they won.

That marriage lasted twice as long as the first. Extracting herself from it was far more difficult than the first time. It entailed an unsorting of sordid indiscretions, not all of them his, and significantly more money than the Strattons—her wealthy previous in-laws—would ever have.

She flew to Paris to celebrate, intending to stay two weeks, which turned into a month, then months, and then years.

"Je suis très content que tu sois revenue," Ray/Roy comments.

He's glad she came back? So now he's flirting. Maybe he was flirting all along. Maybe he has no idea of her connection to what happened. Maybe he's never even heard about the girl lost in the lake.

"Ah, tu parles français?" she asks, and he shoots her a grin.

Her phone buzzes in her pocket. Pulling it out, she sees a text: He's way too young. Hands off.

She whirls around to see Midge, just outside the nearest floor-to-ceiling window, wearing her navy-blue uniform, aviator sunglasses, and a frown. Gesturing at the ladder, she mouths, *Jailbait.*

Kelly turns back to Ray/Roy, glad he can't see out the window from his perch. "You can go ahead and hang the portrait right where it is, thanks. I've got to go outside and deal with a little . . . problem."

She steps out onto the wide terrace, newly adorned with vintage wicker furniture and potted palms. The air smells of roses blooming in the newly restored formal garden below.

"Officer Kennedy, what are you doing out here? Isn't there a law against spying on innocent civilians through their windows?"

"It's Detective Sergeant Kennedy now, and there's definitely a law against *that*." Midge tilts her head toward the front hall.

"Portrait hanging? That's why you're here? You're hauling me off to jail?"

Her teasing grin fades as Midge steps closer, taking off her sunglasses.

Noting the conspicuous absence of twinkle in her blue eyes, Kelly says, "Uh-oh. What's going on?"

"I thought you should hear it from me."

"Hear what?"

"Gordon Klatte . . ."

"Gordy? What about him?"

"He's dead."

CHAPTER
TWENTY-SIX

November 19, 1997

"Hello, Kelly. It's lovely to see you," Caroline's mother greets her at the door on a rainy afternoon.

Kelly resists the urge to respond, *Is it? Is it really?*

But she pastes on a smile as she steps into the foyer, and responds with an equally insincere, "Lovely to see you too, Mrs. Winterfield."

Her own tongue trips over *lovely*, a word somebody's maiden aunt might have used, like, a hundred years ago.

"Caroline's up in her room."

Her room—as if Mary Beth has ceased to exist. As if it's no longer *their* room.

In the almost three months since Caroline revealed that her sister won't be graduating with her class in Mulberry Bay, the topic has rarely come up. If it does, she skirts questions.

But they don't see as much of each other as they used to. Junior year is academically challenging, their extracurriculars don't overlap, and anyway, Caroline's not allowed to have much of a social life unless it involves Gordy. Her parents are increasingly reluctant to sanction shopping malls and movie theaters with the girls, and they absolutely forbid her to attend parties, but they seem perfectly content to let her date him.

"What are you girls working on today?" Mrs. Winterfield asks Kelly.

"We're writing a script."

"A script! Caroline said you were studying together," she says, like a drawing room detective who's just caught the prime suspect in a lie.

"Oh, well, I mean . . . we are. It's for honors English. We have to rewrite a scene from Shakespeare with a modern movie genre spin." Kelly makes a beeline for the stairs.

"Shoes, please?" Mrs. Winterfield calls after her. "We don't want to track mud through the house, do we?"

Yes, Kelly thinks. *Yes, we do.*

She leaves her new leopard-print Wellingtons on the worn doormat that might once have said *Welcome,* and somewhat fittingly, no longer does.

Upstairs, she finds Caroline sitting at her desk in front of an open textbook.

"Chemistry," she says, marking her place and closing it. "Science has never been my thing."

"Yeah, mine either." The room looks pretty much the same as always, but there's an emptiness about it now.

On top of the bookshelf, she sees two framed photographs that weren't here before.

One is a snapshot of Caroline and Gordy. The other is Mary Beth's senior portrait, taken halfway through junior year. She's wearing a black drape across her shoulders and a string of pearls. Kelly's class recently got the photographer's memo about their own upcoming portraits.

"Great picture," she tells Caroline, walking over to the bookshelf.

"Thanks. We were at a church picnic."

"I didn't mean you and Gordy—but that's nice too," she adds quickly. "I meant Mary Beth."

"Oh. Yeah. It's nice." Caroline opens a notebook. "So, I wrote down a bunch of ideas for our project. I think we should do the prewedding scene from *Romeo and Juliet* with a *My Best Friend's Wedding* spin on it. Remember the part where Hugh Grant—"

"Wait, *Romeo and Juliet* is a tragedy. I was thinking we can do the witches scene from *Macbeth* like a Wes Craven horror movie."

Caroline makes a face. "I hate *Macbeth*. And I never saw a Wes Craven movie."

"*Scream 2* is coming out in a few weeks. We should get Talia and Midge and all go."

"Oh, I don't—"

"Never mind. I should know better by now."

"What do you mean?"

"Just . . . you don't really seem like you want to hang out with us anymore. I don't know if it's because of Gordy, or because—"

"It's not Gordy! And it's not that I don't want to hang out! It's . . ." Caroline puts her elbows on the desk, leans forward, and cups the top of her head in her hands, as if she's in pain, or trying to contain some awful thing.

Kelly puts a hand on her shoulder. "What's going on?"

"Forget it."

"Why do you always do this, Car'? You're obviously going through some stuff, but whenever you seem like you want to confide something, you pull back. Is it that you don't trust me? Because you can."

"It's not that." Caroline looks up at her, face etched in misery. "I trust you. But you can't help."

"Try me."

Caroline says nothing, but Kelly sees her glance at the photo of Mary Beth.

"Is it about your sister?" she asks.

"Not just that, but . . . I miss her. Yes."

"Well, is she coming home for Thanksgiving?"

Caroline shakes her head.

"Christmas, then?"

"No."

"What do you mean? Is she never coming home again?"

"I honestly don't know, K. K."

"Well, have you talked to her lately? Is she okay?"

"No."

"No, she's not okay? Or no, you haven't talked to her?"

"Both." She shoots a glance at the closed bedroom door, as if someone might be listening. "You can't tell anyone, okay?"

"I won't."

"I'm not exactly sure where she is."

"She's not down south with your cousins?"

"There are no cousins down south."

"I knew it!"

"It's what my parents told me to say, if anyone was wondering where she was."

Wide eyed, Kelly says, "Your parents told you to lie?"

"They thought it would be easier for everyone."

"Easier than the truth? What *is* the truth?"

"Mary Beth ran away last spring. One morning I woke up and she was gone, and my parents said they'd had a fight—they were fighting a lot back then. And she took off."

Something about the way she says it . . .

"You don't believe that?" Kelly asks.

"It made sense. She was always threatening to go."

"But she had a summer job lined up here. She was going to be a nanny for some rich people."

"I know."

"Did it fall through or something?"

"I don't know. I just . . ." Caroline stands and walks over to the window seat built into the turret.

Kelly thinks she's going to sit down. But she kneels in front of it and gives the molding a firm tug. It pulls away, and Kelly sees a hidden compartment.

Caroline produces something from the depths and holds it up.

"She wouldn't have left without this."

"An American Girl doll?" Kelly asks, recognizing it. She used to have the same one.

"Not the doll, but . . ." Giving the head a twist, she removes it and pulls out a thick roll of cash.

"Whoa!"

"Mary Beth has been stashing money away for a few years. It used to be in her piggy bank, but then she hid it away."

"Probably smart. There have been a bunch of break-ins around here lately. She was saving up for 'Cuse, right?"

"She called it her escape fund. Not just for college. They say money doesn't buy happiness, but Mary Beth said it can buy freedom, and for her, freedom would be happiness."

"That makes sense."

"Yeah. The thing that's been bothering me for months is . . ." Caroline rocks back on her heels and looks Kelly in the eye. "If she ran away . . . wouldn't she have taken her escape fund with her?"

CHAPTER TWENTY-SEVEN

Present Day

Growing up on Fourth Street, Talia heard her share of jokes based on the fact that there are no other numbered streets in Mulberry Bay. No First, Second, or Third Street, and nothing that came after.

As children, trying to make sense of that, she and Caroline decided that it was probably intended to be Forth Street.

"As in, 'increase and multiply, and go forth upon the earth'?" Mary Beth asked when they told her.

"Not as in anything biblical," Caroline said.

Talia, who hadn't even realized Mary Beth was talking about the Bible, said, "We just think that's what it was supposed to be, because it would be stupid to have a Fourth without First, Second, or Third."

"A lot of things are stupid," Mary Beth said. "Including the Bible."

Even now, Talia remembers Caroline's gasp and Mary Beth's laughter.

And even then, Mary Beth was questioning, pushing back. Never when her parents or older sisters were in earshot. Usually only when it was the three of them, swinging on the swing set in the Winterfields' backyard.

Mary Beth had told them that if they pumped their legs hard enough, they could swing up and touch the sky. For a long time, they believed it. But it never happened. Not for Talia or Caroline, and not even for Mary Beth.

Turning the corner onto Fourth Street, Talia exhales in relief. Her house is still there. She can see its twin cupolas rising above the fish scale–shingled mansard roof.

Clown hats, she and Caroline used to call them. On days like today, when the sky was blue with only a few cumulous clouds, they'd lie side by side on their backs on the grass, hoping a cotton ball of a cloud would align with a cupola's point like a pom-pom. It didn't happen often, but when it did, they'd scream "Clown hat!" and laugh themselves silly.

Talia hasn't thought of that in years.

Nor has she thought about the witch tree, as she and Caroline had referred to a gnarled old maple on the corner. Walking home from school, they'd run past it holding hands, terrified that the boughs would come alive like arms and grab them.

New homes have been built where the old ones were razed— neo-Victorians, mostly, in keeping with the neighborhood architecture.

The Queen Anne Victorian where Talia grew up presides over the center of the block, transformed into an architectural confection. The gingerbread trim is intricately painted in creams and roses, and the clapboards are green. A mossy shade, like her mother's eyes, and Talia's too.

The place looks lived in, with cars in the driveway, screens in the windows, a garden hose stretched across the front yard to a vibrant flower bed, and a bike leaning against the steps.

Next door, the Winterfields' house looks like its dowdy stepsister— slightly shabby, with dandelions in the grass, unkempt hedges and straggly perennials along the foundation. It's painted white, all of it, including the gingerbread trim, as though no one could be bothered to embellish the architectural detail.

She intended to drive on past, just checking out the old neighborhood for old times' sake. But she finds herself pulling up at the curb, wondering whether the Winterfields are home. Wondering how they'd react if she stopped in to say hello.

It's what you do, isn't it? When you're back in your hometown and feeling nostalgic, with time to kill and, yes, questions to ask?

She's spent twenty years wondering about Caroline's mom and dad. Whether they've changed, whether they have regrets. Whether they know . . .

Anything.

Only one way to find out.

She gets out of the car without allowing herself to reconsider and approaches the house along the walkway that bisects rectangles of lawn pocked with dandelions. She and Caroline used to pick them for their bridal bouquets when they were playing wedding. And the walkway consists of the same cracked bluestone rectangles that they used to chalk with hopscotch lines; same weedy strips of dirt between them, obstacles for their snow shovels in winter.

The front steps still creak in the same places, the porch floorboards are still worn, and a familiar black metal mailbox hangs beside the front door.

Before she can lose her nerve, she rings the bell, unsure what she'll even say to whichever of the Winterfields opens the door.

It isn't yet time for the conversation she's long imagined having with them, parent to parent, making things right after all these years. That will have to wait. This is just . . .

She isn't sure what it is, but here she is, on their doorstep, waiting for someone to answer the bell, and dammit, nobody does.

She rings it again, waits.

Knocks, waits.

Maybe nobody's home.

Unsure whether she's relieved or disappointed, Talia retreats down the steps and turns to look up at the second-floor turret room Caroline and Mary Beth once shared. How many times, in their teen years, had she seen one of the sisters perched on the window seat up there, looking out like a princess locked in a tower?

She usually assumed it was Mary Beth, grounded for one thing or another. But occasionally, the figure in the window would wave—with her left hand, not her right—and she'd know it was Caroline, watching her head out to join the others for some outing the Winterfields had forbidden.

Even now, there seems to be a shadow behind the lace curtain, almost as if she's still up there, watching the world pass her by.

Maybe she is.

Someone is.

Talia walks up the driveway to check for cars, past the side door leading to the basement stairs, past the garbage cans, past the clump of rhododendrons that bloomed every year around her birthday. Now, there's a fence between her old backyard and this one—not a charming picket fence like the one at Talia's house back in Westchester, but a no-nonsense wall of wood.

The old metal swing set is gone. So is the redwood picnic table. At the back door, the ugly wrought iron railing that replaced the rotting wooden one has been replaced itself, with composite wood.

She knocks here too.

No answer.

She cups her hands against her forehead and leans in to peer through the window. The mudroom looks the same as always. Tile floor, hooks on the wall that hold jackets and a set of keys.

One last knock, and she gives up, heading back down the driveway.

"Hello?" a voice calls.

Talia turns and spies a woman on the porch of her old house next door.

Her instinct is to take off, like a trespasser who's just been caught.

"Can I help you? Are you lost? Looking for something?" She appears to be in her fifties, blond and fit. The kind of woman who populates Talia's wealthy suburban life, but not Mulberry Bay.

Things have changed, though. This woman seems to belong here, regarding Talia with a wary expression.

"Oh . . . sorry, I . . . no, I'm not lost. I . . . grew up here. In your house."

"Really? That's amazing!" The woman sounds like Hayley, who uses *amazing* to describe all sorts of things that are not. "When did you live here?"

"In the nineties."

"When it was a rental, then. My husband and I bought it in '01. It was a mess—all chopped up into apartments, a total gut job."

Trying not to be offended, Talia points at the house next door. "The Winterfields still live here, right?"

The woman's mouth tightens. "They do. You know them?"

"I did, years ago. I was going to say hi, but I guess they're not home."

"They're out of the country, on a mission for their church."

"Do you know when they'll be back?"

"Not for a while. I only know they're gone because I saw a picture of the mission group in the newspaper last week. Stupid, isn't it? Advertising that your house is going to be empty—it's like an open invitation to burglars."

Talia nods. "Have you ever seen . . . do their daughters ever come around?"

"I wouldn't know. They keep to themselves, and . . ." She points toward the side yard. "You know what they say about fences. They're good neighbors."

"The Winterfields?"

"Fences."

Back behind the wheel, Talia takes one last look at the Winterfield house in the rearview mirror. Up in Caroline and Mary Beth's old room, the lace curtains part. Someone is up there, watching her drive away.

CHAPTER TWENTY-EIGHT

Mulberry Bay is crowded on this summer Friday, and parking spaces are few. Ceto leaves the car in the large lot behind the Landing and gets out to walk several blocks back to the town square.

Even Shore Street is busy—fishermen along the pier, boaters at the marina, a farmers' market in the waterside park, customers perusing the Landing's menu posted outside the door, joggers, dog walkers, stroller moms . . .

There are people everywhere, but only one seems to notice her.

A man, shuffling along the sidewalk, wearing a khaki-green army jacket, stops in his tracks and looks right at her.

She hurriedly puts on her sunglasses and raises her hood, something she should have done as soon as she got out of the car.

She glares at him as they pass each other.

Grizzled, shabby, and weather beaten, he doesn't belong in this town filled with tourists and fancy people and working-class old-timers.

But then, neither does Ceto. He can't know that. Yet, hurrying past him, she feels him watching her as though he does know that. As if he knows *her*.

Knows where she came from, who she is, what she's done . . .

What she's about to do.

But of course, that's impossible.

She reaches the corner crosswalk and darts across the street without checking for traffic. A car swerves around her, and another stops short and honks.

She ignores them, hurrying past the signpost that reads YIELD TO PEDESTRIANS.

On the opposite curb, she turns to see that the man is now at the crosswalk.

The cars are waiting for him to cross, but he's just standing there, watching her.

A cauldron bubbles over, and she reaches into her pocket for the gun. One bullet and he'll be lying in a pool of his own blood.

Just like Gordon Klatte.

That wasn't like this, though.

He wasn't supposed to die. She didn't shoot him. The gun was just to let him know she meant business. She only wanted, needed, to talk to him at last.

Why couldn't he understand that? Why couldn't he just listen? Why couldn't he just tell her what she wanted—what she deserves—to know?

Nobody ever listens, and now look. Gordon Klatte is dead.

That may not have been part of the plan, but when it happened— when he toppled over the edge—it was as if a massive burden fell away with him.

She felt unexpectedly euphoric, standing there at the top of the stairs, watching the blood pool and spread beneath his head.

Only later, when she fled, did she realize that her own burden wasn't the only thing she'd lost. Her most precious possession—her most tangible connection to her past—was gone.

She didn't dare go back for it. It could be anywhere—somewhere along the shoreline path behind his house, or in the woods, or yes, on his property.

It's gone forever. That's Gordon Klatte's fault.

And this man, this sidewalk stranger who almost seems to know her, or know something . . .

This man is going to be next. Blinded by rage, heedless of witnesses, she fumbles in her pocket for the gun.

It isn't there.

No, because she left it in the car, thinking it might not be a good idea to walk into a small-town police department armed.

Again, she looks at the man.

He's turned his back and is walking away.

Ceto lets him go for now and walks on, clutching the envelope neatly addressed to Midge Kennedy.

CHAPTER TWENTY-NINE

"Midge, *what*? Gordy was *killed*?"

Midge nods grimly, noting the shock in Kelly's big blue eyes, and that they're fully lined, shadowed, and mascaraed at this hour, unlike her own.

Actually, unlike Midge's own at *any* hour.

Kelly always looks as though she could be on her way to a cocktail party at any hour of the day. She's svelte and long limbed in heeled sandals and a sleeveless violet silk dress, her blond hair tumbling down her back in smooth waves you only get from a styling brush.

Midge would know. She seldom bothers to tame her own coppery curls, courtesy of Mother Nature and currently restrained by her uniform cap and a couple of bobby pins.

Things might be different if she weren't in law enforcement, or if she'd spent a few years in Paris instead of her whole life here in Mulberry Bay, although . . .

Nah. Midge has never wasted much time on her appearance, and Kelly has always been one of those annoying women who's sexy even in sweats and with bed head. And they've always loved each other just the same . . .

Well, almost always.

Back in 2001, as a rookie cop, Midge pulled over a black Porsche Boxster for speeding and erratic driving.

A young man about her age was behind the wheel. Square jaw, razor stubble, unkempt blond wavy hair. He wore a linen shirt with the sleeves rolled up to reveal a Rolex, and Versace sunglasses—at night.

His license identified him as Thaddeus Ward Stratton of Sutton Place in Manhattan, with a photo of a clean-shaven young man in a suit and tie. Same person, better days. He reeked of bourbon and slurred when he asked his female companion to get the car's registration out of the glove compartment.

Midge trained her flashlight beam into the passenger's seat, and her heart lurched.

Kelly, in smudged makeup, a skimpy dress, and a lot of gold jewelry—including a big fat diamond on the fourth finger of her left hand as she held up the registration card.

Her bloodshot eyes widened in recognition. "Midge? That's you? Oh, thank goodnessssss! Tad, this is my bessssssst friend! Midge, thissss issss Tad! We're getting married!"

"Congratulations," Midge said. "Get out of the car, please, Mr. Stratton."

Ignoring Kelly's protests, she administered the field sobriety test and Breathalyzer, both of which he failed miserably. She placed him under arrest, cuffed him, and put him into the squad car.

Returning to the Boxster, she found Kelly in a pool of vomit, passed out with her head thrown back and neck arched. The thin strap of her skimpy top had shifted, revealing familiar dark ink marks on the pale skin above her left breast.

T-I-C-K.

Midge got her home in one piece, doubting she'd remember any of it.

Not long after the incident, she heard that Kelly had run off and married Tad Stratton, and assumed she'd never see her again. Talia either. Or . . .

Well, Caroline was different. But she, too, was gone.

Just as Midge hadn't bargained on losing them all, she never expected them to come back to her, one by one. First Kelly, and now Talia is on her way, and maybe, just maybe—

"What happened to Gordy?" Kelly asks, shivering as though a stiff breeze just swept off the nearby lake, though it's the warmest day of the year so far.

"Blunt force trauma to the skull."

"What? Someone—"

"No! He fell down a flight of stone stairs. He'd been there awhile when his wife found him, and it was, uh . . . too late."

"His wife found him? That's awful. He was at home, then?"

"Yes." Midge wishes she could unsee it all. Gordy's broken corpse, his wife covered in blood, his sons in shock . . .

Kelly sinks into a wicker settee with a tufted floral-print cushion and props her pedicured toes on a matching ottoman.

Midge thinks of her own outdoor space, a back deck that needs a paint job and is furnished with molded plastic chairs she bought at Walmart's Memorial Day clearance sale as a birthday gift to herself.

She and Kelly have always lived in different worlds, but now more than ever. Her friend has truly turned this old mansion into a showplace. A labor of love, she recently called it.

That struck Midge as odd, because Kelly had never been the kind of person who rolled up her sleeves and tackled herculean physical projects. Then again, the Kelly who came home to Mulberry Bay in 2020 was a different person from the spoiled, indulgent young woman who'd left.

"Do you realize how insane this is, Midge?" she asks. "I mean, Gordy dying so young is a horrible tragedy, but just—that it happened *today*, of all days? On the anniversary of . . . you know."

"I know. It's an odd coincidence."

"*Odd?* That's the understatement of the year."

"It was an accident, Kelly. Accidents happen. So do coincidences."

Midge sits in a wicker chair across from her, rubbing her burning shoulder blades. She worked a long shift yesterday before driving her father to an orthopedist appointment in Albany. He insisted on taking her to dinner afterward. Back home late, she stayed up to watch the Rangers-Dodgers game and slept only a few hours before the call came in.

"Midge? Do you think there's any way that Gordy . . ." Kelly pauses to look around, as if expecting an eavesdropper to be lurking behind the potted palms. "You know . . ."

"That he . . . what?"

"Do you think he jumped?"

"Jumped? Why would he do that?"

"Because he's still pining away for Caroline, on the anniversary of her disappearance? If he thinks she drowned in the lake, maybe he wanted to join her there."

"He didn't jump."

"How do you know?"

"Because *Caroline* was twenty-five years ago, Kelly. He's happily married with two sons and a nice life. It was an accident. Do you know how many times I've investigated an accidental fall?"

"Including my mother's."

She nods. While Beverly Barrow's fall wasn't fatal, it was tragic in its own way. It led to the diagnosis that marked the end of an active, healthy lifestyle and the beginning of a decline that continues to this day.

But that isn't why Gordon Klatte was wandering around in the night. No, he was wandering around because . . .

Well, nobody seems to know why.

"How is your mom?" Midge asks.

"Oh, you know . . . the same. Yesterday she told me she had lunch with Rhonda Haskell."

"Isn't Rhonda living in Cleveland with her son?"

"She sure is." Kelly shakes her head. "It's hard."

"I know. I'm sorry."

"It is what it is. Have you told Talia about Gordy?"

"Not yet."

"Should we call her?"

"No. We can tell her when she gets here. It's not as if it's urgent. I'm sure she hasn't seen Gordy in twenty-five years."

"She hasn't even seen *us* in almost that long."

They hadn't seen each other, either, for two decades. Today isn't just the twenty-fifth anniversary of Caroline's disappearance; it's the twenty-fourth anniversary of the night their friendship—with each other, and with Talia—changed forever.

"It'll be good to see her. It seems like she's got everything she ever wanted—the career, the husband, the kids, the house with a picket fence."

"She told you she has a picket fence?"

"I saw it on her Instagram." Kelly pulls out her phone, opens an app, and passes it to Midge.

The photo shows a pair of children, a boy and a girl. He's solemn eyed, half-hidden behind his big sister, who looks very much like Talia had back in their own elementary school days. She's grinning, holding a clarinet to her lips. They're posed in front of a white picket fence draped in a vine with big purple flowers.

It was posted last night, just before seven. The caption reads, "On our way to Hayley's band concert."

Midge hands the phone back to Kelly. "Cute kids."

"Right? It looks like Talia has the perfect life she always wanted."

"Everyone's life looks perfect on Instagram."

"How do you know? You're not even on it."

"I am when I need information for a case. You wouldn't believe the stuff people put out there in public for anyone to see. Anyway, Talia always said she wanted to be married with children, Kelly. You and I never did."

"No, what we *never* wanted was to be dependent on a man to take care of us. And clearly, I'm not good at being married. But I think I would have been a great mom. Guess that ship has sailed, though, huh?"

"Not necessarily. You can always adopt if you really want—"

"I don't," Kelly says, with a glance at the window, where the too-young workman is now bent over a toolbox. She sighs and sticks her thumb into her mouth.

"Well, if you're trying to look younger, sucking your thumb might be a little too extreme."

She laughs. "I've got a splinter, and I can't find the damned tweezers to get it out. You wouldn't happen to have some with you?"

"I'm not a surgeon—I'm a cop. But be careful. That could be dangerous."

"A splinter?"

"A paper cut can be life threatening, Kelly. I once got called to a house where a kid had a nasty infection from an index card."

"Card!" Starting to snap her thumb and forefinger as if she'd just remembered something, Kelly winces. "Ouch. But that reminds me, Midge, I need to show you this crazy—"

She breaks off as Midge's phone rings.

"Wait a second, Kel." Pulling it out of her pocket, she sees that it's Nap Moreau, the medical examiner. "Sorry, I've got to take this."

Kelly nods, sticking her thumb back in her mouth.

Midge answers the call. "Nap? What's up?"

"Where are you?"

"I'm at Haven Cliff. Why? Where are you?"

"At the morgue with the Klatte case, and you wouldn't believe what—"

"Hang on," she says into the phone, quickly getting to her feet and addressing Kelly. "Can the crazy show-and-tell wait? I need to go."

"Sure. I mean, it's not life threatening. It's just . . . go, Midge. I'll fill you in later. You're busy, and I want to make sure you can be here tonight. Thanks for telling me in person about Gordy."

Midge waves without looking back, already heading down the steps toward her car. "Nap? What's going on?"

"How fast can you get here?"

"To the morgue?"

"Yes. I just found something you'd better take a look at."

CHAPTER THIRTY

February 13, 1998

"The thing about having a dance in the gym," Kelly says, standing on the top of a ladder, tying pink crepe paper streamers to the basketball rim, "is that no matter how much you decorate, it's still always going to smell like Midge's feet."

"Hey!" Midge says, kneeling on the floor beneath the ladder, tracing hearts on red poster board.

Caroline, holding Kelly's ladder steady, says, "She just means you're an athlete, and your sneakers and cleats don't smell like . . . roses."

"At least we finally get to *have* a Valentine's Day dance," Talia puts in. She's cross-legged beside Midge, cutting out a poster board heart. "Do you know how hard I had to lobby for this?"

"We totally appreciate our intrepid student council vice president and committee chairman." Kelly descends the ladder and offers Talia a salute. "I just wish we could have had it somewhere else."

"Well, I don't care where it is, as long as I get to go," Caroline says.

"Your parents still haven't said yes?" Midge asks.

"Not yet. It's still a *we'll see.*"

"The dance is tomorrow night," Kelly says. "What are they waiting for?"

"Who knows? They talked to Gordy, and his parents said they'll drive us and pick us up, but . . ." Caroline grabs a roll of tape and starts gathering red paper hearts from the floor.

"They're letting you help decorate, though," Talia says, "so that's a good sign."

"They think I stayed after for extra help in chem." She looks up at the big black-and-white clock on the wall above the bleachers. "I should probably be getting home soon."

"It's snowing like crazy. I'll give you a ride as soon as we're finished." Heading off the predictable protest, Kelly adds, "I'll let you out around the block and you can roll around in the snow so your parents think you walked."

Caroline laughs. "Fine, as long as we go soon."

"We're almost finished," Talia says, checking the list she made in a notebook. "Midge and I will finish the streamers in here while you two go tape these around the doorframe at the gym entrance."

Kelly follows Caroline out into the hall with the paper hearts and a roll of tape, pulling the gym doors closed after them.

"So . . . any news?" she asks.

"About what?"

"You know . . ." Kelly lowers her voice to a whisper. "Mary Beth. What else?"

"Oh. No news."

In the three months since Caroline showed her the secret escape fund Mary Beth left behind, Kelly has waffled between thinking she simply forgot it in the heat of anger, and thinking something horrible must have happened to her.

It wasn't a small amount of money. They counted it.

"Caroline, how did she get thousands of dollars? It can't just be from babysitting."

"And pet sitting." At Kelly's dubious look, Caroline added, "She's been saving up for a long time. So have I."

"How much do *you* have?"

A fraction of what her sister had stashed away, Caroline admitted. But she didn't want to speculate about how or where Mary Beth had gotten the money. Not then, and not since.

Every time Kelly tries to bring it up, Caroline deflects. Like now.

"You've got to stop asking me that every time I see you," she hisses, looking around the deserted hallway.

"But—"

"Shh! Someone is going to hear. My parents would kill me if they knew I told you about . . . you know."

"If you really believe that, Caroline, maybe you should talk to someone."

"If I really believe what?"

"That your parents would kill you. Because if they would kill *you*, then maybe they . . ."

"Maybe they *what*?"

Kelly shakes her head, heart racing. She shouldn't be thinking what she's thinking, and she definitely shouldn't say it.

But she doesn't have to.

"You're crazy!" Caroline says. "You can't possibly believe that my own parents would—"

At the far end of the hall, a door bangs open as a club meeting lets out. Voices, laughter, footsteps.

"I have to go," Caroline says.

"Wait, I'm giving you a ride!"

"I want to walk."

"But what about—"

"Here. Take these." She scurries away, paper hearts fluttering to the floor behind her.

CHAPTER THIRTY-ONE

Present Day

Kelly closes the front door after the workman, whose name, it turns out, isn't Ray or Roy. It's Ron.

"In case you need anything else," he said, handing her his phone number, scribbled on the back of his boss's business card.

"Like . . . ?"

"Anything. Call me."

She shouldn't—jailbait and all—but . . .

She looks up at the portrait of Asa and Edith Winterfield, now hung in precisely the right spot, and scowls at their disapproving gazes. "What? Don't judge."

She tucks Ron's phone number into her bag, along with the playing card, its relevance eclipsed by the news of Gordy's death, though she'd been about to show Midge before her abrupt departure. It can wait until later, but in the meantime, Kelly might do a little investigating of her own.

She pulls out her phone, finds the number for the Woodstock shop, and places a call.

It rings, rings, rings . . .

"You have reached Enchanted Chalet. No one is available to take your call. Please—"

She disconnects the call, opens a search window, and thumb types: *Cartomancy, two of spades meaning.*

The results are mixed. Some sites say that it signifies indecision; others, everything from conflict to betrayal to bad news . . .

No closer to understanding who might have left it, she shoves the phone back into her bag and moves on, crossing into the parlor through an archway framed by velvet curtains. A seamstress recreated them based on a photograph Kelly unearthed in the town historical archives. It was sepia toned, of course, and there was no way of knowing what color the original draperies were.

She chose shades of green and gold, complementing the carved walnut sofa's upholstery. That piece is original, purchased from a Winterfield descendant, along with other family furniture, books, ephemera, and Edith Winterfield's pearl-handled revolver, now displayed in a glass case alongside her needlepoint.

Edith's husband bought it for her shortly before they built Haven Cliff, after an armed robbery at their New York City mansion. The thieves got away with cash, artwork, and other valuables but missed several priceless pieces of jewelry Edith happened to be wearing that particular night, at the opera.

According to local legend—and to Caroline—the Winterfields built a hidden safe somewhere on the Haven Cliff property. Ever since, would-be treasure hunters have been trespassing in an attempt to locate it, but no one ever has.

Edith famously carried her pearl-handled revolver with her whenever she ventured out in Mulberry Bay, uneasy living way up in what she called *the backwoods.* But it didn't do her much good the day she and her husband were murdered in their own home. Unfortunately, they went to their deaths without ever revealing the location of their hidden safe, and the jewels were among a number of missing valuables after the murders.

Every time Kelly looks at the weapon, she thinks of her dad, an avid collector of vintage firearms. He'd have been excited about this find.

Before she began her restoration project, Kelly had never thought about how entire lives end up packed away in dusty attics, unwanted by generations that aren't interested in what happened before they were born, or what might happen after they're gone. She'd been just like them.

Now, though, it's different. *She's* different. She's spent the last few years learning not only about her own family, skeletons and all, but about the Winterfields.

Skeletons and all.

She thinks of Gordy Klatte, dead today at forty-three. Of his children, faced with the unexpected loss of their father, and at a much younger age than Kelly was when she went through it herself. By that time, she'd been married twice, had a successful law career, and lived thousands of miles away from Mulberry Bay. But losing her father . . .

That was the beginning, the thing that made her realize it was time to grow up.

She just didn't actually do it until she came home to Mulberry Bay.

Hearing a rhythmic beeping, she glances out the window and spots a large panel truck backing into the service driveway. It holds the gilt grand piano that once graced the music room of the Winterfields' Fifth Avenue mansion.

She remembers Caroline and Mary Beth, seated at their parents' old upright, improvising a "Heart and Soul" duet in perfect sync. Remembers them laughing about the sticky keys and how it perpetually needed tuning.

They should have had a piano like this.

They should have had *this* piano, a family heirloom.

Kelly imagines the sisters walking through the front door. Imagines handing over the keys to Haven Cliff.

"It's all yours," she'll say, and indicate the portrait of the sisters' great-great-grandparents. "They'd want you to have it."

It might be true.

But more importantly, Kelly wants them to have it.

"I did this for you," she whispers. "Please come home."

CHAPTER THIRTY-TWO

He walks, following his usual route from Shore Street to the lakeside path, toward the woods and the old amusement park and Haven Cliff.

Away from the pier and the park and the restaurant and the farmers' market and all the people, the strangers and the ones he knows, like the person he saw for the first time since that rainy night.

Twenty-four years ago today.

It was raining.

He remembers weather like he remembers dates, and faces.

Some faces.

The sisters who lived on Fourth Street—he remembers them. Remembers what happened to them.

He remembers the things that matter.

He remembers the rain, thunder, lightning.

He remembers the scream, from the woods near Haven Cliff.

He remembers eating mulberries and smelling mock orange in the woods. He remembers Trolley Park Beach, with the old arcade and the boardwalk and the twisted wreckage of rides and the fishing pier, long gone now.

He remembers the canoe, tied to a piling that night.

He remembers pacing beneath the old awning, waiting for the rain to stop.

He remembers footsteps in the woods—not a night creature, but a human one.

He remembers the girl, breathless, crying, emerging from the shadows. She had a flashlight, but it was trained on the path in front of her, and he couldn't see her face until lightning flashed.

For a split second, he could see her face, but it was enough.

He recognized her immediately, just as he did today. She was the same person who'd come to the same spot with the same canoe one year earlier.

The girl who'd lived on Fourth Street so long ago with the yelling man and the quiet woman and the sisters who vanished, one by one.

CHAPTER THIRTY-THREE

Mulberry Bay's town hall occupies a four-story granite building at the intersection of Main and Center Streets, facing the commons. Built in 1890, it's since been an opera house, movie theater, and bus depot, as well as both the post office and library before they designated buildings for those down the block.

Municipal offices fill the main floor, with meeting rooms and the Historical Preservation Society on the second and third. Police headquarters is on the subterranean level, accessible by a separate entrance around the side.

Midge parks in the spot adjacent to the one reserved for the chief. It belonged to her father until his retirement a decade ago. His successor, Walter Jackson, is out on medical leave.

"I hope it's nothing serious," she told Walt when he called her into his office last week.

"So do I," he said with a shrug. "I'm having surgery first thing tomorrow, and the doctor says the recovery period is about eight weeks. If everything goes well, I'll be back in August. You'll be in charge until then."

Climbing out of the car, she catches a whiff of barbecue from the Smoke Shack next door.

It's hardly a shack, occupying the first floor of the stately old savings and loan building, with prices that rival the new steak house. She thinks of frugal Gordy, stopping here last night to surprise his wife with dinner. Of Gordy, dead just hours later.

Of Nap, summoning her to the ME's office, which is her next stop, just as soon as she checks in here.

Entering the station, she finds Dina Randall, a civilian employee, manning the front desk. Fair haired, chatty, and enormously pregnant with twins, she looks up from a dog-eared copy of *What to Expect When You're Expecting*.

"Hi, Dina. Any news from Walt?" Midge asks.

"Not a thing. I'm still hoping he'll be back before I go out on maternity leave, but . . ."

"I know." Midge shakes her head. Still hospitalized and awaiting test results, Walt didn't elaborate on his health, but unexpected surgery is always concerning.

"How's your dad? Did everything go okay with his doctor?"

"Yes. How are things here?"

"Same as always. I put a bunch of reports on your desk that need signatures, and the mail, and an envelope someone left for you. Oh, and when you have a minute, I'm pulling together a supplies order and I wanted to make sure I didn't miss anything."

"Can it wait?" she asks, turning toward her office. "I'm on my way to the ME, but I'll be back at—"

"Wait, the ME—for Gordon Klatte? I heard what happened, and it's the craziest coincidence because he was just in here."

Midge whirls back, wide eyed. "He was *here*? Why?"

"Actually, he was looking for you."

"Looking for *me*?" Midge frowns. "When was this?"

"Yesterday. Maybe an hour or two after you left. Four thirty or so?" Dina frowns. "Or it could have been after five, because, by the way, Jeff was late—*again*."

Jeff works the desk on weekday evenings. Before Dina—often late herself—can go off on a familiar tangent, Midge asks, "What did he say, exactly?"

"Car trouble. As if anyone would believe *that* excuse for the millionth time."

"Not Jeff, Dina. Gordy—*Gordon*—Klatte. What did he say?"

"He just asked if you were here. I said no. That was pretty much it." Dina shakes her head. "I can't believe I talked to him less than twenty-four hours ago and now he's dead."

Midge nods, thoughts spinning. Gordy had been next door at the barbecue place, so maybe he just thought he'd stop in and say hi?

"Did he say anything else? He didn't tell you why he wanted to see me?"

"No. I asked him if he wanted to speak to someone else—you know, to file a complaint or report a crime or something. But he said he'd catch you another time, and then he left."

"Did he seem okay?" Seeing Dina's expression, Midge rephrases the question. "What was his demeanor like?"

"You know—kind of antsy. Just like everyone else who comes in here wanting to speak to the chief."

"Is that what he wanted? He asked for the chief, and since Walt is out, you told him I'm in that role?"

"No, he asked for you, specifically. He called you by your first name too, like he knows you."

"Right, well, he's . . . an old friend."

"I didn't realize. I'm so sorry for your loss."

Midge thanks her and strides to her office, exhaling only when the door is closed after her.

Friend is a weighty word. Gordy is someone she once knew, yes, and someone she occasionally sees around town. But she can count on one hand the number of conversations they've had since the summer Caroline disappeared—always brief, just small talk.

So why, out of nowhere, would he suddenly come looking for her—on the eve of his death?

CHAPTER THIRTY-FOUR

May 9, 1998

Driving along Fourth Street on her way to Talia's birthday party, Kelly fiddles with the radio, trying to find something better than country, talk radio, or Celine Dion's "My Heart Will Go On," which is playing on two different stations. You'd think the rest of the world would be as sick of this song as she is, but—

Hearing a blast of horn, she swerves and just barely avoids slamming into an oncoming car.

Shaken, she pulls over, pressing a hand against her racing heart.

That was too close for comfort. She already scratched the rear bumper by backing into a shopping cart some irresponsible person left in the Walmart parking lot.

Someone knocks on the passenger's-side window.

Looking up, she sees . . .

"Mr. Winterfield?"

Flustered, she opens the door and starts to climb out of the car.

Unfortunately, she hasn't shifted into park or turned off the ignition. The car starts rolling forward, toward Mr. Winterfield's car, parked directly in front of her. She jabs the brake, stopping a few inches from the rear bumper, and emits an expletive.

She shifts into reverse, backs up, puts the car into park, and turns it off.

Mr. Winterfield is still on the curb, in his version of Saturday casual: a short-sleeved plaid dad shirt and yes, slacks. His arms are folded across his chest and he's all but tapping his foot, fixing her with an icy stare from behind his horn-rimmed glasses.

Climbing out of the car, she pastes on a big fake smile. "Hello, Mr. Winterfield. It's lovely to see you."

But he doesn't play as nicely as his wife. Scowling, he asks, "Do you know how dangerous it is to take your hands off the wheel and your eyes off the road?"

"Actually, I didn't take both hands off the wheel, and I was just trying to—"

"You could have killed someone."

"Well, you could have killed someone too. In fact, maybe you did," she hears herself shoot back.

He blinks. "What?"

"Dad? Kelly? What's going on?"

It's Caroline, stepping out onto the porch, holding a colorfully wrapped birthday gift. It's for Talia. They all chipped in to surprise her with the cargo pants she's had on layaway at Contempo Casuals.

Seeing his daughter, Mr. Winterfield shakes his head and says, "There's no way I'm allowing you to get into this car, young lady."

"I'm not. We're just going next door. But—"

"I don't mean now. I mean ever again." He gestures at Kelly with his own car keys, clutched in his hand. "She isn't fit to be behind the wheel."

Caroline shoots a questioning look at Kelly, who rolls her eyes and shakes her head.

"Just remember what I told you," her father says, getting into his own car and pointing at Kelly's. "If I ever find out you've disobeyed me and set foot in that thing, you know what will happen."

Descending the porch steps as he drives away, Caroline asks, "What the heck is going on, K. K.?"

"It was no big deal. He should probably have his eyesight checked. And the way he talks to you . . . I don't know how you can deal with that."

"He's just being protective. You know how dads are."

"That's not how *my* dad is. Or even Midge's dad, and he's a cop. What did he mean when he threatened you?"

"Threatened me?"

"He said if you disobey him, something horrible will happen to you."

"That's not what he said."

"Well, what *is* going to happen?"

"I'll be grounded," Caroline tells her with a shrug. "It's no big deal."

Kelly shakes her head. "Why do you always downplay what goes on with your family?"

"Why do *you* always accuse me of hiding something?"

"Because you *were* hiding something, remember? About your sister."

"I never should have told you that. Now you think my whole life is, like, one big cover-up. Come on, let's go to Tally's. I only have two hours."

"Two hours? But it's Spice Girls Day!"

They laid claim to their Spice Girls alter egos a few years ago. Kelly's Ginger Spice, the leader; Midge is Sporty Spice; Talia is Posh Spice; and Caroline, playing against type, is Scary Spice. It was a slumber party thing when they were younger—getting into character and costume and reenacting Spice Girls videos.

Reviving it for Talia's birthday celebration was Kelly's idea, in part just to be young and silly again, and in part to keep Gordy at bay, because lately, it's either Caroline and Gordy as a package deal, or no Caroline at all.

She seems to be keeping everyone at a distance, even avoiding the cafeteria at lunchtime, saying she has to study, claiming she's failing chem. Then again, her grades really have been slipping in English, Kelly has noticed. She often seems preoccupied in class.

"Why can you only stay for two hours?"

Predictably, Caroline says, "Gordy and I have plans later."

"But you have plans with your friends. Can't you see him another night?"

"This is a special occasion."

"It's Talia's birthday."

"Birthday eve. And tonight is our church youth group's bingo tournament. They have amazing prizes."

"Caroline! Listen to yourself! Church? Bingo tournament? You and Gordy are acting like senior citizens. Can't you just stay here with us?"

"And act like giggly middle school girls?"

"You said Spice Girls Day sounded like a blast."

Caroline softens. "I did. And it does. I don't know why I'm . . . look, I'm sorry, K. K. I miss you so much. All of you."

"What about your sister?"

"What about her?"

"You miss her too, right? I think it's time to do something about it."

"What do you mean? Do what?"

"You need to tell someone she's not with your cousins, like your parents said. If she ran away—"

"She's eighteen. I don't think it's considered to be running away at her age."

"She was seventeen when she left. And if she didn't just leave—"

"She did," Caroline says.

"How do you know?"

"Because I talked to her. She's fine. So you can stop asking me about her."

"What? Where is she? Is she home?"

"No. She's not coming home."

"Then where—"

"I promised her I wouldn't tell anyone. Especially my parents."

"What about Gordy?"

"What about him?"

"Does he know?"

Caroline frowns. "What does that have to do with anything?"

"Forget it. It doesn't."

"If it makes you feel better, no. Gordy doesn't know. Okay?"

It doesn't make her feel better at all. She isn't sure she believes Caroline—about Gordy, or about having heard from her sister.

"Okay. But Car'? If you ever need . . . anything . . . from me . . . just know that I'm here for you. Whatever, whenever . . . no questions asked."

"Thanks." For a moment, Caroline looks as though she's going to say something more.

Then she turns away, heading toward Talia's house, and there's nothing for Kelly to do but follow her.

CHAPTER THIRTY-FIVE

He walks, shuffling along beneath the hazelnut tree.

You don't often find them flourishing so far north. This one, behind an old house on Fourth Street, delivers a prolific crop of nuts each May and June.

He gathers them into a plastic bag and keeps an eye on the girls across the street. For a few minutes, they were standing there talking—arguing, really. Now, they're walking toward the house where Natalie lives on the top floor with her pretty daughter.

Natalie is his friend. She works at the Landing and gives him food.

These two girls are going to visit the daughter. Another girl, the redhead, jogged up the street and went inside a short time ago.

Her father is the police chief who sometimes pulls over to say, "Everything okay with you tonight, bud?" and if the weather's bad, asks, "Do you have a place to stay?"

He's learned that if you nod, the chief will leave you alone. If you don't, he might try to help you, whether you want it or not.

He never wants help.

So he always nods and keeps on moving, whether or not he has a place to stay.

If you keep moving, they can't catch you. They can't lock you up in a bunker and keep you there in the dark and threaten to kill you, every day, every night, until you wish that they would just do it.

So far, that only happened to him once, in Baghdad, six or seven years ago.

But his brain can't seem to forget about that, just like it can't remember other things. So he keeps moving, always moving, even now, even here.

The girls have disappeared inside the house across the street.

He thinks about Natalie's pretty daughter, and about the red-haired jogger.

About the one who drives the red car too fast and doesn't pay attention. She almost hit another car today.

"You could have killed someone," the man who lives next door to Natalie told the girl.

She could have killed him—one day, he was just stepping into a crosswalk when she came barreling around the corner. But she didn't kill him, and his captors didn't kill him, and he keeps moving.

He shuffles away from the hazelnuts, looking at Natalie's house, wondering about the fourth girl, the one who lives in the house with the yelling man and the quiet woman.

There used to be others there. Sisters.

The older two are married and gone. The third looks like the fourth, but they're different. The third was always making a commotion when she was here—fighting with her parents, slamming doors, sneaking out of the house at night, and into other houses . . .

But she, too, is gone.

He was here last June when she was taken away. Waiting for the sun to come up so that he could gather hazelnuts for his breakfast.

He saw the car pull up with a man behind the wheel. He saw the girl come out of the house with her parents. She was crying. The father had a suitcase, and the mother held her arm.

He watched them put her into the back seat, and there was something about it . . .

It wasn't exactly like what happened to him. There was no siege, no guns, no black hood jerked over her head, and yet . . .

The girl was a prisoner, just as he once was. He sensed it.

They watched the man drive her away—the parents from the sidewalk, and he from the shadows beneath the hazelnut tree.

CHAPTER THIRTY-SIX

Present Day

Kelly finds her decorator, Linden, in the library, arranging nine-teenth-century leather-bound volumes on the floor-to-ceiling walnut shelves. Alongside the fireplace, a locked glass cabinet contains the Winterfield family Bible, Edith's journals, bound household ledgers, and several photo albums.

Caroline would want to pore over it all.

Will want to pore over it all.

Please come home, Caroline. It's all yours.

High atop the rolling wooden ladder built into the bookcase wall, Linden is wearing denim overalls that are more fashion statement than utilitarian, and has white earbuds in. He's bobbing his head, making sporadic *ooo* sounds in a falsetto, listening to what Kelly decides can only be Aretha Franklin's "Respect."

Spotting her in the doorway, he descends, pulls out one earbud, and asks, "What's up?"

"Someone dropped off an envelope a little while ago with one of the workmen. Did you happen to see who it was?"

"All I've seen today is books, books, and more books."

"Okay, well, if whoever it is shows up again while you're here, text me. I have to head over to my mom's for a bit." Kelly pulls her keys out of her bag with a wince and an "Ow!"

"Get bit by something?"

"In my purse?"

Linden grins. "This place is cursed, right? There might be a venomous snake in there."

"There isn't, and it's not cursed, other than by a lack of tweezers. I somehow got a nasty splinter."

"Somehow? Girl, that's what happens when you've spent the last few days arranging old wooden furniture. And you don't need tweezers—you need drawing salve. Try the lavender honey one at Wildgreen."

"That sounds like a yogurt flavor. Or your new hair color," she adds, noticing that his platinum blond waves have gone golden blond overnight, with purple highlights. "And I appreciate the tip. I'll try the salve."

She pulls out her notebook and adds it to the shopping list she made earlier.

"It'll suck that nasty splinter out like a Shop-Vac," he promises. "It's foolproof."

"I don't suppose you have any foolproof remedies for a headache that won't quit?"

"Still? Maybe you should get that checked out, Kelly. I know a great holistic healer who specializes in migraines."

"It's not a migraine. It's just stress."

He shrugs, plugs in the other earbud, and goes back to his book arranging and bopping around and singing.

How nice it must be to be Linden, who never seems to have a care in the world. Of course he must—everyone has their share of problems. But he's happy-go-lucky whenever she sees him.

Then again, whenever she sees him, he's on her payroll and earning buckets of money.

Worth every penny, she reminds herself. And then some.

Outside, she can hear the heavy equipment back behind the trees, where the pool excavation has begun.

Today, of all days . . .

The pool.

Gordy.

Caroline.

Again, she glances at the woods.

Just as there are some things she can't seem to remember, there are others she'd prefer to forget.

CHAPTER THIRTY-SEVEN

July 4, 1998

Summer's been a long time coming, but today is the quintessential Fourth of July—clear blue sky, warm sunshine, sparkling lake. Kelly has the convertible top down, and the music is blasting as she, Talia, and Midge head for Caroline's birthday party.

Caroline's been dating Gordy for a year now, so they've seen even less of her than they did before. And when they do get together, she's sometimes accompanied by him, or asks whether they mind if he joins them.

They *always* mind. But they don't always say it. Not even Kelly.

"When was the last time we even saw her alone?" Kelly wonders now, thinking back.

"You mean other than lunch in school?" Midge asks.

"I think it was back in May. Talia's birthday."

On that May Saturday, they'd played their old CDs, singing along and reenacting their favorite video with borrowed clothes from Talia's mother's closet. Caroline stole the show as Scary Spice in a skimpy leopard-skin bustier, singing into a hairbrush microphone.

"That was just like old times," Talia says wistfully.

"Maybe this one will be too," Midge tells her.

Kelly rolls her eyes. "Not with Gordy there. And his parents, and the Winterfields."

"Don't forget Reverend Statham," Midge says.

"Wait, didn't Caroline say he died?" Talia asks. "Or retired?"

"I don't know. I tune her out when she talks about him," Kelly says. "At least we won't have to hear about his spastic colon, like last year."

"Wasn't it a kidney stone?" Midge asks.

"Potato, po-tah-to," Kelly says. "I'm just glad it's a good beach day."

She pulls into a parking spot, turns off the car, and pops the trunk. It's loaded with beach towels and chairs, along with their group gift to Caroline: the *Spice World* movie, newly out on VHS, a subscription to *Seventeen* magazine, and a collection of lipsticks in current shades of dark plum and brown—none of which will please her parents. The Winterfields consider the Spice Girls bad role models for young women, who they believe should only wear sheer pastel lip gloss and shouldn't read *Seventeen* unless they *are* seventeen.

Which Caroline is, as of today.

They lug their stuff toward the usual picnic shelter, where the usual birthday balloons are tied to a post and the usual family members are setting up.

It's been nearly a year since Mary Beth was sent away—or ran away—and a couple of months since Caroline said she'd heard from her. Kelly hasn't told a soul about any of that. Nor has she broached the subject again with Caroline. They haven't seen her since school got out in June. Even if her parents allowed her to hang out with her friends, she's still forbidden to ride in Kelly's car. And since Kelly is the only one *with* a car . . .

Yeah. They haven't seen her.

"Hey, who's that cute guy setting up the volleyball net?" Talia asks, pointing at the clearing near the pavilion.

Kelly follows her gaze. "Ew! That's Dr. Klatte!"

"Not *him*. The other guy!"

She points at a stranger in cutoff shorts, a tank top, and flip-flops. He's unrolling the opposite end of the net. He's medium height with muscular arms, but his face is mostly hidden behind sunglasses and a baseball cap.

Midge squints at him. "How can you say he's cute when you can't see what he looks like?"

"I can just tell. Maybe this party will be fun after all," Talia says. "Hey, there's Caroline. Ooh, I love what she's wearing!"

"Gordy?" Kelly asks wryly. He's adhered to Caroline's side and has a spindly arm draped across her shoulders. He has on swim trunks and a Hawaiian-print shirt in the same shades of blue as Caroline's sundress, as if they coordinated their outfits.

"Come on—it's Caroline's birthday and she's our friend, so let's just be nice, okay?"

"I'm *always* nice," Midge tells Talia.

"*I'm* not, but I'll try." Kelly pastes on a beatific smile and calls, "Caroline! Happy birthday! And Gordy . . . so nice to see you! You're looking dapper! Love the shirt! So festive!"

"I said nice, not overkill," Talia mutters under her breath.

"Let us help you with all that stuff," Caroline says. "Gordy?"

"Oh yeah. Let us help you." He extends the arm that's not clutching his girlfriend.

"Thanks." Kelly puts her heavy beach bag into his hand and feels a little—*very* little—twinge of guilt when the weight nearly takes him down. He's forced to let go of Caroline and grasp it with both hands.

"You know, Kelly, the beach has plenty of rocks. You don't have to bring your own."

Kelly rewards Gordy's quip with a grin, while Caroline laughs like he's Seinfeld doing stand-up.

Midge hands Caroline the gift bag. "*You* can take this. Happy birthday! It's from all of us."

An unfamiliar male twang calls, "What are y'all doing, carrying all that heavy gear?"

Kelly looks over to see the guy in the cutoffs hurrying over, taking off his sunglasses as if to get a better look at them.

He's handsome, all right, but he's at least forty. Maybe closer to fifty.

Much too old to be checking out teenage girls the way he is, asking, "Caroline, who might these pretty ladies be?"

"We might be her best friends," Talia says, and is she actually flirting with this old man?

"Is that so?"

"Lifelong," Caroline confirms. "This is Midge, that's Tally, and that's K. K."

"Midge, Tally, K. K. Pleased to meet y'all."

"Actually, it's Kelly. And who might *you* be?" Kelly asks, definitely not flirting.

"This is our new minister, the famous Reverend B.!" Caroline announces. "I told you guys about him, didn't I?"

"Oh, right." Kelly nods, as if she remembers. "Your new minister. Because Reverend Statham died."

Caroline's jaw drops. *"What?"*

"I mean, he didn't *die*," she quickly amends. "He, um . . ."

"He retired, but he's still alive and kicking, as far as I know," Reverend B. says. "And I'd shake your hands, but y'all sure are loaded down with . . . what *is* all that?"

"Uh, it's beach stuff? Since we are, you know . . . *at the beach*," Kelly says pointedly.

He chuckles. "Let me help you with it, darlin'." He makes a grab for the sand chair she's holding.

She tightens her grip. "No, thank you. I've got it."

He pulls it.

She holds fast.

Is she really going to play tug-of-war?

Well, yes. There's nothing worse than some leering old guy calling her *darlin'* and acting as if she and her friends need his big strong muscles.

"You can take mine," Talia offers, handing over the chair she's perfectly capable of transporting a couple of yards.

"Okay, this guy is totally giving me the creeps," Kelly tells Midge in a low voice as they trail the others toward the shelter.

"Why? He's just carrying a chair."

"But he's . . ." She wrinkles her nose. "Why is Caroline falling all over him? And why is Talia always hoping some guy will come along and take care of her?"

"Her father was never in the picture, so maybe . . . you know."

"Natalie's done a great job of raising her without help from anyone. Shouldn't that make Talia want to be just as independent?"

"There's nothing wrong with wanting a traditional life," Midge says. "My parents are together, and so are yours, so we probably shouldn't judge."

"I'm not judging. I'm observing. And yeah, my parents are together, but they're not dependent on each other. My mom can take care of herself. If I ever get married, I'm going to be the same way."

"Me too. But that's a big *if*," Midge says. "I'm going into law enforcement."

"So? Your dad's in law enforcement and he's married."

"Yeah, but he's a man. It's different."

Kelly nods. "You're right. It sucks, but it is."

"So let's hold each other to being strong, independent women, okay? To never being code two."

"Code two . . ."

"Rescue," Midge reminds her. "You and I will never need to be rescued. We'll be code four forever, right?"

"You got it. Code four forever. No matter what." Kelly's gaze shifts to Caroline and Talia. "I just hope it stays that way for all of us."

CHAPTER THIRTY-EIGHT

Present Day

Midge hurries down the hall to Nap Moreau's office. The door is ajar, and he's sitting at his desk, so intent on the computer screen that he doesn't see her. He's wearing scrubs, and his short dark hair is spiked on top as though he's raked a hand through it a time or two, as is his habit when he's working.

He moved to Ulster County a decade ago with his then fiancée, a Kingston native he met at medical school at Tulane. His arrival coincided with Midge's second broken engagement and first homicide.

They became fast friends as he helped her navigate the complicated forensics of that murder case. A few years later, she consoled him when he caught his fiancée cheating, advising him not to take her back and not to move home to Louisiana.

"You'll never be able to trust her again, and you can't run away," she told him over beers and pinball at the Dive Inn, before it turned fancy. "That's what cowards do."

"You know I'm not a coward, Midge. But if we're not getting married, I never want to see her again. And if I stay around here, I don't think that's possible."

"I get it, but—"

"I don't think you do."

"I ran into my ex-fiancé yesterday at the A&P. He was with his very pregnant wife and their adorable toddler."

"*You* were engaged?"

"Yes, Nap, someone actually wanted to marry *me*." Two someones, but he didn't need to know that just yet.

"I don't mean it like that. Just—you seem content being single."

"I am. You will be too. It just takes time. If you give up this job and go running back to Louisiana, you're going to regret it, and so will we."

"We?"

"All of us who need you here as much you need to be here. A year from now, you're going to tell me I was right about this."

It took far less than a year, but to this day, he thanks her for the sound advice.

She knocks on the doorframe, and he looks up.

"Oh, hey, Midge." His languid southern inflection belies his troubled expression.

"Hey. What's going on?"

"I'm not sure. I found something that seems—well, it might be concerning. Come on downstairs with me. I'll show you."

He pushes back his chair and unfolds his six-foot-five frame, dwarfing her. He may be named for the famous French emperor with whom he shares a family tree, but he doesn't share the other Napoleon's short stature, nor temperament.

"Did I miss something at the scene?" she asks as he leads her past closed office doors to a stairwell.

"No."

"Then what—"

"You'll see."

"But what does it involve?"

"You'll see," he says again. "Patience is a virtue, my friend."

"Not one of mine."

He chuckles and says, "No, but you have plenty of others," in a way that makes her wonder, not for the first time, whether there could ever be something more between her and Nap.

She isn't willing to risk their friendship to find out, and she suspects he shares that sentiment. Either that, or she's completely mistaken about a shared attraction.

The instincts that serve her well in police work have proven pretty useless when it comes to romantic relationships.

Which this is not, she reminds herself as they descend the stairs. He was right about her being content with single life. Being married to a difficult, demanding career is preferable to being married to a difficult, demanding human, especially when your job makes you all too aware of the hazards broken relationships can inflict.

Nap leads her past the autopsy suite, stops at a door marked AUTHORIZED PERSONNEL ONLY, pulls out a set of keys, and unlocks it. He flicks on a light and gestures for her to cross the threshold.

She steps into a small room with a sink, shelves, and cabinets filled with medical equipment. There are no windows, just a door to the adjacent cold chamber, where corpses are held upon arrival.

Without comment, he hands Midge a tube of menthol ointment and a surgical mask. Following a familiar routine, she slathers a dollop of the ointment beneath her nostrils before putting on her mask. Nap does the same and snaps on surgical gloves.

"Ready?"

She nods.

He opens the door and, ever the gentleman, gestures for her to go first. As she steps past him, the woodsy scent of his aftershave mingles with menthol.

Then she's hit with a blast of refrigerated air that smells strongly of chemicals and the faintest hint of decaying remains. Exhaust fans, strategically placed around the room along with deodorizers, are running on high, but she knows they can only do so much. Especially after he opens the metal cadaver cabinet.

"Deep breath," he says, reaching for a handle.

She nods, inhaling a last lungful of clean air.

He pulls the drawer.

There's Gordy—now lying on his back, covered in a sheet up to his shoulders, limbs askew in rigor mortis.

Gazing down at his face, seeking some resemblance to the young man she once knew, Midge sees only gaping eyes, bruise-colored flesh, and the horrific fissure across his forehead.

"He's purple," she murmurs.

"Livor mortis. He died face down, and the blood is pulled by gravity."

She nods, well aware. When she breathes again, she's struck by the stench of death and an equally familiar tide of nausea.

"Doing okay?" Nap asks.

She manages, "Mm-hmm."

"I didn't notice anything to contradict what we concluded at the scene until we got him here and I started my full examination."

He pulls the sheet aside to reveal Gordy's right arm. It, too, is discolored from pooling blood, elbow bent, forearm resting against his stomach, fingers clenched.

"Overall, his injuries are consistent with his fall. But the way he was lying, face down, I couldn't see his hands and arms until we moved him," Nap says. "Even then, lividity camouflaged the extent of the contusions and lacerations, and what I could see seemed consistent with his other injuries. I assumed he'd been scraped and bruised hitting the steps or railing on the way down."

"But now . . . ?"

"But now . . . well, I wouldn't rule out that he was engaged in some kind of struggle before he fell."

Midge gasps, lungs filled with putrid air, thoughts spinning. "Wow."

"Yeah. That's not all. See this?" Nap points a gloved finger, and she leans in.

"His hand?"

"There's something *in* his hand. I haven't attempted to remove it yet, but you can see . . ."

"I don't see—"

Then she does.

She sees the glint of a metallic strand protruding from that fist.

Sees a silver chain with a broken clasp on the end and something dangling from one of the visible links.

Leaning in even closer, she discerns that it's a tiny silver *t*, one of four initial charms she's certain are on the bracelet, though the rest are hidden in Gordy's purple death grip.

T . . . I . . . C . . . K . . .

CHAPTER THIRTY-NINE

August 7, 1998

"Hey, sweetheart, how's about a refill on the coffee?"

Talia stops, halfway to the door, and counts to three before turning back to the man who's been sitting in her station for the past two hours, chain-smoking and reading a newspaper. Rather, pretending to. Mostly, he seems to be checking her out, which . . .

Ew. He's old, definitely midtwenties, and not her type. Not that she has a type, other than anyone closer to her age, half-normal, and reasonably good looking.

She turns back, pasting on a smile. "Actually, I'm about to go on my break."

He raises an eyebrow. "Oh yeah? Where ya going? Want some company?"

Nope. She'll have plenty. She glances at the plate glass window, where the late-afternoon sun shimmers on rippling blue lake water. A red BMW convertible is parked in a spot marked LANDING CUSTOMERS ONLY, ALL OTHERS WILL BE TOWED.

Kelly is behind the wheel wearing designer sunglasses, blond hair whipping in the breeze. There's Midge in the passenger's seat, fresh from her summer job in her red-and-white lifeguard swimsuit, whistle still dangling around her neck. Someone is in the back, too.

It isn't one of the guys Kelly's always hanging around. It's a girl, wearing a big sun hat so you can't see her hair and sunglasses so you can't see her face, almost like a disguise.

Curious, Talia resumes her dash toward the door, unpinning her plastic name badge and tucking it into the pocket of her black uniform pants.

"Wait! What about my coffee?"

"Hey, Natalie?" Talia calls to her mother, behind the register making change for a customer. "Table six needs a coffee warm-up, if you don't mind. I'll be back in half an hour!"

"Sure thing," Natalie Shaw says sweetly, as though she's not only grown accustomed to her own daughter addressing her by her first name but doesn't mind.

That's not the case, but Talia convinced her that it's more professional than her calling a coworker *Mommy*.

She escapes into the warm sunshine, hoping Mr. Coffee will have vacated the table before she gets back. She's seen her share of annoying and downright creepy customers this summer. Of course, it goes with the territory. Her mother, a striking green-eyed brunette, gets hit on all the time and has even dated a few customers.

"One of these days," she says, "I'm going to meet someone who's a nice guy *and* has big bucks."

So far, it's usually either one or the other. Never both, and sometimes neither.

All her life, Natalie Shaw has made do with far less than she deserves, and it isn't fair.

"Don't we all, sweetheart," she says whenever Talia tells her that she deserves Prince Charming and a fairy-tale ending. "Don't we all."

"There you are! It's about time!" Midge calls over the blasting car radio, as Faith Hill sings about "This Kiss."

"Yeah, we've got places to go, things to do, people to see, so move your butt, girl," Kelly says.

Talia grins, swaying her backside in time to the music as she walks toward the car with an exaggerated sashay. A passing pickup truck honks, and a male voice yells, "Yeah, baby!"

Kelly gives him the finger without even glancing his way as Talia ducks into the back seat with the stranger—and gasps.

"Caroline! I didn't know you were coming!"

"Neither did I. I was walking home from babysitting and these two kidnapped me."

"That explains the disguise. Your parents still won't let you get into a car with Kelly at the wheel?"

"I doubt it. But they'll never know. I just wanted to see you all." Caroline looks at the Timex she always wears on her right wrist, being left handed. "I really do have to get home now, guys. I just wanted to say a quick hello."

Kelly backs out of the parking space. "Relax, Cinderella. We'll get you back before midnight."

"Midnight!"

"She's teasing, Car'," Midge says.

"But where are we going?"

"We're just cruising around, same as always. Kelly likes to burn gas and show off her fancy car."

"Well, we're not going far. I have to be back at work in . . ." Talia lifts Caroline's arm and peers at her watch. "Twenty-eight minutes. Hey, where's your bracelet?"

"What?"

"The TICK bracelet. You always wear it with your watch."

Caroline lifts her chin, looking defensive. "Well, I'm the only one. You guys never wear yours."

T-I-C-K . . .

That was the name of the exclusive little club they formed back in elementary school, before Caroline bestowed the nickname Midge uses to this day. Back then, she was still going by her full name.

Talia-Imogene-Caroline-Kelly. *TICK.*

The year they turned eleven, they bought silver charm bracelets with all four initials—lowercase, so no one would know they were initials.

Of course, they vowed never to take off the bracelets.

And of course, Midge was the first to abandon hers. She wasn't a jewelry person, and anyway, athletes weren't allowed to wear it to practice or games.

Kelly soon swapped hers out for a gold Tiffany's bangle her parents gave her for Christmas.

Talia put hers away when the clasp broke, and she never got around to fixing it.

But Caroline stuck to their vow until now.

"I like wearing it," she said, not long ago. "It reminds me that I have all of you, even when you're not around."

"We're always around," Talia remembers telling her. "You're the one who's not."

"I know. I wish my parents would get past this overprotective stage and realize I can't just sit home alone for the rest of my high school career," she said wistfully.

The others exchanged glances, collectively sure it was never going to happen.

They were wrong, though. Caroline isn't sitting home. She's got an active social life . . . with Gordy.

Kelly heads down Shore Street, saying, "Caroline, you can spare half an hour."

"Yeah," Talia says. "Even I haven't seen you, and I'm right next door. I keep checking to make sure I don't see two lanterns in your bedroom window."

"Who am I, Paul Revere?"

"No, it's our signal, remember? *Two* means you're in trouble and we need to rescue you."

"Well, you don't! Everything's great. I've just been busy babysitting, and with church stuff, and we went on vacation the last two weeks in July."

She seems even sweeter and more delicate than she used to be, wearing a linen skirt and blouse buttoned all the way up. Her voice seems more delicate too, nearly an octave higher than it used to be. *It's like she's turning into her mother,* Talia thinks.

"Bible camp!" Midge snaps her fingers.

"Not Bible camp. It was a family retreat."

"Oh, well, that actually sounds like *way* more fun."

Missing Kelly's sarcasm, Caroline says, "It was!"

"Where was it?" Talia asks her.

"Tennessee."

"Tennessee? Is that where Mary Beth is? With your cousins?"

"No, not Tennessee," Caroline tells Talia, and chatters on. "It was amazing, you guys. We went swimming, hiking, rock climbing, and there was this hilarious talent show."

"Did you do your Scary Spice act?" Midge asks.

"What? No! It was family camp!"

Kelly snorts. "So what *did* you sing? 'Kumbaya'?"

"I didn't sing. I played the piano, in a duet."

"With Mary Beth?" Talia asks. "Was she there? Did you do 'The Skaters' Waltz'? I love that."

"No, with Gordy."

"*Gordy?* The sousaphone guy? He came on your family vacation?" Kelly brakes for a stop sign and turns to gape at Caroline.

"He was with *his* family. They've been going there for years, and they invited us to join them."

"Your whole family?" Talia asks. "All your sisters, and the Jims?"

"Well, no. Eve has really bad morning sickness, and Joanna's Jim couldn't take the time off, so it was just me and my parents."

"Eve's pregnant?" Midge asks. "You're going to be an aunt and you didn't tell us?"

"Yes, she's due in—"

"Wait, but what about Mary Beth?"

"She didn't go with us, Midge. But you would be really proud of me—Gordy and I won this crazy swim relay! We had to do four different strokes, and you know how I always had trouble with the butterfly back when we were all in swimming lessons? Well, Gordy taught me how to do it, and I aced it!"

"That's awesome," Midge says, and then there's a long pause, during which "This Kiss" gives way to Paula Cole singing "I Don't Want to Wait," and a car horn beeps behind them.

Talia looks back to see a driver gesturing at the stop sign.

"I'm going, dude! Geez! Hold your horses!" Kelly, who regularly honks at dawdling drivers, moves on.

"I really have to get home now," Caroline says. "But it was so good to see you all."

"So I guess we'll see you again, when? Christmas?" Kelly asks.

"Don't be like that, K. K. You know I haven't been around."

"I do know. And when you are around, you're with Gordy."

"We just miss you, that's all," Talia says quickly.

"Well, I miss you guys too. But it's not like we won't be parting ways next year at this time anyway."

"Parting ways? You mean for college?" Talia asks. "It's not like we'll be apart forever. I'm going to come back for every break, and so is Kelly."

"Yeah, and I'm still going to SUNY Ulster, just like you," Midge reminds her. "So I'm not going anywhere."

Caroline says nothing, staring out the window as Kelly turns onto Center Street.

"Wait, Car'—are you *not* going to Ulster?" Talia asks her.

"I don't think so. I might be going away to school after all."

"You're kidding!" Kelly says. "Your parents are going to let you leave?"

"It's their idea."

Midge, who's always been glad she wasn't the only one planning to live at home next year, offers a hollow, "Wow, that's so great! Where are you going?"

"Pennsylvania."

"Where in Pennsylvania?" Talia asks. "Because I'm going to look at University of Pittsburgh."

"This is outside Philly."

"Bryn Mawr?" Kelly suggests. "Swarthmore?"

Caroline just shakes her head.

A Spice Girls song comes on the radio. In the front seat, Kelly and Midge crank up the volume and sing along.

Talia touches Caroline's arm. When she looks over, Talia mouths, *Are you okay?*

Caroline offers a faint smile and raises a hand at her, thumb pressed to her palm.

For a moment, Talia is puzzled. Then Caroline blinks slowly, once, twice, three times, four, and Talia gets it.

Four fingers, four blinks. Code four.

Translation: *I'm okay. Don't worry about me.*

Talia smiles and nods, and then they both join in, singing along with the music as the summer sunshine beams down and for a little while longer, all is right in the world.

CHAPTER FORTY

Present Day

"Midge? Are you okay?" Nap is asking.

Midge stares down at the charm bracelet clasped in Gordy's dead hand, feeling as though her legs are going to buckle beneath her.

Gordy was looking for her last night, and now . . . this?

"Midge?"

She turns to Nap. "I'm just . . . it's the smell. Can we . . . ?"

"Come on." He puts a hand on her shoulder and steers her out of the cold room. "Why don't you step outside? Get some fresh air?"

"No, I just need to . . ." She sinks into a chair and peels off her face mask. "Can I just sit here for a minute?"

"Sure. I've got to go back in there and, uh, you know. Close the drawer."

She nods.

He starts back into the cold room.

"Hey, Nap?"

"Yeah?"

"You bagged his personal effects, right?"

"I did."

"What do you have?"

"Just his clothes and a gold cross he had around his neck. His wedding ring is still on his hand."

"What about his cell phone?"

"He didn't have one."

"It didn't turn up on the ground near where he landed? And you checked his pockets?"

Poised on the threshold between the two rooms, Nap just looks at her.

"Sorry," she says quickly, "it's not that I think you overlooked it. I'm just thinking out loud. His wife said it wasn't in the house, so I assumed he had it with him out there."

"It wasn't on him. He didn't have pockets in his pajama bottoms. But if it was in his hand, he might have dropped it when he fell."

"I guess we missed it at the scene."

"Guess so." Nap disappears into the next room before she can point out that Gordy might have dropped his phone, but he held on to that bracelet.

And that if his death involved foul play, it would be logical to assume that the bracelet's owner had something to do with it.

Could it be Talia's, with the clasp that broke all those years ago? Or had it been damaged when he yanked it from the wearer's wrist during the struggle?

The answer to that question might be key to uncovering the identity of whoever was with Gordy in the moments before he fell—or was pushed—to his death.

CHAPTER FORTY-ONE

It's barely lunch hour, but the Landing is busy already. People mill around the main entrance, sitting on benches and leaning against blooming planters.

Stepping inside, Talia finds that the counter cash register, glass pie case, stools, and booths are gone. Now there's a hostess stand with a stack of leather-bound menus, and the tables are round, with white linen tablecloths and vases of fresh flowers. The decor is sleek and modern, done in muted grays and blues with black accents.

Waiting for her turn at the hostess stand, she scans the dining room for familiar faces and finds none. Certainly not the one she's looking for. But she's early.

The hostess is in her late teens, with long, shiny hair and a sophisticated air. "Do you have a reservation?"

A reservation? *Here?*

"I don't. I didn't realize . . ."

"I'll add you to the list. Indoors is at least forty-five minutes. The patio might be a little quicker. Table for one?"

"For two."

"If someone is joining you, I can't seat you until the whole party is present." Pen poised over a clipboard, she asks, "Name?"

You have nothing to hide.

"Talia."

"You can wait outside. Someone will come find you when your table's ready."

Back out in the breezy sunshine, she leans against a stone planter and takes in the scenery.

The lake glistens in the midday sun and is dotted with boats and floating geese. The nearby beach is much wider and sandier than she remembers, with two wooden lifeguard stands. There's no roped-off swimming area, but that's probably because it's too early in the season and much too cold.

Unless you're Midge.

Midge, the impish tomboy with the Red Cross whistle around her neck, baseball cap covering her coppery curls, white sunblock smeared over her freckled fair skin.

But the Midge Talia remembers bears little resemblance to the dignified and professional MBPD Detective Sergeant Imogene Kennedy. Talia pored over online photos of her and of Kelly, who doesn't appear to have changed, or aged.

Not physically, anyway. But as far as Talia can tell, based on a handful of phone conversations and text exchanges, Kelly is no longer the impetuous malcontent who didn't give a damn what anyone thought.

Older. Wiser. All of them, Talia included.

As for Caroline . . .

What if she doesn't show up?

What if she does?

Each time the teenage hostess steps outside with her clipboard, there's an expectant stirring among the waiting crowd. Almost an hour into Talia's wait, she emerges to call, "Tillie? Table for two! Tillie!"

Someone pokes Talia. "Hey, I think she's pointing at you."

She looks up, and then at the hostess, who is indeed pointing at her, shouting, "Tillie!"

She hurries over. "I'm not Tillie; I'm Talia."

"Sorry. Where's the rest of your party? I can't seat you unless—"

"She just went to extend the time on the parking meter."

The lie spills out effortlessly. Of course it does. This is who she's become.

The young woman leads her inside and grabs a couple of menus from the hostess stand. "Did you say your name is Talia?"

"Yes! Why? Was someone looking for me?" she asks, wondering if they could possibly have missed each other.

"Maybe. I'll go ask the other hostess. Your table's on the patio. This way."

She leads Talia out another door to a table for two, pulling out a chair facing an adjacent table of fancy-looking women who are likely summer people. They aren't familiar, and they don't look like locals.

Talia thanks her and takes the opposite seat with her back to the other patrons, looking out over the water.

A young college-aged man appears. "Hi, I'm Greg, and I'll be taking care of you today. Can I get you started with some still or sparkling water?"

"Still's fine. For both of us," she adds, when he looks at the opposite seat. "My friend will be back in a minute."

He pours water, hands her a wine list, recites a list of specials that include fresh seafood and expensive cuts of steak, and walks away.

Talia watches a fat gull perched on a piling, idly eavesdropping as one of the women behind her says, "Wait, Marla, did you just say Dr. McElroy was in a car accident this morning? Is she okay?"

"No, it wasn't Dr. McElroy."

"Oh, I thought you said your dentist."

"I did, but I had to switch to Dr. Klatte because my insurance changed."

Dr. Klatte.

About to sip her water, Talia lowers the glass.

"Oh, Dr. Klatte was in a car accident?" another woman asks.

"Not him," Marla says. "It was his son, and—"

"Oh, I heard the sirens out on 28 early this morning," someone else cuts in. "I bet it happened at the intersection where they built those new townhouses. I keep saying there should be a light there."

"It wasn't a car accident, Kim," Marla says. "I'm not sure what happened. All I know is that he died."

"Dr. Klatte's son?"

"Yes, Gordon."

Talia's heart jumps.

They're talking about Gordon Klatte.

Caroline's Gordy.

Greg the waiter is back. "Are you Talia Shaw?"

"I . . ."

Used to be.

She's been an Adler for almost twenty years now, but here in Mulberry Bay, she'll always be Talia Shaw.

"I am," she tells the waiter.

"Someone left this for you." He hands her an envelope that bears her name.

CHAPTER
FORTY-TWO

Present Day

Spying satellite news vans, crowds of people, and a cop directing traffic in the Wildgreen parking lot, Kelly immediately assumes it has something to do with Gordy's death on the anniversary of Caroline's disappearance.

Then she sees that the onlookers and press are gathered around a group of old-timers marching in a circle in front of the store's entrance, carrying signs that read $TOP THI$ MADNE$$ and GET OUT, WILDGREEN!

Heading inside, Kelly overhears a reporter ask a protester carrying a sign that reads I WANT CHEERIOS why she's opposed to the new organic market.

"Because it's too damned expensive! They don't even sell regular cereal!"

Such is life in Mulberry Bay these days.

The store is packed. Kelly sees a few familiar faces but mostly weekenders and summer people. She grabs a shopping basket and opens her notebook to the list. It contains a few things her mother needs, along with the lavender honey salve. She should probably get tweezers, too, in case it isn't foolproof after all. Lingering in the snack aisle, she remembers how much Talia always loved anything salty and crunchy.

Fritos had been her favorite. Caroline's too. Or was it Doritos?

It doesn't matter. The store doesn't have either of those, only organic veggie chips. Anyway, the Talia she once knew so well is now a stranger, just as Midge was for all those years after their rift. Just as Caroline would be if she were here.

Or maybe that isn't so. If Caroline were here—if she never disappeared—then none of this would have happened.

"Kelly?"

She turns, and Rhonda Haskell, her mother's closest friend, envelops her in a hug and a cloud of expensive perfume. "I thought that was you!"

"Rhonda! What are you doing here? I thought you'd moved to Cleveland, but I guess . . . well, you know. Mom gets confused."

Rhonda's smile dims a bit. "Your mom wasn't confused about me, dear. I've been in Ohio since last fall, but I'm back for a visit. I saw Beverly on Wednesday. I stopped over with lunch—that antipasto salad she always loved."

"She mentioned that, but I thought she was just . . ." Imagining things. Living in the past. She so often is. "Did she know you?"

"Of course she knew me. She seemed perfectly fine. We had a nice conversation."

Kelly has seen it before—that temporary facade of normality her mother is oddly capable of pulling off.

The doctor calls it *show timing* and told Kelly it's quite common in dementia patients, as long as the patient remains cognizant enough to grasp that there's a problem.

"But she never does it when she's alone with me, or the caregivers. I'm starting to wonder if the confusion is the act."

"It isn't, Kelly. She's masking her symptoms to avoid embarrassment. Patients can't sustain the pretense for long periods of time, and these episodes typically take a lot out of them."

Now, she asks Rhonda, "You do know she has dementia?"

"Early stages, isn't it?"

"Not anymore. I guess you caught her on a good day."

"I'm glad." Rhonda pats her arm. "This must be so difficult for you. Let me know what I can do to help while I'm in town. I'm here through Sunday."

And this is Friday afternoon. So much for the fleeting hope that someone from Beverly's old life might actually be there for her. Now that she can't play tennis or chair committees, her large group of friends seems to have moved on.

Kelly pays for her purchases, pushes past the protesters, and drives over to Pine Ridge, a hilly neighborhood dotted with large houses set back from the road behind low cobblestone walls. Her childhood home is a three-story brick Colonial with hunter-green shutters and arched, paned windows. The broad front lawn is shade dappled, with big old trees surrounded by patches of pachysandra.

Her mother's perennial gardens are in full bloom, flitting with butterflies and bumblebees. There's a lap pool, putting green, skating pond, and barn that's been converted to a home gym—testimony to the active lifestyle her parents once led here.

Pulling into the circular driveway, Kelly parks her SUV behind the housekeeper's Toyota and the bright-blue Jaguar that now sits as idle as the lady of the house. Her mother is no longer allowed to drive.

Wishing the Advil she took earlier would kick in, Kelly heaves her tired, achy self out of the car and slams the door. There's a burst of rustling overhead, and she looks up to see a large black bird lift off from a nest high in a massive oak tree. She cups a hand against her forehead to block the sun's glare and watches it soar off into the deep blue sky.

Then, glancing away, she catches a curtain's flutter and a human silhouette in an upstairs window.

She blinks, and it's gone.

Either she imagined it, or her mother is in Kelly's old childhood bedroom, perhaps looking for her, having forgotten—yet again—that she's an adult who no longer lives here.

With a sigh, she retrieves the shopping bag from the back seat, wincing when her thumb comes in contact with the handle. God, it hurts.

Everything hurts.

She scowls, finding the front door unlocked. Mrs. Verga, the housekeeper, knows better, as should the caregivers who come and go on a rotating basis. It should be locked—not to keep people out, but to keep her mother in.

She steps into the foyer. The television is blasting in the adjacent paneled media room. Thinking of the person she glimpsed in her bedroom window, she walks to the foot of the wide stairway and calls, "Mom?"

No reply.

"Mrs. Verga?"

Overhead, all is still.

Either she imagined seeing someone, or this house is as haunted as Haven Cliff seems to be, or . . .

She thinks of the envelope someone left for her, with the playing card inside.

She thinks of Caroline, gone twenty-five years today, of Midge's visit and the news she delivered about Gordy Klatte.

Who's going to believe his death is an accident?

Does Midge?

Kelly sensed an uneasiness about her as she relayed the details—as though she were working a case. Then again, that's how she comes across whenever she's in uniform, so maybe that's all it was.

She walks over to the archway and peeks into the media room. Her mother is dozing in the worn leather chair that was once her father's favorite.

For years, Beverly complained about that recliner, calling it an eyesore that clashed with the decor. She complained about the firearms collection as well, saying she wasn't comfortable having guns in the house. She was still holding a grudge over his taking Kelly to a firing range as a teenager.

"Why on earth does a pretty little girl need to know how to shoot?" Kelly heard her mother ask him. "Stop trying to make her into the son you always wished you had."

The words stung. She never forgot them, nor her father's response: "No child of mine is going to be a helpless candy-ass. She's going to know how to be strong and defend herself."

After he died, Beverly couldn't bring herself to get rid of any of his things. Not the gun collection, still displayed throughout the first floor in glass cabinets, and not the recliner, which she's since adopted as her own favorite spot.

Her slipper-clad feet are propped on the footrest. She's clutching the corner of a pale-blue quilt, as a toddler would a beloved stuffed animal.

In this position, with her head back, mouth open, silvery hair mussed, she looks like a haggard old woman. There's no hint of the sleek, sophisticated blonde smiling from the framed photo with Kelly's dad on the mantel.

It was taken on their twenty-fifth wedding anniversary. They're all dressed up, Dad in a tux and Mom in silver sequins. Kelly remembers that party so well—her parents laughing together, dancing to their song, Billy Joel's "Just the Way You Are."

She believed, then, that they would gracefully grow old together, golfing and lunching at the country club, seeing shows, traveling the world, visiting Kelly wherever she landed.

"Kelly?" Her mother is awake, reaching for the lever to raise the chair into an upright position. "When did you get here?"

"Just now." She goes over to her mother and presses a kiss to her cheek, then shows her the shopping bag. "I stopped and bought a few things for you. Come on into the kitchen."

Bev gets to her feet to follow her, still clutching the quilt. She's wearing a long-sleeved T-shirt and yoga pants she used to don for workouts. Now even spandex sags on her frail frame.

In the kitchen, Kelly can hear the washer and dryer running downstairs. She steps into the mudroom, opens the door to the basement, and calls, "Mrs. Verga? Are you down there?"

"Yes. Doing laundry."

Kelly closes the door and returns to the kitchen to put away the groceries, showing her mother what she bought.

"I got you some organic strawberries, see? It's June, so they'll be sweet. And here's that whole-grain bread you love. I bought some turkey too, for sandwiches."

"Sandwiches!" Beverly echoes, like she's just solved a riddle. "You want a sandwich! An after-school snack!"

"No, thanks, Mom."

"Tell me about school. Did you pass your test?"

"Yes," Kelly says, because it's easier, sometimes, to go along. Then, glancing at the window, she says, "Look, Mom!"

"A hummingbird!" Beverly moves closer, watching the tiny creature dart around the red glass feeder hanging out there.

She's always loved hummingbirds and designed vibrant flower beds to attract them to the yard. Most of the plants are perennials, returning year after year even now that Beverly no longer tends to her gardens. She used to be out there from March until November, weeding, mulching, deadheading, and battling herds of deer.

"Look what they did last night!" she'd fume, waving nibbled foliage and flowerless stems in disgust before dumping them on the compost pile.

"Don't get so worked up. It's just nature, Bev," Kelly's father would say.

"Well, it's *human* nature not to tolerate these beasts chomping and trampling their way through my gardens, destroying my hard work."

On a recent morning when Kelly took her outside to sit in the sun, she noticed a clump of beheaded roses and claimed she'd seen a group of armed "outlaws" sneaking around in there after dark.

"Outlaws? And they were armed, Mom?" Kelly asked with an inward sigh. "Are you sure?"

"Yes, they had your father's pistols, and machetes," she said in that matter-of-fact way of hers, where if you don't pay attention to what she's saying, only to how she's saying it, you can believe she's entirely lucid. "They were cutting all my roses and they're going to sell them at the fair."

"What fair?"

"The fair!"

At times, she can be so oddly insistent that Kelly ends up feeling as though she's the one who's forgotten or overlooked a detail.

In this moment, though, Beverly is benign, pivoting away from the window as if she's just realized something. "Kelly! Your friend . . ."

"Midge?"

"Midge!" Her mother beams. "Midge is your friend, yes. She's . . . she's the police officer!"

It seems she isn't stuck in the past right now. Nor was she when she mentioned lunch with Rhonda Haskell.

"That's right, Mom," Kelly says, opening the freezer. "Midge is a police officer."

"No! Not her!"

"Yes, she is. She's a detective sergeant now." About to put the gelato into the freezer, she sees a pair of Beverly's reading glasses on the shelf. With a sigh, she takes them out, puts the gelato in, and closes the door.

"Yes, but not her. I mean the other one."

"My *other* friend? Talia?"

"Talia," Mom repeats. "Yes, Talia's a nice girl. But she's not here."

"No. She lives downstate. But I told you she's coming to visit this weekend?"

"She is? That's nice."

"So that's who you were talking about? When you said something about my other friend?"

"No. Not Talia."

"Not Talia? And not Midge?"

"The *other* one," her mother says again.

"Caroline?"

"Caroline! Yes. Caroline Winterfield. Such a sweet girl."

"Yes. And she *was* my friend, Mom, but . . ."

"Oh dear. Did you girls have a falling-out?"

"What? Why would you think that?"

"You said she *was* your friend. But not anymore?"

"Mom, what do you mean?"

"That must be what it was about, then," Beverly says, seemingly to herself. She gives a little nod.

"What must be what?"

"That must be what Caroline wanted to talk to you about."

"What do you mean?"

"She probably wanted to make amends."

"Mom, I don't understand. Caroline . . ."

"She was here, looking for you."

CHAPTER FORTY-THREE

Sitting at the umbrella table, Talia stares at the object she just pulled out of the envelope addressed not to Talia Adler, but to Talia Shaw.

It's a playing card.

On one side, there's a photo of the town hall.

The other is imprinted with a black two of spades.

She looks around, heart pounding, scanning the people at other tables. No one is paying any attention to her.

The conversation at the table behind her has resumed.

"Gordon Klatte—isn't he the one whose girlfriend drowned on prom night?"

"Yes, the Winterfield girl."

"What? When was this?"

"Oh, years before you moved here," the first voice says. "They never found her body."

"Here we go, ladies!" Greg is back with the wine and their entrées.

Talia looks down at the playing card in her hand, and then at the envelope.

Only someone from her past would use her maiden name.

But very few of them even know she's in Mulberry Bay.

And only one knows she was planning to have lunch here at the Landing.

Unless . . .

"Talia Shaw?" the clerk in the minimart read aloud when she handed him the wrong credit card.

So many people were in earshot. What if one of them overheard, and . . .

And what? Followed her here? Left her an envelope?

She turns to scan the patio again, looking for a familiar face among the strangers and finding none.

She pushes back her chair, jumps up, and hurries for the exit, clutching the playing card in her trembling hand.

Two of spades.

Two.

Code two.

CHAPTER
FORTY-FOUR

"*Caroline* was here?" Kelly asks, staring at her mother. "When?"

Beverly is offhand. "I don't know. A little while ago."

Not helpful. For her, years ago can seem like a little while. And she gets testy very quickly whenever Kelly presses her for details, especially if she senses any doubt.

She pastes on a smile. "Well, I'm sorry I wasn't here, but I'm so glad you had a chance to visit with her. How is she? I haven't seen her in so long, I can barely remember what she looks like."

"Mmm." Beverly busies herself folding her quilt.

"What does she look like, Mom? My friend Caroline?" she adds, in case her mother's already lost the conversational thread.

"*You* know what she looks like, Kelly! She's your friend!"

Beverly opens a drawer filled with pots and pans, sets the quilt inside as if it belongs there, and closes the drawer.

Kelly turns away, trying to think of another way to ask about Caroline. It would help if she knew whether Beverly saw a teenager, which would indicate a delusion, or a middle-aged woman, in which case . . .

Is Caroline really back in town?

If Caroline really was here at the house a little while ago, where is she now?

What if Mom saw middle-aged Caroline as teenage Caroline, just as she so often sees middle-aged Kelly as teenage Kelly?

"You want an after-school snack!" she'd said just now, and "Tell me about school."

Whenever Kelly's friends came over in the old days, her mother would chat with them for a minute or two and send them up to Kelly's room.

What if she really had glimpsed someone in her old bedroom window?

Kelly makes a turkey sandwich, cuts it in half, and puts it on a plate with some baby carrots. She sets it on the table.

"Here's your lunch, Mom."

"I'm not hungry." Beverly stares out the window.

Kelly casually removes the quilt from the pots and pans drawer and drapes it over the back of a chair. "Sit down. You'll be able to watch the hummingbirds while you eat."

"They're such pretty little things, aren't they? Here and gone so quickly that sometimes it's hard to tell they were even there."

"A lot of things are like that." Kelly clears her throat. "Like Caroline. She was here. Is she gone now?"

"Who?" Beverly takes her quilt from the chair back, sits with it spread across her lap like a napkin, and picks up her sandwich.

The rare glimpse of clarity has once again been enveloped by fog. No wonder Kelly doesn't miss San Francisco. Visiting her mother is the next best thing.

In the front hall, she notices an empty glass case that had held one of her father's prized possessions, an antique Smith & Wesson revolver he inherited from his grandfather. It had reportedly once belonged to the sharpshooter Annie Oakley, and he said it was worth a fortune.

She hurries upstairs to her childhood bedroom, calling, "Mrs. Verga?"

No answer.

"Mrs. Verga?"

She eyes the closed door at the far end of the hall. Behind it, a narrow back stairway leads to the third floor, intended to house the domestic staff when the house was built around the turn of the last century. It also leads down to the mudroom. From there, you can go out the back door, or into the kitchen, or you can descend to the basement, where Mrs. Verga is doing laundry.

What if she was the one Kelly saw in her room upon her arrival? What if, after spotting her, the housekeeper crept down several flights of stairs undetected and acted as though she'd been in the laundry room the whole time?

But why? There's no reason for her to sneak around the house when she has free rein of it all day every day, and certainly no reason for her to be in Kelly's old bedroom.

She doesn't clean in there, other than dusting and vacuuming once a season, if that. It's been unoccupied and vacant since the summer Kelly eloped with Tad.

She hesitates outside the room, resisting the strange temptation to knock.

What if someone really is in there?

Caroline? Caroline's ghost? An armed intruder?

Kelly throws the door open.

The room is deserted and undisturbed. She takes in the cherry furniture and tailored fabrics with aqua and red stripes and patterns. It all seemed so chic in her teenage years, when all her friends' rooms were ruffly pastel pink with whitewashed wood.

The paperback novels on the shelves were high school favorites, with a smattering of textbooks.

The closet and bureau are full of clothes that are now vintage.

The adjacent bathroom contains expired medication and decrepit cosmetics and hair products. She certainly had the opportunity to sort through it all during the four years she lived here before moving to Haven Cliff. But she'd stayed in the guest suite, avoiding this room with all its memories of happier times, when her friends were her friends, and her father was alive, and her mother was clearheaded.

Now, Beverly has a team of caregivers who do overnights on a rotating schedule. Kelly pulls it up on her phone to see who was on duty last night.

Rayanne—Kelly's least favorite of the mostly competent crew. It isn't that Rayanne is incompetent, but she's young, and new at this, and spends a lot of time texting and posting on social media when she's supposed to be . . .

What? Watching Beverly sleep?

Kelly doesn't have a problem with the caregivers who read, watch television, or knit to pass the long overnight hours. But Rayanne strikes her as a little too distracted while she's on the job. It's something she needs to address with the girl or with the agency that employs her, but she hasn't had the time or energy.

She dials Rayanne's number and gets voicemail.

"This is Kelly Barrow, Beverly's daughter. I know you were here overnight, and you're probably catching up on your sleep now, but I'm just wondering if by chance you know whether anyone stopped by the house? Mom says someone did, but . . . well, you know. Just give me a call back if you can, okay? Thanks."

She hangs up, wondering why she even bothered. Rayanne isn't the type to promptly return a call, and Kelly has no idea when the Caroline sighting even took place. For all she knows, it was thirty years ago.

She takes the back stairway down to the basement.

When her parents bought the house, it was a regular old cellar with clammy stone walls and cobwebs in the rafters. They'd renovated it soon after, creating a thousand square feet of living space with hardwood floors, recessed lighting, and high-end electronics, furniture, and appliances. There's a wine cellar, a media room with a wet bar, a kitchenette, the guest suite with a full bathroom, and a large laundry room.

The housekeeper is there, ironing sheets. A stout woman with long, gray-streaked hair, Mrs. Verga is either much older than she looks, or much younger. Kelly can't remember which it is, only that Beverly often commented about it back when she knew what she was saying.

Mrs. Verga is humming to herself. She stops when she sees Kelly, but the iron keeps gliding across the white percale. "Is everything all right?"

"Not really. Do you know what happened to that revolver of Dad's that was in the front hallway?"

"There are a lot of revolvers of your father's in the front hallway."

"The special one in the glass case. The one that used to belong to Annie Oakley."

"I have no idea," Mrs. Verga says. "I certainly didn't take it."

"I didn't think you did, just . . . it's valuable. I hope it hasn't been stolen."

"Did you ask your mother? She's always moving things around lately."

Right. Reading glasses in the freezer, a quilt in the pots and pans drawer . . . the gun will probably turn up in the oven.

"Anyway," she says, "Mom told me she had a visitor?"

"Rhonda Haskell stopped in, yes."

"That's not what I meant, but since you brought it up . . . you knew about that? Were you here?"

"Yes."

"Don't you think you should have mentioned it to me?"

"Your mother told you about it." She sets down the iron and lifts the sheet. It's the fitted kind that's impossible for anyone other than Mrs. Verga to transform into a neat rectangle. That has always bothered Kelly more than it should.

"My mother isn't exactly a reliable eyewitness."

The woman just looks at her, mouth pursed, hands flying as they double and smooth, double and smooth, double and smooth the sheet.

Kelly meets her gaze and asks, "Was anyone else here?"

"With Rhonda? No."

"Not with Rhonda. Mom said an old friend of mine stopped by."

"Which friend?" Mrs. Verga is very busy with that fitted sheet, unfurling it and starting the folding process all over again.

"It was Caroline Winterfield. My friend who went missing, years ago. Do you remember her?"

"Everyone remembers her."

"But she wasn't here, was she? Recently?"

"I didn't see her."

"Did the overnight nurse say anything about her being here?"

"No."

"All right, well . . . thanks."

Kelly turns to go, wishing she hadn't brought it up.

Then Mrs. Verga asks, "Did you check the cameras?"

CHAPTER
FORTY-FIVE

October 26, 1998

"Ms. Barrow. So nice of you to join us," Mr. Hayes comments as Kelly slides into her seat, late for class as usual. "Please open your text to page 201. Quite fittingly, we're discussing *The Taming of the Shrew*."

Kelly opens her book and glances across the aisle at Caroline, intending to share an eye roll with her. But she's busy writing something in her notebook.

Settling back into her seat, Kelly half listens to Mr. Hayes and half plans her costume idea for the Halloween party Saturday night. Originally, she and her friends were going to go as Poseidon, Oceanus, Hydros, and Ceto, the water gods that coordinate with their pedestals in the woods behind Haven Cliff.

But yesterday, Caroline announced she could no longer be a part of it.

"Let me guess. Your parents won't let you go to the party?" Kelly said.

"No, they will . . . as long as I go with Gordy."

"Okay, well . . . maybe he can be a god too. He can be Hydros."

"*You're* Hydros."

"I can be one of Ceto's children. They were all evil monsters, like Ceto. I can be Medusa. I can get a bunch of those dollar-store rubber snakes and make them into a wig, and—"

"K. K., Gordy and I are going as Harry and Hermione."

"As who?"

"They're characters in the Harry Potter book. We have it all figured out."

"Sounds like you do." Kelly knew she sounded more snippy than hurt, but that's always been her style.

Having promised Midge and Talia that she'll come up with an even better costume idea for the three of them, she's absently watching Mr. Hayes write something on the board and weighing the idea of Rachel, Monica, and Phoebe from *Friends* when Caroline reaches across the aisle and puts a folded piece of paper in front of her.

Puzzled, she opens it and sees a scrawled note.

K. K., I need a huge favor. Life or death. I hate to ask, but there's no one else. Are you free after school and later tonight?

Wide eyed, Kelly turns to Caroline and sees that her expression is troubled, and expectant.

She nods, and jots, *I'm free. Whatever you need.*

She passes the note back to Caroline, who quickly writes something else and returns it.

It says, *Meet you at your car after the last bell. Tell no one. Promise.*

At three o'clock, Kelly is in the driver's seat, engine running, in the student parking lot on a hill behind the school.

For most of October, the skies have been blue, and the trees were a glorious autumnal tapestry. Kids lingered here after school, blasting music from car radios, goofing around with friends, maybe sneaking a smoke. No one is hanging around on this monochromatic rainy afternoon. A cold wind scuttles the last few dead leaves from the branches, a reminder that the long Catskill winter is looming.

The Fourth Girl

A figure hurries through the empty parking lot in a hooded black raincoat, unrecognizable until Caroline opens the door and ducks into the passenger's seat.

"Thanks, K. K.," she says, breathless. "Let's get out of here before someone sees me."

Kelly promptly shifts into drive. "Where are we going?"

"To the Thruway. How much gas do you have? I'll pay you back."

"Don't worry about it. I've got a full tank."

Caroline exhales and leans back, closing her eyes as though she's just escaped a harrowing ordeal.

Kelly exits the parking lot and waits until they're past the school, with a row of yellow buses loading at the curb, to ask, "Car'—are you going to tell me what's going on?"

"I just have to run a quick errand. We should be there by five thirty, and we can get home at eight, and I told my parents I'm babysitting for the Bennetts."

"That's a five-hour quick errand. Where are we going?"

"Syracuse."

Ah, 'Cuse.

"Mary Beth is there."

"Yes." Caroline unzips her backpack and rummages inside.

"We're picking her up?"

"No. We're giving her this." Caroline shows her the American Girl doll. "She needs her money, K. K. She doesn't sound good. I'm so sorry I had to ask you, but I didn't know what else to do."

"It's okay." Keeping her left hand on the wheel, Kelly reaches across and touches Caroline's shoulder with her right. "I told you, anything you ever need, Car'. I'm here for you."

"Thanks," she says in a small voice, turning to stare out the passenger's-side window, chin propped on her fist.

Kelly stops at a light and flicks on her turn signal to head toward the Thruway.

"So, Syracuse—that's where she's been all this time?"

201

Caroline hesitates. "It's where she is now. That's all I know."

"Who else knows about this?"

"Only you."

"Not even Gordy?"

"He's close to his parents, and they're close to mine, so . . ."

"So you don't trust him."

"Of course I trust him—with everything except this."

"Because you think that if you ask him to keep something in confidence, he'll tattle?"

"Tattle? We're not preschoolers on a playground! It wouldn't be right to burden him with the truth. He always feels obligated to do the right thing."

"So you turned to the girl who always does the wrong thing."

"It's not like that, K. K. My sister is in trouble. I'm the only one who can help her, and . . ." Her voice breaks.

And Kelly is the only one who can help Caroline.

She makes her turn and heads toward the Thruway, Syracuse, and Mary Beth.

CHAPTER
FORTY-SIX

Present Day

Talia drives, following a route she took countless times when she lived here.

From the Landing, she takes Shore Street past the park where they celebrated all those birthdays with Caroline, and where she introduced them to Gordy.

Now he's dead.

What the hell?

Do Midge and Kelly know?

Does Caroline?

She passes the Dive Inn, rendered nearly unrecognizable. Her mother sometimes stopped there for a drink after her shift. Talia remembers the stories she told about the people—the men—she met there. She pictures her, sipping her beer at the bar.

"Beer, Mommy? But you like merlot."

"When in Rome, Talia. When in Rome. Never order wine in a dive bar," Natalie said with a laugh.

Gazing at the Dive Inn, she wouldn't be surprised if there's a wine list now, and wonders what her mother would think of the makeover.

"Never trust a woman with a facelift or a man with a toupee, Talia."

Oh, Mommy. So full of those little nuggets of wisdom. So full of life. Always optimistic, even on the darkest day. Always believing in that elusive happily ever after.

"Oliver's a keeper. He really is."

That's what Natalie told her about Oliver before introducing Talia to him, way back in December 2000. A keeper. She didn't believe it then, or for a long while, but she was wrong. Oliver and Mommy had fifteen years of wedded bliss before he died of old age. Talia, who wept bitterly the day he married her mother, wept even sadder tears at his funeral.

Her mother's death two years ago was unexpected. Ben thought that it was better than watching someone waste away from a terminal illness, as his own father had.

But there had been plenty of time to prepare themselves and the kids for her father-in-law's death. When it came, it was a relief. No more helplessly witnessing a loved one's pain and suffering, or wondering which season, which day, which breath, would be the last.

She never imagined that the quick hug she gave Natalie Shaw that July morning on the train platform would be a final goodbye.

"I really would love to have you up to visit over Labor Day," her mother had called back as she boarded the northbound train. "With the kids, and Ben. Don't you think it's time?"

"I don't know . . ."

"Promise you'll at least consider it, Talia. They've never been to Mulberry Bay. The lake is warm and beautiful then."

"The lake is never warm, Mommy!" she returned with a laugh, in lieu of a promise she wouldn't keep, and then the train pulled away and her mother was gone.

Forever.

It's so wrong that the woman who loved to belt Aerosmith's "I Don't Want to Miss a Thing" is now missing everything. That Talia's back here in Mulberry Bay without her. That Talia is here—anywhere—without Ben and the kids.

She needs to get out of here. She needs to drive straight home right now and come clean to her husband . . .

In which case her marriage will never be the same.

Okay, then she can drive straight home right now and tell Ben some story about car trouble, or a mix-up with the dates for the yoga retreat, or food poisoning . . .

Mommy, again: "It's always best not to lie to a man you love. But sometimes you have to, and when you do, you stick with it for the rest of your life. You never, ever, ever let him know, because once he knows . . ."

He'll never believe another word you say.

Yeah.

So if she does go home and come up with some story to tell Ben, she'll have to play out the chosen charade for the entire weekend.

That sounds exhausting, and daunting.

Even more exhausting and daunting than staying to do what she came here to do, and say what she came here to say, and see the people she wants to see.

No, *needs* to see them. Right now, she misses her friends so desperately that she can't fathom how she's gotten along without them for all these years. Can't believe she tried to erase them from her life and go on as if they, and Mulberry Bay, never existed.

She presses a trembling hand to the spot just above her racing heart.

T-I-C-K forever.

How many times, over the years, has she considered having the tattoo removed? She consulted a number of experts, but they all told her the same thing. The ink could be removed, but she'd be left with a scar.

Either way, a scar.

Mommy: "If you say you're going to do something, no matter how hard it is, then you do it."

"Okay," Talia says aloud. "I'll do this. I just wish . . ."

So many things.

This doesn't feel like home. Everyone has left. Everything is different.

A figure catches her eye—a frail-looking old man shuffling along the sidewalk across the street. He pauses beneath a mulberry tree and tosses litter to the ground.

No—not litter. A bird swoops down to get it.

Bread.

He's holding a piece of bread, and he's tossing crumbs to the birds.

The Walking Man.

Talia whispers, "Thanks, Mommy."

Not everyone has left, and not everything is different. Kelly and Midge asked Talia to be here, and she is here, and she's not going anywhere until she sees this through.

And Caroline . . .

Meet me at the Landing, Talia texted last night. It will be easier to see Midge and Kelly later if we see each other first.

Busy with Hayley's band concert and Caleb's anxiety and the million things she had to do before her departure, she didn't see the reply until she was getting ready for bed.

I'll be there. What time?

Talia was early.

Caroline, it now seems, was earlier.

She looks down at the two of spades card, face up on the passenger's seat.

She can't go home yet—back to Ben, and her children, and her life that has nothing to do with what happened here. She has to see this through.

Jaw set, Talia drives on, out along the lake toward Haven Cliff.

CHAPTER
FORTY-SEVEN

The cameras . . .

Kelly hurries back upstairs.

How could she forget?

Four years ago, fearing that her mother might decide to go for another wee-hour walkabout after being released from the hospital, Kelly looked into various ways to keep her safe.

A surveillance system seemed like the best idea, but that was in late March 2020, with the lockdown in full swing. House calls weren't even being made by doctors, let alone home security installers.

She ordered a few motion-activated cameras online and mounted them outside the front and back doors, configured to alert Kelly's phone at the slightest motion and to record for sixty seconds. Unfortunately, that included *all* movements made by wildlife and the weather, which meant constant notifications and hours of footage daily, none of which involved her mother.

Fed up with being alerted every time a raindrop fell or a spider spun a web, Kelly quickly gave up on the cameras, deleted the app, and bought Beverly a high-tech watch with a GPS locator. It wouldn't prevent her from wandering but would allow Kelly to track her when she did.

If she did.

She didn't.

Yet the more time Kelly spent with her mother that spring, the more she came to accept that she couldn't leave her. Not just because of the pandemic and travel restrictions, but she could never again live in France, with an ocean between them. Mrs. Verga was right about that, *and* about the cameras, still in place at all the doors, and likely in working order.

But if Caroline really was here, her image might have been captured in the video footage that's available to view on the app for thirty days.

If Kelly reinstalls it on her phone, she can check the footage for a human figure amid the raccoons and coyotes, moths fluttering past the lens, foliage stirring in the breeze.

Reaching the top of the steps, she hears Beverly talking to someone in the kitchen, saying, "All right, then, I'll tell her."

Kelly's heart jumps, and she pushes the door open, expecting to see . . .

Caroline?

No. Of course not Caroline.

Her mother is alone at the table, sandwich half-eaten, carrots untouched.

Either she was talking to an imaginary companion or Kelly is hearing things again.

Fun choices.

She spies her notebook on the table. Is it closer to her mother than it was when she left the room? It seems so. She grabs it and sees that it's no longer open to the shopping list but to a different page, one covered in scrawled notes.

"Everything okay, Mom?"

"Of course." Beverly smiles.

"Who were you talking to just now?"

"Your friend Midge."

Kelly's heart sinks. First Caroline, now Midge. She should have known. Her mother is stuck in the past, not—

Then she realizes that Beverly has a phone in her hand.

Kelly's phone.

"Mom, can I see that, please?"

Her mother hands it over.

There was, indeed, a call from Midge just moments ago.

"You answered my phone?" she asks Beverly.

"Yes. It rang."

"Well . . . thank you."

She leaves the room to return the call.

Midge picks up immediately.

"That was fast."

"You talked to my mom?"

"Just for a second. She sounds good. Listen, I need to ask you something. I can't tell you why I'm asking, but just . . . keep it to yourself, okay?"

"Sure. What's up?"

"Do you remember our charm bracelets?"

CHAPTER FORTY-EIGHT

October 26, 1998

Kelly and Caroline reach their destination at five twenty, ten minutes ahead of schedule despite stopping at a service station to ask directions to the address Mary Beth gave Caroline when she called the house yesterday. Aware that their parents always go to their Bible studies class on Sunday afternoons, she correctly guessed that Caroline would be home alone to answer the phone.

The conversation was brief. Mary Beth asked her sister to bring the money she left behind, saying she needed to pay off some debts, buy some food, and find a new place to live.

"Where is she living now?" Kelly asked—one of many questions she had that Caroline couldn't seem to answer.

"Are you sure this is the right street?" she asks Caroline as she skirts around potholes and broken glass, past sketchy-looking characters loitering outside seedy row houses.

"It's right. Slow down. I'm trying to see the addresses."

"If I slow down, we're going to get carjacked, kidnapped, killed, or worse," Kelly mutters, aware that the red BMW is drawing stares from the loiterers.

"Number 302 . . . 304 . . . That's it. That's 306. Stop."

Kelly hits the brakes, puts the car into park, and follows Caroline's gaze to a dilapidated yellow brick duplex. One of the first-floor windows is boarded up, and the vinyl awning hangs at a precarious angle above the stoop.

"That can't be it. There's no way Mary Beth is—" She gasps as someone raps on her closed window.

It's a scruffy teenage boy with stringy hair poking from beneath a knit cap. He gestures for her to roll down the window. She flips him the finger and turns to Caroline. "This is crazy. We're out of here."

She's about to hit the gas when she hears the kid shout something that sounds like, "Winterfield."

"Wait!" Caroline says. "What's he saying?"

Kelly looks at him again.

"You here for Mary Beth Winterfield?" he calls, loud and clear.

Kelly nods.

"Don't move. Keep the doors locked."

He scurries toward the duplex. He's wearing clothes that might be grunge cool if he were onstage with Pearl Jam, but here, are plain old grungy.

"What is going on?"

"We need to get out of here," Kelly tells her, reaching for the gear.

"No!" Caroline grabs her hand before she can shift into drive. "He told us to wait here."

"Yeah, like sitting ducks." Kelly eyes the row house, then the rear-view mirror, seeing a menacing-looking trio of young men approaching the car.

"But he knows my sister!"

"How do you—" Kelly breaks off as the door opens and the kid reappears, accompanied by . . .

Someone.

She assumes it's a young boy—tufted short hair, scrawny in flannel and denim—until Caroline lets out a sob, throws open her door, and rushes at the young boy who isn't a young boy at all.

211

Gaunt, with bad skin and glassy eyes, she bears no resemblance to the beautiful, lithe Mary Beth Winterfield, who'd worn the trendiest clothes and real perfume.

But it's her—it has to be her—because Caroline is hugging her and crying. For a moment, Mary Beth stands stiff and frozen, seeming dazed. Then she hugs her back, holding on tightly.

In the rearview mirror, Kelly sees that the three guys are heading for the passenger's-side door Caroline left wide open, with her backpack on the floor. Kelly quickly shoves it under the seat.

The kid in the cap shouts something at them, and they skulk away. Kelly reaches to close the door, but he sticks his head in.

"Don't worry," he says. "I won't let anyone mess with you. Sweet car. Where'd you get it?"

Ignoring the question and doing her best to do the same with the body odor wafting from his clothes, she asks, "How do you know her?"

"Who, M.? She's my old lady."

"Nice." Kelly rolls her eyes.

Caroline and Mary Beth are walking toward the car now. Caroline has an arm around her sister, whose movements are slow, almost robotic. Maybe she's just overcome with emotion. Maybe she's on something.

"Hey," she says to Kelly when they reach the car.

"Hey. Are you . . ."

Yeah, no. Of course she's not okay. It's a ridiculous question, and one Kelly doesn't bother to finish. Instead, she says, "Get in, Mary Beth."

"What?"

"Get into the car. You need to come back with us."

Mary Beth steps back, out of Caroline's embrace.

"What the hell are you talking about?" the kid asks, eyes narrowed at Kelly beneath the brim of his hat.

Kelly ignores him. "You can't stay here, Mary Beth. This is dangerous."

"Who the hell are you to tell her what to do?" the kid asks, and pokes Mary Beth. "Yo, M., go back inside. I'll handle this."

"Now who's telling her what to do?" Kelly asks.

Caroline shoots her a warning look. "Nobody's telling anybody what to do."

"Did you bring the money?" Mary Beth asks.

"Yes. But—"

"Can I have it?" She holds out her hand.

"Only if you give me your phone number."

"Yeah, I don't have one of those." Mary Beth shrugs, hand outstretched like she's waiting for Caroline to count cash into it and be on her way.

Caroline looks like she's about to cry.

The kid in the hat looks like he's going to punch her if she does.

"So, what? If I need to talk to you, I just show up here and knock on the door?" Caroline asks. "Is that what I do?"

"No!" Mary Beth says quickly. "Don't do that."

"Yeah, that could be a bad idea." The kid nods at the house. "They don't like *visitors*."

"Then how am I supposed to find you, Mary Beth?"

"I'll call you sometime on a Sunday, like before," she tells Caroline.

"Next time you need something, right?" Kelly asks. "You call her, and she comes running. What happens if she needs you? Doesn't it work both ways?"

"You don't need me for anything," Mary Beth tells her sister. "You're way better off without me."

"I'm not. We're family. I love you. And . . ." Caroline glances at Kelly and takes a deep breath. "And I'm not leaving you here with your money until you tell me how to find you."

"Forget this bullshit." The kid leans into the car again, looking around like he's expecting to see a bag of cash. "Where's the money, princess?"

Kelly gives him the finger for the second time since they've met.

He snarls, "You little—"

"J. T.! Shut up!" Mary Beth pulls him back, out of the car. "I'm dealing with this."

"Mary Beth," Caroline says, "why are you here, with him? Why can't you just get into the car and—"

"And what? Come home? Like they want me back? Like they'll even let me in the house?"

"You can stay with me," Kelly says. "My parents won't care. We have a huge house, and—"

"Yeah, I'll bet you do," J. T. says. "A nice big mansion to go with that fancy car, right? I'll come too. How about that?"

"Shut up, J. T.!" Mary Beth steps between him and Kelly and turns to her sister. "I need a pen."

"There's one in my backp—"

"I've got one," Kelly says quickly, reaching into the console and grabbing a ballpoint.

"What about something to write on?"

Caroline looks at Kelly, who says, "Just write on your hand."

She nods, clicks the pen with her left hand, and holds it poised over her right palm.

"Okay," Mary Beth says. "You won't need me. You know you won't. But if you do, call this number."

She rattles off ten digits.

Caroline writes them on her hand. "Is this for the place where you're going to be staying?"

"It's a pay phone. A friend of mine will pick it up. Tell him you're looking for M. He'll know where to find me."

"But—"

"That's it, Caroline. That's the best I can do. If you need me, I'll help you, even though—"

When Mary Beth breaks off, Kelly prompts, "Even though . . . ?"

"Even though it's been the other way around lately. And that sucks, because I'm the oldest."

Caroline shakes her head. "The twins are the oldest. They're the ones who should—"

"Oh, please. They only look out for each other. It's always been that way. The two of them, and the two of us."

Funny—in all the years Kelly has known them, Mary Beth and Caroline have never seemed to like each other, let alone love each other.

Suddenly, the bond between them might as well be a cord. Elastic, stretched thin, frayed, but unbroken. Considering the home in which they were raised—the way their parents are, the way the twins are—Kelly realizes the sisters must have sometimes felt as if it were just the two of them against the world.

"Well, now it's just me," Caroline says in a wobbly voice. "I miss you so much. I wish you could come—"

"Yeah, well, I can't. Not ever." Mary Beth looks over her shoulder, where J. T. is glowering. "Now I need my money, and you need to get out of here before he gets pissed off."

"Pissed off?" Kelly follows her gaze. "Aw, but he's such a sweetheart."

He curses at her.

She contemplates giving him the finger a third time but blows him a kiss instead.

"Cut it out," Mary Beth tells her in a low voice. "You don't want to mess with him."

"Please come with us," Caroline says, clutching her arm. "I'll talk to Mom and Dad. It'll be—"

"For the love of God, just give me my money and get the hell out of here!"

Pale and trembling, Caroline nods. "Where's my backpack, K. K.?"

Kelly retrieves it from beneath the seat.

Caroline unzips it, pulls out the doll, and thrusts it at her sister. "Here's your money," she manages to say, climbing back into the car and turning to Kelly. "Let's go home."

Kelly nods, shifts into drive, and pulls away from the curb. In the rearview mirror, she sees Mary Beth standing on the curb, clutching the doll against her chest like a lost little girl.

CHAPTER
FORTY-NINE

Present Day

"Kelly?" Midge says into the silence on the other end of the phone line.
No reply.

The call must have dropped. Some areas around here have sketchy coverage, but she's in the heart of town. She'd been so distracted after leaving the morgue that she neglected to take her usual shortcut, so she's crawling along Main Street in Friday-afternoon traffic.

"Kelly?" she says again and is about to hang up when she hears a reply.

"Yeah, I'm here. It's just . . . the charm bracelets? Of course I *remember* them. Why?"

"Do you still have yours?"

"I'm sure it's somewhere."

"Somewhere, like at your mom's house? Or somewhere, in Paris?"

She laughs. "Yeah, no, Midge, I definitely wasn't wearing it in Paris."

"So you didn't take it with you when you moved out?"

"I didn't move out—not like normal people do, with suitcases and boxes full of stuff they want to keep. I eloped, remember? Well, you don't *remember*, because we weren't speaking back then, but there was barely enough room in Tad's stupid Porsche for my toothbrush."

"So the bracelet is still at your mother's house?"

"Probably. My old bedroom is a shrine."

"Can you look for it?"

"Now?"

"Well, you're there, and it's kind of important."

"I'm in the middle of looking for something else right now, and it's kind of important too."

"What is it?"

"It's . . ." Kelly hesitates. "You know my dad's firearm collection? Well, the most valuable gun isn't where it's supposed to be."

"Annie Oakley's revolver? Do you think it was stolen?"

"I don't. You know my mom. She's always moving stuff around. I just have to look for it."

"Well, while you're at it, please look for the bracelet too. Okay?"

"Are you just feeling nostalgic? Or is there a reason you're asking?"

"There's a reason. I can't explain it right now. I'm on a case, and I need to get—"

"Wait, Midge? There's something else. My mother thinks that Caroline was here last night, and we both know how she is, but . . . someone delivered a playing card to Haven Cliff."

"A *playing card*?"

"Yes. The two of spades."

"What does that mean?"

"At first I thought it was some kind of tarot thing, but then my mother said Caroline was here, and now I'm wondering if she left it."

"Why—"

"Because it's a two, Midge."

"You said."

"Think about it. Think about what today is. Think about Caroline. Think about a two."

"What—" Then it hits her. "A two. Code two."

"Right."

"And you think Caroline left it for you?"

"Maybe. I saw the person who delivered it. Only from a distance, out the window. They came and went on foot."

"And they, what, slid a playing card under your front door or something?"

"No, it was in an envelope with my name on it."

Kelly goes on talking about a woman who left the envelope with a workman, but Midge barely hears her, remembering something.

Earlier, at the police station, Dina left a stack of mail and papers on her desk. There was an envelope with Midge's name printed on it.

Not *Detective Sergeant Kennedy*, but MIDGE KENNEDY, in block lettering.

She left it there without bothering to open it, in a hurry to get to the medical examiner's office.

"Kelly, sorry, I've got to go. I'll meet you back at Haven Cliff in a little while. See if you can find the bracelet. And make sure you have that card."

She hangs up quickly, before Kelly can say another word, with a twinge of guilt. If Gordy's death was a homicide, she needs to keep certain information to herself, at least for now. But if Caroline is in town . . .

Five minutes later, Midge is back in her office.

The envelope is right where she left it. She puts on a pair of gloves before she opens it, just in case . . .

But she knows what she's going to find.

A playing card with a photo of Mulberry Bay printed on one side, and a two of spades on the other.

CHAPTER FIFTY

December 19, 1998

Six days before Christmas, Talia and her friends are browsing backlit glass display cases filled with trinkets only Kelly can afford. An oasis in the crowded, echoey, twinkly shopping mall, the jewelry store is decorated in tasteful white lights and white poinsettias, the "Nutcracker Suite" piped over a speaker.

There's only one other customer, a guy returning an engagement ring. He's in his late twenties, maybe early thirties, with prominent dark eyebrows and five-o'clock shadow. Talia decides he looks a little like Billy Bob Thornton in *Armageddon*, the movie she and her mom rented from Blockbuster last night.

The saleswoman, prim in a red cardigan and emerald holly leaf brooch, inspects the ring as if she suspects the guy might have removed a diamond baguette or two. At last, closing the black velvet box with a satisfied snap, she says, "I'm so sorry your engagement didn't work out."

"Oh, Sherry said yes. But she wants something more permanent than a gold ring."

"Ah, something in platinum, maybe?"

"No, she wants us to tattoo each other's names around our ring fingers."

"I see. That certainly is permanent," the saleswoman comments with a tight smile.

"Ooh, you guys, check out this one." Kelly points at a diamond-encrusted dinner ring. "Isn't it gorgeous?"

"For your mom?" Midge asks.

"For me!"

"I thought you were getting something for your mom! Hurry it up! Some of us just want lunch."

"I like this white-gold one." Caroline points to a dainty solitaire setting. "It's pretty, isn't it?"

"Pretty," Talia agrees, trying to make out the mostly hidden price tag on a pair of dangly gold hoops that are her mother's style.

"Sorry, I can't hear you because my empty stomach is growling so loud." Midge cups a hand to her ear. "What's that?"

"This ring. I just wondered what you thought of it."

"Oh, you know her, she won't like it unless it's battered and deep fried," Kelly tells Caroline. "But *I* personally think it's way too plain."

"Not for me. I like simple." Caroline holds up her left hand and turns it back and forth, as if envisioning the ring on it.

"Wait, why are you even looking at diamonds?" Midge asks. "If you tell me Gordy is going to propose soon, I'm going to barf."

"I thought you have an empty stomach," Kelly says.

"I do. But watch me."

"You don't like Gordy?" Caroline seems wounded.

"Of course she does! We all like Gordy," Talia says quickly. "Right, guys?"

"We *like* him." Midge isn't entirely convincing. "We just think you're way too young to be . . . you know . . ."

"Thinking about marrying this guy. Or any guy," Kelly says. "Now help me pick out some earrings for my mom so that we can get out of here. How about those chandeliers?"

Talia shakes her head. "Those look like something you'd see in *Vogue*. Or, like, on Mary Beth. Are you getting her anything, Caroline?"

"I . . . no. She's not . . . I'm . . . not."

"She's not coming home for Christmas *again?*" Talia asks, frowning. "What's up with that?"

"Nothing's *up* with it. She's just not coming home, okay?"

"Okay."

Talia sees Caroline and Kelly exchange a glance, as if there's something more to it.

Before she can ask about it, Midge says, "Let's get out of here. I'm starved."

"No lunch until we at least find something to give each other," Caroline tells her.

After considering choosing secret Santa names, or each of them getting something for everyone, they'd decided on a group gift this year.

"Here?" Midge groans. "I'm not a jewelry person, guys! No more charm bracelets!"

"How about necklaces with all of our birthstones?" Kelly suggests, pointing to a display. "A garnet for me, emeralds for Midge and Talia, and a ruby for Caroline."

"That would be nice," Caroline says. "What do you think, Talia?"

"I think there's something you're not telling me and Midge."

"What do you mean?" Midge asks.

"I feel like Caroline and Kelly have some secret," Talia tells her.

Kelly shrugs. "It's Christmastime. Everyone has secrets."

"Not about Christmas."

"About what?" Midge asks.

Before Talia can figure out how—and whether—to elaborate, the saleswoman walks over to them, having dispatched her customer with his ring refund.

As Kelly explains what they're looking for, Talia thinks about how Caroline has never been big on talking about her family. But if there was something to say about Mary Beth, she'd have said it to Talia before the others, since she lives right next door and knows them best. She and Caroline have known each other longest and have always been closest.

"What a lovely keepsake!" the saleswoman says. "A lot of people can't maintain even one lifelong friendship. You're very blessed to have each other. Now, let me just price that out for you . . ." She flips pages in a catalog, presses buttons on a calculator, and names a figure.

"For all four?" Kelly asks.

"Each."

They look at each other, shaking their heads.

"How about if we do sterling silver instead of gold?" Kelly asks the woman.

"That would bring it down some, but . . ." Again, she works the calculator. Again, she names a price they can't afford.

"It's a shame you weren't all born in January," she said. "The garnet is the least expensive gemstone by far."

"That's ironic," Talia comments.

"How about if I buy the necklaces for everyone?" Kelly asks. "I'll put it on my dad's credit card. I bet he won't even notice."

"But this is supposed to be something from all of us, for all of us," Caroline points out.

"We'll have to think of something else," Talia says.

They thank the woman, who tells them to come back if they change their minds.

"Hey, why don't we treat each other to Arthur Treacher's?" Midge suggests, back out in the mall. "That's affordable."

"As a *Christmas* gift?" Kelly asks as though she suggested they dine on live maggots.

"Ground Round, then?"

"God, Midge! We don't want lunch!" Talia says. "We want something special that will commemorate our lifelong friendship and, you know, how blessed we are to have each other. And you know what? Sherry has a good point."

"Who?"

"Sherry! The guy's fiancée?"

"Which guy?" Caroline looks around.

"The one who looks like Billy Bob Thornton," Talia says.

Kelly nods. "Oh, he was hot. Too bad he's engaged."

"He was saying that his fiancée wants a tattoo instead of a ring. What if we—"

"Ooooh! That's genius!"

Talia grins. "Isn't it?"

"Let's do it!"

"You mean get tattoos?" Midge asks.

"We can do our initials, just like before," Talia says.

"Those were bracelets. Tattoos are permanent," Caroline says.

"That's the whole point."

"My parents would kill me," Caroline says.

"You have to stop saying that all the time," Midge tells her. "Nobody's going to kill you. Nobody's ever going to find out. My parents wouldn't be thrilled either—believe me."

"Same here," Kelly says.

Talia shrugs. Her mother won't mind. She has a couple of tattoos herself, including Talia's birthdate inked above her navel, "so that I never forget what it was like to carry you when I was pregnant, so much a part of me, my beautiful daughter."

"I don't know," Caroline says. "It seems kind of extreme. Why don't we see if we can find a different mall Santa and do the picture?"

"Because that's lame," Kelly says, though it was her idea in the first place. "We need to do this instead. T-I-C-K forever! I love it! Midge? Are you in?"

She hesitates. "I guess so. Yeah, I'm in."

"So am I. We can get them right here, close to our hearts." Talia touches the spot just above her left breast. "Your parents will never see it, Caroline."

"God knows Gordy won't either," Kelly says, grinning. "Not until the wedding night, anyway."

Even Caroline laughs at that. "Okay," she says. "I'm in. But we'd better do it before we chicken out."

Less than an hour later, they're in Woodstock, where a pleasantly stoned geriatric hippie offers them a group rate and asks who wants to go first.

Kelly volunteers.

"Does it hurt?" Midge asks her when the buzzing starts.

"Like a mother," she manages through clenched teeth, adding as the others exchange nervous glances, "if you guys back out, I swear I will come after you with this needle weapon thingy and tattoo your faces!"

They don't back out, and yes, the experience turns out to be more than excruciating.

But in the end, it's worth it. It proves that they belong to each other. That no matter what happens and no matter where they end up, they're a part of each other's lives forever.

CHAPTER FIFTY-ONE

Present Day

Memories bombard Talia as she drives out to Haven Cliff.

One moment, she can't believe she waited this long to come back; the next, she wonders why she ever agreed to subject herself to this.

She made the decision on her last birthday, when she was feeling utterly vulnerable, nostalgic, heartsick, homesick. It was hard enough to turn forty-three on the heels of yet another "the team has gone in a different direction" email after Talia's fourth—fourth!—interview for a job for which she's overqualified. And when you've lost your mom, and your birthday coincides with Mother's Day weekend, the last thing you feel like doing is celebrating.

She was out running errands when her cell phone rang that afternoon, and *Unknown Caller* flashed across the dashboard screen.

She picked up, and a voice blasted over the speakers—familiar and yet not, lower, huskier than it was in their youth, but still recognizable.

"Happy birthday, stranger."

It took her a moment to force a response past the rush of emotion in her throat.

"Kelly?"

She heard a sound on the other end—a laugh, or maybe it was a cough, or . . . a sob?

"Yeah, it's me. I, um . . . I . . . Happy birthday! How are you?"

"Good. I'm good. How are you?"

"I'm back home in Mulberry Bay. Guess where I'm living? Never mind, you'll never guess in a million years. Haven Cliff."

"What?"

"Yeah. I bought it. So I'm back, and Midge never left. She's detective sergeant now at the MBPD."

"Wow, that's . . . I . . . I haven't been back there in forever. My mother is . . . she's . . . she . . ."

"I know. I'm so sorry, Talia. She was amazing."

Talia shouldn't have been surprised that Kelly knew about her mother's death, having said yes when the funeral director asked if she wanted the obituary sent to the *Tribune*.

At the time, the question was unexpected, and she hadn't given it much thought. Natalie had lived there through much of her life.

Only later did Talia realize that if the man who got Natalie pregnant and then left her—the man whose name Talia never knew, the man she refuses to consider a *father*—if that man still lived in the area, he might have seen the obituary.

Well, good. She wanted him to know that Natalie had done so well for herself. That she'd built a wonderful life on her own; that she'd been loved.

And maybe, too, that the daughter he never acknowledged didn't need a damned thing from him and never will.

Talia certainly wasn't hoping he might see her name and track her down, wanting to make amends. And if he did, by chance, ever reach out to her, she'd just hang up on him or slam the door in his face. It's what her mother always said *she'd* do if he ever dared show up. It's what she'd want Talia to do as well.

That's what she's been telling herself for two years now, ever since she found herself orphaned. That turning her back on the man who abandoned her would be satisfying, for her sake, and her mother's. It's what he deserves.

Most days, she believes it, just as she believed she'd be better off if she never set foot in her hometown or saw her old friends again in this lifetime.

Then came her birthday, and the call from Kelly.

"I miss you, Tal'. Midge does too. We're hoping . . . we were thinking . . . maybe we can all get together. I know you haven't been back in years, but don't you think it's time?"

She remembered her mother's last words, that day on the train platform. "I really would love to have you up to visit over Labor Day . . . Don't you think it's time?"

Talia opened her mouth to tell Kelly that it wasn't; that it would never be time. Instead, she found herself responding with a choked-up "I don't know."

Kelly made her promise to think about it.

Hanging up the phone that day, she had a sudden urge to call Ben. It's what she normally does when something happens. He does the same.

"You'll never believe who just called me," she'd say.

Only Ben had never even heard of Kelly, or Midge. He knew next to nothing about her hometown.

If her mother were still alive, she'd have understood. Over the years, aware that Talia had drifted apart from the girls and cut her ties with Mulberry Bay, she'd never once pushed Talia to talk about what happened. If the subject ever came up—and after a while, it rarely did—Natalie accepted that Talia didn't want to talk about it.

Now, she did.

And there was only one person who'd understand.

She opened her text message app and scrolled back, back, back, back . . .

Their last exchange had been almost a year ago. Talia had reached out in mid-June to say, Thinking of you today. The response: a heart emoji.

That day, her forty-third birthday, Talia texted the same thing she'd have said to Ben, or her mother. You'll never believe who just called me.

She pressed send, and with a whoosh, off it went to Caroline.

Talia slows the car and flicks her turn signal.

Haven Cliff is just ahead.

She wonders if it might be all fancy now that Kelly's in charge. She's always had expensive taste.

But the entrance is still enveloped by woods, and the lane is still narrow, rutted, and dirt. It passes between familiar stone pillars supporting an arched iron banner that reads HAVEN CLIFF. There are woods and wildflowers on either side of the winding drive.

Around the last bend, the mansion comes into view.

She hits the brakes and stops to take in the stone masterpiece, awed at the transformation. It looks like something out of an architectural magazine, or a history book. The mansion she saw only in ruins and in faded historical archive photos for all those years has materialized in grand and glorious living color.

She pulls up to the portico and turns off the engine.

Getting out of the car with the flowers she bought for Kelly, she looks toward the familiar path that leads to the pool site.

An aquatics company's van is parked there now. She can hear heavy machinery operating nearby. Unfazed, several deer are grazing on the lawn.

She opens the trunk, pulls out her bag, takes a deep breath, and heads for the house. There's no going back now.

No looking back either.

If she did—now, with a glance over her shoulder, or on the way here, with a peek in the rearview mirror—she'd realize that she's being followed.

CHAPTER
FIFTY-TWO

Ceto stopped just short of the last stretch of driveway, the part that circles around in front of the house. Here, the lane is bordered on either side by shrubs and trees, with a convenient spot where she can pull off into the thicket, her car all but concealed.

She climbs out, pats her pocket to make sure the gun is here, and moves through the trees until she has a clear view of the house.

Earlier, there were several other vehicles out front—Kelly's car and several trucks and vans belonging to workmen and delivery people. They're all gone.

There's only Talia, parked near the portico and carrying bags and a big bouquet toward the front door.

The pool company van remains on-site, operating excavating equipment way back in the woods with a maddening, incessant rumble and clatter.

Ceto sees Talia knock on the front door. She waits for a bit, then knocks again.

When no one answers, she seems to hesitate.

Then she turns the knob.

The door opens, and she disappears into the house—alone inside, Ceto guesses.

But not for long.

CHAPTER
FIFTY-THREE

March 6, 1999

A light snow was falling when the girls left Mulberry Bay to drive to the movie theater in Kingston to see *Blast from the Past*. Ten minutes later, it's become a raging whiteout.

Talia, white knuckled, is stuck with designated driver duty once again, creeping along behind a salt truck. Kelly's BMW is in the body shop, being repainted after her latest fender bender.

"It wasn't my fault," she's saying now, recapping the accident for Caroline. "The guy in front of me slammed on his brakes."

Midge, seated beside Talia in the passenger's seat, says, "Because a little kid ran out in front of his car."

"Right, but is *that* my fault?"

"Isn't a rear-end collision always the fault of that driver?" Talia asks.

"Not if there are extenuating circumstances. The road was slippery—and the weather is also not my fault." Kelly heaves an exaggerated sigh and pulls out her new pink Walkman. "You know what? I'm going to plug in and listen to music until we get to the movies."

"What are you listening to, K. K.?" Caroline asks.

"The new Britney Spears. Here, you can listen too." Kelly leans toward her.

"No!" Talia says. "Your giant head is blocking my view in the rearview mirror!"

"Me? Midge is the one with the giant head, and you know it."

"I am," Midge agrees cheerfully, "but my giant head isn't a dangerous obstruction right now."

"It is for me." Kelly pokes her from behind.

"You guys! Stop!" Caroline says. "I never get to see you and I missed you all so much and now all you're doing is bickering."

"You're right." Talia quickly changes the subject. "How do you like being an aunt?"

Caroline was excited back in January to report that her sister Eve had delivered a baby boy.

Now, though, she gives a lackluster shake of her head. "I guess I'd like it if I ever got to see him. But my sister is ridiculous about germs and being around people. Anyway, they might be moving. My brother-in-law is interviewing for a job in Kentucky. If he gets it, Joanna and Jim are saying they might go too. And she's pregnant too."

"Joanna is? That's great!" Midge says.

"Tell her that. Her morning sickness is even worse than Eve's was."

"Maybe it runs in the family," Talia says.

Caroline nods. "My mom says it does. I'm just bummed that they're all moving away and I'll be a stranger to my nieces and nephews."

She's so glum Talia asks, "But what else is new with you, Caroline? Something good must have happened since we saw you."

"I'm trying to think, but . . . Oh! Last weekend at church, we had this thing where . . ." She hesitates. "Never mind."

"No, what?" Midge asks.

"Tell us," Talia says. "We all want to know. Right, Kelly?"

"I'm listening," she says, one earbud in her ear, the other dangling from her hand.

"Okay, well, you guys remember Reverend Bauer, right?"

"The new minister?" Talia asks.

Midge nods. "The young guy, right?"

232

"Well, he's not *young*. His kids are our age," Caroline says. "But he's a lot younger than Reverend Statham, and he's like a regular guy, you know? He wears jeans and sneakers, and he's always laughing and joking around. He's the best."

"Wait, is this the guy who was at your birthday party last summer?" Midge asks.

"Yes! Everyone loves him."

"Really? He gave me the creeps."

"K. K.! You can't say that about a minister!"

"I just did. Between that fake southern drawl and—"

"It's not fake! He's from Alabama."

"—the way he was ogling all of us," Kelly says over Caroline's protest. "I know a perv when I see one."

"Ogling? He was not ogling!" This time, Caroline raises her voice. "He's just friendly! And what perv would organize a purity ball?"

"A *what*?" Kelly asks.

"It's this beautiful event where you get all dressed in a gorgeous white gown and your dad wears a tuxedo and escorts you and you get a gold ring, see?"

Talia glances in the rearview mirror to see Caroline holding up her left hand, a gold band flashing on her fourth finger.

"Wait, Car', this sounds like a wedding," Midge says.

"I guess it is, kind of. You vow to wait for true love and your wedding night."

"You mean . . . this guy Reverend B. makes girls vow in front of everyone not to lose their virginity?" Kelly asks in horror.

"No one *makes* you do it. You *want* to do it, because it's the right thing."

"Wait, you actually did this? At your church?"

"Yes. It's basically a dance, for fathers and daughters. And the dads vow to protect their daughters' virginity."

"Wow," Midge says. "That's really . . . um . . . I mean, it's . . ."

"Sick!" Kelly, never one to mince words, yanks out her other ear-bud, eyes blazing. "I *knew* he was a jerk, but this is crazy!"

"Don't call my father a jerk!"

"Not your father, Caroline! Your minister!"

"Don't call him a jerk either!"

"Guys, come on! Stop shouting! I'm trying to drive!" Talia says.

"Sorry!" Kelly lowers her voice. "But, Talia, don't *you* think it's crazy?"

Talia bites her lip and shakes her head, reluctant to further upset Caroline.

"How about you, Midge?" Kelly asks. "I know *you* think it's crazy."

"I think . . . I mean, it's just hard to know what's going to happen in the future," Midge says. "How do you know you're not going to meet some great guy and fall in love and—"

"I *am* in love with a great guy. And Gordy and I are going to wait for marriage. What's wrong with that?"

"It's not the waiting," Talia says. "At least, that's not what's bothering me. It's the whole idea of making this public pledge about something that's really . . . private."

"Exactly. Why is the minister involved in this decision?" Kelly asks. "And why is your *dad* involved?"

"Because that's what a purity ball is."

"I've never heard of it. I can't believe it's even a *thing*," Midge says.

"Well, it is."

"I guess we just don't understand it. If it were me, I'd be . . ." Talia swaps out *mortified* for "uncomfortable."

"I was, a little. But everyone else was doing it, so . . ."

"*We* weren't doing it," Midge points out.

"Maybe you should put less pressure on yourself about the future and not worry about what anyone else is doing," Talia suggests.

"Yeah, you need to relax and live a little," Kelly says. "That's what college is for. And while we're on the subject, I don't think you should be going to the same school as Gordy. He might be jealous if you went out with anyone else."

"Of course he'd be jealous! And I'd never do that."

"Why? Did the purity brigade make you pledge not to date anyone other than Gordy?" Kelly asks.

"Of course not. And there is no purity brigade. No one is making me do anything I don't want to do."

"Are you sure?" Midge asks. "There's no pressure from Reverend B., and your parents, and Gordy?"

Caroline is silent.

"How do *you* feel about all this?" Talia asks, trying to catch her eye in the rearview mirror. But she's looking down, arms folded. "That's what we're trying to understand."

"I feel like you're all attacking me. That's how I feel." Caroline sounds like a wounded little girl.

It's strange, Talia thinks, that every time they see her, she's one step closer to becoming . . . what? Either her mother or a child? Is she aging, or regressing?

"We just worry about you, Car'," she says gently. "It kind of seems like . . . well, sometimes, it's like . . ."

Midge jumps in. "It's like your whole life has already been mapped out."

"So has yours, Midge. You know where you're going to college, and that you're going to major in criminal justice and be a cop and live in Mulberry Bay forever."

"That's different."

"How?"

When Midge hesitates, Kelly answers for her. "Because, Caroline, your future has been decided *for* you. Not *by* you."

"Come on, Kelly. You're only going to Dartmouth because it's your parents' alma mater, and you're planning on law school because it's what *they* want, not what *you* want. Because if you don't, they won't pay."

Even Kelly doesn't argue with that, saying, "Fair enough. But parents are supposed to pay for their kids' educations. They're not supposed to handpick their boyfriends."

Not that she's had any serious ones. Kelly dates around—a lot.

"I don't know," Midge says. "I'm sure Bev and Bill would have plenty to say if you brought home some guy who isn't up to their standards."

Kelly shrugs. "Which is why I never bring those guys home. And this isn't about me; it's about the way Caroline's parents served her up to Gordy. I wouldn't be surprised if they gave the Klattes a cow to seal the deal."

"That's not how it is!" Caroline protests. "Gordy and I really love each other."

"And you're sure you're doing this because you want to?" Talia peers at her in the rearview mirror. "You're sure you're okay with it?"

Caroline makes a fist, leans forward, and gives four steady raps on the dashboard.

"What are you do—oh!" Midge says, and laughs. "Code four! Well, good. I just hope it stays that way."

"Yeah, Car', we love you," Talia says. "And if you're happy, then we're happy."

"I'm happy."

Talia doesn't miss the slight hesitation in her voice, and she's pretty sure the others don't either.

But no one says anything about it, and they drive on through the blinding snow in silence.

CHAPTER
FIFTY-FOUR

Present Day

Midge asks Dina about the person who dropped off the envelope, but she says that whoever it was came while she was distracted, on a phone call with dispatch. She doesn't even know whether it was a man or a woman, recalling only that they were wearing a dark-blue or black hoodie and sunglasses. They dropped the envelope on Dina's desk and left without saying a word.

"I'm sorry, Midge. I really didn't think much of it. What was in the envelope? Is something wrong?"

"Just . . . if they come back, or if anything like this happens again, or if anyone comes here looking for me . . . keep them here and call me right away, Dina."

Back in the car, she heads home to change into her uniform. Gordy's death is a homicide investigation now.

She weighs whether to tell Kelly about that yet—or that she, too, received an envelope containing a playing card.

But first things first. She can't move forward with the assumption that Caroline was at the Klatte home last night until she confirms that Kelly and Talia are in possession of their bracelets.

Stopped at a light, she finds Talia's number in her contacts and dials. It rings right into voicemail.

Maybe it's on Do Not Disturb while Talia is driving or she's in a zone with spotty service. Or maybe the phone is set to block calls from numbers that aren't in her contacts and she hasn't added Midge. Maybe the battery has run out. Maybe it's simply turned off.

Midge doesn't leave a message.

The light turns green, but an SUV is blocking the intersection several cars ahead of her. It has a Vermont license plate, a luggage rack piled high with bags, and two bikes strapped to the back, and the driver is trying to make a left in a spot where no one who lives here would ever attempt to do so.

Tourist traffic may be good for the local economy, but at times like this, Midge misses Mulberry Bay's ghost town days.

At last, the SUV turns, but so does the light, back to red.

Midge notices a line of people on the sidewalk near the Municipal Building. It must be Mulberry Sorbet Day, a relatively recent annual tradition, with the mayor himself dishing up free scoops of the local delicacy to anyone who wants it.

But no, that event is on the first day of summer, still a week away.

Anyway, this line stretches past the Municipal Building, all the way to the Smoke Shack next door—barbecue-craving customers, that's who they are.

Again, she thinks of Gordy and that unexpected takeout dinner for his family last night.

And Gordy, coming to see her at police headquarters.

Both events were out of character. So which had been the catalyst?

Something tells her he didn't decide to pop in to say hi because he was in the neighborhood, getting takeout. They don't have that kind of connection.

Or *any* connection, other than Caroline, twenty-five years ago.

All right, so maybe the barbecue dinner was his cover story for his wife, because he broke his weeknight pattern in coming to talk to Midge when he should have been home waiting for her, and cooking.

What did he plan to say?

She remembers his corpse at the bottom of those stairs.

She imagines Caroline, standing in the darkness at the top. Caroline, taking off into the night.

It's what she does, isn't it?

What she did.

She runs. She hides.

She comes back.

But does she murder people?

Maybe it was an accident.

Gordy had scratches on his hand and a bracelet in his grasp.

That doesn't mean he wasn't alone out there. Anyone could have been with him.

Anyone with Caroline's charm bracelet?

It doesn't have to be Caroline's.

If Talia or Kelly lost theirs, some random person could have found it.

Someone who had no idea of the significance of T-I-C-K but kept the bracelet for twenty-odd years and happened to be wearing it last night while struggling with Gordon Klatte before he fell—or was pushed—to his death on the anniversary of Caroline's disappearance?

Come on, Midge.

Why is she trying so hard to ignore the obvious?

Because Caroline is her friend, and she's spent years keeping her secrets, protecting her?

Midge is a cop now, with a job to do.

A good cop, who relies on evidence, not assumption, and explores every angle of a case.

Especially a homicide.

She puts on her turn signal, heading toward her house. The route takes her along Fourth Street, where Talia and Caroline once lived.

The Winterfields still do, but they, like Gordy's parents, are away on the church mission trip. Midge saw the article about it in the newspaper last week and has been meaning to admonish the editor. Break-ins might be rare in Mulberry Bay these days, but it's better to post photos about people's travels after they're back home again.

She rarely sees Caroline's parents. They've never been entrenched in the local community. Their social life revolves around their church, which is in Kingston, and they kept to themselves long before Caroline disappeared. They didn't even join the search parties in the days after the disappearance.

Midge overheard her mother tell her father, "If that were one of our kids, I'd be out there on my hands and knees, crawling through fields and streams and screaming myself hoarse."

"Yeah, well, not everyone is as fierce as you are, Gena. Maybe they can't bear to be out there, just in case they find . . . something."

"You know those people have always been standoffish. It's their *child*. If it were mine, I'd be doing everything in my power to find her."

"As far as I can tell, for them, it's not about what's in their power. It's about trusting in a higher power."

Her mother snorted, which surprised Midge. It wasn't as though Gena Kennedy was the beatific type who'd never said a bad word about anyone. She certainly wasn't one to keep her opinions to herself—especially about the Winterfields, as she'd always liked Caroline and thought her parents were far too strict with her.

But Mom was also a staunch churchgoer, and it wasn't like her to make light of faith—their own, or anyone else's.

"Don't tell me you wouldn't be praying, just like they are," Dad said.

"Oh, I would. But it's not all I'd be doing. And I'm not judging these people, believe me. But their behavior is making me wonder if they might—"

"They don't."

"You don't even know what I was wondering, Bobby."

"I do, and it's my job to look into this from every angle. I'm telling you; the parents don't have anything to do with whatever happened. She drowned in that lake."

"Unless they finally smothered that girl like they did her sister," Gena said darkly.

"You may not agree with their parenting, but I interviewed them and they're not killers."

"You really believe what they said about Mary Beth choosing to finish high school out of state, living with some relatives no one ever heard of?"

"No. I don't believe that."

"Then you think they might have—"

"Mary Beth got into some trouble, Gena. Remember that rash of neighborhood burglaries a few years back?"

Midge listened, wide eyed, as her father told her mother that Mary Beth had been responsible for them. One night, she was caught breaking into a house where she sometimes babysat. The family was supposed to be away but had changed plans at the last minute. She'd been arrested for criminal trespass, caught with a bag full of jewelry, video games, and small electronics she intended to sell or pawn.

"I had no idea," Midge's mother said, echoing her own thoughts.

Unlike Kelly, who fawned over Mary Beth, and Talia, who'd once called her soulless, Midge had never paid much attention to her. They had so little in common, aside from Caroline, and she hadn't been around the last few years. Midge hadn't even considered her whereabouts until Caroline brought it up in June.

If she had, she might have suspected that Mary Beth Winterfield wasn't just a free spirit who hung out with a fast crowd and liked to tease her younger sister and her friends.

Soulless suddenly didn't seem like much of an exaggeration after all.

"She was a juvenile offender. Her name was never released. The homeowner was furious with her until he saw how her parents reacted when they showed up."

"How did they react?"

"Let's just say her mother was devastated and her father was apoplectic. And that poor kid was a wreck. Crying, and so sick to her stomach, she kept throwing up. The homeowner decided to drop the charges, and the records were sealed."

"I guess it makes sense that her parents would send her away after that, or that she'd run away. But don't tell me Caroline got herself into trouble too. I'd never believe that."

"You never know what goes on in families' private lives, Gena. But no, she wasn't in any trouble that I know of."

"So you don't think she ran away?"

"She wouldn't have gotten very far without anyone seeing her. Not if she had no money, no car, and no one to help her."

"Maybe she had all of those things."

"There's no evidence. And Midge and the other girls are just as devastated as everyone else. If their friend ran away, we'd know about it."

At that, Midge was swept by a tide of guilt so fierce she nearly barged into the room and confessed everything she knew. Which wasn't *everything*, but . . .

But enough.

Even now, she can't quite believe that her parents trusted her so blindly, or that they underestimated the power of friendship at that age. That they didn't consider that when you're seventeen, your allegiance is with your friends. That you'll make promises and keep secrets for people who matter more than your family, or other adults, or the authorities. That you'll protect them at any cost.

That's what they were doing, she and Kelly and Talia. Protecting Caroline.

The shared burden created an irrevocable bond among the three of them that first year.

Then came the first anniversary of Caroline's disappearance—the night they kept their promise and revisited Haven Cliff.

The night it all fell apart.

CHAPTER FIFTY-FIVE

June 15, 2000

He walks, worried about the crying girl who rowed away in the canoe, wondering if she was the one who screamed up in the woods at Haven Cliff.

That's where he's heading now.

Maybe she saw a snake. Maybe she was bitten.

But she didn't seem injured when she emerged from the woods. Nor did she seem sad.

She was hysterical. Incoherent. Maybe even in shock.

He'd seen soldiers behave that way after seeing one of their fellow hostages beheaded.

Not him. He learned, back when he was a child and his father was still around, that if something horrible happened, you had to be quiet about it, because if you weren't, something even worse would happen to you.

So he didn't cry, and he didn't talk. He had nothing to say, and no one to say anything to.

He just walked. Around and around and around the tiny room where they kept him.

Now, he walks outside, free to go wherever he wants to go. But he still doesn't cry, and he still doesn't talk, because he still has nothing to say and no one to say anything to, and because the words are pushed deep down inside of him, with the screams and the tears and the fury toward his captors. Toward his father.

He climbs the old stone steps that lead up from the beach to the picnic shelter perched on the cliff. Some nights—most nights—teenagers hang around on the beach, and in the shelter. But not tonight.

He follows the trail through woods that are soft and clean in the rain, alive with night creatures and fluttering moths and buzzing insects. He climbs over fallen limbs and a tree or two, toppled in the storm a few nights ago.

There are footprints in the mud along the trail, heading toward the old swimming pool site where teenagers hang out. Not at night—only in the day. And only the four girls, including Natalie's daughter who no longer lives in Natalie's house.

She's away at college, he overheard Natalie telling a customer last fall.

"You must be one proud mama," the customer said.

"Oh, I am. I miss her, but . . . she needed to get away, after . . . well, you know."

The woman said she did know.

He knew too. About the girl who was supposed to have drowned out here a year ago tonight, the last time there was a canoe on the beach.

Now there was another canoe, and a scream, and a girl crying as if she'd seen a fellow hostage beheaded. He walks even faster, following the footprints up into the woods at Haven Cliff.

Two sets of footprints going in.

But only one set coming back out.

CHAPTER FIFTY-SIX

June 15, 2000

Midge, Kelly, and Talia waited for hours up at the pool site, calling for Caroline, hoping she might be nearby, might hear them and come back.

Now it's dawn, and they're making their way back along the trail toward the mock orange grove. They walk in silence, and the woods seem hushed, as if every living creature is as numb with exhaustion as they are.

They reach the car, and Midge unlocks the doors, but no one makes a move to get in.

It's as if they've reached an unspoken decision to wait a little longer. Wait for something more. Because even though they got what they wanted, it wasn't enough. It will never be enough—just knowing that Caroline got her fresh start. *They* will never be enough, just the three of them, without her. They're supposed to be four.

Talia leans against the car, hugging herself, shaking her head. "I just really thought she was coming home. Like, for good."

"I never thought that," Kelly returns. "I never even thought she was going to show up tonight."

"Guess we were both wrong."

"Guess so."

Midge shrugs, uncertain what she thought before. Now, though . . . now that the long-awaited night has drawn to a conclusion, that doesn't matter. What matters is where they're going to go from here. What they're going to do next.

What they *have* to do.

Kelly yawns and rubs her eyes. Her fingertips come away sooty with makeup. It isn't like her not to notice, or care. Even at this hour.

But then, this isn't like any of them—the oppressive quiet that hangs like the damp chill Midge didn't even notice until this moment.

She shivers, thinking of bed, and home, and her parents, who think she's sleeping over at Talia's. They have rules, even though she's about to be a college sophomore. They like to say things like, "As long as you're living under this roof . . ."

She's grateful for them anyway. Grateful, and guilt ridden.

"This has to stop," she says softly, shaking her head. "We can't do this anymore."

Kelly and Talia say nothing in response. Maybe they're too exhausted, too lost in their own thoughts, to even hear her.

Maybe that's better. Maybe now isn't the time to discuss this, anyway.

High overhead, a bird chirps.

And Talia says, simply, as if in answer to the bird, "No."

Midge waits.

Another bird calls to the first.

Talia says nothing more.

Midge looks at Kelly. She's shaking her head, but not in her usual frustrated-with-Talia way. She's a stranger, with those dull, black-rimmed blue eyes and spiky hair that looks white in the moonlight.

"Kelly, you know this is wrong, what we've been doing. For a year, a whole year, we've been—"

"No, Midge, *you're* wrong!" Kelly says. "We *have* to do this. We gave our word. How is going back on our word the right thing to do?"

"We gave it a year ago. We didn't know any better back then! We didn't realize how awful this was going to be. We didn't have time to stop and think about it. We just said yes."

"Because she was our friend. Because that's what friends do."

"There's way more to it than that," Midge says. "Do you know what this is doing to people? To her parents? And Gordy? Her sisters? This is destroying people's lives. We have to tell the truth."

"That would destroy *our* lives, and our parents' lives. Especially yours, Midge," Kelly adds. "Yours, and your father's . . . What do you think is going to happen to him, hmm?"

Midge says nothing. Kelly is right.

She turns to Talia, leaning against the car, chewing her lip. "What do you think?"

"I think we need to remember what Caroline asked us to do, and why."

"I don't know if that even matters anymore," Midge tells her. "She's the one who caused all of this!"

"Well, we can't undo it," Kelly says.

"No, but we can make it right. We can stop lying!"

"We aren't lying!"

"We're not telling the truth. Isn't that lying?"

"Not by my definition."

"It is by mine."

"Stop!" Talia shouts, and Midge sees tears rolling down her face. "Just stop!"

They fall silent.

The woods have come alive now, birds twittering a dawn chorus all around them. The sun is up, casting misty rays through the trees.

"I just know that I can't keep doing this," Midge says at last. "It's eating away at me."

"Well, it isn't *your* decision to make," Kelly tells her. "It's all of ours."

Midge is silent.

"What, you don't agree? You think you're the only one whose opinion matters here?"

"Of course I don't, Kelly. I'm just trying to make you see—"

"And *I'm* trying to make *you* see. But you won't. So, let's just do this the democratic way. We'll vote. I say no. Talia?"

"I say no."

"But—"

Kelly cuts off Midge's protest. "Majority rules. That's that. It's over."

And so it is.

The discussion.

Their friendship.

CHAPTER
FIFTY-SEVEN

Present Day

Midge pulls into the driveway of the three-bedroom cape she bought from her parents a decade ago. Just as it was never enough house for Bobby and Gena Kennedy, raising five children in it, it was too much house for Midge, then in her early thirties and single.

She'd grown tired of rentals and roommates, and her parents were weary of working and winters. They bought a Myrtle Beach retirement condo but spend summers here in Mulberry Bay, staying with Midge now that the rental market is so steep.

She parks in the driveway, behind Uncle Father Tom's sedan. He comes over for lunch with her dad on Fridays, while her mom keeps her standing hair appointment at Le Shag.

Midge waves at a neighbor mowing his lawn across the street, then pauses on the doorstep to suggest that a pair of skateboarding middle schoolers next door wear their helmets.

"We're just staying on the sidewalk," the older one tells her.

"Doesn't matter. You can still fall and hit your head on the concrete. You'll thank me someday when you're not maimed for life with a trau-matic brain injury—or worse," she adds, thinking of Gordy.

And that she's officially become her father. He was always policing the neighborhood kids, much to Midge's embarrassment.

But in this job, you bear witness to the worst moments in people's lives. It's human nature to want to spare others from avoidable consequences.

"Dad?" she calls, stepping into the house. It smells of fried onions and bacon.

"In here, Midge!" her dad responds from the kitchen.

She finds him and Uncle Father Tom sitting at the table, surrounded by the remnants of a hearty lunch.

"Imogene!" Her uncle, Mom's brother, always calls her by her full name.

He does the same with Mom, who goes by Gena. They're both named for Midge's grandmother, but even she wasn't the first Imogene. The name goes way back to Ireland in their family tree, as do the red hair and freckles Midge shares with her mother and uncle, though his ginger hair is long gone.

She plants a kiss on his bald head, and one on her father's cheek as he pulls out a chair for her.

"Sit down and I'll get you a plate, Midge. There's plenty left."

"That's okay. I'm just stopping in for a minute to grab something. I'm working a case."

"What's going on?"

"We had a 10-55 early this morning that looked like an accident, but now . . ."

"It doesn't?"

"Right."

"What's a 10-55?" her uncle asks.

"Coroner's case," Dad explains, picking up his coffee cup. "What happened?"

"The victim fell down a flight of stone stairs."

"Wait a minute—is this the Klatte fellow?"

"Klatte!" Her father sets down his cup.

"How did you know?" Midge asks her uncle.

"I stopped at the bakery on my way here to pick up those scones your mother likes, and everyone there was talking about it."

"Bad news travels fast," Midge says, looking around for the white bakery bag. "I'll take a scone, though, if you got them."

"I didn't, sorry. They had run out. The place was mobbed."

"Summer people," Midge says.

"Is this Gordon Klatte?" her father asks her. "The one who . . ."

"Yes."

"The one who . . . ?" Uncle Father Tom echoes, looking from Dad to Midge.

"The one who was dating Midge's friend who drowned the summer they graduated."

"Ah. Caroline Winterfield, was it?"

"Good memory," she says, nodding, edging back toward the door. This isn't a conversation she wants to be having right now—or ever. Not with her father. The subject of Caroline rarely comes up, but if it does, it's quickly dropped. She told him many years ago that it's too upsetting for her.

"That was a terrible loss," Uncle Father Tom says. "So is this, it seems. The way they were talking about Mr. Klatte in the bakery, he was a cross between Saint Michael and Christ himself."

Her father rubs his unshaved chin. "I don't know about that, but he's led a solid life in all the years since Caroline went missing. Back then, I was so sure he had something to do with whatever happened to her. I was wrong."

"How do you know that?" Midge asks.

"My gut is telling me."

Her gut is telling her that it's more than that.

"Dad?"

He shrugs, tight lipped.

"Well, like I said, I'm not so sure Gordy's death was an accident, and this is the anniversary of Caroline's d—" She clears her throat, changing *disappearance* to "drowning. And he stopped in to talk to me yesterday, but I wasn't there, and I have no idea what he wanted. So, if there's something you know that I should know . . ."

Her father glances at her uncle, who promptly pushes back his chair and stands. "If you two will excuse me, I'm going to go make a few phone calls, check in with the rectory."

The minute he's out of earshot, her father asks, "Why don't you think Gordon Klatte fell down those stairs by accident?"

"Why don't *you* think he had anything to do with what happened to Caroline?" she asks in return.

"Because he and I spoke about it."

"When you questioned him? I remember you said you thought he was hiding something."

"That's what I thought back then, right after it happened. And for a long while after."

"What changed your mind?"

"He did. I happened to run into him at Stewart's one day, seven, maybe eight years later. I'd heard he'd gotten married out of college and settled back here in Mulberry Bay."

"Not something he'd have done if he was guilty of something," Midge comments. "Once he got away, he'd have stayed away, don't you think?"

"I do. He was with his wife the day I saw him, and she was expecting."

"And you talked about *Caroline*?" she asks, incredulous. "In front of his wife?"

"Not then. We made small talk, you know . . . But he called me a few days later and asked if he could come talk to me. I'll admit, I thought he might want to confess something. The Klattes—they're faithful, churchgoing people. I thought maybe he'd made his peace with God and had decided to turn himself in."

"For killing Caroline." She forces herself to look him in the eye. Even after all these years, and despite the fact that he's no longer in law enforcement and she is—even now, she can't tell him the truth. Even now, she intends to carry Caroline's secret to the grave.

And she might never know what secrets Gordy Klatte carried to his.

Her father nods. "That's what I thought he was going to confess, but that wasn't it. He told me it was his fault that she drowned because he wasn't taking care of her as he should have been that night."

Midge bristles. "Taking *care* of her? She wasn't a Tamagotchi."

"A what?"

"You know . . . Okay, you don't know, but . . . that attitude of Gordy's was part of the problem. All those men who think women are fragile and need protection. What did he say, Dad? About that night?"

"That he was intoxicated. And that he'd lied about that when I questioned him, because he was underage. He thought he'd be arrested, and then his college admission would be rescinded, and his parents would disown him."

Caroline's voice echoes back over the years. *My parents would kill me.*

"So Gordy really was hiding something."

"I can always tell."

"Why do you think he came to see me yesterday, Dad?"

"That, I don't know."

If only she could tell him about the two of spades. But there's no way to do that without sharing more information about the past, and Caroline, than she can reveal.

She pushes back her chair. "I've got to get back to the Klattes' house. I need to take another look around and question his wife again."

"You don't think it was a domestic?"

"No! I mean, you never know, but in this case . . ."

"Go with your gut, Midge."

"Always. Thanks, Dad."

She kisses his cheek and hurries to her bedroom on the second floor.

When she bought the house, she briefly considered moving into her parents' old room downstairs. But that would mean being uprooted whenever they visited, or making them sleep on the second floor, which consists of two gabled bedrooms and a small half bath.

She opted to make over the room she shared with her sister when they were growing up. Their three brothers occupied the identical room across the hall, which now serves as Midge's home office.

She keeps her off-season clothing in the closet there, along with a few boxes containing childhood keepsakes. Now, she lugs them out and starts digging, reminding herself that this isn't the time to browse and reminisce.

The first box contains yearbooks, photo albums, and scrapbooks filled with sports clippings from her glory days as a high school athlete.

The second is filled with VHS tapes, DVDs, and CDs, though she no longer has the means to play any of it.

In the third, she digs through miscellaneous mementos—her lucky baseball glove, rubber-banded stacks of greeting cards, souvenirs . . .

Aha.

She plucks a small white cardboard box from the depths.

She pauses before lifting the cover, stamped with MULBERRY BAY JEWELERS in scrolled gold font. For all she knows, the box is empty. It's not like she's checked it lately—or ever.

But when she shakes it, she hears a rattle.

And when she opens it, she sees the bracelet, tarnished but familiar.

T-I-C-K.

One down, three to go.

CHAPTER FIFTY-EIGHT

With her mother settled in front of the television again, Kelly opens the front door to check the camera.

Not only is it still there, but as soon as she steps in front of it, a green light indicates that it's seen her and has started recording.

Back in the kitchen, she smears lavender-scented goo over her throbbing, swollen thumb and wraps it in gauze. Then she takes a water bottle from the fridge and picks up the notebook she somehow left on the counter this time.

Dammit. Really?

She takes the back stairs up to her old bedroom, closes the door, and opens her phone.

There's a text from Midge, asking again about the bracelet.

Dammit again. *Really?*

Ignoring it, Kelly reinstalls the camera app on her phone. According to the download meter, it's going to take a few minutes.

Her head is aching again—actually, it never stopped. She steps into the bathroom and checks the medicine cabinet for ibuprofen. There's only Tylenol, and it expired in 2003.

The app is still downloading.

Kelly paces, wondering why Midge asked her yet again about her bracelet, and what to tell her.

The truth?

Why can't the right thing to do ever be the easiest?

Sometimes, it seems as though she's going to spend the rest of her life making up for the selfish, reckless person she once was.

She'll tell Midge about the bracelet face-to-face. When they spoke earlier, she'd been busy on the job, obviously in a big hurry to get off the phone.

Kelly hears a ping. Ah, the app has popped up at last. Clicking on it, she sees a log-in window, asking for her username and password. She remembers neither.

It takes a full five minutes to recover the username from an old email account for which she's also forgotten the log-in information.

Back on the camera app, she finds that she now needs to reset the password.

"This is ridiculous," she mutters, massaging her temples with her good thumb and forefinger in an effort to relieve her headache as she waits for another emailed link.

Why is she even wasting precious time and energy on this right now? She needs to get back to Haven Cliff. The house is empty. Linden had texted her, saying he was the last one out and wanting to know if he should lock the door.

Don't bother, she'd written back. I'll be home in a few.

Just as she decides the app will have to wait until later, the email clicks in, and she quickly resets the password. Logging into her old account, she blindly accepts the cookies. All she wants to know is whether it's still active.

It is, thanks to an autorenewal setting that's been paying the subscription on her credit card for the past few years. She can hear Midge scolding her that she should pay more attention to things like that.

If you knew how many cases of credit card fraud I have to deal with, Kelly . . .

Midge and her warnings.

Midge, wanting to know about her charm bracelet.

Midge, who can sniff out a lie like a hound can a corpse.

Kelly scrolls down to the front door video footage.

As she expected, there's a month's worth. Hours and hours of minute-long clips recorded all day, every day.

There's no way she can wade through all of it. Not now, anyway. Maybe she can take a quick look, though, just to see . . .

She starts with last night. It must have been before ten o'clock, her mother's usual bedtime. She checks the eight o'clock footage, watching only the first few seconds of each recording. Most, as she suspected, show swaying branches, marauding raccoons, flitting insects.

Her phone rings.

Probably Talia, at Haven Cliff and wondering where she is.

But it's an unknown caller.

She ignores the call. Back to branches, raccoons, insects . . .

The phone rings again.

Unknown caller again.

Kelly ignores it again.

Raccoon . . . deer . . . wind . . . spider . . .

Person.

She gasps.

Last night, at 9:11 p.m., someone came to the door.

CHAPTER FIFTY-NINE

"Come on, Kelly," Talia says, listening to the phone ringing on the other end. "Answer!"

It rings into voicemail again, just like before.

With a groan, Talia hangs up.

It's a landline phone, not even cordless, sitting on an antique desk in the front parlor. It looks like something out of an old movie, but when she picked it up, there was a dial tone.

Of course she didn't know Kelly's cell phone number, saved as a contact in her own phone. But there was a notepad on the desk that conveniently lists several numbers, mostly subcontractors. Kelly's was right at the top.

Too bad she isn't answering.

Oh well. She'll probably be back any second, and she won't mind that Talia let herself into the house.

Deciding to explore while she's waiting, she returns to the hall and leaves her bag where she dropped it by the front door, beneath the watchful gaze of a couple she recognizes as Caroline's murdered great-great-grandparents, Asa and Edith Winterfield.

If things had turned out differently for them, Caroline's life would never have unfolded the way it had. She always said that her great-grandfather resented being raised as a penniless orphan, and that his disappointments and challenges had left a mark not only on her grandfather, but her father as well.

To Talia, that sounded like an excuse for his unforgiving disposition, but who was she to judge? At least Caroline's dad, unlike her own, raised his children.

She heads up the grand staircase, wishing Kelly and Midge were here and wondering where Caroline is right now. The more she thinks about it, the more certain she is that Caroline left the two of spades to let Talia know she's around. For whatever reason, she isn't yet ready for a face-to-face reunion.

Or maybe she was the one lurking in her parents' house on Fourth Street, aware that they're out of the country.

It wouldn't be the first time—

Hearing a noise below, she stops and looks back, down the stairs.

"Hello? Kelly?"

All is still.

She shrugs and moves on, reminding herself that she likes old houses; that she's always lived in them; that she's never seen a ghost.

But this is Haven Cliff. There are worse things than ghosts, and she probably should have waited in the car until Kelly gets home.

The wide upstairs hallway is carpeted, with elegant gaslit sconces and gilt-framed family portraits lining the walls. Closed doors too. Talia isn't comfortable peeking behind them, but she studies the faces in the paintings and photographs, aware that these people were Caroline's ancestors. She sees a resemblance in some.

As she wonders what Caroline's life would have been like if her branch of the family had inherited their share of the fortune, she hears movement in the hallway below.

"Kelly?" she calls, moving again toward the stairs. "Hello?"

No reply.

She listens, hearing only the distant rumble of heavy machinery outside.

She must have been mistaken.

CHAPTER SIXTY

June 15, 2000

He walks, following the two sets of footsteps through the mud toward the huge rectangular crater that was once a swimming pool.

He's seen photos of it in the Historical Preservation Society. He knows that it was bordered by a brick colonnade and that the pedestals beneath each of its four archways held statues. He's looked up the names etched in the old stone and discovered that they belong to Greek water gods. Poseidon was tempestuous, Oceanus noble, Hydros benevolent, and Ceto a sea monster.

He used to see the girls sitting on the pedestals in the sun; used to hear them talking and laughing, arguing, crying. Never screaming, never frightened, never hysterical . . .

Not until tonight.

The double set of footprints stops near the pedestal marked Ceto, beside the swimming pool.

The hole is huge, and deep. Dangerous. He always gives it a wide berth.

Tonight, he walks to the edge.

Peering over, he spots a broken body in the depths of the hole. That shouldn't catch him by surprise, but it does. He presses a fist to his racing heart and closes his eyes, remembering another time and place, another broken body.

His fellow soldier, fellow captive. His comrade, his brother-in-arms, his friend.

Those remains were tossed into a pit much like this one, exposed not to rain but to relentless desert sun.

His friend.

Broken, bloodied, headless.

He deserved a proper burial.

So does the girl.

He turns and looks around, spying a splintered, leafy branch on the ground beneath a towering oak. He grabs it and starts dragging. It's heavier than it looks. He heaves it over the edge, and he winces when it lands far below with a thud. It isn't quite on top of the girl, but its branches obscure one of her arms.

It's a start.

He looks around for another branch and sees several, scattered by the storm. One by one, he drags them to the edge of the pit and pushes them over. It's a grim, rhythmic process, like shoveling dirt into a grave. He's back in time, back in a distant, war-torn land, doing for the dead girl what he'd been powerless to do for his dead friend.

A proper burial. No living person will have to bear witness to the horror.

He didn't know her, yet he'll mourn her just as he does the long-dead carousel children. He'll remember her, because he always remembers the things that matter.

He'll remember, too, the other girl. The one who got into the canoe and paddled away in the night, leaving her dead in the pit.

CHAPTER
SIXTY-ONE

Present Day

When the Klatte house comes into view, Midge sees that cars now clog the driveway and are parked along the side of the road. She pulls up on the shoulder behind an SUV sporting a pair of bumper stickers.

One says, LET GO AND LET GOD. The other is identical to the sticker that was plastered on her own family's car in the old days, when Midge and her siblings were playing sports at Mulberry Bay High. Same maroon-and-white design, same font that reads GO WILDCATS, same black cat logo. It's one of the few things that hasn't changed around here.

Walking toward the house, Midge notes that the visitors seem to be mostly local. Several cars along the road and driveway have Wildcats bumper stickers, and most also display resident parking stickers.

A somber group of teenagers sitting on the front steps falls silent as she approaches. You don't have to be a cop in uniform for that to happen, and the kids don't have to be up to something. It's universal at their age—the clannish wariness when an outsider enters their realm, especially an adult.

This bunch strikes her as particularly wholesome, though you never know. The other night, she responded to a call about a party that involved trespassing, underage drinking, and illegal fireworks. Every kid there was fresh faced, clean cut, polite—and wasted.

She sees the older Klatte son with his girlfriend by his side. Midge met her briefly earlier. Her name is Sarah, and she's a wisp of a girl with a wisp of a voice.

"Hi, guys," Midge says, and they murmur polite greetings. She turns to Mike. "Are you hanging in there, kiddo?"

"I guess so."

"Is your mom inside?"

He nods.

"Mind if I go on in?"

He shakes his head, and the kids scooch to either side of the top step to make room for her to get by.

The house is filled with somber people speaking in hushed tones. Most are familiar faces she's seen around town.

The air feels close and too warm, strongly scented with brewing coffee, perfume, and a large vase of sympathy flowers still in its florist packaging.

Seeing Midge, a pair of middle-aged women break off a quiet conversation. One is Sarah's mother, also named Sarah, also wispy in every way.

"I'm Detective Sergeant Kennedy with the MBPD," she says. "I'm sorry to bother you all at a time like this. I just need to speak with Mrs. Klatte."

"I'm not sure where she is," Sarah says.

"Do you mean she isn't home?"

"No, I just . . . hang on a second." She steps away, leaving Midge with the other woman.

"You're a family friend?" Midge asks her.

"Yes. My son is in Noah's class. Gordon is their soccer coach. Such a good man. I just can't believe this happened to him."

"It's a terrible shame."

"I don't know why anyone would go walking down there in the middle of the night. I don't care how stressed you are. At that hour, you stay inside and walk on the treadmill. Or, I don't know, read a book, watch TV . . ."

"Gordon was stressed?" Midge asks, keeping a neutral expression.

"That's what my son said."

Hmm. Amy told Midge that he's been fine. And that he never goes down to the lake if he can help it.

"And your son knows because . . . ?"

She shrugs. "I guess Noah told him."

"We meet again," a male voice says, and Midge turns to see Reverend Parker, back with Sarah. "How can I help you, Detective?"

"I need to speak with Mrs. Klatte."

"She's upstairs resting, under sedation. Maybe I can help you. What is this in regard to?"

"What kind of sedation?"

Sarah answers before he can. "Just Valium. She needed to calm down. She's been beside herself, poor thing. I don't think anyone can blame her for taking medication, under the circumstances."

Midge nods, eyeing the crowded living room through the archway.

There are folding chairs now, and boxes of cookies, deli sandwich platters, a case of water bottles. Crumpled napkins and water rings on tables, crumbs on the floor. Clutter everywhere, people everywhere.

They're here to lend support, she knows. In a small town, it's what you do.

But no, she definitely can't blame Amy Klatte for taking a Valium and retreating to her bedroom.

She spots Noah in a corner of the couch. Like his brother, he's wearing khakis and a nice shirt and is surrounded by other kids his age. Noah, though, appears to be in a world of his own, shoulders slumped, scrolling through his cell phone.

Again, looking at the boy, she sees his father as he was at that age.

Again, she reminds herself that what happened to Gordy has nothing to do with his high school sweetheart's purported drowning exactly twenty-five years ago.

That *his* death, on *this* day, is nothing but a bizarre coincidence.

She quickly excuses herself from the pastor and women and walks over to the boy. "Hey, Noah."

He looks up with red-rimmed eyes. "Hi."

"Your mom's upstairs resting, huh?"

"I guess so."

"Are your grandparents here yet?"

"They're in Haiti, on a church mission. I don't even think they know."

"I mean your mom's parents. Or other family members? Your aunt?"

"No."

She was hoping to speak with someone other than this poor kid, who's already been through so much. But she does have a job to do.

"Has your dad's cell phone turned up, by any chance?"

He gapes at her. "What? No! Why?"

"Your mom couldn't find it, and you said he had it in his hand last night when you went to bed, didn't you?"

"I didn't say that. He had the remote control. Why?" he asks again. "Is something wrong? Is that why you're here again?"

"This is all routine, Noah. Don't worry. I'm just wondering if you can tell me anything else about your dad's mood last night? Or lately?"

"What do you mean?"

"Was he under pressure at his job, do you know? Something like that?"

"I guess so. Isn't everyone?"

She tries a different approach. "Is that why he was outside last night, do you think? To clear his head? Maybe he couldn't sleep and he was planning to walk along the lake for a while?"

"Yeah." He doesn't meet her gaze. "I mean, I don't know for sure, but that's what I think."

"So he's done that before?"

"I guess so," he says again.

Midge nods but recalls her father's words about Gordy after Caroline disappeared: "I've been doing this long enough to listen to my instincts. My instincts are telling me that this Klatte kid isn't sharing everything he knows."

Now, they echo back as Midge stares at his son, wondering what he's hiding.

Noah shifts his weight on the couch.

"Did you get something to eat?" Midge asks. "There's a lot of food around, huh?"

"Yeah."

"It seems like a lot of people around here care about your family. I know it doesn't help much now, but it's a good thing. Your dad . . . did he have a lot of friends?"

"Yeah."

"Is there anyone here that you think I can talk to?"

"About my dad?"

"Yes."

"I don't know. You should ask my mom."

She nods. "Okay. I will, as soon as I have a chance to talk to her again. But can you please give me your dad's cell phone number?"

"Why?"

"In case the phone turns up somewhere. We need to verify that it's his."

He recites the number, and she jots it down. She'll need a search warrant, regardless of whether it turns up. She can use the carrier's records to check Gordy's text and call logs.

"Thanks, Noah. Before I go, I just need to have one last look around outside, okay?"

He nods and looks down, quickly swiping a hand against his eyes.

She resists the urge to assure him that everything's going to be okay.

It isn't. Not for a long while.

She reaches into her pocket, takes out a card, and hands it to him.

"This is my number. Tell your mom I was here, and ask her to give me a call, okay?"

"Okay."

She turns away, then back to him. "And, Noah? If you ever need anything, you can too."

"I can . . ."

"Call me. Anytime." She hesitates, watching him closely. "*Is* there anything you need?"

Before he can answer, a woman's voice calls from the kitchen, "Hey, Noah, do you know where your mom keeps the coffee filters?"

He rolls his eyes but calls back politely, "I think so. Coming."

"Wait, Noah? Just tell me—do you need anything?"

"Yeah. Coffee filters." He heaves himself off the couch and makes his escape, adding over his shoulder, "I'll tell Mom you were here."

Midge heads back toward the door, detouring close to an open box of doughnuts. No powdered sugar–covered jelly ones, but she snags a glazed twist and pauses to wolf it down in a couple of bites.

She grabs a napkin and another doughnut for the road and sees a trio of elderly women watching her, eyebrows raised.

"I missed breakfast this morning," she tells them. "And, you know . . . cops and doughnuts, right?"

They don't return her smile.

Outside, the kids are still hanging around on the front steps. Again, they curtail their conversation when they see her.

"Hey, Mike? I wanted to speak with your mom, but she's not available. Will you please ask her to call me?" She holds the doughnut in one hand and hands him a card with the slightly sticky other.

Mike shoves it into his pocket with mumbled thanks.

"I've got to go out back to wrap things up," Midge tells him. "I won't be long. Okay?"

"Uh-huh."

Unlike his younger brother, Mike seems fully engaged with his peers, especially the girlfriend, who's still right by his side.

Midge gets a Gordy-and-Caroline vibe from the couple, and not just because Mike is Gordy's son. There's something familiar in the way his arm is around her shoulders—it seems more possessive than leaning on her for support. Familiar, too, is the girl's demure disposition.

Maybe Sarah has always been this way. Caroline wasn't.

Midge and the others noticed the changes in her as she settled into her relationship with Gordy that first year. She remembers how Caroline deferred to him whenever he gave an opinion, even if her own differed.

In the Klattes' backyard, birds are flitting around the feeders, and a young buck is snacking on the tangle of multiflora at the edge of the woods. He regards her warily for a moment, then goes back to his brambly white blooms.

The sun is hot and directly overhead now, and Midge's stomach rumbles a reminder that she's now skipped breakfast *and* lunch. She should have snagged a sandwich along with the doughnuts, because they're not putting a dent in her appetite.

She eats the second one as she stands gazing around the yard, looking for anything she might have missed earlier.

Like Gordy's cell phone lying in the grass.

Or a dropped wallet that belongs to Caroline?

She moves to the top of the stone stairs. The grass is worn away in this spot, probably from foot traffic. There are no signs of a struggle, but this isn't an interior scene with white carpeting and fragile objects. Outdoors, it can be difficult to tell.

She finishes the doughnut and licks her sticky-sweet fingers as she descends the stone stairs to the bloodstained bluestone patio, belatedly glancing back up at the house to make sure no one is watching. All in a day's work for her, yes, but respect for the grieving family always comes first.

She thinks of Louie, eating chocolate-covered peanuts while standing over the corpse with flies buzzing around. He killed one with his bare hand and then went right back to eating with it. The insect's remains are still embedded on the rough wooden railing.

No one would go up or down these stairs without using it for support.

Locard's Exchange again: Gordy's assailant's fingerprints might be on it, or . . .

Midge starts to turn away, then whirls back.

Or that person might have taken part of it with her.

Microscopic evidence, or maybe something larger.

Like a splinter.

CHAPTER SIXTY-TWO

He walks, following the sound of heavy machinery up the trail through the woods to Haven Cliff, wondering what's going on.

He thought construction was completed at the mansion. It looks finished. Maybe he was mistaken.

About that.

About a lot of things.

Like the familiar face he glimpsed earlier, on Shore Street.

He was so sure it was the girl from Fourth Street—the one with the disappearing sister, and the canoe, and she looked exactly as she had that night, but—

No.

Oh no.

Reaching the edge of the woods, he stops short. The heavy machinery making all the racket isn't up at the house. It's right here in the clearing.

He shakes his head in disbelief.

Twenty-four years ago, he stood in this very spot, incredulous, watching a backhoe complete the job he started, filling in the old pool. It was almost as if he summoned it through sheer will, giving the dead girl . . . well, not a proper burial, but a burial just the same.

Now, it's the opposite.

Now there's an excavator, digging, digging, digging where the pool used to be.

He turns away and he walks, away from the hole and the girl and the past. Walks quickly, with his head down, through the woods, toward the old picnic shelter with the stone fireplace and the tire swing and the steps leading back down to the lake.

He's almost there when a shadow falls across his path, and a voice says, "Hey, old man, where are you going?"

CHAPTER SIXTY-THREE

March 20, 2020

"This is not life as usual. Accept it. Realize it, and deal with it. Sick individuals should not leave their home—"

Kelly aims the remote and turns off the television, silencing the governor.

For her, life as usual ended the day she flew home from Paris.

Shortly after, her life itself nearly ended.

She started sniffling shortly after they pushed back from the gate at Charles de Gaulle. By the time she climbed into the back seat of a car service sedan for the hundred-mile trip from JFK to Ulster County, she couldn't stop shivering, and the dryness in her throat quickly went from a tickle to soreness to a cough.

Coughing into her hand and fishing a soggy tissue out of her pocket to blow her nose, she was aware of the driver's uneasy glances at her in the rearview mirror.

Kelly pressed her clammy forehead against the cold window, listening to the news radio station blabbing on about the mysterious epidemic, watching the swirling snow, thinking she had never felt more alone in the world.

That was just the beginning.

She didn't just have the sniffles, a cold, or the flu. She had the dreaded virus.

She knew it the moment she got Michel's text saying that his husband had been diagnosed and was hospitalized, and now he was symptomatic as well. He found someone to look after Bijou in case he, too, became incapacitated.

Remembering that last tarot reading—the tower card, with its message about upheaval looming—she vows she'll never again take a psychic message with a grain of salt.

Quarantined in this house, cut off from the outside world, she's been sicker, and more terrified, than she's ever been in her life. The doctors she was able to reach advised her to call the county health department. When at last she got through there, the health department advised her to call her doctor.

Her mother—the one person in the world who would have taken care of her—is out of reach, needing care herself. The hospital staff is overwhelmed—doctors don't return calls, nurses are harried and vague. Beverly isn't asking them the right questions about her situation beyond the twisted ankle—or if she is, she's forgetting the answers or choosing not to share them with Kelly.

"Don't worry about me," she says, every time they talk. "I'll be fine. Just get better."

Kelly had little appetite as the illness progressed, and the battle for survival left her utterly depleted. Today, though, she woke up famished.

She goes to the kitchen, where sunlight spills through the big window over the sink, reminding her that this is the first day of spring. Not that there are any signs of it yet. The yard is all bare branches and muddy slush piles, and the wind is blowing. It looks cold out there.

She can't remember the last time she stepped outside or had the energy to even consider it. And now, whether she's sick or not, she's still going to be a prisoner.

Deal with it, the governor said.

Fine. Kelly Barrow is no candy-ass. But dealing with it would be a lot easier if she just knew what was going on with her mom, and Bijou, and Pierre and Michel, both of whom are now hospitalized and out of touch.

Dealing would also be easier if she had something decent to eat.

With a lockdown looming this weekend before she's completed her illness-mandated quarantine, it appears that she might have gotten this far only to starve to death. She absolutely will *not* ask Mrs. Verga to drop off groceries. She and the housekeeper haven't spoken since they exchanged angry words in the hospital waiting room that first night. As always, she accused Kelly of being selfish and neglecting her mother. As always, Kelly's knee-jerk reaction was to defend herself and deflect, and yet . . .

Mrs. Verga, who's been wrong about so many things, might be right about this.

Weeks of isolation provide plenty of time for soul-searching, and when you contract an illness you might not survive, you can't help but reflect on the life you've lived. Kelly found herself questioning every choice she's ever made, realizing that she could have done many things differently. She could have done so much better.

In her darkest moment, on a night when she lay feverish and struggling to breathe, she promised herself that if she got through this and had a second chance, she'd change.

A pretty big *if*, even now.

Is this how it's going to end for her? For her mother? Both of them wasting away, forgotten by the world?

She's never been one to feel sorry for herself, but—

The doorbell shatters the silence.

Looking through the front window, she sees a police car parked in the driveway. Her stomach lurches, and if it weren't empty, she'd probably vomit right here and now, because she knows what it means.

They've come to tell her that her mother has passed away.

She throws the door open.

The first thing that hits her is that no one is there, followed closely by . . .

The bitter wind. She was right. The sunshine is deceptive.

And then . . .

There's a twenty-pack of toilet paper sitting on the mat.

Bewildered, she bends to grab it.

"Oh, good! You're alive."

The voice is muffled but familiar. She looks up to see a uniformed figure, face all but hidden behind an N95 mask. She'd be unrecognizable but for the voice and the red curl poking from the blue cap.

"Midge!"

"Hi, Kelly." She gives a casual wave, as if this isn't the first time they've seen each other in almost twenty years.

Kelly waves back and gestures at the doormat. "What's this?"

"Toilet paper. Guess you haven't seen it in so long you've forgotten what it looks like, huh? You're not the only one. But I heard that Walmart was getting a shipment this morning, so I got there when they opened. Word travels fast around here. You wouldn't believe the line. We were only allowed to get two, so I got one for myself and one for you."

"You brought me . . . toilet paper?"

"It's the cheap brand—not soft and cushy. But then, you never were a candy-ass, so I'm sure it'll be okay," she adds over her shoulder as she heads toward the car.

Kelly emits something that's intended to be a laugh but comes out sounding more like a sob.

"Wait, Midge—don't go. I—"

But she's still walking.

Of course she is, because they're not friends, and she owes Kelly nothing.

"Please, Midge. Please, before you leave, I just want to say . . ."

I'm sorry?

I'm scared?

I need you?

"I'll be right back. I just have to get something."

"No, never mind. Forget it. I'm sick, and I don't have a mask."

"I know."

"You know? You know that I don't have a mask? Or you know that I'm sick?"

"Both." Midge is at the car now, reaching inside. "I ran into Mrs. Verga yesterday. She said you were deathly ill when you flew home and that your mother told her it was COVID."

Midge closes the car door and walks back toward Kelly, loaded down with . . .

"Are those groceries?" Kelly asks.

"Yes, and I got you some medical stuff too—every store is sold out of hand sanitizer and masks, and we're supposed to hoard what we have on the job, but . . ."

Midge wiggles a hand that's gripping the bag, and Kelly sees a surgical mask dangling from her fingers, before she blurs and disappears in a blinding tide of tears.

She's crying—maybe the first time she's ever done that in front of anyone, or maybe she never has. She wipes her eyes on her sleeve, then blows her nose on it, loud and hard.

"Holy crap, Kel'. You could have waited. There's a box of tissues in one of these bags. Anyway, when I asked Mrs. Verga if you were okay, she said I was crazy if I thought she was going to come anywhere near you or this house. So I figured, you know . . ."

"Got it. This is a . . . what's the police code for welfare check?"

"It's a friendship check, Kelly. Not an obligation. I'm here because I care."

"Thank you," she says softly, not sure she believes that. "And police code reminds me . . . you haven't . . . Caroline isn't . . ."

"No. I haven't. She isn't."

"And Mary Beth?"

"No."

"How about Talia? Have you seen her?"

"Not once." Midge shakes her head. "She's married. Lives downstate."

"Natalie?"

"Remarried, moved away."

"And the Winterfields? They're still here?"

"They are. Still in the same house. I never see them."

"That's strange. It's not that big a town."

"Well, it's pretty easy to avoid someone if you want to."

"You think Caroline's parents want to avoid you?"

Seeing the look on Midge's face, she realizes she meant it the other way around.

"Midge, we did what we had to do. What she asked us to do. It couldn't be any other way. She made us promise never to tell, no matter what happens."

"I know she did."

"You haven't told, right? You haven't—"

"No!" Midge shivers, and maybe it's because of the wind.

"Hey, it's cold out here," Kelly says. "You're busy, and I'm germy. They're saying infected people should even mask outside. If I exposed you to—"

"You didn't. We're far enough apart, and the way this wind is blowing, I'm sure it's good. But if you go get a coat and put on the mask, you know . . . maybe you can sit on the steps, and I can sit over there . . ." Midge tilts her head at a wrought iron bench beneath a tree. "And we can catch up. I don't think I've seen you since the night I—"

"Arrested my first ex-husband?"

"I was going to say saved your life."

"Same difference," Kelly says. "I just didn't know it at the time. Now you're saving it again."

"Don't get too excited. They were out of almost everything, and there was only one flavor of ice cream—rum raisin."

"I love rum raisin!"

"No, you don't. You love chocolate fudge brownie with caramel swirl."

"I do. And, Midge? I love you too—for doing this," she adds, because neither she nor Midge has ever been much for mushy.

Midge nod and offers a gruff "No problem."

Translation: *I love you too.*

CHAPTER SIXTY-FOUR

Present Day

Does Midge really believe that Kelly—*her* Kelly—has a splinter stuck in her thumb because she was out here last night, pushing Gordy Klatte to his death?

"Everyone has something, or someone, they'd kill for," her father once said.

"Even you, Dad?"

"Even me. I'd kill to protect my family. If someone was trying to harm any one of you, well . . . that's all it would take."

As a teenager, Kelly blamed Gordy for taking Caroline away from them.

But that was long ago. Surely she hasn't been harboring a murderous grudge against him all these years. Even if she has, she wouldn't have acted on it . . .

Would she?

Midge pulls her phone from her pocket and sends a quick text.

Did you find the bracelet?

She watches for the three dots that will mean Kelly is writing a reply.

They don't appear.

Maybe Kelly's busy with her mom, or driving, or Talia is there and they're catching up.

Should Midge just call her?

It's not *that* important, is it?

It might be. But does she want Kelly to know that? Not if she suspects—

Come on, Midge. This is Kelly. Your best friend. Of course she didn't kill Gordy.

But if someone did, then Midge is on a case. That means she better choose very carefully when and where and with whom to share certain details.

She consults her notebook and dials—not Kelly's number, but the one Noah gave her.

With any luck, she'll hear Gordy's phone ringing somewhere nearby.

The call goes directly into voicemail. The outgoing message is automated, a robotic voice informing her that the person she's trying to reach is not available.

Yeah, no kidding.

She runs through the usual options.

Gordy's phone might be on Do Not Disturb or set to block unknown callers.

It might be in a no-service zone.

The battery might have run out.

It might be turned off.

But it didn't vanish off the face of the earth.

Midge surveys the area. If Gordy dropped it during the fall, it has to be close by. It might have landed along the stairs, or on the ground close to where he was found.

The terrain on either side of the flight is mostly rocks and dirt, with a few straggly saplings poking up. The phone should be fairly easy to spot there, especially with the sun to catch its reflection. She sees nothing and turns her attention to the stone patio.

It's surrounded by pachysandra. She bends over and parts some leaves with her hand, belatedly spotting poison ivy vines twining through the clump.

No, thank you. She finds a stick and pokes around until she startles a snake that slithers away.

Yeah, that's enough of that. If the phone is in there, it's going to be difficult to find. She needs to get forensics back here, with a search warrant in hand.

About to place the call, she hears footsteps overhead and looks up.

Noah Klatte is standing at the top of the stairs.

He zeroes in on the bluestone stained with his father's blood and grips the gatepost to steady himself.

Midge hurries up the stairs toward him. "Noah?"

"I just wanted . . ." He takes a deep breath. "Earlier you said . . ."

Again, he glances at the bloodstain.

Midge steers him back. "I said that I'm here for you. That you can call me if anything—"

"Yeah. And there *is*. There's something . . ."

"Something you need from me?"

"Kind of the opposite. But you have to promise not to tell, because it's bad. Really bad."

CHAPTER SIXTY-FIVE

The image on Kelly's phone is grainy, the female figure cast in shadows. It's impossible to get a look at her face and make out her features. But she has a slight build, with long brown hair, and is wearing glasses.

It could be Caroline.

She just stands there on the doorstep almost for the entire duration of the clip, reaching for the bell, then hesitating. Then she visibly takes a deep breath, reaches again, and rings.

The clip ends.

Kelly watches it over.

Over again.

Midway through the fourth viewing, she notices something that takes her breath away.

As she fumbles with her gauze-wrapped thumb for the button to freeze the image, the phone rings. Unknown, yet again.

She ignores it, yet again.

Focused on the app, she hits pause and zooms in on the woman's hand as she reaches for the doorbell.

Not only does she appear to be left handed, but there's a bracelet around her wrist.

A silver charm bracelet.

CHAPTER SIXTY-SIX

Promise not to tell . . .

It's bad. Really bad . . .

Midge stares at Gordy's son. His eyes are tortured.

Her heart sinks. Is this boy responsible for his father's death? Were they together outside last night? Maybe they got into some kind of argument?

"Noah, I can't make a promise like that," Midge says quietly. "Not until I know what it is. But I can promise that I'll help you, whatever it is."

"But my mom can't know. Please. She can't know. It would kill her."

"What can't she know?"

No reply. Tears roll down his cheeks, and his shoulders heave.

"I'll bet your mom is stronger than you think," she tells him.

He just shakes his head.

"I know she loves you very much, and that you love her," Midge says tightly, remembering how he comforted Amy this morning, hysterical in her bloody nightgown.

"I do. That's why . . ."

Again, he breaks off, unable to go on.

Midge waits. Then she says, "Look, Noah, whatever you did, you have to—"

"It's not what *I* did!"

"Then who? Your brother?"

"No." He makes eye contact at last. "My dad."

"What did your dad do?"

Silence.

"Did you see something? Hear something?"

He nods. "His phone."

"You heard him on the phone?"

"No. There was this text . . . I saw it. Yesterday, a few of them, and then . . . last night."

"You saw it yesterday? And last night?"

"No, it was *from* yesterday and last night. I saw this morning, after . . . after."

"Okay, Noah, let's sort through this, because I'm not sure I understand. Where's the phone now?"

"I hid it."

"Why?"

"Because I told you, my mom—she can't know about this."

"Wait, back up. Where did you get the phone?"

"It was right there." He points to a spot a few feet away, near the top of the steps. "I saw it lying in the grass when we came back up . . . after we . . . after my mom found him."

"So you and your brother heard her screaming, and you came outside and found her there with your dad. That did happen, just the way you said it did, right?"

"Right."

"And then you came back up—all three of you?"

"Yeah. And my mom—she kind of ran up the steps. She had her phone in her hand, and she was dialing 9-1-1. Mike was right behind her, and then me, and then I saw my dad's phone. It was just lying there, you know? So . . . I grabbed it, and I shoved it into my pocket. I didn't know what else to do."

"Okay. What happened next?"

"My mom was on the phone with 9-1-1, and she just kept screaming, and so did Mike. They were both . . . they just . . . they fell apart. So I grabbed the phone and I talked to the operator. I told him to send help, even though . . . I just thought maybe they could save him."

"You did the right thing." Midge clears her throat. "And then what? Did you look at your dad's phone?"

"No. I forgot about it, because there was a lot . . . my mom and Mike were a mess, and then the paramedics came, and you came, and people were here. Reverend Parker told me and Mike to go get dressed. And when I got up to my room and started changing, I remembered the phone. So . . . I don't know why. I looked at it."

"There was no passcode on it?"

"There was, but I knew it. It's 1125. It's a Bible verse—John 11:25. You know it, right?"

"I should, but . . ."

"It goes, 'I am the Resurrection and the Life. Whoever believes in me, even though he has died, he shall live.' My dad . . ." He breaks off and clears his throat before adding a hoarse, "Sorry. It's hard."

"I know it is. So when you looked at the phone, what did you see?"

He takes a deep breath. "A text. It was the last one he got. It said, 'I'm by the lake. Come down. We need to talk.'"

"Who was it from?"

"Some woman. Her name is Caroline."

CHAPTER
SIXTY-SEVEN

"Hey, old man, where are you going?"

He walks. Away from her, past the stone fireplace, toward the shelter and the tire swing and the steps to the beach.

"Old man!"

She can't be talking to him. If she's just a kid, he can't be an old man. He must have gotten confused about the time, just like he had when he was a captive in that dark room.

The longer a hostage was kept, the more dangerous the situation became. Without a watch or electronics or windows to show sunrises and sunsets and seasons changing, he had no way of knowing how long he'd been there.

Two days? Perhaps two weeks?

Two years, he learned after the rescue.

He lost two years of his life. But he didn't lose his life. Not like his friend.

And so time passes, and he keeps track of the things that matter. The people who matter.

The girl—

He was so certain she mattered. How could he have been wrong?

Now, there's no mistaking the hardness in her eyes, like his captors' eyes. The eyes of someone capable of inflicting tremendous suffering and lethal pain.

She's dangerous.

He walks away, toward the house, thinking of the other girls.

They should know. He has to tell them.

Now, at last, he has something to say; someone to say it to.

"Old man," she calls again. "You'd better stop. Stop right now."

He walks.

He hears something then. Louder, closer than the construction equipment in the clearing.

It's just a tree snapping, and it's the strangest thing, because the sun is shining and there's no storm and there's no war. It's just a tree snapping, and it's so close, and it's going to fall, and it might fall on him, and he'd better walk, and so he does.

One step, two steps, three steps . . .

The tree doesn't fall.

He does.

CHAPTER
SIXTY-EIGHT

Racing home to Haven Cliff, Kelly thinks about the left-handed woman on her mother's doorstep, wearing a silver charm bracelet. The letters were obscured, little more than silvery glints, but she's positive that they're letters, and the letters spell T-I-C-K.

Caroline.

Her mother was right. She really was there last night, at Kelly's childhood home.

Last night . . .

Gordy died last night. An accident.

She tries Midge again.

Still no answer.

Kelly doesn't bother to leave a message. Midge is on a case. When she sees the missed calls, she'll get in touch as soon as she has a chance.

She turns into Haven Cliff and barrels down the lane toward the house. No such thing as speeding here, on her private property.

The windows are down, and the excavators are still rumbling and scraping back in the woods, but another sound reaches her ears—a distant bang.

Fireworks? At this time of day?

A fawn jumps out in front of her car, as if startled. Kelly hits the brakes and swerves, narrowly avoiding hitting the animal as she skids and spins to a stop at the edge of the thicket, branches scraping the side of the car.

The fawn disappears into the trees on the other side of the lane. Kelly puts her car in park and waits a few moments to see if its mother follows. No sign of her. Scanning the woods beyond the boughs resting against her car, she sees movement.

Not a doe.

Wait, it's not even movement.

Just the sun, glinting off something shiny where there should be only foliage and wood.

Kelly gets out of the car into blinding sunshine and reaches back in to grab her sunglasses. They aren't there, and how can they not be there when she's certain she—

Oh. She's wearing them.

But she is not her mother.

She is *not*.

She just can't be expected to keep track of things—possessions, facts, things she needs to do, things she's *done*—when she's this achy and exhausted, feeling as though her skull is clamped in a vise that someone is squeezing, squeezing, squeezing.

It will be okay, though. She just needs to . . .

What? What do I need to do?

"What is going on?" she mutters, grabbing the top of the open door to steady herself, lightheaded and needing a moment.

Maybe it's the damned sun. The heat. It's warm today. Though not that warm, and there's no humidity.

Maybe she's dehydrated. She reaches back into the car, grabbing the water bottle she brought from her mother's fridge. Sipping, she finds that it's cold, and nearly empty.

She's not dehydrated.

She looks down at her thumb, still wrapped in gauze. Is it infected, like Midge said? Is she dying?

"No way."

She tosses the empty bottle back into the car and looks again at whatever's glinting in the sunlight.

Probably just a swath of flaccid Mylar that escaped a balloon bouquet, or a piece of scrap metal from God knows where.

But when she steps closer and parts the branches, she sees an unfamiliar car hidden in the thicket.

CHAPTER
SIXTY-NINE

"Her name was *Caroline*?" Midge asks Noah, managing to keep her voice level, her gaze steady. "Are you sure?"

"Yeah."

She holds her breath, cheeks puffed, trying to process it, trying to think of some way this isn't what it looks like.

Midge! Stop! Do your job!

She thinks of Gordy, coming to see her yesterday, for the first time in . . . ever.

Now it's starting to make sense.

She exhales and asks, "Where's your dad's phone?"

"I told you; I hid it."

"I understand, but this is a serious matter, Noah. I'd like to take a look at it."

It isn't true. There's nothing she'd like less, in the whole world, than to face concrete evidence that her friend . . .

She looks down at the bloodstained bluestone.

Her friend did *this*?

Gentle Caroline?

You haven't seen her since you were kids, Midge. People change . . .

Noah is shaking his head. "My mom can't know!"

"The phone is evidence in a police investigation, Noah. I'm so sorry, but I'm going to have to see that text exchange."

"You can't."

"I understand that you hid the phone because you're trying to protect your mother, but—"

"I didn't hide it, okay?" He pulls a phone out of his pocket. "It's right here. But you can't see the texts because I deleted them."

She sighs. There are ways to retrieve deleted texts. But that will take time.

"I'm sorry," Noah says, "and I'm praying for forgiveness, because I know it was wrong. But so was leaving that text there. My mom would be . . . she loves him so much. And she thought—I thought—that he loved her too."

"I'm sure he did."

"Then why was he meeting some woman in the middle of the night without telling my mom? I'm not stupid. I know why."

Midge exhales through puffed cheeks, then asks, "What did the texts say, exactly?"

"Well, I didn't read them all, but the last ones said she was coming over because she needed to talk to him. He said no, don't. She said she was coming anyway. She said she'd come the back way, from the path by the lake, and not to worry because no one would see her. He said no—he just kept saying no. And then she said she was already there, coming up to the yard."

Midge's phone buzzes with a call.

"Hang on," she tells Noah, and checks it.

Kelly.

She ignores it for now, going back to Noah, sensing that he's ready to bolt.

"Do you know what time that was?"

"Late."

"How late?"

"I don't know, but . . . I mean, I think she was texting him while we were watching the game, toward the end, because he had his phone. And he gets mad at me and Mike when we do that. He's always telling us we need to be in the moment. But he wasn't."

"How long was it going on?"

"The game?"

"No, I mean the communication between your father and Caroline. Did you read all the texts? Back to the beginning? Or—"

Her phone buzzes again. Kelly again.

"Sorry, Noah, I'd better get this," she says, and answers the call. "Hey, I'm on a case right now, so I—"

"Midge! You need to get to Haven Cliff right away. Something strange is happening here."

CHAPTER SEVENTY

Talia is in the library, gingerly flipping through an old album filled with sepia photos of Haven Cliff, when she hears a door open, footsteps, and Kelly's voice calling her name.

She jumps up, leaving the album on a table, and hurries into the hall, forgetting to be anxious until she catches sight of Kelly.

She looks so very like herself, Talia thinks, and then: *She looks nothing at all like herself.*

The Kelly she remembers was a beautiful, sophisticated blonde, yes. But she rarely lost her cool, and her voice had a distinctive edge.

This woman is flushed and flustered, clutching the bouquet Talia left by the door. She stops short when she catches sight of Talia. When she speaks, she sounds like she's about to cry. "You came! You're here! And you're okay!" She throws her arms around Talia.

It's the first time she's been hugged so fervently—by an adult, anyway—since the days of greeting her mother at train stations and airports. She manages to hold back her tears until she realizes Kelly is full-blown bawling.

When at last they let go of each other, Kelly takes tissues from her bag and hands one to Talia before blowing her nose, loud and long. "Sorry. I'm kind of a mess lately."

"You? Never. You look exactly the same. You even smell the same, like fancy French perfume."

"It's just lavender salve. I've got a splinter." Kelly waves the bouquet, and Talia sees that her thumb is bandaged. "Did you bring these flowers?"

"I did."

"Thank you. They're beautiful."

"No, they're wilted and bedraggled, especially compared to this." Talia gestures at a nearby pedestal that holds a professional floral arrangement of lilies and trailing vines.

"They're *beautiful*. Come on to the kitchen and I'll get them into water," Kelly says, leading the way to the back of the house. "Sorry I wasn't here to let you in, but there's some stuff going on. You won't believe this, but Gordy Klatte—"

"Died. I know. That's crazy. I don't know the details."

"Neither do I, other than that it was an accidental fall." Kelly fills a crystal vase with water and peels the tissue and cellophane away from the limp bouquet.

"An accident? On this day? Exactly twenty-five years after Caroline—"

"I know, right?" Kelly grabs shears and begins cutting the flower stems. "A little too coincidental, isn't it? And I have other stuff to share."

"About Gordy?"

"Indirectly."

"I have stuff to share too. But I wanted to tell you *and* Midge."

"She should be here in a few minutes." Kelly puts the flowers into the vase, picks it up, and says, "Come on. I can give you a tour, and we'll find a nice spot for this."

"I did some snooping around already, and I can't believe what you've done. Do you remember that you once said you couldn't imagine why anyone would ever want to buy it?"

"Did I?"

"You did. What changed your mind?"

"It's a solid real estate investment."

"That's bull, Kelly. I'm sure there are plenty of other properties around here."

"That's *exactly* what Midge said."

"Yeah, well . . . we know you."

They're in the formal dining room. The din from heavy machinery floats through the open screens on a warm summer breeze.

"Why Haven Cliff, though, Kelly?"

"Because it was there?"

"That's the thing. It *wasn't* there. It wasn't *here*. You had to build it from scratch."

"Mmm." Kelly moves the centerpiece of roses and freesia to the sideboard and puts Talia's bouquet in its place. She stands back to admire it, then moves it an inch in one direction, a millimeter in another.

"Kelly? I was looking at those old photos just now, and it seems to me that everything inside and out is an exact replica. Every detail. It's like you're trying to recapture the past—not even your past."

Kelly meets her gaze and nods. "It's Caroline's past. Her family's past."

"Yeah. I figured."

"Back in those days, when we were all together, and friends . . . I was so caught up in my own life that I never noticed how badly she was hurting."

"We all were. I think about that all the time. About whether we could have helped her before it was too late."

"That's why I did this, Talia. In case it's not too late. So that if she ever comes back, she'll have Haven Cliff."

"You're going to hand it over to her? No strings attached?"

Kelly nods. "I can afford it. And a Winterfield should live here."

"Maybe, if Caroline knew this was here waiting for her . . . maybe it would make a difference."

"Yeah. Too bad there's no way to let her know."

There is. But Talia can't tell her that without the rest of it. She'll wait for Midge.

"Come on," Kelly says, leading the way back to the hall. "Let's go get your bag out of the car."

"I already did, with the flowers."

"The flowers were on the floor."

"On the floor? I left them on top of my suitcase, right—" Talia starts to point at the spot just inside the door.

It's empty.

The bag is gone.

CHAPTER
SEVENTY-ONE

December 13, 2000

Talia's mother has a boyfriend. Oliver is rich, divorced, retired, and lives in Florida most of the year. But he has a summer house in the Catskills. He and Natalie got together in August, right after Talia left for school.

He flew Natalie to Boca for Thanksgiving to meet his children and grandchildren. Talia was invited too, but she chose instead to spend the holiday in New Jersey with her roommate Mei-Xing and her family.

Now, on her first night home in Mulberry Bay for Christmas break, her mother is at a country club gala with Oliver, whom Talia assumed would be spending Christmas and New Year's with his own family like a normal father and grandfather. But Mommy said he missed her too much, so he's here, and they'll be celebrating the holiday with him.

Just the three of them, which she supposes is better than having to meet his huge family. Then again, that might be preferable to feeling like a third wheel.

Either way, she has a feeling this Christmas is going to suck. If only she could go back in time so that she could crash Midge's merry household, or Kelly's family's elegant open house.

Or even further back in time, to when Caroline was right next door.

The Winterfield house is dark. No plastic crèche on the lawn, no garland on the railings, and the place looks deserted.

"They're visiting the twins and the Jims and the grandkids," Mommy said, wearing a fancy red dress and leaning into the bathroom mirror to curl her eyelashes. "Down in Tennessee, maybe? Or Kentucky? I guess it was too hard for them to be here over the holidays after . . . what happened."

"Yeah. It's hard for everyone."

Alone in the apartment, Talia wanders into the living room—dark and stark, still without a tree or decorations. Mommy promised they'll do it all tomorrow—then remembered she has to work a double shift to make up for being off tonight.

Talia glances out the window at the Winterfield house, missing Caroline desperately.

Missing the others, all of them. T-I-C-K . . .

She wonders whether the four-way friendship would have fractured if Caroline were still around.

Maybe—

She frowns and leans closer to the window.

Someone is inside the house next door, moving through the first floor with a flashlight.

Talia is out of the apartment and down the stairs like a shot, cutting across the yard to the Winterfields' back door. She finds it unlocked and pushes it open a crack before stopping to consider that it might not be Caroline. It might be a prowler . . . an armed prowler.

She starts to pull the door closed again, but it's too late.

Whoever's in the house is right there in the kitchen, and the flashlight beam catches and blinds her, and she's certain she's about to die.

Then she hears a familiar voice. "Talia?"

CHAPTER SEVENTY-TWO

Present Day

The deafening sound of those excavators must have drowned out the gunshot, because no one comes running out from the site to investigate.

Yes, it was spectacularly stupid, shooting someone in broad daylight. But for Ceto, it was also cathartic, like plunging into a refreshing pool after a hot, tense afternoon. She allows herself to bask in the exhilaration for a few moments, floating on a tide of relief.

Then the heated fury simmers once more, because it wasn't enough. It wasn't one of them . . . the three women she came to find. No, just some old geezer who got in her way.

She steps back to study her handiwork.

The tire swing is still moving, gently rocking its macabre, bloody burden, propped against the chains. His mouth is gaping in a silent scream, and his eyes are wide and fixed on her.

She turns away, thinking again of the women, wondering what they thought of the gifts she left for them, whether they've compared notes yet. Whether they've figured out the meaning.

Two—code two.

Spades, well . . .

Spades are shovels. Shovels dig.

Up at the pool, enormous shovels are digging into the ground, right where, as girls, they abandoned their friend that night.

It's time they acknowledge what they did.

It's time they're punished for their sins, like Gordon Klatte.

Back at the old picnic pavilion, Ceto moves two large stones at the old fireplace.

The bag is still there, right where she stashed it.

The phone is still inside.

She presses a button and waits for it to power up.

CHAPTER SEVENTY-THREE

"Something strange is happening here . . ."

Kelly's words have been ringing in Midge's brain as she drives back to Haven Cliff from the Klatte home, where something strange is also happening.

It seems something strange is happening everywhere today, and her instincts are telling her that it's all connected.

The drive takes only a few minutes.

Parking in front of the portico, she spots Kelly on the steps, talking animatedly to a stranger.

Attractive, middle aged, brunette, sunglasses . . .

A stranger, yet familiar.

The woman turns, spotting her as she gets out of the car.

"Midge! Is that you?"

That voice . . .

"Talia!"

They hug, and it's awkward and then it isn't. Talia shoves her sunglasses up over her forehead, and Midge can see those green eyes, and the decades fall away.

"Midge," Kelly says, "I'm sorry I dragged you over here. I know you were on a case. But something's going on, and you need to know."

She quickly tells Midge that there's an unfamiliar car parked just off the lane approaching the house.

"It's an old Hyundai, pretty beat up. We just checked and it's gone now, but I got a picture of it earlier—make, model, license plate. The work crew said it doesn't belong to anyone on the job now. Normally, I'd think it was hikers who didn't know this was private property, but it looks like someone tried to hide it."

"Maybe it was hikers who know it's private property," Midge suggests.

Kelly frowns. "Maybe, but I keep thinking about the person who was here earlier and delivered that envelope—"

"The playing card," Midge says. "Someone left one at the police station for me, but—"

"Wait, a playing card? Was it a two of spades?" Talia asks.

"You got one too?"

"It was left for me at the Landing, in an envelope with my name on it," she tells Midge. "I was going to show you guys, but I had it in my bag, and . . ." She looks at Kelly.

"Someone stole Talia's bag from inside the house," Kelly tells Midge. "She left it by the door. We've looked everywhere. It's gone."

"Not someone," Talia says. "It has to be Caroline. No one else would—"

"Wait." Midge puts a finger to her lips, looking around. "Let's go inside and talk privately."

CHAPTER SEVENTY-FOUR

June 5, 1999

Slipping into her room at dawn, Talia sits on the window seat to take off the heeled sandals she borrowed from her mother. They're a half size too small, and her feet are killing her.

Other than that, it was a perfect evening. She and Paul went to the mall to find him a bow tie and cummerbund that would match Talia's prom dress. Then they ate dinner at the Ground Round, went to a late showing of the new Julia Roberts romantic comedy, *Notting Hill*, and drove up to Overlook Mountain to look at the stars.

Talia presses her forehead to the window and gazes at the night sky, thinking about their date and wishing she didn't have to be up in a few hours to work the breakfast shift at the Landing. Business has been slow lately, but Sunday mornings always bring a church crowd—mostly old people who order toast and coffee, ask for extra jelly packets and pocket them, and then tip her in small change.

With luck, she'll be finished in time to meet Kelly at Midge's softball game. She's pitching, and they're planning to cheer her on. Caroline can't go, of course, because her Sundays are encompassed by church.

But she probably wouldn't have gone anyway. She's been lying low lately, even more so than usual. Talia and the others no longer even see her at school, now that the regular schedule has given way to the final exam schedule.

Glancing next door, Talia is startled to see a figure stealing through the shadows along the side of the Winterfields' house.

A prowler?

No—it's Caroline.

What in the world is she doing?

Sneaking out, it seems . . . although she's barefoot, wearing a white nightgown, and heading for the backyard.

Caroline stops at the small concrete pad where the garbage cans are waiting to be dragged to the curb for pickup. She lifts the lid on one and stashes something inside. *Way* inside, bending over to shove it down.

CHAPTER SEVENTY-FIVE

Present Day

Satisfied there are no intruders in the house, Midge returns to the library, where Talia and Kelly are waiting.

"All clear?" Kelly asks.

"All clear. Whoever stole the bag must have grabbed it and taken off. But I sent the car's license plate number to be traced." Midge closes the doors behind her and settles in a chair beneath a painting of Asa Winterfield, scowling as usual. She scowls back, asking, "Why do you people never smile?"

"Maybe he doesn't want anyone sitting in his seat." Kelly points to a framed photo that shows Asa, sitting in the same chair, positioned in the same spot in the room. Beside it, there's a photo of his wife in the carved wooden rocker Talia now occupies.

"I hope Edith doesn't mind that I'm in hers," Talia says. "Not that I believe in ghosts, although living in this place, I might. Do you?"

Kelly hesitates before answering. It isn't like her.

"Maybe I do, sometimes," she says, wincing as she sits down again on the settee.

"Are you okay?" Talia asks.

"I'm just tired and achy. Stiff knees. We're getting old, guys."

"How's the headache?" Midge asks.

"Same as always. It won't quit."

Talia says, "Uh-oh. Stiff knees, headache, tired . . . that sounds like Lyme disease."

"I don't have a bull's-eye rash."

"Not everyone does," Talia tells Kelly. "Or maybe you did, but you missed it. That's what happened to my friend Mei-Xing last year."

"Mei-Xing . . . wasn't she your college roommate?"

Talia turns to Midge. "She was! How'd you know?"

"You used to mention her a *lot*."

"And here I thought you guys were tuning me out."

"I'm so sorry," Kelly says. "I did a lot of not-so-nice things back then. I'm not that person anymore."

"None of us are who we used to be," Midge says. "And we all have things to apologize for."

Talia nods. "Especially me. But you should get checked for Lyme, Kelly. Mei-Xing had stiff knees and a bad headache too, and all these other crazy symptoms."

"Crazy . . . like what?" Kelly asks.

Talia ticks them off on her fingers. "Fevers, fatigue, forgetfulness, insomnia. And some neurological issues like seeing things, hearing things . . . She thought she was going crazy."

"So did I, or . . ." Kelly shakes her head. "I thought it might be something . . . hereditary."

"Where there are deer, there's Lyme," Talia says. "A tick can be lethal. Mei-Xing is fine now, but she was late stage by the time they diagnosed it. You need to get tested, Kelly."

"You do. You haven't felt good for a while. It can't wait." Midge pulls up a number on her phone, presses send, and hands the phone to Kelly. "Here. Tell them you need lab work."

"You have Kelly's doctor programmed into your phone?" Talia asks.

"She's everyone's doctor," Midge says. "And when you have elderly parents living with you, you've got her on speed dial."

Kelly gets through to a receptionist, who transfers her to the nurse, whose voicemail picks up. She leaves a message, disconnects the call, and hands the phone back to Midge. "There. Satisfied?"

"I will be when they call you back."

"Which will be next week. It's a Friday, and this isn't an emergency."

Midge rolls her eyes. "So, getting back to those playing cards Caroline left for us . . ."

"What makes you think it was her?" Kelly asks.

"Who else would it be?"

"Midge is right," Talia says. "On the first anniversary, she let us know she was okay, just like she promised. Today is the anniversary, and I think she's letting us know she's in some kind of trouble. Two of spades. Code two."

Midge nods, digesting this, thinking of Gordy. "Talia, do you remember our charm bracelets?"

"How could I forget? T-I-C-K forever, right?" Talia reaches into her pocket and produces hers. "The clasp is broken, so I can't really wear it, but it felt right to bring it this weekend, for old times' sake."

Ah, two down, two to go.

Midge turns to Kelly. "I have mine too. What about yours?"

"I'm sure it's somewhere."

Again, Midge thinks of Gordy. Of the wooden railing on that stairway. Of the bracelet in his hand, and the splinter in Kelly's.

"Did you look for it?" Midge asks her. "At your mother's? Like I asked you?"

"It wasn't there."

"Are you sure about that?"

"Pretty sure, but I was mostly worried about finding the Annie Oakley revolver, so . . ."

Sensing Kelly's unease, Midge fixes her with a gaze she usually reserves for suspects. Which Kelly isn't, she reminds herself. "Did that turn up?"

"Not yet."

"Uh-oh. What happened to the Annie Oakley revolver?" Talia asks.

"It's misplaced. Why do you keep looking at me like that, Midge?"

"Like what?"

"Like you're thinking . . . something. About me."

Midge forces herself to glance at Kelly's injured thumb. Forces herself to remember Gordy's devastated son, who believes his father had something to hide; that there was another woman.

She doesn't doubt that someone was texting Gordy to meet outside last night.

She just isn't so sure it was Caroline.

"I am thinking something about you, Kelly," she says. "I think you're lying about your charm bracelet."

CHAPTER SEVENTY-SIX

June 11, 1999

An hour after they've taken the last high school final exam of their lives, Midge, Kelly, and Talia are at Haven Cliff.

Caroline summoned the three of them here to break what she said is some intensely personal and private news. Kelly offered to pick her up, but she was riding her bike over, saying that no one can know they're even meeting her this morning.

Kelly pulls into their usual spot, by the mock orange grove. The morning is gray and cool. It isn't raining, and there's none in the forecast, but she presses the button to put up the convertible top. She learned the hard way always to do that, having left it open one clear May night and finding it full of snow the next morning.

"What do you think she wants to tell us?" Midge asks as they start walking up the trail toward their spot.

"I'll bet it's about Mary Beth," Kelly says.

"Why?"

"*Why?* Because she's been gone for two years, Midge! That's why."

"Caroline said she's—"

"I know what Caroline *said*, but . . . I don't know. I feel like there's a lot more to it."

"Like what?"

"I don't know. There must be some reason she never wants to talk about her sister. Maybe she's finally ready to tell us what's going on with her."

"Kelly, we're here to listen to whatever she wants to say to us, not push her to discuss the things she doesn't want to," Talia cuts in.

"Anyway, I don't think this is about Mary Beth," Midge says. "I think it's about Caroline. Maybe she broke up with Gordy."

Kelly brightens. "You think?"

Talia shakes her head. "That's not it."

"How do you know?"

"Because they're going to prom. No one would break up this close to prom."

She's probably right about that, Kelly thinks as they follow the trail. It's cool and peaceful here, hushed except for their footsteps and the birds singing overhead.

Caroline loves this place. That's why she suggested Robert Frost for their sophomore honors English project.

"Some of his poems feel like they were written about Haven Cliff, K. K.," she'd said, two years and a lifetime ago. "About our woods . . . 'lovely, dark and deep.'"

Things were so different back then. Caroline was different. Happier, more innocent. Mary Beth was still in her life, and Gordy was not.

Which of those things—Mary Beth's departure, or Gordy's arrival—triggered the change?

Maybe both. Maybe neither.

Maybe it just happens . . . young women grow up, friends grow apart.

It's June, after all. Their school days, and their intertwined lives in Mulberry Bay, are coming to an end. Nothing Caroline is about to tell them can change that.

Maybe Kelly shouldn't be trying to hold on to something—someone—that will soon be part of the past anyway.

Not just Caroline.

Midge and Talia too. All of them.

T-I-C-K . . .

Maybe they were young and naive, believing anything is forever.

CHAPTER SEVENTY-SEVEN

Present Day

Kelly opens her mouth to protest Midge's assumption that she's lying about the bracelet—which, itself, would be a lie.

Midge is right.

Kelly shakes her head. "You're good, Detective Sergeant Kennedy."

"I know how to read people. Especially you. What's going on with your bracelet?"

"I don't have it. It's long gone. I was so angry with you that last summer . . ." She turns to Talia. "And with you too."

"*Me?* Why?"

"Because you just took off, like Caroline."

"I went to college!"

"But you never came back. You never looked back. It's like you wanted to forget everything about Mulberry Bay. Including me."

"I did," Talia says softly. "I'm sorry."

"You did the same thing yourself, Kelly," Midge points out. "You left too."

"Yes. But I'm back now, and I'm staying forever, and we're friends again. Isn't that all that matters?"

"Right now, the bracelet matters. If yours is gone, where is it?"

She takes a deep breath. "It's in the bottom of the lake, Midge. After you arrested Tad, I tied it to the biggest rock I could lift, and I threw it off his boat."

She waits for a reaction.

It isn't the indignant one she expects.

Midge grins. "That's so *you*, Kelly."

Relieved, she nods. "It *was* me. Not anymore. If I were smart back then, I would have thrown him overboard with the rock too."

"Wait, who's Tad?" Talia asks.

"My first ex-husband."

"Your *first*. Wow, we've got a lot of catching up to do."

"We'll have time," Midge says. "But right now, we need to focus on Caroline."

"We do," Talia agrees. "And I need to tell you both the real reason she was running away."

Kelly frowns. "It wasn't to get away from her parents and Gordy?"

"That was part of it, but there was more. A lot more. One night, I—"

She breaks off as Kelly's phone rings.

"Ignore it," Kelly says.

Midge shakes her head. "No, pick it up. It might be the doctor."

Kelly looks at the screen, not recognizing the number. "I don't think it's the doctor. It would say 'medical center.'"

"Just answer it!" Talia says.

With a sigh, she does.

A male voice explodes on the other end, so loud she holds the phone away from her ear.

"Kelly! Where are you?"

"Who is this?"

"It's Raoul."

"Who?"

"Raoul, with Aquascapes."

Raoul. Aquascapes . . . Why is he shouting at her?

"Where are you?" he asks again.

"I'm home. Why?"

"And you don't know?"

"Know what?"

"Listen, I'm on my way. My crew is out there. They called me, and . . . just meet me out by the pool, okay? I'll be there in about five minutes."

"I'm in the middle of something right now. I can't just . . . whatever it is, can you please handle it? Right now, that pool is the least of my worries."

"It isn't about—I can't—it's . . . look, my excavation guys found something. They called me right away, and I thought I'd better get ahold of you, before I call the police, but—"

"The police! What? Why would you—"

"It's bones. Someone was—"

"Bones! An animal . . ."

"No. Human bones. Buried in your pool."

CHAPTER
SEVENTY-EIGHT

June 11, 1999

Caroline is waiting for them in the swimming pool clearing, sitting on her stone pedestal, reading a book, her bike propped against the base.

She waves when she sees them.

"She's nervous," Midge says.

Kelly squints at her. "How can you tell from here?"

"Because she closed that book without keeping her place."

"That doesn't mean—"

"Yes, it does. You need to pay attention to details, Kelly. If she were actually reading it, she would have—"

"It's that Harry Potter book. She's probably read it a million times. She doesn't need to keep her place."

"You guys, stop!" Talia hisses. "Why are you always bickering?"

"We're not bickering," Kelly tells her. "We're discussing."

"Well, let's discuss with Caroline."

When they get closer, Kelly gets a good look at Caroline's face and can see that she's been crying. Her heart sinks.

"Thanks for coming, guys. I just . . . I've got something to tell you." She climbs off her statue.

Talia reaches out and lays a reassuring hand on her forearm. "It's okay, Car'. Whatever it is, you can trust us."

"Do you promise you won't tell anyone? Not even your parents?"

They look at each other and nod.

"Not now, and not ever. You have to swear to God . . . or, no, swear on your lives," Caroline amends, with a glance at Kelly, who frequently professes that she doesn't believe in God.

Mostly, she just does it to get a rise out of Caroline, for which she now feels guilty.

"I promise, and I swear to God, and I swear on my life," Kelly assures her.

Midge and Talia do the same.

"Thank you. I . . . I just can't take this anymore." Caroline pauses, biting her lip and avoiding eye contact.

"What can't you take?" Midge asks.

"My parents, the way they are, and Gordy, the way he is . . . and all these plans . . . You guys were right. My whole future has been mapped out for me. I feel like I don't have a say in anything."

"Because you *don't*," Kelly says. "They're controlling you. And you're letting them. You—"

"I know! I get it now. So . . . not anymore. It's going to stop. I'm going to stop it."

"Good for you!" Midge gives her a thumbs-up. "It's time to start standing up to them."

"That's not what I mean. I have to go."

"Go where?" Talia asks her, wide eyed.

"Away. That's all I can share."

"With Gordy?"

"No! Gordy's one of the reasons I'm leaving."

"So, wait, you're . . . what? Running away? All alone?"

"Not exactly. Not alone. Someone is helping me, but I can't say who. And I'm not running away. Remember what you said about Princess Diana, K. K.?"

"That she should never have married Charles in the first place. She would have been way better off if she'd—"

"No! I mean the night she was killed in that car crash!"

"Oh . . ." Kelly frowns, thinking back. "What did I say?"

"That she was more of a prisoner than a princess. And what if she faked her death so that she could go live her life in peace and privacy?"

Kelly nods. "I mean, I don't think that anymore, because someone probably would have seen her by now, you know?"

"What does this have to do with anything?" Midge asks.

"It's what I have to do."

"You're going to . . . what? Fake your death?"

"I'm going to go away. On prom night. It's my only chance. My parents gave me permission to stay out late because I'll be with Gordy. By the time anyone figures out I'm gone, I'll be far enough away that no one will ever find me."

There are tears in Caroline's eyes, but Kelly senses her conviction. Her shoulders are squared, and even her voice sounds different. It isn't as high pitched and girlish, somehow. It's almost as if she's putting on some kind of act now, wanting them to believe she's strong and brave . . .

Or maybe she *is* strong and brave. Maybe she's been suppressing who she really is, allowing the people who want to control her to believe they can push her around. Maybe she's had the upper hand all along, tamping down her determination and even suppressing her natural voice.

"But where are you going?" Midge asks. "Do you have money?"

"Some. I've been babysitting for years, and it's not like I've spent any of my earnings."

"But how long can you live on babysitting money?"

"I've got a plan. The less you guys know, the better. People are going to ask you, and you won't be lying when you say you have no idea where I am. I wasn't going to tell you any of this, but then I realized . . . you three are the only ones I'm leaving behind who really matter to me.

You've never hurt me, or tried to control me, and I can't let you think I'm dead."

"You're going to disappear forever?" Talia's question is a wail.

"Not forever. I'll come back someday, when my life is my own. I promise."

"But how will we know nothing horrible happened to you out there?"

"Because it won't, Tally. I'll be okay."

"No," Midge says. "No way. You have to let us know. That's the only way I'm going to agree to this. You have to call us or write to us."

"I can't call or write, Midge. That would leave a trace. Someone might find me."

"You're not a fugitive, running for your life." She hesitates, peering at Caroline. "Are you?"

"Not the way you think, but . . ."

"Then we need to set up a secret meeting," Kelly suggests. "So that we can make sure you're okay. Before the summer's over and I have to leave for Dartmouth."

"No. That's too soon."

"Then when? Winter break?"

"No," Talia says quickly. "What if there's a blizzard or something on the day we're supposed to meet?"

"Well, you and I will both be away at school until next spring, so . . . how about exactly one year from prom night?" Kelly suggests. "We meet right here."

"What if someone sees me around town?" Caroline asks.

"They won't if we meet at midnight."

"I don't know . . ."

"If you can't promise us, we can't promise you," Kelly says. "It's only fair."

"You said you didn't want us to believe you're dead, but that's exactly what we're going to think if you just take off and we never hear from you again." Talia wipes tears from her eyes. "We're going to wonder for the rest of our lives what ever happened to you."

"Not only that, but we're going to look for you," Midge puts in. "And I'm going to be a detective, so, you know, I'll hunt you down no matter where you're hiding."

Caroline smiles through her own tears. "I'm not hiding. I'm just . . . going away."

"Right," Talia says. "You're going away, and then you're coming back to see us. A promise for a promise. Got it?"

"Got it."

"Do you swear to God?" Kelly asks, knowing that Caroline, of all people, would never do that without meaning it.

Caroline hesitates, then nods. "Yes. I'll meet you guys in this exact spot exactly one year after I leave. I swear to God."

CHAPTER SEVENTY-NINE

Present Day

Asa Winterfield had built Haven Cliff on an old burial ground, if you believe local lore. It's the reason Haven Cliff is cursed, if you believe in curses.

Talia reminds herself of this as she follows Midge and Kelly in grim silence out to the pool site. If human remains have been unearthed, they're likely ancient.

With the machinery silenced, everything seems preternaturally hushed. Insects hum, birds chirp, trees rustle. The air is thick with blooming mock orange.

They reach the clearing.

Talia's eye falls on the spot where there had once been a heap of bricks. There's a colonnade now, with an archway above each pedestal.

Poseidon, Oceanus, Hydros, Ceto.

Kelly, Talia, Midge, and Caroline.

They'd perch on those stone slabs for hours, legs dangling, sorting out their problems, and the world's.

Now the sky is blue, the sun is shining, and the air is infused with dense floral perfume, and it's as if she's stepped through a portal to another June afternoon.

When Caroline summoned them here that day, saying she had big news to share, Talia was so sure she knew what was coming.

She was wrong.

Reaching the clearing, she sees the backhoe, the yawning hole in the ground surrounded by heaps of dirt, the workers standing around it like mourners at a grave.

A man in a hard hat spots them as they walk toward the edge of the pit.

Midge, so official in her uniform, shows her badge. "I understand you found . . ."

"A skeleton. Yeah. You want to take a look?"

Midge nods, turning to Kelly and Talia. "I'll look. You don't have to—"

"I need to see," Kelly says, moving to the edge.

Talia shakes her head, but her legs carry her forward. Her heart is pounding, even though whatever is down there—ancient human remains—has nothing to do with her.

The last time she was out here, they came to meet Caroline on the one-year anniversary of her disappearance.

June 15, 2000.

That night too, heavy machinery was parked at the pool's perimeter. They were scheduled to begin filling it in first thing the next morning.

Talia looks into the pit. Chunks of white plaster are scattered across the dirt. A limb, a head—one of the missing statues.

Maybe it's Ceto, the primordial sea goddess. Caroline's statue.

Dread slips over her.

There's something else, poking out of the earth.

Something pink, and plastic, and she recognizes it, even all these years later.

She looks again at the white shards.

Those aren't broken pieces of what was once a statue.

A leg bone . . . a skull . . .

It's a skeleton.

CHAPTER EIGHTY

June 15, 2000

It's past midnight and the rain is falling in earnest when they reach the end of the overgrown path from the mock orange grove.

Midge is in the lead, her flashlight trained on the terrain to guide them along.

Kelly is behind her, picking her way over uneven ground in heeled shoes more suitable for dancing than hiking.

Talia brings up the rear. Her legs are limp, her heart is racing, and so is her mind. Now that Caroline is back, she needs to stay.

She doesn't have to return to her parents' house. They're not even around. Both of the twins and their husbands moved away, and Natalie told Talia that the Winterfields are spending the summer with them, thinking of moving too.

"I guess I can't really blame them," she said. "There's nothing holding them here anymore. I'm sure they want to spend time with their grandchildren. Eve's little boy is a toddler now, and she's pregnant with her second. Joanna has a baby girl."

"That's nice," Talia murmured, thinking of Caroline.

"This is it, you guys," Midge says, and the beam shifts to illuminate the large clearing.

"Caroline?" Kelly calls. "Where are you?"

Midge sweeps the light from the weedy field to the rusty posts that once held the tennis net, to a row of crumbling brick pillars and rubble, to construction equipment poised alongside a yawning rectangular hole in the ground that was once a pool.

Talia expects to see Caroline sitting on her stone pedestal, waiting for them.

She isn't there.

It's empty.

They walk slowly toward it.

"Caroline!" Talia calls in a choked voice.

"You promised you'd be here!" Kelly yells. "What the hell?"

"She promised us, *and* she swore to God," Midge says. "She must be coming. She'd never break a vow to God."

Wouldn't she?

Talia thinks of the purity ball and how Caroline vowed to keep her virginity until her wedding night.

They walk slowly toward the pedestals, Midge and Kelly still calling her name, still looking for her as the flashlight sweeps the surrounding woods, still believing that she's going to be here, still believing in her, in this friendship.

T-I-C-K forever.

Yeah, right.

Talia takes a deep breath. She has to tell Midge and Kelly what really—

"Look!" Midge focuses her beam like a spotlight.

"Look at what?" Kelly asks, and then: "Oh!"

Talia sees it too.

Four coins—pennies—lying on the block of stone etched CETO. Caroline's stone.

"It looks like someone was sitting there," Talia says slowly, "and loose change fell out of their pocket. That's all it is."

"No, it isn't. Look at how they're arranged. Neatly, in a row. Someone deliberately put them there. *Caroline* put them there."

Kelly shakes her head. "How do we know that? It could have been anyone."

"No, it was her!" Midge insists. "Four pennies. Not two. *Four*. Don't you see?"

Talia frowns, and then it hits her.

"Code four!"

"Exactly. She was here, just like she promised. She's letting us know she's okay."

CHAPTER EIGHTY-ONE

Present Day

Midge stares into the depths of the hole.

There are bones.

There is something else.

Something pink and plastic. Something that makes no sense, unless . . .

Unless.

But no, the remains can't be Caroline's, because Caroline didn't die that night.

She was alive one year later, alive at Haven Cliff, leaving them a sign that she was okay, just as she promised.

Caroline is alive now, in Mulberry Bay, texting Gordy . . .

Gordy.

Caroline was with Gordy last night, and now Gordy is dead, and what if Caroline is dead too?

What if—

But no, even if something had happened to her since last night, she'd be a corpse like Gordy, not a skeleton.

Midge turns to Raoul, the site manager. "I'm going to need to clear the area. You can leave the equipment, but everyone has to go."

He nods, not questioning her, and turns to the crew.

Midge faces Talia and Kelly, hoping they didn't see it—the telltale pink plastic there with the remains.

But they're wide eyed, both of them, and she knows that they saw it. Knows that they're thinking what she's thinking.

"You should go back to the house," Midge says.

Kelly shakes her head. "This is my property. I need to be here."

"This is *my* jurisdiction, and these are human remains; it's my job to investigate."

Her *job*. There's no room for emotion now.

"Sergeant Kennedy?"

She turns back to Raoul. The crew is scattering.

He asks, "Do you need me here?"

"No, you can go too. I'll be in touch when you can get back to work, but . . ." She shakes her head. "I have to file a report and get the ME over here. The investigation is going to take some time."

He looks at Kelly. "I promised you a pool by the Fourth of July."

She emits a choked laugh. "It's okay."

Raoul walks away, leaving the three of them alone together to stare into the pit.

"Midge." Talia touches her arm. "I know what you're thinking, but it isn't her. Down there . . . that's not Caroline."

"Talia, no one wants to accept this, but—"

"It isn't Caroline! It's not like she was one of those teenage girls you hear about on *Dateline* or some true crime podcast. We all knew she was running away that night."

"Maybe she was *planning* to run away and something happened to her."

"Like what?" Kelly asks. "Like she just happened to be abducted, and murdered, within a few minutes of walking away from us? That's way too big a coincidence."

It is, Midge knows.

Just like Gordy's death, today.

"Do you know how stupid we all were, running around Haven Cliff in the dark?" she asks Talia and Kelly. "Cliffs, bears and bobcats, the lake, and that pool . . . it was an accident waiting to happen. And I think . . ." She pauses, taking a deep, shaky breath. "I think Caroline might have fallen in somehow."

"She didn't. They searched for her after she disappeared."

"I know they did. But they were focused on the lake. She went toward the lake. Everyone thought she'd drowned *in* the lake. They could easily have missed her."

"Okay, that's true. But how could they have not noticed a corpse when they filled it in a year later?"

Midge shrugs. It isn't likely.

But her friends are in denial. She needs to make them see.

"The Walkman is there, Kelly. Your pink Walkman. You gave it to her that night."

"I know, but she was alive a year later. She let us know she was okay. Code four, remember?"

Of course she remembers.

On the first anniversary of Caroline's disappearance, they expected to find Caroline waiting for them in the woods. Instead, they found four pennies, neatly lined up on her pedestal, the one marked Ceto.

Midge shakes her head. "What if someone else left them there?"

"Who would have known about it?" Kelly asks.

"She might have told Gordy. Or he could have overheard us talking about it. Or someone else did—some random person who thought it would be a good prank."

"That's sick and twisted."

Midge shrugs. "People can be cruel, Kelly."

"No," Talia says. "It was Caroline. She was alive then, and she's alive now."

"We all want to think that," Kelly says, "but—"

"I don't *think* it. I *know* it. I was about to tell you guys, but then this happened . . ." Talia waves a hand at the hole in the ground. "I've been in touch with her, and she's alive."

"You've seen her?" Midge asks.

"I haven't seen her, but we've been texting."

Midge thinks of Gordy, who was getting texts from Caroline.

Or . . .

From someone who claimed to be Caroline.

"I stopped at her parents' house this morning," Talia tells them. "They're away, but I think I saw Caroline looking out the window of her old bedroom."

"You *think* you saw her?" Midge asks. "You're not sure?"

"I'm pretty sure."

"Well, I know for a fact that she's here," Kelly says. "I have proof. Come on back to the house and I'll show you."

CHAPTER EIGHTY-TWO

June 15, 1999

As always, there's a fire in the stone fireplace, coolers full of beer and booze, music blasting from a boom box.

But tonight, everyone is in formal wear, straight from the prom.

Kelly's gown is slinky and black, with spaghetti straps. Her date was the star baseball pitcher from Mulberry Bay's archrival high school team. His prowess cost the Wildcats the state championships. That was fine with Kelly, always more of a rebel than the rah-rah type.

Not Midge. She's here with Mulberry Bay's star shortstop. They're both wearing the school colors—her dress is maroon, and so is his bowtie, with a white tux.

Talia's green gown matches her eyes. She's head over heels in love with her boyfriend, Paul. He's in the school band with her and is equally gorgeous.

The weather is exceptionally warm and sticky for June, just as the forecast predicted, cooperating with the plan Caroline laid out for them.

Quite a few people brought swimsuits along and are down on the beach. Midge and Talia encourage their dates to go, promising to meet them soon for a swim.

"Are you sure?" Paul asks Talia. "I thought you hate swimming in the lake, especially at night."

"It's prom night!" she says.

"Yeah, it's tradition," Kelly says.

"Is it?" Paul asks.

"Definitely. We just need a few minutes to, uh, you know . . . talk about what everyone wore to the prom," says Midge, who wouldn't know a potato sack from a Vera Wang.

Seeing her date furrow his brows, Kelly says, "Unless you guys love Joan Rivers on the red-carpet fashion as much as we do?"

They do not, and beat a hasty retreat.

In the weeks leading up to tonight, the prom and this party have been all the four girls have talked about.

Then Caroline told them her plans, and everything, from that moment on, has been about her. They're preparing to say goodbye. Yes, it was coming anyway. But not this soon. And she's not going off to college. She's going . . .

God knows where. And they won't see her for a whole year.

She's wearing a white gown, looking ethereal in the firelight with layers of tulle floating around her.

Gordy, in a rented black tuxedo, seems to be sticking closer to Caroline than usual. Maybe he's being extra possessive because there are so many other guys around. Maybe he's paranoid because they both told their parents they were attending the school-sanctioned after-hours pancake breakfast at the gym.

Or maybe he senses that something is going on.

"Do you think he knows?" Kelly whispers to Midge and Talia as they settle on a bench by the fire.

"No way. She made us swear on our lives not to tell anyone, including him, so why would she?"

"Maybe she didn't tell him. Maybe he was spying on her, or eavesdropping, or . . . I don't know. For all we know, he has her bugged."

Midge rolls her eyes. "Oh, come on, Kelly. He's not James Bond!"

"But look at the way he's Velcroed to her."

"He's *always* Velcroed to her."

"But especially tonight." Kelly tilts her head to indicate Gordy and Caroline, standing off to one side, separate from everyone else.

They aren't talking to each other, or even looking at each other. They're just staring into the crackling fire, which is as forbidden as everything else going on here tonight.

"I think it's time." Kelly makes a move to get up, but Talia grabs her arm.

"Wait! Not yet!"

"We said we'd help her do this," Midge says gently. "There's no reason to prolong it. We need to let her go."

"I know, but . . ."

"We have to," Midge tells Talia. "It's time to put Kelly's famous superpower to good use."

Kelly stands, bats her eyelashes at them, and walks toward the cooler.

She's always been able to talk any guy into just about anything. Or out of anything. Like tonight, she convinced her own date not to attend the after-party. He was already worried that some of the baseball guys might try to gang up on him, so she didn't have to push too hard.

This next feat is far more daunting.

She grabs a couple of beers and makes her way over to Caroline and Gordy.

"Hi, guys. Isn't this a blast?" Kelly asks. "Aren't you glad you came?"

"Definitely!" Gordy says.

Caroline nods, her smile tight, looking as though she can't find her voice.

Kelly's own sounds a little hoarse as she asks if either of them wants a beer.

"We don't drink," Gordy tells her.

"But it's prom night."

"So?"

"Hey, Caroline, can you come here for a second?" Midge calls from the bench.

"Be right there!"

Caroline looks again at Kelly, who longs to throw her arms around her and tell her she's doing the right thing.

"I'll be back in a second," she tells Gordy, who starts to follow her. "Stay here, okay?"

"But—"

"Hey, Gordy? I need to tell you something," Kelly says.

Wary, he asks, "What?"

She laughs, hoping it doesn't sound forced. "Don't worry. I just wanted to say that I'm really glad you decided to let Caroline come tonight."

"What do you mean?"

"Just . . . you guys miss all the parties. I'm glad you let her come to this one."

"Why do you keep saying 'let her'?"

"Oh, do I?" She shrugs. "I guess those were her words. We were talking about all the stuff she wasn't allowed to do and how she was so excited about tonight. I don't suppose she . . ." She lets that hang in the air for a second. "Never mind."

"You don't suppose she what?"

"Nothing, just . . . she probably didn't mention the champagne, huh?"

"What champagne?"

"She bought a special bottle for the two of you to have tonight."

"How would she do that? She's not twenty-one."

"Oh, Gordy." Kelly pats his arm. "See? I knew I shouldn't have said anything. Wait, where are you going?" She tightens her grip as he starts toward Caroline.

"I need to ask her about this, because . . ."

"Wait, Gordy, don't. It'll only make her more upset."

"She's upset?"

"Lately? Yes. Doesn't she seem like it?"

He considers that and nods. "Yeah. But what's she upset about?"

"I think it's all getting to her. Graduation, and college coming up so fast. Everyone's a little wistful right now about all the things they wish they'd done. Even me." Not true, but Gordy seems to be buying it. "What do *you* regret?"

"Me? I don't—"

"Oh, come on, Gordy. You can't tell me that you haven't wondered what it would be like not to play it so safe all the time."

"I don't play it safe. I just follow the rules. And the laws," he adds pointedly.

"Not always."

"Yes. Always."

"You're here, aren't you? You lied to your parents about where you are. And you ignored the No Trespassing signs. So, see? You broke the law, and it's not so bad, is it?"

He scowls.

"Now, where were we? Oh! I know you love Caroline. That's why I'm so glad you let her come tonight and—"

"Cut it out, Kelly. I'm not some . . . some . . ."

"Want a beer?" she asks, popping the top off the second bottle and holding it out to him.

"No! I'm just—"

"You're just saying you're not a saint, and you like to have a good time. Right."

"No! That's not—" As he gestures helplessly with his hand, she puts a beer into it.

She taps the bottle with her own and says, "Cheers, Gordy. Let's party like it's 1999."

"It *is* 1999."

"All the more reason."

He looks at the beer. Then he takes a cautious sip.

"Whoa!" Kelly says. "Guess they were wrong about you."

"Who was wrong?"

"Everyone. They're always saying you're not cool, but you are."

"Drinking isn't cool, Kelly."

"That's not what I mean. But it's prom night. Everyone is loosening up. Even Caroline, see?"

He follows her gaze, seeing the bottle in her hand. "That's water."

"Vodka."

"It is not."

It isn't, but he doesn't seem so sure.

"Bottoms up, Gordy."

She isn't proud of it. She's only doing it for Caroline's sake.

Okay, maybe there's also a tiny part of her that resents all that righteousness of his.

All right, it isn't a *tiny* part of her. It's been building for a long time. For Kelly, it hasn't been easy, or much fun, to be around someone who wears virtue like a badge of honor.

Gordy is just . . .

He's too damned good for his own good.

Caroline, by contrast, is just . . . *good*. For all her moral fortitude, she never seems to judge Kelly. Not like Gordy does.

That isn't Kelly's only problem with him.

If Gordy hadn't barged into Caroline's life, she wouldn't find it necessary to disappear from Kelly's. From all their lives.

So, yes. Tonight, she wants to see him falter. Fall.

"By the way," she says, "have you heard anything about Reverend Statham's spastic colon?"

"His what?"

"Isn't that what he has? Wait, let's sit on this bench, okay? My feet are killing me. Now, tell me about it."

He does, almost mindlessly sipping from the bottle every time she clinks her beer against his. *Pavlov's dog had nothing on Gordy Klatte,* she thinks.

Halfway through the first beer, she sneaks a full one into its place. He doesn't notice then, or when she does it again . . . and again.

By that time, they've rejoined the others on the bench by the forbidden fire.

It's Midge who looks after Gordy when he throws up all over his rented tux.

It's Talia who suggests that she and Caroline go down to the beach for a swim—completely out of character for a girl who wouldn't jump into cold water even if she were on fire, but the party is in full swing, and no one bats an eye.

"Wait, you know what? I forgot my bathing suit in the car. I'll meet you down there," she tells Caroline.

"Sounds good. See you in a few."

Talia gives her a quick hug and heads back toward where the cars are parked.

Midge hands her a flashlight. "Careful," she says. "It's really dark."

"Take this too," Kelly says, handing her a small sack.

"What is it?"

"You'll see."

She's sure the money she tucked in there will come in handy, but the real gift is her pink Walkman. Caroline's been coveting it for months. Kelly was planning to get her one for her birthday next month, but she won't be here.

Caroline nods, takes the flashlight, and turns away quickly.

Fighting back tears, Kelly watches her walk off onto the wooded trail with her flashlight guiding the way.

She never looks back.

CHAPTER
EIGHTY-THREE

Present Day

"It's Caroline," Talia says, leaning in over Midge's shoulder to see the video on Kelly's phone screen. "It's definitely her. Don't you think, Midge?"

"It *could* be her, based on her size, and the glasses . . ."

"*And* she's left handed, and she's wearing the bracelet. And Kelly's mom talked to her. She did, right? You said she did."

"I did, but my mom . . ." Kelly clears her throat and looks at Midge.

"Her mom has dementia," Midge tells Talia.

"I'm so sorry. That's rough, Kelly."

"It is." Kelly takes a deep breath and lets it out. "Most of the time, when she says something happened, it either didn't or it was years ago. But once in a while, she knows what she's talking about."

Midge hears her father saying the same thing. And how many times has she said it herself?

I know what I'm talking about. I've been doing this long enough to listen to my instincts.

Her father was dead-on about Gordy hiding something. It just wasn't what he thought.

She looks at Talia. "You said you've been texting with her?"

"Yes. On and off, for years. If I had my phone, I'd show you. But it was in my bag, like the playing card."

"When was the last time you heard from her?"

"Just yesterday."

"What was it about?"

"She knew I was heading up here today. I said it was going to be a reunion, and I told her to meet me for lunch at the Landing so that we could see each other first. I didn't tell anyone else I was going there. She had to be the one who left the card for me."

"For all of us," Kelly says. "I saw her—I saw the person who left it for me. It could have been her. Just like the person in the video could have been her."

"It had to be her," Talia says. "And she needs help. Code two."

"But if she knew where to find us, why not tell us herself?" Midge asks.

"Maybe she's afraid."

Kelly frowns. "Of what? What's going on in her life? Where has she been all these years?"

"She made me swear I wouldn't tell you guys the whole story, but I think it's time that you knew."

CHAPTER EIGHTY-FOUR

June 5, 1999

Forehead pressed to the window, heart racing, Talia watches Caroline in the yard below. She quickly replaces the garbage can lid and looks around furtively, as if she's making sure no one saw her shove that package way down inside.

But she doesn't look up; doesn't notice Talia watching from her third-floor window.

She turns back toward the house, takes a few steps, then rushes back to the garbage can.

Seeing her open it, Talia is certain she must have had second thoughts about throwing away whatever it was.

But instead of reaching in, Caroline bends over the open can, so far in her head is no longer visible.

What in the world . . . ?

Then Talia hears the retching sounds.

Caroline is sick.

She's sick, and Talia has to help her, poor thing.

She hurries to the door, down the stairs, out into the night.

Cutting across the yard, she can see Caroline still standing beside the can, arms wrapped around her stomach as if that might calm the nausea.

"Car'? Are you okay?"

She whirls around. Seeing Talia, she presses an index finger to her lips, warning her to be quiet, and shoots a look at the house.

All is still and dark.

"What are you doing out here?" Talia whispers.

"What are *you* doing out here?"

"I asked you first."

"I was just . . . taking out the garbage."

"Yeah, no. What's going on?"

No reply.

"Come on, Car', it's *me*. You can trust me."

"There's nothing to—"

"I saw you getting sick." She points to her bedroom window, overlooking the yard. "And I saw you throwing—"

All at once, it hits her.

"Throwing away the garbage, Tally. I just said that."

"Throwing up," Talia says. "You were throwing up. *And* throwing something away. Are you drinking?"

"What? No!"

"I'm not judging! I won't tell anyone." She indicates the garbage can. "What was it? Vodka? Beer? Wine?"

The way Caroline returns her gaze, brows knit . . . it's almost as if she's surprised by Talia's assumption. Her eyes are clear and sharp. She doesn't seem drunk at all.

"I, um . . ." She pauses to swallow. "I was . . ."

Then she gags and turns back to the garbage can, vomiting into it again. Talia leans in and holds her hair back, hoping she's not contagious. The last thing she needs right now is a stomach bug during finals, with the prom coming up, and with precious little time with Paul.

When Caroline lifts her head again to look at Talia, she's crying.

"Please don't tell anyone," she says softly. "Tally, please. Promise me. My parents would kill me."

"For being sick?"

"For being pregnant."

CHAPTER
EIGHTY-FIVE

Present Day

Kelly sits in stunned silence as Talia leans back in the rocking chair and exhales, as if she's relieved to have finally told them everything.

And everything is a *lot*.

She pictures Caroline, racked with morning sickness, hiding a positive pregnancy test in the garbage can.

"And she *swore* it wasn't Gordy's baby?" Midge asks Talia.

"Yes. It was the first thing I asked her. They made that chastity vow, remember?"

"Vows can be broken," Kelly points out. "I know that better than anyone."

"But do you honestly think Caroline cheated on him? You think she slept with *someone else*?" Midge asks.

"I don't know." Kelly rubs her temples, wishing the doctor would call, wishing the headache would go away, wishing this—all of this—would just go away.

"It had to be Gordy," Midge says. "If there was someone else, she'd have told us."

Talia nods. "And she'd have broken up with him. I just don't get why she thought she had to lie to me about it, though?"

"Because she loved him, Tal', and she was probably trying to protect him," Midge points out. "It's how they were raised. Their chastity, their faith—it was everything to them. I mean, if Gordy tortured himself with guilt for years about having a few beers on prom night, imagine how the two of them felt about premarital sex?"

"He felt bad about the beers?" Kelly asks. "That was my fault. I pushed him into it."

"It wasn't your fault. We were all just doing our part to help Caroline. Talia, when she told you she was pregnant, did she also tell you she was going to run away?" Midge asks.

"No. I found that out when you guys did. She was just really upset and confused. She kept saying she didn't know what to do."

"You mean she was thinking of not having it? Or giving it up?" Kelly asks Talia.

"No! The opposite. She wanted that baby. But she said her parents would send her away and she'd be forced to put it up for adoption."

"Why would she think that?" Kelly asks. "Did they know about it? Did they say that?"

"No, she hadn't told them. But it's what they did to Mary Beth."

Midge nods. "They sent her away too, as soon as she got into trouble. But *Caroline* didn't break the law."

The way she says it—with the emphasis on *Caroline*—makes it sound as though Mary Beth *had* broken the law.

Talia shrugs. "She might as well have, as far as her parents were concerned. Anyway—"

"Wait a second," Kelly says. "Midge, are you saying the Winterfields sent Mary Beth away because . . . what, she committed a crime or something?"

Midge hesitates, and Talia answers the question for her. "No, it was because she was pregnant."

"Mary Beth was pregnant?" Kelly asks, just to be sure. "So, Caroline was pretty much following in her footsteps?"

"Exactly. The Winterfields would have sent her away to the same so-called home for unwed mothers where they sent Mary Beth."

"So that's where she went?" Midge rubs her chin.

"Yes, and she told Caroline that it was a horrible place. They were brainwashing these pregnant girls, making them feel like sinners who needed to be punished. They were basically used as human incubators, and their babies were taken away and sold to rich people who were looking to adopt healthy infants with wholesome white mothers."

"But isn't that illegal?" Kelly asks.

"Hell yes, it's illegal," Midge says.

"And it's exactly what happened to Mary Beth. She never got over it."

Kelly thinks of that long-ago day in Syracuse, remembering Mary Beth's gaunt, vacant eyes, the run-down neighborhood, the punk who called her "M" and his "old lady."

A lump rises in her throat. No wonder Mary Beth's life took such a tragic turn. No wonder Caroline, thinking the same thing was going to happen to her, had to run away.

"Did that minister help Caroline escape?" Midge asks. "Reverend B.? I always thought it might have been him, the way she talked about him . . . she really trusted him."

"No, not him." Kelly shakes her head, remembering something. "I know who it was."

CHAPTER EIGHTY-SIX

September 16, 2006
Danbury, Connecticut

The prison's visiting room is warm, close, and crowded with people. Many are children, shepherded by harried young fathers or world-weary grandmothers, here to see their incarcerated mothers. Babies and toddlers are crying, and so are a few of the grandmas.

Talia has found herself close to tears a few times during the endless visitor processing and waiting period, wondering what she's even doing here, certain it's a mistake.

But then Carlena, a friendly young woman with a broad smile that reveals a shiny gold front tooth, takes her under her wing like she's a new girl at a school in a tough neighborhood. She's here to visit her girlfriend, who's doing time for money laundering.

"How about your gal?"

"My . . . gal?"

"The friend you're here to see. What's she in for?"

"Drug trafficking."

"How long?"

"Twelve years."

"Sucks. Ever been in prison?"

"No, I haven't seen her in . . . six years."

"I don't mean to *visit*."

"Oh, you mean . . . *me*? Have I been *in* prison? No. You?"

"Jail, yes. Prison? Hell no. Hey, here they come. Good luck."

It's such a strange thing to say, as if Carlena senses, somehow, that Talia is here on a mission. But there's no time to ponder it, because an armed guard is escorting an inmate in green drabs to the plastic chair across the table from her.

Talia hasn't seen Mary Beth Winterfield since the December night she mistook her for Caroline, and then for a prowler at her parents' home. Back then, she was gaunt and emaciated. Now, she's equally unrecognizable, carrying too much weight, skin sallow, hair stringy.

Talia starts to rise and reach out to embrace her, but there are so many rules—strict ones, about physical contact. She can't recall whether hugs are forbidden, and a handshake seems far too formal, so she stays seated.

But Mary Beth reaches across the table and gives her hand a hard squeeze, and Talia sees tears in her eyes as she settles into the chair.

"Wow. When I saw your name on my visitors' list, I thought I was tripping, but . . . none of that here, you know? So how'd you find me?"

"Google."

"No kidding. I'm on Google?"

Unsure Mary Beth knows what Google even is, she says, "Yes. If a person, or a thing, exists, it's pretty much on Google."

Caroline, however, is not. Talia plugs her name into the search engine every so often just in case she pops up, but she never does. Of course not, because people who fake their own deaths and disappear don't use their own names in their new lives.

Mary Beth, however, was relatively easy to find, prominently featured in news coverage about a series of drug trafficking arrests in Syracuse. By the time Talia came across it last fall, Mary Beth had been sentenced to twelve years in prison.

At that point, it seemed like a bad idea to reconnect. Talia was busy launching her marketing career in Manhattan, still trying to put Mulberry Bay and her memories behind her.

Yet Caroline was never far from her mind. Mary Beth was her only link to her lost friend. And she happened to be incarcerated within an hour's drive of New York.

Once Talia made up her mind to visit, she had to get permission, and wait all spring and most of the summer to be scheduled. Then she had to rent a car for the day, lie to her roommates about where she was going, and make sure she followed the instructions right down to the very specific dress code.

"How have you been?" Mary Beth asks.

"Fine." She bites back the reciprocal question, since the answer is pretty obvious.

"Are you still in Mulberry Bay?"

"No. My mom moved away right after I saw you that night."

"Which night?"

"That night at your parents' house?"

Mary Beth looks puzzled. "I haven't lived there in years."

"No, I know, but I saw you . . . you don't remember?"

"Sorry. I forget a lot of stuff. Most of it is on purpose, but some things . . ." She shrugs.

So she has no recollection of that night? Of the things she told Talia about Caroline?

"I was using. Did you know that?"

Talia shakes her head. It seems impolite to admit she assumed that was the case.

"Don't ever start, okay? Promise me you won't."

Promise me . . .

She thinks about Caroline and opens her mouth to ask about her.

But Mary Beth speaks first. "So, yeah . . . thanks. You don't know what it means to me."

"Oh, it's . . . I mean, drugs have never been my thing, so—"

"Not that. I'm talking about your being here. I never expected . . . Well, most of the time, it seems like no one on the outside even remembers I exist."

All around them, people are talking, arguing, laughing, crying.

Talia tries to think of something to say and comes up with, "You don't get many visitors, then?"

"None."

"None? Not . . . what about your family?"

"I'm dead to them, Talia."

"You mean your parents?"

"And my sisters."

"Even Caroline?"

A shadow crosses Mary Beth's face. "Oh, she's . . . uh, yeah, sometimes I see her."

"She's in Syracuse? It's kind of a long way from here."

"Syracuse?"

"Isn't that where you were living? With Caroline?"

Mary Beth processes the question for longer than it takes to provide the simple "Yeah."

"And she's still there?"

"I don't think so."

"You don't know?"

"I've been in here for months, okay? It's not like I'm keeping track of stuff on the outside. I can't even if I wanted to!"

"I know. I know, I'm so sorry. I just thought . . ."

"You thought you'd come and see me so that I could tell you how to find my sister. Didn't it ever occur to you that if she wanted to talk to you, she would?"

"So you're saying . . . she doesn't. Is that it?"

Mary Beth stares at her. "I don't know."

"Okay, well . . . can you just tell her I was here? When you see her again. Just let her know I'm thinking of her and that I'd love to see her again."

"What if she says yes?"

"What do you mean?"

"What if she wants to see you? I mean, I know she didn't before, but maybe she's changed her mind."

"I really hope she has."

"I'll let you know," Mary Beth says. "Next time you're here."

Talia doesn't know what to say to that.

"Ah . . . you weren't planning to come back, were you?"

"No, of course I will. If you want me to."

"Like I said, I don't get many visitors, so . . . why not. Oh, and did they tell you that you're allowed to make a deposit into my account?"

"Which account?"

"It's, you know, to spend in the commissary. I like to buy music."

Music . . .

Talia has a flash of a young Mary Beth sharing a piano bench with Caroline, their hands flying over the keys in a flawless "Skaters' Waltz."

"Sure," she says, her voice thick with emotion. "I'll find out how to make a deposit so that you can buy some music. And I'll come back to visit again."

"You promise?"

"I promise," Talia says. "If you promise to tell Caroline what I said."

CHAPTER EIGHTY-SEVEN

Present Day

"So Mary Beth is the one who helped Caroline get away that night," Midge says after Talia has dropped another piece of the puzzle into place. "I didn't realize they were even in touch at that point. How did you figure that out, Kelly?"

"I knew Mary Beth had given Caroline a phone number so that she could reach her in case of an emergency."

"Why didn't you ever mention that?" Midge asks.

Kelly shrugs.

Midge lets it go. They've all kept their share of secrets where the Winterfields are concerned.

She nearly slipped and revealed one of her own minutes ago, when she assumed Mary Beth's parents sent her away because of her arrest. It isn't her place to divulge sealed police records—especially when she only knows about this one because she was eavesdropping.

As a police chief, Midge's father never had much sympathy for anyone who committed a crime, including youthful offenders. But Midge remembers that he felt sorry for Mary Beth, mentioning that she'd been sick to her stomach, throwing up.

Morning sickness?

Could her pregnancy have been the motive for those burglaries?

Had Mary Beth, like Caroline, known what was in store for her and been desperate for a way out?

"So Mary Beth was forced to give up her baby for adoption," Midge says, and Talia nods. "What about Caroline? She had hers, and kept it?"

"She miscarried."

Kelly gasps. "Oh no."

Midge clasps a hand to her mouth, speechless. She wasn't expecting such a cruel twist.

"That's why she couldn't bear to see us again," Talia goes on. "She was devastated, and she wanted nothing to do with her past, and . . . who am I to judge her for that? I felt the same way, for a long time."

"So did I." Kelly looks at Midge. "You're the only one who stayed. But then, you've always been the strongest one of all of us."

"Or maybe the weakest. Maybe I just never had the guts to leave."

Talia shakes her head. "No, Midge. Cowards run away."

"But Caroline wasn't a coward."

"Not Caroline. She was so brave, trying to save her child. I guess I was just thinking about me. I let go so easily."

"Talia, you're the one who never gave up looking," Kelly says. "You're the one who found Mary Beth."

"Yeah. I visited her every once in a while. Before she was paroled a few years ago, I finally got her to give me Caroline's number."

"How?"

"How do you think?"

"Did you bribe her?"

"Yep. Not a lot of money, and I was positive the number she gave me was fake. When I tried calling it, it rang into one of those robotic voicemails. I left a message, and a few days later, I got a text back from Caroline."

"You must have been shocked," Midge says. "What did she say?"

"Just that she was glad to hear from me and that she was okay. We've texted on and off ever since. It's always brief, just basic stuff. She doesn't talk about her life now, and she doesn't want to be found. She says she prefers that people keep right on believing that she's dead."

"But now she's come back to Mulberry Bay?"

"Maybe it's time. Maybe—" Talia clears her throat. "Sorry. I'm getting emotional, but it's just . . . it's been so damned hard, living with what we did. Carrying that secret around for twenty-five years."

Midge nods. "I feel like I've spent my whole life trying to make up for it, one way or another."

"Me too. I was so reckless, and selfish . . . a spoiled brat." Kelly pauses. "I mean . . . don't everyone jump in all at once to disagree."

Midge flashes a faint smile. "But what we did, for Caroline . . . that wasn't reckless, or selfish."

"Right. We were trying to protect her. *Save* her," Kelly adds. "Because they were smothering her. All of them, including Gordy."

"And now he's dead," Talia says. "What happened, Midge?"

"It looks like an accident." She keeps the *but* to herself.

Talia, however, seems to hear it loud and clear. "It *wasn't* an accident?"

"I'm investigating it. That's all I—" Midge's phone buzzes.

Kelly's does the same, simultaneously.

Looking down, Midge sees a group text from an unknown number.

Tally, K. K., & Midge, I'll meet you at midnight at our spot.

It's signed with a pair of black spade emojis.

CHAPTER EIGHTY-EIGHT

Dusk has fallen over Haven Cliff.

In the dining room, the table is set with linen, silver, and Haviland Limoges. Lit tapers in twin crystal candelabras illuminate the droopy centerpiece.

"Seriously, I won't feel bad if you toss those flowers right into the garbage," Talia tells Kelly as they sit down to fragrant, beautifully garnished platters of grilled chicken and roasted vegetables Kelly's chef prepared.

"Why would I do that?"

"Because they're half-dead and they look ridiculous alongside all these gorgeous professional arrangements."

"Talia, those can't ever hold a candle to a wildflower bouquet from someone I love."

Talia smiles. "You have impeccable manners, Kelly Barrow."

"It's not manners. I mean every word of it. I never lie."

"Except about the charm bracelet," Midge says, spearing a roasted potato with her fork.

"Except that," Kelly agrees, wishing she hadn't brought it up, despite the quirk of a smile that indicates she's only teasing. "I'm really sorry about that, Midge. And, Talia, thanks again for the flowers, *and* for helping me get to the bottom of what's going on with my health."

Earlier, the doctor called back, asking Kelly to come right down for blood work before the lab closed. Talia accompanied her to the lab, and then to the pharmacy. Though the results won't be back for a few days, the doctor suspects Lyme disease and has preemptively started her on antibiotics.

"I'm glad I could help," Talia says. "And you can't take your medication on an empty stomach, so you'd better start eating."

Kelly smiles and reaches for the platter of chicken. "You must be a great mom."

"Oh, I am—when I'm not skipping town without telling my children and husband where I'm really going. I hate that I did this."

"But we understand why you did it," Midge says. "We're all in it together. Twenty-five years of lies, for Caroline's sake."

"Yeah, well, she can thank us tonight." Kelly deposits a piece of chicken on her plate. Her stomach is churning, and it's not from the medication.

"She can, *if* she's the one who sent that text," Midge says.

It was sent to all three of them, including Talia's number, meaning that whoever took her bag might also have seen it. She confessed anyone can access her data, because she removed the security password years ago.

Midge, of course, was aghast.

"Why would you do that, Talia? Do you know how many people come to me to report fraud because someone got into their phone or computer?"

"I guess I never thought about that. It just seemed like a hindrance to punch in a code every time I wanted to do anything."

"But what about your husband?" Kelly asked. "If you were texting back and forth with Caroline for all these years, and now making plans with us to come here this weekend, weren't you worried he might find out?"

"No, because we trust each other. He'd never snoop on my phone."

Kelly, with two cheating ex-husbands under her belt, bit back a comment. She hopes Talia is right.

"That group text could have come from anyone," Midge reminds them.

Kelly shakes her head. "Caroline's the only one in the world who ever called me K. K."

"And she's the only one who ever called me Tally. It had to be her."

Midge shrugs, poking at a piece of chicken with her fork.

"If it wasn't from Caroline," Kelly says, "then where do you think she is?"

"I have no idea."

"Well, I know where she isn't," Talia says, setting down her fork. "She isn't lying dead in that pit outside."

"*Someone* is," Midge says.

"It could be anyone, like you said about the text."

"Anyone who had the pink Walkman Kelly gave Caroline? I can't imagine her ever parting with that."

"What if she didn't?" Kelly asks, remembering something. "What if someone borrowed it without asking?"

Midge turns to her with a questioning look.

"Remember how Mary Beth was always helping herself to Caroline's stuff?"

"I do," Talia says. "It drove Caroline crazy. She used to take her clothes, her makeup, her jewelry . . . and then she'd lose it, or stain it, or break it."

"Her jewelry?" Midge asks.

Talia shakes her head. "I know what you're thinking, Midge, but she wouldn't have taken Caroline's charm bracelet. That wasn't her style."

"No. But a Walkman would have been," Kelly says.

"Those remains don't belong to Mary Beth, because I saw her," Talia reminds them. "At her parents' house, and in prison."

"But maybe she took the Walkman and sold it or pawned it to whoever is buried in that pit," Midge says.

Kelly nods. "Still . . . how did whoever it is end up there? I can't make it make sense."

"I can't either," Talia says. "But I'm sure it's not Caroline, and that she's going to show up to meet us tonight."

Midge shakes her head. "To meet *me*. This is police work now. It might be dangerous. If she had anything to do with Gordy . . ."

"But she asked for all of us to be there," Talia points out. "If she's lurking somewhere and sees that it's just you, there's no way she's going to show."

"That's true. She'll know it's a trap, especially if she really is the one who . . . you know." Kelly can't even bring herself to say the words.

"I still say there's no way Caroline is capable of killing someone," Talia says. "If she was with Gordy last night, it was an accident."

"If it was an accident, why did he struggle with her?" Midge asks. "Why was her bracelet in his hand? Why didn't she call for help?"

"There has to be a good reason for all of that. I know it. I know *her*. We all do. She's not—"

"We *knew* her," Kelly cuts in. "When we were kids. But we grew up."

"*You* sure did. I can't believe all you've accomplished."

"Yeah, well, I was an entitled spoiled brat as a kid," she tells Talia. "And for most of my adult life too. Ask Midge. I've come a long way."

Midge nods. "We all have. None of us are the girls we used to be. Including Caroline."

"She went through hell," Talia says.

"Exactly. And how can she not blame Gordy for some of that?" Kelly asks. "Or all of it?"

They're silent for a moment, digesting this.

Then Talia says, "What about my bag? Why would she steal it? I just don't understand that."

"We don't know that it was her," Midge points out. "It could have been anyone. Kelly's had so many people in and out of here, doing work on the house. And the door was unlocked. But you can file a report, when you're ready."

"I will, as soon as we get through tonight and I can talk to Ben. I'm going to tell him everything. No more secrets."

"Good. I'm no expert when it comes to marriage, but I've learned some hard lessons from my failed ones." Kelly leans back and pushes away her plate.

Talia follows suit.

Midge takes one last nibble of chicken and does the same, leaving the rest untouched.

"You guys didn't eat much. Was the food okay?" Kelly asks.

"It was amazing," Talia says. "I'm just nervous about tonight."

"Midge?"

"Not nervous, but—" She breaks off as her phone rings.

She looks at it and excuses herself, striding out of the dining room. Kelly and Talia look at each other across the table.

"I'm going tonight," Kelly says in a low voice. "No matter what she says. She can't go out there alone."

"I'm going too. We have to. We're her friends."

"Midge's, or Caroline's?"

"Both. And we have to make sure nothing happens to either one of them."

Kelly nods, thinking again of the skeleton buried in her pool.

Haven Cliff may encompass an old graveyard, but early settlers weren't buried with Walkmans.

"Talia? If that's not Caroline or Mary Beth in the pool, then who is it?"

"I keep wondering the same thing. What if—"

"I'm back."

They turn to see Midge in the doorway, looking pensive.

"Everything okay?" Talia asks her.

"They traced the plates on that car stashed by your driveway. It's registered to Ceto Winterfield in Syracuse."

CHAPTER EIGHTY-NINE

Present Day

As they make their way through the mock orange grove just before midnight, Midge is in the lead with a flashlight. Kelly and Talia are right behind her, just like that last time.

Allowing them to accompany her is the hardest decision Midge has ever made.

She knows she should have insisted they stay behind, just as she knows she should have called Nap as soon as she saw the skeleton.

But there are *should*s, and then there are *can*s.

As in, she *can* do this on her own terms.

This is her case. It's her suspect.

It's *Caroline.*

Ceto.

It seems that's what she's calling herself these days.

The car's registration gave Midge little more to go on, other than an address in Syracuse. An online search revealed that it's a large apartment building in an impoverished neighborhood. She placed a call to the local precinct, hoping someone there might be able to shed more light on Ceto Winterfield's existence, but it sounds like they've got their hands full tonight with violent crime. Every night, most likely.

For now, she's on her own.

Well, on her own with Kelly and Talia.

They might be right. If she were to show up alone, Caroline—or whoever was behind the group text—might sense that it's a trap and bolt.

No. Not *whoever*.

It was Caroline. It had to be Caroline.

Ceto.

Who else would even know the significance of that name?

It makes so much sense . . .

So little sense.

There are facts, and then there are instincts.

She relies on both to do her job. Typically, one supports the other.

The facts seem to indicate that Caroline is alive, living as Ceto, delivering envelopes, stealing luggage . . .

Killing Gordy.

Midge's instincts tell her Caroline can't be a killer—that those skeletal remains are Caroline's.

She should have called Nap. Why hadn't she called Nap?

Because she'd no longer have control of the investigation. Forensics would have the entire area cordoned off. There would likely be press snooping around, given Haven Cliff's involvement. Everyone in the area would know about it, including Gordy's killer, who would probably slip away and disappear forever.

Gordy's killer . . .

Instinct: Caroline isn't a killer.

Fact: the bracelet in his death grip could only belong to her.

Picking her way along the trail, Midge hears her father's words ringing in her ears.

"Everyone has something, or someone, they'd kill for . . ."

Earlier, she even considered Kelly a suspect, but no. It has to be someone with a far more personal connection to Gordy Klatte.

They've reached the clearing. In the moonlight, the backhoe looms alongside the pit.

Amid the chatter of birds, frogs, and crickets, Midge picks up a faint rustling somewhere in the shadows, just beyond the flashlight's glow.

It might be an animal. All the way here, she could hear woodland creatures darting away from the path, taking cover in the trees.

But this feels different.

Instinct: someone is lurking. Watching them.

"Caroline?" she calls. "Is that you?"

There's no reply.

"What do we do now?" Talia whispers.

"We wait."

"Maybe she left something, like last time," Kelly suggests.

Midge nods. "Let's check."

They start toward the stone pedestal.

Again, Midge hears movement in the shadows, as though someone is tracking them.

She stops. "Caroline? Are you here?"

Silence.

"Caroline?" Talia calls. "We want to see you."

Kelly chimes in. "Please, Caroline. We've missed you so much."

More rustling, this time less furtive.

Then a figure emerges from the trees.

Midge gasps.

"It's her!" Kelly says.

"Caroline?"

"Hi, Talia." Squinting, she lifts a splayed hand to her face, palm out. "Midge? That's you, right? With the flashlight? Do you mind turning it off? You're blinding me."

She obliges, but not before noticing that Caroline looks haggard, at least a decade older than forty-three. The years have been cruel to her.

"I've been wondering about you for years," Kelly says as she walks toward them. "I've been so scared that you weren't even alive."

"Oh, I am. Sometimes barely, but I'm alive."

"Where have you been?"

"Come on, Kelly. We both know that doesn't matter."

Kelly.

Not K. K.

She stops, about ten feet away. Close enough now for Midge to see her face.

To see her eyes.

And now she knows, for certain, where Caroline has been all these years.

Not living in Syracuse, mourning the loss of a baby she desperately wanted.

Not living as Ceto, texting Talia, texting them all to meet her here at midnight.

Not here. Not living.

Midge's instincts had been correct when she saw those bones.

They're Caroline's.

But the lies . . .

The lies belong to the woman in front of her.

Mary Beth Winterfield.

"What happened to your sister that night?" Midge asks quietly.

Mary Beth falters, then recovers, defiant. "To Mary Beth? What do you mean? What happened to her which night?"

"Midge?" Kelly asks. "What are you talking about?"

Midge turns her head slowly, deliberately, to look at the excavation site, then back at the woman in front of her.

"You can stop pretending," she says. "We know who you are."

"Midge, what—" Talia breaks off in a gasp as she realizes the truth.

It's Kelly who says her name, though it's a question, asked in dread. "Mary Beth?"

"No! It's me, Caroline. Come on, you guys know that. Talia, *you* know. You texted me to meet you at midnight, and here I am."

"I didn't text you," Talia says. "I couldn't have, because—"

"Because *you* texted *us*," Midge cuts in, as the slightest hint of doubt tries to edge into her brain.

Talia was about to say that her phone had been stolen.

What if the message about meeting at midnight really didn't come from Mary Beth? What if someone else has Talia's phone? What if Midge was wrong about Caroline?

Can they possibly be working together?

Either way, Mary Beth is putting on one hell of an act. "I don't know what you're talking about. I didn't text you. I'm here because you asked me to come. And hey, I promised I would, right? On the anniversary of my disappearance?"

"*Caroline* promised," Midge says, and then pauses, hearing a sound, back in the trees. A twig snapping. A raccoon, or some other night creature, or . . . an accomplice?

"Caroline is dead," she goes on, watching Mary Beth's face. "She never ran away and lived with you."

"You think you know everything, don't you, Midge? But you're wrong. You're dead wrong."

Part of her wants more than anything to be wrong about this.

But if she is—if Caroline is alive, and the sisters are working together—then she isn't the Caroline Midge and the others knew and loved.

Which is worse?

Whichever is more dangerous, she tells herself. And that would be two sisters.

She keeps her voice level. "Oh, I definitely don't know everything. I'm wrong a lot. But I don't believe Caroline ever left Haven Cliff on prom night. I think she's been right here all along, buried in the pool."

"You're right," Mary Beth says, and smirks, as if aware of Midge's fierce stab of grief, before going on, ". . . about being wrong."

Again, she hears movement in the woods.

Mary Beth, too, seems to hear it, turning toward it, then whirling back to Midge. "What was that?"

"A raccoon? A squirrel?"

"Or maybe a coyote—there's a den back there," Kelly says.

"This is a trap, isn't it? That's why you made me come out here, because you wanted to—"

"We didn't *make* you do anything," Midge says. "You came here on your own."

Mary Beth points at Talia. "You said you wanted to help me."

Talia flinches. "Of course we want to help you."

"Just like you wanted to help Caroline," Kelly says. "Remember that, Mary Beth? You were the big sister, and it was the two of you against the world."

"Talia said that you rebuilt this house for me?"

"I built it for *Caroline*." Kelly turns to Talia. "But when did you tell her that? You didn't even know until you got here."

"I didn't tell her. She must have been hiding, listening to us talking about it."

"You actually think I'm hanging around this place, what? Spying on you? Eavesdropping?"

"And helping yourself to other people's belongings," Kelly says.

"And texting me," Talia adds, "pretending to be your sister."

"Way to hold a grudge. That was ages ago."

"It was hours ago."

Mary Beth shrugs. "Yeah, sure. Whatever you say."

Midge takes over the conversation, sensing Mary Beth's restlessness.

"I still think I'm right about Caroline," she says. "I don't think she's alive."

"You're not just wrong, Midge. You're forgetful. Or crazy. Didn't she come back here a year later to let you know she was okay, just like she promised?"

"I don't think she did. I think you left those nickels on the pedestal," Midge says. "And you've been texting Talia, and doing the same with Gordy—messaging him, pretending to be Caroline. Why? Is he the one? He hurt her? So you wanted to hurt him?"

"What? No! I don't know what you're talking about. Gordy? Pennies on a pedestal?"

Pennies.

Midge had said *nickels.* Deliberately.

Talia gasps. "So you really did—"

Midge whirls to give her a warning look. Talia and Kelly need to let her handle this. It's delicate, and she has training. She knows how to keep things from—

Too late.

She feels movement behind her, and then something nudges her between the shoulder blades. It's a gun. Mary Beth has a gun.

"I did what?" she asks, her voice dead calm.

Don't say it! Midge screams at Talia with her eyes.

But there's no way she can see Midge's expression out here in the dark. She has no idea about the muzzle poking Midge's back.

"Gordy," Talia whispers. "Oh my God, Mary Beth. You killed Gordy."

Midge feels Mary Beth tense. Feels the gun jabbing.

"Gordy? Gordy Klatte? He's dead?"

"Come on. You know he's dead," Kelly says. "You killed him."

"Now I get it," Mary Beth says. "So that's why you lured me out here. All of you. You think I'm a murderer."

"*We* didn't lure *you.* We're here because Caroline said she would be. We're here for her." Midge keeps her voice as steady as her right hand, inching toward her holster.

"Oh God," Talia says. "Mary Beth, please tell me Caroline isn't . . . she's . . ."

Mary Beth sighs. "You believed it, then, huh? I was never sure. I thought maybe . . . but no. You actually believed it."

"What? I believed what?" Talia asks as Midge's hand creeps toward her weapon.

"That you were talking to Caroline," Kelly tells her. "But it was Mary Beth all along, pretending to be her."

"Sorry, Talia. I did what I had to do. Then, and now. Always."

"Did *you* do this? To Caroline?" Talia gestures at the pool. "Did you hurt her? Did you put her there?"

"Did I *put* her there? She was my sister! Do you think I'm some kind of monster?"

"We don't," Kelly says. "I always thought you were amazing, Mary Beth. I wanted to be just like you."

"Trust me. You don't want that. Nobody wants that."

"Mary Beth, I know what they did to you. I know you only wanted to keep your baby."

"My baby," she says on a choked laugh, or sob. "How do you know—"

"I know how hard everything was for you, after all that," Kelly says. "And I know you loved Caroline."

"Of course I did," Mary Beth says. "She was my sister. Of course I loved her."

"She was your little sister," Kelly says. "The twins . . . they only looked out for each other, right? But you always looked out for Caroline."

Mary Beth says nothing.

"I was with her, remember?" Kelly goes on. "That day in Syracuse? You gave her your number so that she could call if she ever needed you."

"That's what she did, right?" Midge asks. "She called you because she needed you?"

"Of course she called me. Who else would she call? Not any of *you.* You were just friends, not family. You didn't know . . ." She shakes her head.

"We didn't know what the two of you had gone through, in that house, did we?" Midge says. "We couldn't help her. You were the only one who could help her, because you understood exactly what your parents might do if—"

"*Might* do? What they did."

"Right. What they did to *you*," Kelly says. "I'm so sorry, Mary Beth."

"Yeah, sure you are," Mary Beth mutters.

"Thank God you were there for her," Talia says. "Thank God you helped her."

"I did. I helped her, because . . . I couldn't let them take her baby too."

"What happened that night?" Midge asks quietly. "The night she died?"

"You mean you don't *know*?" Her tone is mocking. "Come on. You're the detective. You tell me."

"I don't know. I wasn't there."

"Why don't you guess? Come on. Take a shot. What do you think happened?"

"I think Caroline did something to upset you."

"Yeah? How about you, Kelly? What do you think happened?"

"I think you were trying to help her, like you said. I think that's all you wanted to do. Be the big sister, and help her, because she needed you."

"And?"

Kelly shrugs.

Mary Beth turns to Talia. "And . . . ?"

"And something . . . went wrong. She did something, or she said something, or—"

"She said something, all right. She said she'd changed her mind about staying with me! She said she wanted to stay here!"

"Here . . . you mean, your parents' house?" Midge asks.

"In Mulberry Bay. With all of *you*. She said you would help her with the baby. I wasn't enough."

"I don't think Caroline would ever have said that to you, Mary Beth," Kelly says. "You were everything to her. She missed you like crazy when you were gone."

"Yeah? Then why did she want to leave me? Why did she want to take the baby away from me?"

"Just like before," Midge says softly. "That's it, isn't it? If Caroline and her baby were allowed to stay here, well, you probably felt like *your* baby was going to be taken from you all over again."

"I couldn't let that happen."

"Of course you couldn't." Midge's hand starts to close around her pistol.

"I couldn't let her do that. I couldn't—" Mary Beth breaks off, grabbing her wrist. "What the hell, Midge. Don't you dare. Don't you *dare*! Don't move. I'll shoot you. I swear I will."

Midge sees Kelly's eyes widen, and Talia's jaw drops as they realize what's going on.

"You don't want to do this, Mary Beth. I know you don't. Killing a cop is murder one."

"Do you think I care about that? About breaking laws, and punishment? Do you have any idea what I've been through? How I've spent most of my life?"

"I'm sorry," Midge says. "I can help you."

"No. *I* can help *you*. You wanted to see my sister. I can make that happen. For both of us."

"What are you doing?" Talia shrieks. "What are you talking about?"

"I'm just giving Midge what she asked for. She said she came here to see Caroline."

"You're *sick*," Kelly says. "What happened to you? I used to think you were this beautiful, amazing person, but . . ."

"I was. Remember me that way. Please? Because there's no one left who does." She sounds like a wistful little girl. Then her voice hardens again. "Now come on, Midge. They don't need to see this."

She feels the gun, nudging her to move.

"This isn't you, Mary Beth," Talia says. "I know you."

"You *knew* me. A long time ago, before—"

"You were like a big sister to me. That's why I visited you for all those years. I cared about you."

"No, you acted like you cared about me, Talia, but you were only trying to get me to tell you about my sister. I thought you were there for me. I thought you were going to offer to help me when I got out of there. You knew I had nowhere else to go, and you—"

"I *did* try to help you! I gave you money!"

"To give you Caroline's phone number. That's what you wanted. Now it's Midge's turn to get what she wants. Walk, Midge. Walk."

She walks.

Mary Beth propels her toward the dark woods, leaving Talia and Kelly behind.

It doesn't make sense. Why would she leave witnesses?

Because she doesn't care.

Because she's made up her mind about whatever she's going to do, and nothing else matters.

Midge clears her throat. "Mary Beth . . ."

"Hey, I'm sorry. Really, I am. I never meant for any of this to happen."

"Think about Caroline. Think about what she'd want."

"Sweet Caroline, everyone used to call her, remember?"

"I do. It fit."

"God, I loved her. She was the only one who . . ." She clears her throat and mutters, "Never mind."

"She was the only one who what? Loved *you*?"

"She *cared*."

"She did."

"So damned much. About me. About everyone. And everyone let her down."

"I didn't," Midge says. "And they didn't. Kelly, and Talia . . . we were all there for her, beginning to end. We'd have been there now, if she were . . ."

Alive.

Tears spill from Midge's eyes as she allows the truth to wash over her.

Mary Beth must have blamed Gordy. That's why she's here. She did to him what she did to them. She got him to meet her outside in a remote spot where no one would see them. Where no one could help him.

She was pretending to be Caroline, wearing Caroline's bracelet.

When did he realize the truth?

He struggled with her, alone out there in the night. He fought for his life, and lost.

Now Midge, too, knows the truth. Midge, too, is alone in the night with this deranged woman. Midge, too, is determined to fight for her life.

But Midge is going to win.

They're past the old picnic pavilion, on the path that leads down to the lake. The very spot where she last saw Caroline. Midge looks at the benches, the fireplace, the tire swing . . .

Someone is there, on the swing.

For a split second, she thinks it's one of those ghoulish life-size dummies she's seen on lawns at Halloween—houses where people go all out, with fake gravestones and dry ice smoke in cauldrons.

But this isn't that. This isn't fake.

Midge registers what it is, who it is, what Mary Beth is capable of.

She twists and makes a grab for the gun.

Mary Beth falters but recovers quickly. Of course she does. All those years in prison . . . you never let down your guard.

She grabs Midge's arm and twists it painfully behind her back.

There are sirens, now, in the distance. Kelly or Talia—they'll have called for help.

Code two.

There's no way they can get here on time.

Closer to her ear, she hears another sound: a weapon chambering a round.

She feels cold, hard metal pressed against her temple.

This is it, then.

It's all over.

This is where it ends.

"I'm sorry, Midge," Mary Beth says. "But I'm coming with you. It won't be so bad. Anything will be better than—"

Midge hears the gunshot.

Yet somehow, she's still standing, still breathing, still alive.

Mary Beth crumples at her feet.

How . . .

She looks up, around, bewildered, and sees Kelly, with a pistol in both outstretched, trembling hands.

"Midge. Oh, God, Midge. Is she . . . ?"

Midge quickly crouches and presses a hand to Mary Beth's throat. She has a pulse.

"She's alive."

It's a leg wound, and she's losing a lot of blood. Midge hurriedly takes off her belt and wraps it around Mary Beth's thigh and loops it through to tighten it.

The sirens are closer.

"Talia called for help. She'll show them where we are," Kelly says. "Do you think they'll get here in time? For her?"

"I think so," Midge says, pulling the makeshift tourniquet tight. Mary Beth moans. "It's going to be okay. Just hang in there. Kelly, here, hold this while I check something."

Kelly crouches beside her.

Midge hurries over to the tire swing. She can see that he's dead before she touches his hand, hard and cold. No need to check for a pulse.

Kelly gasps, seeing him. "What the hell? Is that—"

"The Walking Man."

"What happened?"

Midge shakes her head, unable to speak, and returns to Kelly. Crouching beside her, she says, "Here, let me. I'll take over."

"Oh, God, Midge. I didn't mean to . . . I can't believe I . . . but she was going to—"

"I know. But why are you carrying a weapon?"

"I grabbed it, just in case, because I was scared. Of her. For us."

"Is it Annie Oakley's?"

"Edith Winterfield's."

"You saved my life, Kelly."

"Yeah. I guess that finally makes us even."

CHAPTER NINETY

At dawn, they leave the house and walk back up the trail.

This time, Kelly leads the way into the woods.

There's no fog this morning. Beyond the treetops, the sky is visible, a deep purple streaked pink and gold in the east. There are no sirens today either. Only birds singing high in the branches, overlooking the silent procession.

She, Midge, and Talia are all clutching wads of soggy tissues and bouquets, like a trio of bridesmaids who mistakenly found their way to a funeral.

The flowers are mock orange, sweet and fragrant, freshly cut from the grove.

Kelly can hear soft weeping behind her—Talia? Midge?

Likely both.

All through this long, strange, dark night, they've taken turns breaking down and comforting each other—never all three of them at once, though. That's how it's always been with the three of them.

How it was with the four of them.

They were strong for each other.

It's Kelly's turn now, and she manages to keep her composure even when they reach the clearing, where Caroline's remains lie in the cavernous pit that's been her grave.

The medics sedated Mary Beth, and she was unconscious when they transported her to the hospital.

Maybe, eventually, she'll reveal what happened the night Caroline disappeared—and died. Maybe she never will.

Now, whenever Kelly remembers how Caroline walked off toward the path to the beach, she imagines her doubling back through the woods to the pool, where Mary Beth must have been waiting for her.

Maybe Mary Beth was trying to do the right thing when Caroline asked for her help in running away and raising the baby.

Maybe not. Maybe she believed helping raise her sister's child would somehow make up for being forced to give up her own.

Maybe she had something darker in mind all along.

Maybe Mary Beth said something, or Caroline sensed something, that made her uncomfortable—or frightened.

Clearly, Mary Beth saw the change of heart as a betrayal. That could have made her snap, given how unstable she was when Kelly and Caroline saw her in Syracuse.

Drugs, prison time, all that loss . . .

Her entire adult life has been a tragedy.

Maybe Caroline's death was an accident.

Maybe not.

Either way, Caroline must have told her about the plan to come back here on the first anniversary. And about code two, and code four.

So, a year later, Mary Beth was the one who left those pennies on the pedestal, wanting them to believe Caroline was still alive.

Or, who knows? Maybe she was so far gone that she believed she *was* Caroline.

Or believed she was Ceto, anyway. That seems to be what she's been calling herself—Ceto Winterfield.

Yet she seems to have gotten clean and has managed to stay out of trouble the past few years.

Why this, then?

Gordy's murder, the attempt on Midge's life . . .

"It's hard to guess motive when you're talking about someone who's mentally ill and probably delusional," Midge said.

"She didn't seem that way when I saw her in prison, though," Talia said. "Or in all those texts where she was pretending to be Caroline."

Kelly thought about her mother and show timing. Maybe Mary Beth, too, was able to mask her mental confusion.

Or maybe she really has been stable.

Talia's invitation for "Caroline" to meet them back in Mulberry Bay this weekend might have caused her to spiral into all those memories. All that sorrow.

All that rage.

Toward Caroline's friends, and toward Gordy . . .

"Why, though?" Talia asked. "Why Gordy?"

"She probably saw him as responsible for starting the whole thing," Midge said. "And she might have felt like he took her place in Caroline's life after she was forced out of it."

Kelly nodded. "Right. Remember how jealous *we* were? I'll bet Mary Beth felt the same way about Gordy."

"And about us," Midge said grimly. "But who knows? There will always be questions. This isn't Nancy Drew, or Scooby-Doo, guys. In real life, crimes are rarely tied up neatly."

Talia's missing luggage hasn't turned up.

Nor has the missing Annie Oakley revolver.

Does it matter? Any of it?

Not to Kelly. Not now. It won't bring Caroline back.

She stops at the edge of the pit but avoids gazing into the depths.

Tilting her head back, she looks instead at the sun, glowing in the sky.

Midge clears her throat. "Someone should . . . someone has to say something."

"You should," Kelly tells her. "You're the one who made sure we could do this before . . . you know."

"I can't." Her voice is hoarse. "Talia, you do it."

"I can't," she chokes out on a sob. "Kelly."

Kelly nods.

For a moment, she closes her eyes, uncertain what to say.

Then it comes to her—the Robert Frost poem that's been flitting at the edges of her consciousness, the one about the woods, and promises. The one Caroline believed was about Haven Cliff.

She recites the poem's last stanza like a prayer, eyes still closed: "'The woods are lovely, dark and deep, But I have promises to keep, And miles to go before I sleep, And miles to go before I sleep.'"

She opens her eyes, raises the bouquet to her nose, and inhales the fragrance one last time before letting go.

"We love you, Caroline," Talia says softly, throwing her own flowers into the grave and squeezing Kelly's hand.

Midge stands for a moment, clutching her bouquet, tears running down her cheeks. Then she steps forward and tosses it—up, not down, so that the white blooms sail briefly toward the sky before showering down all around them, into the earth.

"How long do we have?" Kelly asks her, clasping her hand as she steps back.

"As long as we need," Midge says.

They stand there for a long time, silent, holding hands, lost in their own thoughts.

Kelly stares at the pedestal across from her, remembering Caroline, sitting there on that warm June day, chin held high, tears in her eyes.

I'm going to go away. On prom night . . . no one will ever find me.

At last, Kelly utters the words she said to Talia on her birthday back in May. The words that led Talia here. Led to this.

"It's time."

They let go of each other's hands. Let go of Caroline.

Midge takes her phone from her pocket, dials, and says quietly, "Nap? . . . Yeah . . . yeah, it's fine. Send them up here."

They retrace their steps, back along the trail to the mock orange grove, where the medical examiner's van has been waiting.

Kelly sees a team unloading equipment from the back. A tall man in a suit waves Midge over, and she turns to Talia and Kelly. "I've got to speak with the ME. Are you guys okay?"

Kelly nods. "Go ahead. We're fine."

Midge leaves them, and Kelly puts an arm around Talia, who's wiping tears from her eyes.

"We're not *that* fine," she says, leaning her head on Kelly's shoulder. "At least, I'm not."

"Yeah. Me either. But we've got each other, and she's got a job to do."

"What do you think is going to happen to Mary Beth?"

"It sounds like she's going to pull through. I wasn't exactly shooting to kill—not that I'm a great shot."

"Are you kidding? You're amazing. But then, you never were a candy-ass, Kelly Barrow," Talia adds with a grin.

She laughs. "Now there's a phrase I haven't heard in years."

"What I meant was, do you think she's going back to prison? I guess I know the answer. I just hate thinking of her in that horrible place."

"I know. But look what she did to Gordy and the Walking Man. And what she tried to do to Midge. And Caroline . . ." Kelly shakes her head.

"I know all that. And she was never my favorite person, believe me. Not like she was yours," Talia adds.

"It was a long time ago. And sometimes, you just see what you want to see." She sighs. "Come on. Let's go inside. I'll make coffee."

"In a minute. Ben should be up now. I need to call him, if you don't mind my using your phone?"

"Not at all." Kelly hands it over.

"Thanks. We've got a lot to talk about. I'll see you inside in a bit."

Kelly nods, heading back toward the house alone, needing coffee, covering a yawn.

"And miles to go before I sleep," she whispers aloud, remembering.

Remembering all of it, poetry and music and parties and laughter and bickering . . .

She closes her eyes, allowing the memories, and their voices.

"You guys know Gordy, right?"

"We've got places to go, things to do, people to see, so move your butt, girl!"

"Sorry, I can't hear you because my empty stomach is growling so loud."

"It's not like we'll be apart forever."

"I miss you so much. All of you."

It was just yesterday, and it was a million years ago.

She opens her eyes and finds herself looking at the house.

It catches her off guard. Somehow, she expected to see it in ruins. But this is now.

Haven Cliff gleams like a jewel in the early-morning light. She takes it all in—the granite facade and portico, the turrets and balconies, the grillwork above the roof, the gardens beneath the windows. She spies a hummingbird darting around the garden.

She smiles, thinking of her mother.

Then, catching another fluttering in the corner of her eye, she turns just in time to see someone.

It's a girl in a white dress, luminous in the golden sun.

Kelly blinks and she's gone.

Maybe she's a ghost.

Maybe she was never there at all.

Maybe Kelly's just seeing what she wants to see.

Or maybe this time, she wanted to say goodbye.

And so, just in case she's still watching, from wherever she is, Kelly lifts her fingers to her lips and blows a kiss at the spot where she was. "Sleep well, my friend."

Acknowledgments

With gratitude to my agent, Laura Blake Peterson, and my editor, Megha Parekh, who made this happen.

To Charlotte Herscher, for her patience and tireless developmental editorial work, and to the team at Thomas & Mercer.

To Holly Frederick, James Farrell, and Eliza Leung at Curtis Brown, Ltd.

To Alafair, Alison, Kellye, Laura, Megan, and Sarah, who hand-held and pep-talked.

To Mark, Morgan, and Bryce, who tolerated writer-me for months on end.

And especially to Brody, who did the above *and* plotted it with me.

About the Author

Photo © 2023 Patti Looney Photography

Wendy Corsi Staub is the *New York Times* bestselling author of more than ninety novels, including *Windfall*, *The Other Family*, and *Dying Breath*. She is also the author of the Lily Dale Mystery series, the Foundlings trilogy, the Mundy's Landing trilogy, the Nightwatcher trilogy, and the Live to Tell trilogy. Wendy is a three-time finalist for the Simon & Schuster Mary Higgins Clark Award and has won an RWA RITA Award, an RT Award for Career Achievement in Suspense, the 2007 RWA/NYC Golden Apple Award for Lifetime Achievement, and five WLA Washington Irving Prizes for Fiction. Wendy lives in the New York suburbs with her husband, their sons, and three rescue cats. For more information, visit www.wendycorsistaub.com.